DEATH OF A LESSER MAN

DEATH OF A LESSER MAN

An Inspector Stride Mystery

Thomas Rendell Curran

BOULDER PUBLICATIONS

Library and Archives Canada Cataloguing in Publication

© 2011 Curran, Thomas Rendell
Death of a lesser man / Thomas Rendell Curran.
ISBN 978-0-9865376-2-2

I. Title.

PS8555.U68D42 2011 C813'.6 C2010-907250-2

Published by Boulder Publications
Portugal Cove-St. Philip's, Newfoundland and Labrador
www.boulderpublications.ca

Design and layout: Vanessa Stockley, GraniteStudios.ca
Cover image: Alex Nikada / iStockphoto
Cover design: Alison Carr
Printed in Canada

Newfoundland
Labrador
We acknowledge the financial support of the Government
of Newfoundland and Labrador through the Department
of Tourism, Culture and Recreation.

We acknowledge financial support for our publishing program by the
Government of Canada and the Department of Canadian Heritage through the
Canada Book Fund.

For

Donald Wilfred ("Fred") Curran, MM (1896–1922)
Newfoundland Regiment No. 122

France, October 1916

The shell fragment struck him in the midsection and knocked him to the ground. When he tried to stand again, there was no life in his legs. Using his arms, he dragged himself to a shell crater, rolled over the lip and down the side, and came to rest at the bottom in a pool of water. For a long while he could only lie still, looking up at the patterned blue-white sky, listening to the tumult that continued above.

The pain came soon enough, heavy and enveloping. He pushed himself backwards on his elbows until he reached the side of the crater and he lay there, exhausted. After a minute, he looked down. The front of his tunic was shredded. His intestines, no longer under the protective shield of skin and muscle, glistened in the afternoon light.

The pain continued, and grew worse, and as he drifted in and out of consciousness, his sense of time deserted him. But he knew that he was dying, and his worst fear now was that it would take too long. He looked around for his rifle, but it was nowhere in sight.

Sometime later he was aware that he was no longer alone. Another soldier was there, kneeling beside him, holding a pistol in his right hand. The dying man recognized him as an officer from his own Regiment. He looked at him for a moment, nodded, then closed his eyes and let his head fall back against the side of the crater. He heard the familiar sound of a revolver being cocked.

CHAPTER 1

St. John's, Newfoundland
September 1947

Sir Alexander Bannerman would not have been pleased. The Governor of Newfoundland from 1857 to 1864, Bannerman, erstwhile classmate of Lord Byron at Marischal College in Aberdeen, was a no-nonsense Scot noted for his sense of what was right and honest, and what was not. And contrary to the colonial stereotype, Bannerman was also a generous man. He demonstrated that quality in the last year of his governorship, when he donated a piece of his own land, on the south side of Circular Road, for the creation of a public park. It would be the first park established in the city, and when it was officially opened in 1891, it was named after him.

What would have made Governor Bannerman frown was a noisy, and—as it was soon discovered—violent disturbance late on a Monday night in the middle of September. A heavy rain was falling at the time, one of the first good showers after more than two weeks of unusually hot, dry weather, and there were few people out and about. But it was still warm. For anyone who liked to walk in the rain, this was a good night for it.

Harrison Rose liked walking in the rain, or, indeed, in any kind of weather. He took a solitary walk every night around midnight before finally turning in. It was his established routine and he had stuck to it for years, no matter what the weather or the season. He would leave his home on Circular Road at about 11:45 and walk for at least a half hour, sometimes longer. Only the route varied, and even that not by a lot. Rose was a man of routine, a quality drilled into him—literally—from his early youth: a virtue in many circumstances, but not, as things turned out, in all.

He walked in an easterly direction, along Circular to the junction with King's Bridge Road, and from there along the path by Quidi Vidi Lake. Sometimes he would do the full circuit around the lake, a route that brought him past the

American military base at Fort Pepperrell on the return trip, and from there back to King's Bridge Road. From King's Bridge, whether he walked the short route or the long one, he always went down to the junction with Military Road, headed west, and eventually walked across Bannerman Park to Circular Road, and on home.

Harrison Rose made it to the middle of Bannerman Park at about twenty-five minutes past midnight. It was then that the noisy disturbance took place. It was also at, or close to, that same moment that Harrison Rose was shot and killed.

For once there was at least one policeman near the scene, and he was within hearing distance when the shots were fired. And not just a beat cop, but an inspector with the Newfoundland Constabulary. Eric Stride lived on Circular Road, not far from Bannerman Park. Stride was the only unmarried officer on the Force not living in the police barracks attached to Fort Townshend, the Constabulary headquarters. At 12:25 that evening, as on most evenings, he was still up and about. More often than not a poor sleeper, Stride preferred to stay awake as late as possible, forcing himself if he had to.

When the disturbance that resulted in Harrison Rose's death took place, Stride happened to be standing by the bedroom window of his flat on the third floor of his house, looking out at the rain, listening to its soothing patter on the roof and eaves, and on the leaves of the tall trees in his yard. Only minutes earlier he'd pulled the window open to let some cooler air into the room, still uncomfortably warm from the recent hot weather.

At first Stride didn't think—didn't want to think—that the sounds he heard were gunshots. Circular Road was a quiet, tree-lined street in an affluent neighbourhood, very affluent in fact, populated for the most part by well-to-do families, people with money and position in St. John's society. Government House and the Colonial Building, the nominal seat of government, were not far away. Gunshots were out of place in this neighbourhood. But Eric Stride had heard a lot of gunfire in his lifetime. Almost every week he took himself off to target practice, using the .38 Colt Detective Special that he often carried with him in contravention of Constabulary regulations.

So, when the first wave of puzzlement had passed, Stride knew damn well that what he had heard were gunshots. First one shot, and then another about thirty seconds later. If there had been only one, he might have disregarded it as his imagination playing tricks, but the second shot confirmed what he knew he'd heard the first time.

After he heard that second shot, he put in a quick call to Constabulary headquarters at Fort Townshend, and then he retrieved the Colt revolver from his bedroom. He threw on a raincoat and ran downstairs, heading for Bannerman Park.

When he reached the sidewalk in front of his house, he made a quick survey of the street, but his main focus was directed towards the park. He set off on a fast trot in that direction, angling over to the south side of the street, his Colt in his right hand, all the time on his guard, in case someone with a gun should suddenly appear. He reached the eastern end of the park in less than a minute, and there he came to a halt and looked around. Then he began moving ahead again, slowly, scanning the area, straining to see through the dark and the rain. He moved into the park itself, staying close to the line of fence. Still seeing no one, and no sign of life save for an occasional car passing by on Military Road to the south, he quickened his pace, but moving cautiously still.

Minutes later he came upon a body of a man lying on the ground, close to the base of a large maple tree. A scattering of newly fallen leaves lay on the grass beside him.

Stride took a last, careful look around the area, but still he saw no one. He moved close to the body and reached out with his left hand to feel for a pulse, placing his fingers on the man's neck just under the chin. He found no pulse and felt no movement in response to his touch. When he drew his hand back, his fingers were wet and sticky with a mixture of blood and rain.

The man was lying on his back but tilted to the left, his right arm draped across his torso. His eyes were open and staring, seeming almost to express outrage that this insult had been inflicted upon his person. Stride turned the man's head and saw on the left side the small entrance wound of a bullet, so neatly circumscribed that it seemed impossible that it could have caused his death, or produced the large amount of blood that ran over his chin and down over his clothing.

Stride reached his left hand under the man's blood-stained raincoat and into his jacket, looking for identification. He found a wallet in the right inside pocket and was pulling it out when he heard a sound off to his left, from the direction of Military Road. A uniformed policeman was coming towards him, his nightstick held at shoulder height, making ready to strike.

Stride raised his right hand as a caution, forgetting for the moment that it still held the Colt. There was a muttered "Jesus Christ!" from the constable, who took a stumbling motion backwards. Stride took a closer look at the man and recognized him as one of the younger constables on the Force.

"It's all right, Kennedy, put the stick away. It's me, Inspector Stride."

The constable stopped his nervous retreat and leaned closer, relief washing over his features.

"I'm sorry, Inspector, I didn't recognize you." Tom Kennedy slipped the nightstick into the sling under his rain cape and moved closer. He crouched down beside Stride and looked at the body. "He's dead?"

"Yes." Stride turned Rose's head to show Kennedy the head wound.

"Jesus Christ," Kennedy said again, breathing the words as much as speaking them. "No exit wound?"

"The bullet's still in there," Stride said. "You heard the shots? That's what brought you here?"

"I was down by the Garrison Church, St. Thomas's, when I heard what I thought was a gunshot. Then I heard a second one, and I thought I'd better take a look. You never know, right?" Kennedy glanced at the body again, his focus on the man's head. "But I didn't expect anything like this."

"Did you see anyone on the street on your way here?"

Kennedy looked back towards Military, then shook his head. The movement scattered rainwater from the hood of his rain cape onto Stride and the body.

"No, sir. I saw a couple of cars on the street, but there didn't seem to be anything unusual about them. And at that point I didn't know there was anything up. Where were you when you heard the shots?"

"At home." Stride pointed in the general direction of his house. "I live just over there. I've already phoned Fort Townshend. We should be getting some assistance soon."

They both looked across the park in a westerly direction, towards the intersection of Military and Rennie's Mill Road. Two sets of headlights were moving in their direction. As they watched, the first vehicle, a black sedan, moved on past. The second and larger set turned left onto Rennie's Mill, then right onto Circular and pulled up to the curb near the place where Stride had entered the park. It was the Constabulary's workhorse van, the Black Maria.

"Go fetch them, Kennedy. I'll stay here. But give me your flashlight."

The constable nodded and gave Stride the flashlight. He headed across the park towards Circular. The Black Maria was parked now, and two uniformed policemen were standing beside it peering into the darkness. Then one of them spotted Kennedy coming towards them and raised a hand in recognition.

Stride opened the wallet and went through the contents. He found a driver's licence tucked into a side pocket. Using Kennedy's flashlight, he read the name of Harrison Rose. He took another look at the body, studying the face from different angles. For the first time he recognized the dead man as one of his neighbours. He had sometimes seen Rose walking on the street, but more often driving in his car, a black Rover from pre-war days.

He had never met Harrison Rose, although occasionally he had nodded to him as they passed each other on Circular Road, and once or twice they had exchanged a few words about the weather before Rose went on his way, tapping the metal tip of his cane on the sidewalk. Stride stood up now and looked around for the cane. He had never seen Rose walking without it.

Then, Kennedy's voice came to him from close by, from the direction of Circular.

"I found this, sir. It might have been the dead fellow's." Kennedy was approaching, the other two uniforms following close behind him. He held a cane at shoulder level. "I found it just over there."

"It's probably his," Stride said. "He always had one with him when he was out walking."

"You know him, sir? The dead man?"

Stride shook his head and the water dislodged from his hair streamed down over his face. The rain had not let up any since he'd left his house, and he realized for the first time that he was almost soaked through to the skin.

"I know who he is," Stride said. He took the cane from Kennedy. It had a considerable heft. There were many nicks and scratches on the hardwood, but he couldn't tell if the damage was new or not. "His name is Harrison Rose. He lives—lived—down the street from me."

Stride looked at the three constables standing in the rain, waiting for him to give them directions and define their role in the investigation that was about to begin. He dug into his imperfect memory for names.

"Westcott and Skanes, isn't it?" The constables nodded and took a half-step forward. The two men looked almost enough alike to be brothers, both of them young, tall and slender. "All right, this is a crime scene, and the weather be damned, we have to get started. One of you get to a phone and get hold of Noseworthy." Constable Kevin Noseworthy was the Constabulary's evidence officer. "Use the call box on Rawlins Cross. And put in a call for Dr. Butcher." He wiped rain from his face and did up the top button of his raincoat, much good it would do. "Do you have any more oilskins in the van?"

"We have two, sir," Westcott said.

"I'm already bloody soaked, but bring me an oilskin anyway. Then go back to Fort Townshend and pick up a couple more. And some kind of canopy. Dr. Butcher will want the body, and himself, out of the rain when he does his preliminary examination."

"Canopy, sir?" Westcott looked puzzled.

"There must be something like a canopy back at Fort Townshend." In truth, Stride really had no idea if the Constabulary had one. "Ask Dickson if we have something that will do the trick. He's on duty tonight."

"I'll do my best, sir. Do you want me to get hold of Sergeant Phelan, too, while I'm at it?"

Stride looked at the constable. He hadn't even thought about Harry Phelan, his partner for four years. He decided the lapse was due to the lateness of the hour, together with the consuming anxiety of the situation.

"Yes, of course. Pick him up when you go to fetch Noseworthy. And give Kennedy your flashlight." Westcott gave Kennedy the light and started across the park in the direction of the Black Maria. Stride looked down at the body of Harrison Rose, and at the rain pelting down on him. It didn't seem right. He unbuttoned his raincoat, a new mackintosh he'd bought only a month earlier, and draped it over Rose's body. He noticed for the first time that Rose was wearing leather gloves. He pushed them under the raincoat too.

Then Westcott was back, holding out an oilskin. Stride took it from him and slipped it on. If anything, it made him feel even less comfortable, pressing his wet clothes against his skin.

The constable headed back across the park, going towards the Black Maria.

"All right," Stride said. "Side by side, arm's-length separation, and we'll do a walk-through. Keep an eye open for shell cases, and make note of anything else that looks even marginally relevant. I don't care what it is. Noseworthy can decide later if it's useful."

They lined up, side by side, double arm's-length apart, and began the established procedure, slowly walking over the scene, eyes focused on the ground, their search assisted by the modest illumination from three regulation constabulary flashlights. The rain continued to fall.

CHAPTER 2

They had a canopy in place over the body before Thomas Butcher arrived at the scene. Stride thought he'd seen it used at a garden party at Fort Townshend the previous summer.

On the first walk-through of the scene they found two shell cases of the same calibre, each with ejection marks that indicated a semi-automatic. That matched the number of shots Stride had heard. They made note of everything in the area of the body that looked remotely interesting, leaving it all in place until Noseworthy had gone through with his evidence bags, his camera and his notebook. There really wasn't very much. The park had been busy on the weekend—large numbers of people enjoying the unusually warm September weather. The park cleaners had come through early on Monday morning, and the place, while not quite spick-and-span, was notably free of litter. And then the rain had started, and the park was all but deserted after that.

Harry Phelan had come along with Noseworthy in the Black Maria, with two additional uniformed policemen. Now Harry was standing under the canopy looking down at the body, smoking a cigarette, waiting for Butcher to arrive so that they could get on with it, finish up all that could be finished up on this night, and then go back home to bed. He'd told Stride that he thought that he might have a cold coming on, some kind of early response to the change in the weather.

Stride sympathized, managing only a muted reaction in his own sodden and uncomfortable state. He gave Harry the number of Rose's house on Circular.

"Take a uniform with you to the house and see if there's anyone there. When you come back, leave him there. We'll need to have a guard on the house for the next couple of days."

"Was Rose married, sir?"

"I don't think so. As far as I know, he lived alone. I only knew him by name, just a nodding acquaintance. I've never seen a woman with him. Maybe he's a bachelor, or a widower. I don't know."

"Next of kin might be a problem."

"We can worry about that later. When Noseworthy's finished, and Butcher gets here and does his preliminary, we'll have the body taken to the General Hospital for the autopsy."

Phelan opened his umbrella, collected a uniformed constable, and set off down the street. On their way, they passed Thomas Butcher making his way across the park in the direction of the canopy, holding an umbrella. Butcher's black Rover was parked on Circular.

"A grand night for a garden party, and no mistake," was Butcher's comment when he saw the canopy that had been set up. "And not a mosquito or blackfly in sight."

"We're counting our blessings, Thomas."

Butcher stepped under the canvas out of the rain. He furled his umbrella and turned his attention to the body on the ground, still covered with Stride's coat.

"Is that your mac, Eric?" He gave Stride a questioning look.

"Yes, it is."

"Very charitable of you, old man. It's almost new, isn't it?"

"It used to be," Stride said. The coat was sodden now, and blood from Rose's wounds had seeped into the fabric in two places, near the head and on the chest. In spite of the amount of blood, it hadn't fully registered with Stride until now that Rose had been hit more than once. The head wound had captured all his attention.

Butcher knelt down and pulled the coat back from the body, folding it as he moved it away, taking note of the location of the bloodstains and carefully probing the chest area with the fingers of his right hand. He lifted the coat completely away from the body and looked up at Stride.

"Noseworthy can take this now, Eric. He'll have to bag it as evidence. I'll need to look at the bloodstains later. You'll want it back, I suppose?"

"I suppose." Stride looked at the coat and shook his head. "Or maybe not."

Butcher continued his probing of Rose's body, focusing on the chest area. Stride directed a flashlight beam to assist him. He opened the clothing—the topcoat, suit coat and shirt—and then pulled the undershirt back. When he was done, he rearranged the clothing more or less to the position it had been in before he'd started his examination, and turned his attention to the head.

After a few minutes he stood up and took out his silver cigarette case and lighter.

"Three wounds," Butcher said. "Two in the chest, plus the head wound. I think any one of the three might have been enough to kill him. The head wound, certainly."

"We found two shell cases," Stride said. "Both of them from the same weapon, probably."

"A semi-automatic."

"Yes." Stride borrowed a cigarette and a light from Butcher. He'd left his own back at his flat. "The thing is, Thomas, I heard only two shots."

"You heard the shots?" Butcher turned and looked in the direction of Stride's house on Circular. "Yes, I suppose you would have. But your house is a distance away, Eric. You might have missed one of them."

"I suppose. But I was standing by an open window, and I heard only two. So did the constable on the beat." He looked towards Kennedy, who was standing next to Skanes under the canopy. "I can't argue with the number of wounds, though. There's three, and that settles it."

Noseworthy came back from his picture-taking and his first assessment of the scene.

"Nothing much of importance out there, but we'll take another look tomorrow. Well, later today, when it's light and, hopefully, the rain has stopped. Although the forecast isn't promising. I did find two cigarette butts under a tree back there." He turned and pointed to the left. "They might mean something— the shots could have come from there. But almost everyone in this town smokes cigarettes from about age twelve on."

Stride took the two shell cases from his pocket and gave them to Noseworthy. He looked at them under the beam of his flashlight, lining them up on his palm, rolling them back and forth, comparing the ejection marks. He took his time. Then he looked at Stride.

"I'll take a closer look later, but I think they're both from the same weapon. Nine millimetre, semi-automatic. But you've figured that out already." He looked at Butcher. "I've got all the snaps I need, Dr. Butcher. You can take him away whenever you're ready."

Stride spoke to Westcott and Skanes. The two constables nodded and went off in the direction of the Black Maria, parked now on Circular Road in front of Butcher's Rover. Two minutes later they came back with a stretcher.

"You say the fellow lives down the street from you?" Butcher was shaking rainwater from his umbrella, making ready to head back to his car.

"Yes, he does. Did. His name's Harrison Rose. His house is closer to King's Bridge Road."

"Harrison Rose." Butcher looked thoughtful. "And that's where Phelan was off to?"

"Yes." Stride looked towards Circular Road. Phelan was walking back towards them now, and he was alone.

"There's no sign of life in the house," Phelan said when he reached the canopy. "We knocked and we rang the bell, but no one answered. I took a quick look around the back, and the place is locked tight. There's a light on at the back, in what looks like the kitchen. I left Donovan there to keep a watch on the house. Under the circumstances, though, I think it might be a good idea to send another uniform to stand watch with him, one in front and one in back. If there's someone running around out there with a pistol, two warm bodies are better than one alone."

"I agree," Stride said. But it would be two unarmed warm bodies, Constabulary procedures being what they were. "Send the other uniform who came along with you in the Black Maria."

"Doyle," Phelan said. "Michael Doyle."

"Right." Stride looked at the policeman named Doyle, determined to match name with person the next time he ran into him. "You'd better go along with him, Harry, and make sure they both understand the situation. There's someone out there, armed and probably dangerous."

"I'll pass it along, sir. It will help keep them awake while they stand watch."

"And make sure they stay in touch with each other every couple of minutes."

Phelan nodded and moved off towards the group of uniforms.

"I didn't know Harrison Rose personally," Butcher said. "But I do know who he is."

"Yes?"

"Rose isn't from here, originally."

"I think I probably knew that, from his accent, the few times I spoke to him. But you'd met him?"

"Only casually, on one or two occasions. He's English, but I think he's lived here for a long time. Someone told me he had a military background. British Army, I think, but don't quote me on that."

"You know more about him that I do, Thomas, and he was a neighbour of mine. Mind you, I'm not especially gregarious."

"Each to his own. You know, it occurs to me that if Rose was ex-army, he was probably in the Great War. Jack McCowan was over there."

McCowan was Stride's district inspector. Thomas Butcher knew many of the Great War veterans who were living in Newfoundland. During that war he was a surgeon in the British Army and, for a time, attached to the Newfoundland Regiment in France.

"He might know something about him. Rose was late fifties. That would be about McCowan's age."

"What do you think of it, Thomas?" Stride borrowed another cigarette. "I've never seen anything like this before. Not in St. John's."

"A man takes three well-directed bullets from a semi-automatic in the middle of a public park, the fatal shot looking like a *coup de grâce*? No, I haven't seen anything like this before, either. I know it's odd, given the hour and the weather, but I wonder if Rose was meeting someone here this evening."

"Like the man who shot him?"

"Or woman. Or perhaps Rose was in the habit of taking walks late at night, rain or no rain, and someone had paid attention."

"And was waiting for him when he walked through the park."

"That would seem to be one possibility." Butcher looked at his cigarette, made a face, then snubbed off the lit end and dropped the butt into his coat pocket. "Well, I'm off home for a nightcap and a few hours sleep. I have surgery at eight, but only one, fortunately. I'll be able to do the post early this afternoon, say about two? But if that's not convenient, I can schedule for a better time."

"Two sounds about right, but I'll call first."

Stride watched while Butcher made his way back across the park in the direction of Circular Road. He took a final long drag on his cigarette and then, just as Butcher had done, pinched off the end and placed the butt in the pocket of his oilskin. This was a crime scene, after all.

The windows of the second-floor sitting room of Government House faced west towards Bannerman Park. Rodney Gilbert, a senior aide to Governor Sir Gordon Macdonald, came into the room and went to the window. He pulled back one of the drapes.

Gilbert was in his late thirties, tall and willowy. His hair was reddish-brown, and slightly longer than the current fashion. He had it cut that way because he believed it gave him a professorial air.

"There's something going on in the park," Gilbert said. "You can't really see anything from here, but I heard a commotion from downstairs while I was catching up on my correspondence. And there's two vehicles parked on Circular near the park. One of them's the police van, that thing they call the Black Maria."

"It sounds serious," Barnes Wilson said. Wilson, a major in the British Army, was the Governor's aide-de-camp. He was as tall as Gilbert, but heavier, with the appearance of a former athlete. And he was older than Gilbert, in his early fifties. Although Wilson had a rented flat in town, he sometimes spent the night at

Government House in one of the guest bedrooms. He closed the book he'd been reading but kept his thumb between the pages. "You went out and had a look?"

"Yes, I did. And I think it is serious. I kept my distance, but I got close enough to see that they've put up some sort of canopy just inside the park. And, you know, I thought I heard shots a little while ago. Two of them."

"Shots? You're sure about that?" Wilson picked up the drink that stood on the table by his left elbow. "You don't suppose it was just a car backfiring?"

"I think I know the difference, Barnes. A gunshot sounds nothing like a car backfiring, except in films. And bad films, at that."

"I'll take your word for it, old man. And if it matters, I happen to agree with you."

"About hearing shots?" Gilbert turned away from the window and looked across the room. "You heard them too?'

"No, I didn't hear any shots. What I'm agreeing with is their not sounding like a car backfiring." He sipped his whisky. "If there were shots, maybe they happened when I was in the loo a while back."

"I'm wondering if I should go out there again and find out what's going on. His nibs won't be pleased to learn that there's some kind of a fracas just next door, and his staff can't tell him what it's about."

"His nibs will probably also not be pleased if one of his senior aides goes wandering out into the night and has his picture taken at a crime scene. If that's really what it is that's going on out there."

"Yes, well, there is that," Gilbert said. He pulled the drape shut again. "Do you think I should alert him, though, just to be on the safe side?"

"I don't suppose it can do any harm. He does like to be kept in touch with things. Just give me fair warning, though, old man. If he catches me tippling whisky, I'll get another lecture about the temperance ideal and be made to stand in the corner again. And you know how I hate that."

Gilbert laughed.

"It is a bloody pain, isn't it? I'd never even met a real teetotaller before, not until I was posted here. And no one even thought to warn me that Government House was the bloody Sahara of foreign postings. Worse even than being posted someplace in Arabia, with all their mad religious laws. And in St. John's of all places, a city almost awash in beer and rum."

"Colourful language, old man, but not really accurate. This supposedly solemn and god-fearing house holds admirable supplies of booze. Nothing brings on the urge to tipple like being in the employ of an ardent drysider. I don't know anyone working here in this pile of granite who doesn't have a private stash. Rumour even has it that you've got a couple of jugs squirrelled away in your digs down among the socks and the unmentionables."

"Yes, well, a fellow has to look after himself, make the best of it."

"Think of it as wartime grimness extended, old man. Someday soon they'll appoint a new Governor for this rock within the roiling sea, and civilization as we remember and adore it shall be restored."

"We can always hope," Gilbert said.

"I know I bloody well do." Wilson took another sip of his whisky and opened his book again.

"Well, I'll take your advice and see if his nibs is still awake. If he is, I'll give him the word about the doings next door. Cover the bases, as the Yanks like to say."

"You do that, old man. Just keep me in the picture." He smiled up at Gilbert. "As our side likes to say."

When Gilbert left the room, Barnes Wilson closed his book and picked up his glass. He sat for a minute longer, thinking, then got up and went to the window. He pulled the drape back. Gilbert was right. He couldn't see anything of what might be going on in the park from the window. He accepted Gilbert's word that it probably was something serious. He considered going out for a look himself, but decided not to. He was no more willing to be a part of whatever it was than Gilbert had been. Even less so.

Wilson looked at his watch. It was past one now. He'd got very interested in the book he was reading, and hadn't realized how late it was. He checked his watch again, and made the conversion to London time. It was not quite five in the morning there. He thought about that for another minute, then pulled the drape back into place and went back to his chair and his glass of whisky. He looked at the book on the side-table, but decided he wouldn't read any more that evening.

CHAPTER 3

It was going on two when Harry came back to the park after posting Doyle and Donovan at Rose's house. The rain had let up a little, but it was still coming down steadily.

"How bad is your cold, Harry?"

"Too early to tell, really. It's the time of year for it, but the weather's still warm, so maybe it won't amount to anything much."

"We'll hope not. I think we're going to be especially busy with this one. This isn't like anything we've seen before."

"You found Rose's wallet still in his pocket, so it obviously wasn't a robbery."

"I think it's something very different," Stride said. "And just now, I want to have a look at Rose's house."

Phelan looked back towards the street.

"The Black Maria should be back soon from delivering the body to the General," he said. "Noseworthy's stuff is piled there on the curb. Maybe we should have him wait for a bit?"

Stride nodded and walked over to where Noseworthy was standing under an umbrella.

"Harry and I are going to have another look at Rose's house. I want you to stay here until I'm sure there's no reason for us to go into the place."

"Harry said it was locked tight, and nobody was home."

"That's probably the case, but I want to have a look myself."

"Right, sir. I'll load my stuff aboard the van when it comes back, and I'll meet you there."

Harrison Rose's house was on the north side of the street and the driveway sloped gradually downwards as the land fell away in the direction of Empire Avenue, into the shallow valley created by Rennie's River. Towards the bottom, the driveway curved around to the right, behind the house, and ended at a garage painted with the same colours as the house, white with a dark green trim.

Stride went up onto the veranda and turned the knob on the front door. The door had a double lock: two deadbolts above the doorknob, three inches apart. The front windows were covered with heavy drapes. He went back to the driveway and along it to the garage at the bottom. The double garage doors were shut and padlocked, but there was a side door. When Stride tried that, he found it was also secured with a deadbolt. A small double window afforded him a look inside. Harrison Rose's black Rover was there.

A flight of nine steps led up to the back door of the house, rising to a landing about five feet square, bordered by a wooden railing. A light shone through the window, just as Harry said. The cellar door was under the landing, set close to ground-level, with two concrete steps leading up to it. Stride went to the cellar door and turned the knob. The door was locked. He climbed the steps to the back door and tried that, with the same result.

"No one home, and no sign of forced entry." Stride leaned against the railing and stared at the door for a minute. "I want to get in there now. I don't want to wait until morning."

"We'll need a court order to do that, sir. It might be a challenge to find a judge up and about this late."

"If one is, it's likely to be Justice McGinn. He told me once he only needs a couple of hours sleep a night. And anyway, I don't mind waking him up. He owes us one."

"If you don't mind, sir, I'll let you make the call."

"I don't mind at all. I'll go over to my place and do that. In the meantime, talk to Noseworthy again and make sure he stays put. Once we get into Rose's house, we might need him."

Phelan made a gesture in the direction of Circular.

"The Black Maria's just come back."

"Give him a hand to load his stuff and then drive back here. Wait for me. I'll be back as soon as I make the call."

"And if you can't get the court order?"

"We'll go in, anyway." He held up a ring with four keys on it. He'd taken it from Rose's pocket. "McCowan might give me a lecture about it later, but I've had lectures before."

Stride let McGinn's phone ring six times before giving up. He took off the oilskin and stripped off his wet shirt. The air in his flat was warm, and it felt good after wearing wet clothing for a couple of hours. Then he went to the bathroom and towelled himself dry. He pulled on an undershirt and a sweater, and took his old raincoat, the one he thought he wouldn't have to wear again, from the hall closet. He found his cigarettes and lighter and left the flat.

Harry and Noseworthy were waiting on Rose's veranda.

"You got the court order all right?" Phelan said.

"I'll pretend I did. And you'll pretend you didn't hear me say that."

"McGinn wouldn't go along with it?"

"I didn't talk to McGinn. Either he's not at home, or he isn't answering his phone. And I just didn't feel like calling anyone else. It doesn't matter. It's time we got started."

He found the right keys for the front door on the second try. He pushed the door open and stepped into a vestibule. There was a clothes closet on one side and a boot rack on the other. The floor of the vestibule was expensively tiled. The hallway beyond was richly carpeted in a deep brown colour. A hemp mat lay in the middle of the vestibule. Stride wiped his feet before stepping on the carpet.

There was a study to the left of the vestibule, and to the right was the living room. He continued on down the hall to the kitchen.

The room was neat and tidy, towels hanging on racks, rows of cabinets on two walls, and what looked like a broom closet at the far end. A pantry door on another wall, partly open, showing boxes, cans and bottles on shelves. The stove and refrigerator were new, both of them run on electricity, both of them white. Many homes in the city still used iceboxes and coal-fired stoves.

Noseworthy stepped into the kitchen behind Stride.

"Do you want me to do anything, sir? It doesn't look like anyone's been in here. This isn't a crime scene."

"No, it isn't. I think all we'll do at this stage is look around the place, get a feel for it, collect anything that looks useful. Tomorrow we'll come back and do a proper search." He looked at his watch. "It's too bloody late to do much tonight."

"What are we looking for, sir? Anything in particular?"

"A journal or diary would be useful. It might tell us things about Harrison Rose. Maybe give us an idea of why someone would ambush him in the park."

"Assuming that's what happened," Phelan said. He'd followed Noseworthy into the kitchen and was admiring the fittings. "I think Kit would probably trade me in for a kitchen like this."

"And then who would she cook for?" Noseworthy said.

"The next handsome man who comes along, I expect."

"They say a change is as good as a rest."

"Let's get on with it," Stride said. "Kevin, you take a look upstairs. Harry and

I will do the study. If there's anything personal to be found, it will probably be there."

A search of the study yielded some correspondence and a collection of manila file folders containing household accounts, bills and receipts. Twin bookcases held a large number of volumes, some of them leather-bound, the majority of them war histories. Most were about the Great War, with a smaller number on the more recent conflict. A few others covered earlier wars—in the Sudan, the Crimea, South Africa, Ireland—the great variety of places the Union Jack had travelled in the company of cannon and musket, and then in later years with machine guns, artillery and military aircraft.

A collection of pictures hung on two of the walls in the study, taken in a variety of locales. Some of the pictures might have been taken in France, or in Belgium, but three of them were in a strikingly different environment. In one of those, a young officer who was probably Harrison Rose sat atop a camel, with a pyramid for a backdrop and a grinning Egyptian guide holding the reins of the barely tolerant beast. In another picture in the same grouping, taken in a desolate, hilly locale, the same young officer stood with another soldier, perhaps a few years younger than he was—a corporal, judging from the stripes on his sleeves—who had his hands behind his back in the stand-at-ease position. Rose himself struck a jauntier pose, hands on his hips, smiling, a pipe clenched in his teeth.

"Butcher was right," Phelan said. "Rose was in the army." He tapped a finger on the picture of the two men. "This one looks like the Dardanelles."

"Gallipoli?" Stride took a closer look. "I think you're probably right."

"Bloody awful show, Gallipoli. One of Kit's uncles was there. The Newfoundland Regiment arrived there in September of 1915. God's arsehole, Kit's uncle called it. Awful heat when they arrived, almost no fresh water, swarms of flies, never mind the Turkish artillery and snipers. And then in November the weather turned freezing cold, and there were terrible rainstorms, even floods. Some of the British troops actually drowned in their trenches, and others froze to death on the firing steps."

Stride looked at the photograph a moment longer, trying to draw a mental picture of the life Harrison Rose and his corporal might have shared in Gallipoli, recalling some of the things he'd read and heard about the campaign there. He tasted the bitter irony that Rose had survived that horror, and the even worse horrors he likely went through in France and Belgium, only to be gunned down here in St. John's in peacetime.

He sat at Rose's desk and opened and shut the drawers. Then he sat back and frowned. "There's no sign of a journal or a diary. Odd, for a military man. But maybe it's somewhere else."

They left the study and went upstairs.

There were five rooms on the second floor. One of them, at the far end of the hallway, was a bathroom. The door next to the bathroom, probably a bedroom, was closed. The three other doors were open. One of those, they found, was also a bathroom. That was a surprise, not the usual arrangement for a house like this. The other two were bedrooms, nicely furnished, but small. The largest room was the master bedroom, behind the closed door. The main bathroom was larger than Stride would have expected for a house like this, for almost any house, in fact. There was a double sink, a bathtub and a separate shower stall.

Noseworthy turned and looked at them as they came into the bathroom.

"I think this was probably a bedroom originally," Phelan said. "Twice the normal size. The man liked his comforts."

"I think so," Stride said.

The master bedroom had a practical, utilitarian, feel to it, the signature of a military man who'd led an organized life. That dovetailed with Stride's recollections of the man he had sometimes seen walking on the street—the erect posture, the almost ceremonial use of the cane that he carried with him. A large double bed sat in the middle of the room, the headboard against the far wall, flanked by matching dressers.

A large clothes closet contained six dark-coloured suits, all on wooden hangers. But there was a woman's clothing there also, two dresses and three blouses. On a shoe rack underneath, side by side with six pairs of highly polished men's shoes, three black and three brown, were two pairs of women's shoes.

"He may not have had a wife," Phelan said, "but he apparently didn't lack for female company."

"Apparently not," Stride said. "I wonder if she's a local woman, or someone who visits from outside the country."

Stride pulled open the drawers in the two dressers. One dresser held Rose's clothing, the other a woman's, but while all the drawers in Rose's dresser were full, the woman's dresser was only partly used, with an assortment of clothing and a zippered bag containing cosmetics. It reminded Stride of the arrangement in his own flat. Dianne Borg kept some things at his place, but most of her clothing was in the house she shared with her husband, Marty Borg, an American army officer stationed at Fort Pepperrell. Stride found himself wondering if Rose had a similarly complicated arrangement in his own life. That raised another possibility: Rose might also be involved with a married woman. It was a potentially important point.

Noseworthy had remained in the large bathroom. Now he came back into the master bedroom.

"The man knew what he liked," he said. "And he didn't pinch pennies. That bathroom is about half the size of the place where I'm living. You've noticed the female attire?"

"I've noticed," Stride said. "I think that's all I want to do here now." He looked at his watch again. "Let's call it an evening, and start over again in the morning."

"That suits me," Phelan said, and Noseworthy nodded.

"I noticed the pictures in the study," Noseworthy said. "British Army, from the insignias on Rose's uniform. It looks like he was in the First War, in Gallipoli as well as the Western Front. I wonder if he knew any of our lot back then?"

"It has to be a possibility," Stride said. "It could explain why he's living here, instead of somewhere in England."

"It could at that," Noseworthy said.

Stride went back to his flat and hung his raincoat in the hall closet. A hot shower was next on his list of things to do. Never having liked baths, he'd had the shower installed earlier in the summer. He stood under the shower for what seemed like a very long time, but was not quite five minutes. He cranked up the temperature of the cascading water one small notch at a time to as high a level as he could stand, until the chill of the night's events were washed out of him.

He towelled himself dry and wrapped himself in a heavy bathrobe, then made a pot of tea. He added a tot of rum to the steaming mug, then sat at his desk in the second bedroom, which he was in the process of converting into an office. He sipped the tea, fought off the temptation of a cigarette, and recorded the evening's events in his notebook, point by point, from the sound of the two shots, still clear in his mind's ear, to his discovery of Rose's body lying in the rain on the grass in the park.

Everything that happened after that became less his own, falling into the established routine of an investigation—the search for evidence in the park, the quick tour through Rose's house. The only part of the scenario that was fully his was the part that had occurred before Kennedy came across the park, nightstick in hand, ready to strike him down.

He went back through it a second and third time, starting from when he stood by the open bedroom window: the sound of rain falling on the house and the trees, the sudden gunfire, the small amount of time it took him to realize what it was he'd heard, the phone call to Fort Townshend, finding his revolver. Perhaps two minutes in total, no more than that, but probably no less. Then running down the stairs to the outside, across and along the street and into the park. And the discovery of Rose's body. Then Kennedy and the nightstick again.

He'd heard only two shots. He was certain of that. If there was a third shot, as there had to have been because the number of wounds on Rose's body left no room for doubt, that third shot had to have been separated from the first two by as much as two minutes, the amount of time that elapsed before he was into the stairwell and more or less out of earshot of anything happening outside.

The question was, why? He tried to put himself in the gunman's place, standing under a tree in the dark, taking careful aim, pumping two rounds into Rose's chest, and then ... what? Waiting for two minutes to crawl by while he did nothing? Unless he was a fool—and the care with which Rose had been dispatched seemed to argue against that likelihood—the gunman had to know that the two shots would have been heard by someone. Even the thirty-second gap between the two shots Stride had heard was odd. And then, after an even longer pause, stepping forward and firing a third round into Rose's head, the *coup de grâce* as Butcher called it. And then, only then, running from the scene, scarcely two minutes before Stride appeared from the direction of Circular Road, and another minute before Kennedy came into the park from Military.

He went through it all again. Then, another thought, and one that dropped another question mark into the mix. Two shell cases only. Skanes had found them, not far from the same tree where Noseworthy had found the cigarette butts, a dozen feet from where Rose's body lay. But where was the third shell case? They had gone over the area, done it carefully, and more than once. It was frustrating to believe they could have missed it, but it was raining hard, and it was dark. The likelihood was that one of them had trod on it and pushed it into the ground, under the grass, or under the leaves that were scattered about. They would look again in the morning.

Still, there had to have been a lapse of time between the first two shots and the third, the period when Stride was out of earshot: time enough for the shooter to change his position, move closer to Rose, now lying on the ground, and pump the fatal shot into his brain from close range. But two minutes? Ten or fifteen seconds would have been plenty of time.

He went back to his notes and went over them again, making a few small additions. Then he screwed the cap back on his pen, blotted the page dry, and closed the notebook. He was tired now, even sleepy, his body and mind relaxed—halfway to being numb—from the hot shower and the tea and the rum. He gave in to the temptation for a cigarette to go with the last of the tea. He didn't want to think any more about Harrison Rose and gunshots and wounds and tricky questions of timing. He wanted to put all of it aside until morning, when he would start over again, assembling the bits and pieces, lining up the similarities, teasing out the contradictions, trying to make sense of the whole thing.

He rolled his chair back from the desk, smoked his cigarette and drank the last of his rum-spiked tea. And when he had done that, he turned out the light and went off to bed.

CHAPTER 4

I t was just past nine when Kitty Phelan opened the door for Stride and led him down the hallway to the kitchen where Harry was working on a second cup of tea and reading the sports section of the *Daily News*. A plate with traces of egg yolk and toast crumbs was pushed off to one side. An ashtray held a burning cigarette. Phelan gave Stride a tired look and snuffled with a kind of resigned pride.

"The cold's worse?"

"Let's just say it's not a lot better."

"He's suffering mightily," Kitty said. She was a tiny woman with dark hair and skin so fair that it bordered on pale, and an abundance of energy. Where her husband was relaxed and easygoing, Kitty Phelan almost glowed, most of the time seeming to hover an inch or two above the floor. "And if you give him the slightest encouragement, Eric, he'll go into his dying swan act. You don't want to face that this early in the morning." She went to the stove and picked up the teapot. "There's a decent cup in here, if you're interested?"

"Very interested," Stride said. He took a seat at the table and lit his first cigarette of the day.

"Any good news in the paper?"

"The Dodgers finally have a lock on the pennant." Harry laid the newspaper on the table and dabbed at his nose with a handkerchief.

"And the Yankees already have theirs sewn up," Kitty said. "So, there's good news and bad. I don't see the Dodgers taking the Yankees in the World Series, even with Robinson's black magic working for them. It was a miracle they got this far."

"You have to have faith," Harry said. "This year will be different."

"Baseball doesn't run on faith, love. It's pitching, hitting, running and a decent helping of luck. Faith is for Sundays, sacraments and other imponderables." She placed the cup of tea in front of Stride, milk in first and the tea poured in after, the way he liked it. "You're looking well, Eric, all things considered. You couldn't have got much sleep last night."

"In fact, I did all right. I had a hot shower followed by a tot of rum, and then I went into a kind of coma for about four hours."

"That might help you deal with his lordship here. I think he's still a bit comatose. Mind you, it's hard to tell sometimes."

Harry grunted from behind his handkerchief, blew his nose one more time, then picked up the paper again.

"There's an item here on page six about a disturbance in Bannerman Park last night. It has Alex Greene's name attached."

"I didn't see him there last night," Stride said. "And he's never been the shy and reluctant type."

"I didn't see him, either. Or any other reporters." Phelan double-folded the paper and gave it to Stride. "And maybe he wasn't there. He might have got the basics from a stringer who happened by, and then wrote the story from that."

"Could be. There isn't a lot here, and nothing about a body. But Butcher's name is mentioned, so it comes to the same thing." He gave the paper back to Harry. "It really doesn't matter very much. And I'm happy enough that it's Alex who's had the first kick at it. He's less of a nuisance than some of the others in his trade. We can expect a few of them to show up sometime today."

"I'll have my 'no comment' line ready, and refer any and all of them to my superior officer."

"And I'll send them along to talk to McCowan."

"And he'll tell them to bugger off, like as not."

"Until we get a chance to brief him on our progress, he will."

"That sounds like a cue for me to get moving."

"You read me correctly," Stride said. He swallowed the last of his tea and started down the hall.

They stopped at Bannerman Park on their way to Harrison Rose's house to see what progress the two constables, Westcott and Skanes, had made in their search for additional evidence. The rain had slackened a little, enough that Stride and Phelan didn't need umbrellas when they walked into the park.

A large area, including the place where he'd found Rose's body, was roped off, and the entire park had been closed to the public while the investigation was going on. But that, as might have been expected, had a contrary effect. When word spread that something involving the police was happening in the park, gatherings of curious onlookers lined up at various points around the park, on Military and Circular Roads, and on Rennie's Mill. Clusters of umbrellas decorated the perimeter, like strange black mushrooms coaxed from the ground by the persistent rain.

Stride caught Skanes's attention and went over to where he was standing.

"We haven't found anything much, sir. Candy wrappers, more cigarette butts, a couple of bottles, and that's about it."

"No sign of the third shell case?"

"No, sir. We've raked the grass and sorted through the leaves, but no sign of it. If it's still here somewhere, it's probably been pushed underground."

"Keep looking. If you don't find it, we might need to locate a metal detector."

The suggestion drew the same reaction from Skanes as did his mention of a canopy the night before.

"I don't believe we have one of those at Fort Townshend, sir."

"I don't think so, either," Stride said. "But if it does come to that, we might be able to borrow one from the Canadian army, or from the Americans."

"So, you want us to keep looking?"

There was a resigned quality to Skanes's tone, not quite a pleading, but a hint that he thought this was already a bad use of their time and energy. They'd combed the area thoroughly, he said, marking their progress with small pennants on wooden pegs, and going back and forth over the ground more than once.

Stride surveyed the scene, newly surprised at how large the park actually was, the number and variety of trees, the many flower beds. It wasn't a place he visited often, hardly ever, in fact. His nature was to stay away from anywhere people gathered in any significant number.

"Give me your best judgement, Skanes. Do you think it's worth going over the area again?"

"Maybe one more time, sir." He hesitated before going on. "But it might be better to have another crew take over. I'm not trying to bum out on this, but when you go over a place time and time again, you end up looking at the same spots instead of new ones. It's like being lost in the woods; you go around in circles."

"I know what you mean," Stride said. "Switch jobs with the men patrolling the perimeter. I can leave that with you?"

"Yes, sir. I already talked to them about it. We were just waiting until someone gave us the go-ahead."

"And now you have it." Stride looked towards Circular Road, and then up at the sky. The rain had started coming down harder again. He turned his coat collar up. "Mr. Noseworthy will be along in a little while, and he'll make the final decision on how much more time you need to spend here."

He started back towards Circular Road and the MG. Another uniform was talking to Phelan. When he got closer, he saw that it was Tom Kennedy, the young constable with the nightstick from the night before.

"I thought you'd still be home in bed, Kennedy."

"I caught a couple of hours shuteye after I came off duty, sir, but then I was wide awake and I couldn't get back to sleep. So I came on down to see if I could be of any help. I've never worked on a murder investigation before. I figure the experience will be useful."

"It will," Stride said. "And I'll never turn down an offer of extra help."

"I checked with District Inspector McCowan first, to see if it would be all right. I thought I should do that."

"I can't imagine that he thought it wasn't all right."

"No, sir, he didn't. He said for me to come on ahead. As it happens, I have a few days leave, and I might as well put them to good use."

Stride saw that Harry was listening to this with a bemused expression. The uniforms weren't famous as volunteers for extra, unpaid duty. He was probably thinking the same thing that Stride was, that Kennedy might be a comer, someone with ambitions. Assuming he wasn't just brown-nosing, always a possibility.

Kennedy at least looked like a good prospect: his uniform fitted him well, and it was neatly pressed. About two inches shorter than Stride's six-two, he was trim and fit, in sharp contrast to some of the older officers on the Force, whose girth seemed to grow in rough parallel with their years on the beat.

"We'll be knocking on doors this morning to see if anyone saw or heard anything last night. We'll start with the houses nearest Rose's place, and then work our way along. Make a note of anything and everything, especially any contact anyone might have had with Rose."

Kennedy looked down the street in the direction of Government House.

"There, too, sir? Government House, I mean. They might have heard something. It's right next to the park."

"Interesting thought," Phelan said. "I can't remember anyone questioning someone at Government House about a case. At least, not since the riots in '32, and even that was dicey, I was told."

"It is an interesting thought," Stride said. "I'll think about that one for a while. For the time being, though, we'll concentrate on the regular folk."

"I knew who Mr. Rose was, but not a lot more than that." Mary Holden lived on Circular with her husband and three children, three doors away from Harrison

Rose. She was a well-dressed woman in her early forties, with blonde hair just turning softly, and attractively, grey. Stride sometimes saw her walking her dog on the street, but they hadn't met. "Such an awful thing to have happened. I thought Mr. Rose was a nice man, very polite, very much the gentleman. He always said 'good morning' or 'good afternoon' when I passed him on the street. Of course, he was English, and it showed. I think I would say he was very proper."

"Did you talk to him at all?"

"I don't think we ever had a real conversation, just the occasional chat. It wasn't that he was standoffish or anything. He was always pleasant enough. It was more to do with our different situations, I think. And the age difference. But we were neighbours for going on ten years."

"Ten years. That's when you moved here, or when Mr. Rose did?"

"When we moved here. Don and I, and the children. Mr. Rose was already here. I think he'd lived here for quite a while by then."

"Did he always live alone?"

"As far as I know, he did. Although he did mention that he'd been married once. That was just in passing, and I don't remember that he said much about it."

"He might have been a widower, then?"

"I don't know, but I don't think so. My impression was that he and his wife were separated. Perhaps they were divorced, I don't really know." She looked thoughtful. "I don't think she ever lived here, in the city, I mean. But I think he has a daughter somewhere. He mentioned that one time, again just in passing, probably when I told him that Don and I had two daughters of our own."

"Did she ever visit him?"

"The daughter? Not since we've been here. Certainly, I've never seen her." She looked thoughtful again, more serious this time. "At least, I don't think it was his daughter I saw him with."

"You saw him with someone? A woman?"

"Yes." She smiled uncertainly. "A couple of times I did see him with a woman, younger than he was, but not young enough to be his daughter, I don't think."

"Recently?"

"Yes. It was just last month. Well, sometime in the summer, anyway."

"Could you describe her for me?" He caught her look of uncertainty. "If we can locate her, she might be able to help us in our investigation."

"Of course." Mary Holden thought about it for a moment. "I'd say she was about my age. Late thirties, or maybe early forties. Dark hair, cut quite short, but nicely styled. And pretty. Yes, I would say she was pretty, a good-looking woman." She looked at Stride, almost asking for approval. "Does that help?"

"Yes, it does. Can you tell me anything else about her, or about them?"

"Oh, dear. Have I put my foot in it, now, telling tales about the poor man?"

"I'm sorry?"

"What I mean is, I don't think I was supposed to have seen them together. It was their reaction, I think, the furtive look they had when I saw them, as though they were pretending not to be together, if you know what I mean. I wondered if there was something going on. Well, I might as well say it, I suppose. I wondered if she might be someone else's wife." She paused again. "Now I almost feel as though I have done something wrong, said things I shouldn't have."

"I understand," Stride said. "It's a difficult situation. We need all the information we can get about Mr. Rose. Try not to worry about it." Her smile showed some relief. "It might be necessary for me to talk with you again, Mrs. Holden."

"I suppose so," she said. "Well, you know where I live."

"I didn't find anyone who knew Rose very well," Phelan said. "Everyone said he was polite, and a gentleman, but none of the people I talked to really knew him, I don't think, other than to say hello, or just have a casual conversation on the street."

"It was the same with me, Inspector," Kennedy said. "I talked to people at six houses, and no one said they knew Mr. Rose very well. It looks as though he kept pretty much to himself."

"I think it's because he was English," Phelan said. "A generally standoffish lot, the Brits." He smiled at Stride and Kennedy. "That's a personal opinion, of course."

"We won't put it writing," Stride said. "Did anyone mention seeing him with a woman? One of the people I talked to said she'd seen him with a woman sometimes, someone younger than he was. She seemed to think there was something going on between them."

"That would go along with the clothing and the cosmetics in his bedroom," Phelan said. "But no one I talked to mentioned seeing him with a woman." Kennedy nodded agreement. "I guess if there was something going on, they were careful about it."

"It would seem that way," Stride said.

"I did talk to one gentleman who knew Rose a little better than the others," Phelan said. "A Mr. Winter. He told me that Rose went to his church, the Cathedral, Church of England. Which is what you'd expect. Apparently he attended service almost every Sunday. And when he wasn't at the Cathedral, he went to St. Thomas's."

"It's closer to his house."

"And there's something else Winter told me. Rose was invited to stand for election to Vestry a few years ago. At the Cathedral. That's the lay body that runs a lot of the church affairs. There's about a dozen members of Vestry, altogether, and they're elected by the congregation."

"He didn't accept?"

"He politely declined, Winter said. And he gave me the impression that people were a bit miffed when Rose turned down the invitation. It's something of an honour to be asked to stand for Vestry, and almost no one ever says no."

"Interesting," Stride said. But if Harrison Rose wasn't outgoing, that wasn't very different from Stride himself. It didn't have to mean very much.

"I think Mr. Noseworthy's here," Kennedy said. The Black Maria was moving down the street towards them.

"He'll be making another search of the house," Stride said. "As long as you're here, Kennedy, you can assist him and Sergeant Phelan. You'll get some more experience in murder investigations."

"Thank you, sir, I'll do that."

"I'm going over to Government House and see if anyone there has anything to tell us. I'll catch up with all of you later."

Rodney Gilbert was talking on the phone when Stride was ushered into his office in Government House. He held up an index finger and then pointed towards a chair near his desk. He made a few small grunting noises that signalled assent to whatever it was his caller was saying, and then excused himself, adding that he would be calling back. He stood up and extended his right hand.

"It's Inspector Stride, I think? We met once, last year at a garden party here at the rock pile."

Gilbert's accent, upper-class Brit, went nicely with the decor of Government House. So did his appearance. His neat brown suit had a tailored look, and it draped nicely over his slender frame.

The decor of Government House was all that a viceregal residence should be. Stride had been inside on several occasions, always suitably impressed with the furniture and the trappings: the large portrait of the King over the mantelpiece in the hall, the faded battle colours of the Newfoundland Regiment hanging in a niche in the passage that led into the main part of the house. And then there were the frescoed ceilings, created—ironically enough—by a Polish artist, Alexander Pindikowsy, in the late 1800s, as part of his fifteen-month prison term for issuing forged cheques on the Commercial Bank in St. John's.

Rodney Gilbert's office was more utilitarian than ceremonial, but it was well appointed with quality furniture. The centrepiece was a large desk in dark walnut. The chair that Stride sat in had a leather seat and back, and the wood matched the desk. A framed portrait of King George and Queen Elizabeth hung on the wall over his desk.

"I remember," Stride said. "It rained halfway through and we all retreated inside until it stopped."

"You're right, it did. But at least the rain did stop that day, not like what's going on out there now. I suppose you're here about the shooting last night. I'm assuming, then, you must have got my message?"

"Message?"

"Well then, you didn't get it," Gilbert said. "I called Fort Townshend this morning, asking for an update on the situation. There's a security concern, of course, at least until the affair's sorted out. I left a message for the investigating officer to call me."

"It's probably still there, waiting for me to pick it up," Stride said. "But I came back down to the scene from home. I didn't go to Fort Townshend this morning."

"Well, you're here now, so no harm done."

"You had something to tell us about the shooting?"

"I can give you a bit of information. I was working late last night, catching up on correspondence, after a late-night meeting with Governor Macdonald, and I thought I heard shots. That was about 12:25. I know because I made a note of the time. The information I had from Fort Townshend this morning was that Colonel Rose was shot at about that time, so that's probably what I heard."

"But you weren't certain at the time that they were shots?"

"I was pretty certain, but not positive," Gilbert said. "One doesn't expect to hear gunfire in this neighbourhood, so my natural scepticism kicked in straightaway. Later on, when I asked one of my colleagues about it, he said he hadn't heard anything. But by then you'd started your investigation in the park next door, so I knew my initial reaction was probably correct."

"How many shots did you hear?"

"Two," Gilbert said.

"Two shots. You're certain of that?"

Gilbert looked at him.

"Yes, I heard two. Is there some question about the actual number?"

"Mr. Rose was shot three times, twice in the chest and once in the head."

"Really. Well, I suppose I must have missed one. This building's built of granite, and the walls are pretty thick. Perhaps two of the three shots were so close together they sounded like one. I don't know what else to say."

"That might have been it." But Gilbert's statement had renewed Stride's own puzzlement about the number of shots fired.

"You referred to Mr. Rose as 'Colonel,'" Stride said. "Was he still in the army?"

"No. He left the service quite some time ago, I believe."

"Do you know when that was? When he left the army?"

"No, I don't have a date. We do keep some information on Britons living in Newfoundland, but we don't keep detailed files. What we have on Colonel Rose is that he left the service sometime after the First War. I expect more information is available in London, but we don't have it here. But I can add that we also know that Colonel Rose was in business here in St. John's. We don't have information on the nature of his business, but that sort of thing really isn't our concern. We'd only keep information of that sort if the individual volunteered it, and he didn't. Anything beyond that might give a chap the impression we were keeping tabs on him, and that might not go down very well."

"Probably not," Stride said.

"Do you have any idea yet what it's all about? Was robbery the motive?"

"We don't think so. Colonel Rose still had his wallet on him."

"And the house wasn't burgled?"

"No. We were in the house last night, and there was no sign anyone had been in there."

"So you really don't know what it's all about?"

"No, we don't. In fact, we don't know a lot about Colonel Rose just yet."

"And you're hoping I can help you," Gilbert said.

"Yes."

"Well, I'm afraid I don't know very much about him, apart from the obvious. As I explained, we don't keep files on our people. And that's assuming he was still one of ours. I believe he'd lived here for a long time."

"Do you know how long?"

"Ten or fifteen years, I think. But don't quote me on that."

"We've reason to think that Colonel Rose might have been involved with a woman," Stride said. "Would you know anything about that?"

"Good lord, no. It's my understanding that Colonel Rose lived alone. I knew that he'd been married, but his wife wasn't living with him. I don't think she'd ever been here, in fact."

"Can you tell me anything about his marital situation?"

"Not much more than what I've said already. I knew he'd been married, and also that he had a daughter somewhere. In fact, it was Colonel Rose himself who told me that, at one of the functions here at Government House."

"So, you did know him."

"Oh, not really," Gilbert said. "I've probably met most of the Brits who live in St. John's, at one time or another. But I didn't really know Colonel Rose, not in any real sense."

"He and his wife were separated, then? Were they divorced?"

"I believe they were. But to be honest, I don't really know. I'm not even sure she's still alive." Gilbert caught Stride's expression. "And before you ask, I'll say I don't know why I said that. More impression than fact, really."

"Colonel Rose didn't say that she was dead?"

"I don't think so, but it's my impression that she might be. I'm sorry, I don't think this is very helpful. Probably more confusing than anything else."

"No, it's all right," Stride said. "You said he had a daughter somewhere. Do you know where she is?"

"In England, I believe. But, again, that's more by way of impression than known fact." He smiled again, less grim this time. "I hope I haven't muddled things for you, Inspector. Look, let me think about this for a while. If I come up with anything I think is useful, I'll get back to you."

"I'd appreciate that," Stride said.

"The general number at Fort Townshend will get you, I suppose. Or do you have a private line?"

"The general number will do it, but you can call me at home if you need to." Stride took a card from his wallet. It had both his office and home phone numbers. The cards weren't Constabulary issue—he'd had them made up himself. It was more convenient than having people go through the bother of writing down his name and number. He hoped it would start a trend on the Force, but he had his doubts about that. The rate of change in some Constabulary procedures could be almost glacial, a one-legged route march up the north face of Everest in the dark of night. He stood up. "I appreciate this, Mr. Gilbert. You've been very helpful."

"I hope I have." Gilbert took a card from his desk drawer and gave it to Stride. They walked down the hall together towards the main entrance. "If there's anything else you think I can help you with, please don't hesitate to ask."

"I'll do that."

"And may I ask for a quid pro quo?"

"Of course."

"Can you let me know how things go? Just the occasional update, you understand, nothing formal. Just call it in. My personal number is on the card I gave you."

"I'll do that," Stride said.

"Unless Governor Macdonald decides he wants more, in which case we'll be in touch on a more formal level. But I don't really anticipate that happening."

CHAPTER 5

Stride stopped on Circular Road in front of Government House and lit a cigarette. It was still raining, but the air was fresh, cooler than it had been for the past week. The Black Maria was still parked in front of Rose's house, but there was no one in sight. He thought again about the number of shots he'd heard, but still couldn't square his memory with the three wounds on Rose's body.

He looked to his right and saw a man walking towards him from the direction of King's Bridge Road. A red umbrella completely hid the man's head and shoulders, but the familiar long, loping stride told him it was Alex Greene.

"An early morning for you, Alex," Stride said, when Greene was close enough to hear.

"A very late evening, actually. I haven't managed to make it to bed yet."

"Places to go and people to see?"

"In a manner of speaking. I got caught up in one of those complicated late-night parties that move around from house to house. You know the drill."

"I did, once upon a time. But it seems you stopped by the newspaper office at some point."

"The old newsman's reflex. I was in the neighbourhood and went on in. And for once it was productive. A stringer had just phoned in news of a gathering in the park, close to your place, and he recognized Tom Butcher as one of the celebrants. That told me it was something worth looking at. I massaged his notes into the short piece you read in this morning's rag."

Greene's gaze shifted from Stride to Harrison Rose's house and the Black Maria.

"But perhaps you've done a bit more work since then?" Stride said.

"Yes, I have. The party finally broke up around seven, and I've been out and about. What I have so far is that a gentleman named Harrison Rose is dead, shot last night in the park."

"You got that from someone at the General Hospital?"

"That's one of my sources. Is it official yet?"

"Not yet. We can't release the name until the next of kin have been notified."

"Is there a next of kin? I wasn't aware that Rose had any relatives in the vicinity."

"We think he was married at one time, but we don't know anything about his wife. We believe he has a daughter, but we haven't confirmed that, either. And all that's unofficial, too."

"Understood," Greene said. "I suppose Jack McCowan will entertain questions at some point?"

"That's the drill from our side. But I don't know when that will happen. For one thing, I haven't had a chance to sit down with McCowan and give him a briefing. Sometime later today, probably."

"For the briefing, or the entertainment of questions?"

"There isn't any timetable."

"I see you're still working on the house. Noseworthy and Harry are there, I suppose?"

"Yes, they are. How much do you know about Harrison Rose, Alex? I'm getting the impression you know something about him."

"I don't know anything about the shooting, but I do know a little about Rose."

"Such as?"

"For one thing, I know he was a colonel in the British Army from the Great War. Also that he was attached to the Newfoundland Regiment for a time."

"I didn't know that. I suppose that could explain why he's living here now."

"It might. He joined the Regiment in Gallipoli in 1915, but I understand that was a month after they'd got there."

"There are pictures in his study that look like they were taken in Gallipoli. Do you know if he was still with them at Beaumont Hamel in 1916?"

"For the bloodbath on the first day of the Somme? Yes, he was. Jack McCowan can probably tell you more about that than I can. He was there."

"Yes, he was. What else do you know about Rose?"

"Not a whole lot," Greene said. "I did meet him once, two years ago, when I was doing a story on the Great War, comparing it to the most recent one. Someone gave me his name and suggested he might be worth talking to."

"And did he agree to that?"

"No, he didn't. He wasn't rude or anything. Very polite, in fact, in that nice

English way. But he also had nothing to say to me, or said he didn't. He was quite definite about that. Your turn, now."

"We don't know very much at this point, Alex. There's no evidence that robbery was the motive."

"You heard the shots from your place, I suppose?"

"Yes, I did. From what we've seen of his house, Rose was obviously well off. Do you know anything about that side of his life?"

"I know that he was in business here, and had been for quite a while. I think his business has something to do with wood, timber." Greene laughed. "Those tall, firm things with bark and leaves." He laughed again. "Forgive the sorry humour. I think I'm in need of some sleep."

"You're forgiven." Stride looked down the street. Tom Kennedy was coming out of Rose's house, carrying a file box, one of the kind the Constabulary used for storing evidence. He slid it into the back of the van. "I have to get back to work, Alex. There are things I need to be doing over there."

"I understand. But I'll be in touch, if that's all right."

"We've been through this place pretty thoroughly," Noseworthy said. "It will take us a while to sift through everything we've collected."

"Was Kennedy any help?"

"He was. I didn't expect to see him here today. Wasn't he on patrol duty last night, about the time Rose was shot?"

"Yes, he was. He's here this morning on a volunteer basis."

"Really. Well, he did help. For one thing, he managed to find a large ring of keys in the back of a drawer in the master bedroom. I've tried them out and most of them are for doors and cupboards here in the house. A few of them didn't fit anything. I'm guessing they're for Rose's business office. That's at the Newfoundland Hotel, by the way. A number of small companies have offices there."

"Any sign of a personal journal?"

"No. There's some personal correspondence, and a bunch of household files, and we've boxed it. We might find more information when we go through his office at the hotel. In the meantime, we'll take everything we've collected from here back to Fort Townshend, Kennedy and me. I'll start sorting it later today."

"We've confirmed that Rose did have a daughter," Phelan said. "There was a letter from her in the correspondence file. Her name's Catherine Darnell."

"The letter was from England?"

"She probably lives in England, but the envelope was postmarked Boston.

She's visiting with friends. The letter also said she'd be arriving here sometime soon."

"Here? In St. John's?"

"That's what she wrote."

"There wasn't an arrival date?"

"No, sir."

Phelan gave Stride the letter. He read it through, then gave it to Noseworthy to put in an evidence box.

"I talked to one of the Governor's aides at Government House," Stride said. "He didn't have a lot to tell me about Rose. Nothing that adds to what we already know. But he did tell me he'd heard the shots last night. Two of them."

"Two shots," Noseworthy said. "The same as you heard. I don't understand. It doesn't match up with the number of wounds."

"We heard what we heard," Stride said. "I know it doesn't make sense, but there it is. And the fellow I talked to, Rodney Gilbert, he made a note of the time, and it fits. About 12:25."

"I've been thinking about the number of shots I heard," Kennedy said. Stride hadn't seen him come into the kitchen. "Last night, after Dr. Butcher said Colonel Rose had three wounds, I had to wonder if I'd got the number of shots wrong. But I don't think I did, sir. I'm positive I heard only two shots, and I really don't think I could have missed one. They weren't right together. First I heard one shot, and while I was still wondering if I'd really heard what I thought I did, there was a second shot. That's when I came on along to the park."

"Well, it's a mystery," Noseworthy said. "And in somewhat the same vein, we did find a revolver upstairs. A Webley Mark V, in a leather holster, tucked away on a shelf in a cupboard. The Mark V's a brute of a weapon, a .455 calibre. We also found three boxes of cartridges, same calibre. I'm guessing it's the weapon Rose carried with him in the war. It was standard British Army issue back then. And it's in mint condition, freshly oiled."

"And?" Stride could see that Noseworthy was working his way towards something else.

"We found an open box of cartridges in the study, in a drawer in Rose's desk. They're .38s."

"But you didn't find a gun to match."

"No, we didn't. Which tells us that Rose might have owned a .38 at one time."

"Maybe he loaned it to someone," Phelan said. "Or it's out for repair. I'll call around to the local gunsmiths when we get back to the Fort."

"You can do that while I'm briefing McCowan," Stride said. "There's a chance he knew Harrison Rose from his time back in the First War. I ran into Alex Greene and he told me that Rose was attached to the Newfoundland Regiment in Gallipoli in 1915. He was also at Beaumont Hamel the year after that."

"It's more than a possibility," Noseworthy said. "I spoke to McCowan before I came back down here. He told me he did know Rose from back then."

Jack McCowan rested his chin on his hands while Stride went through his briefing on the murder of Harrison Rose. He included the information on the inconsistency between the number of shots he'd heard and the number of times Rose had been hit.

"Very odd," McCowan said when Stride was finished, but he didn't add anything to that. "And you say Noseworthy found a Webley Mark V in Rose's house? I'm not surprised. A lot of the chaps carried the Mark V in the First War. I had one for a while, myself, but I switched to the Browning .45 semi-automatic. An American weapon. I still have it, in fact." McCowan picked up his cigar and sat back in his chair. "What's your take on it so far, Eric? It obviously wasn't a robbery."

"I'm not sure, sir."

"But you've had a thought or two."

"Yes. It has the look of an ambush, sir. An assassination."

"I have to agree with you. But your suggestion only raises more questions. We'll keep that part of it to ourselves for the moment, and deal only with what we actually know to be fact. Understood?"

"Yes, sir. Noseworthy told me you knew Rose from your time in the war."

"Yes, I did. And I do know a bit about him. Not very much, but it might help. I've also met him on a few occasions since, here in St. John's. We weren't friends, and I didn't know him all that well. I actually got to know him better during the First War than I did after he moved here. Sounds odd, I know, but that's the way it was."

"I ran into Alex Greene earlier, and he told me a little bit about Rose, although not much."

"I suppose that had to do with the article he wrote on the war two years ago. He interviewed me at the time, and told me he'd tried to interview Harry Rose as well. Well, I can fill in some of the blanks. Rose was with our Regiment for about two years, altogether. We had quite a number of British officers with us over there, at different times. Senior officers for the most part, major and higher."

"I understand Rose was a colonel."

"Eventually he was, but not when he was with us. When he first came to the Regiment, he was a captain, and a newly minted one at that. He was career army, joined up a couple of years before the big show started in 1914. He'd been wounded in the first Ypres, in October of '14, and he was invalided back to England. But he'd done well at Ypres, been decorated, in fact. He was promoted to Captain about that time, and when he got out of hospital, he joined our Regiment in Gallipoli, on Suvla Plain. That was in October of 1915. When he got there, I mean. We'd been posted there in September. He was with us until the last stages of the withdrawal in January of '16. And he stayed with us when we were sent to France for the big push that summer."

"Greene said Rose was with the Regiment at Beaumont Hamel on July 1."

"Well, yes and no. He was with the 10 percent. It isn't generally understood, but not everyone in the Regiment went over the top that day. It was standard practice to keep 10 percent of each regiment, each battalion, in reserve, to re-supply after the primary objective had been reached. Of course, on July 1, 1916, none of our objectives was reached, and almost the entire Regiment were casualties—killed, wounded or missing. It was a bloody disaster. Our lot just about had the worst of it, although our lads weren't singled out for special punishment, whatever some people might think. We lost 310 men, killed that day, but all told, the British Fourth Army had more than 19,000 dead. In a single day. The figures still leave me numb."

McCowan sat back in his chair and stared at the tip of his cigar and he fell silent for a long moment.

"Well, enough of that. Rose stayed with the Regiment for another year and a bit, got promoted and then he moved on."

"You knew him fairly well back then?"

"Not really, no. We were assigned to different companies in the Regiment. Also, Rose was a more senior officer than I was."

"Was he a good officer?"

"Interesting question, Eric. Are you thinking his war record might have something to do with this?"

"I wasn't, no, but I probably will now. At least wonder about it."

"Well, we have to think about all the possibilities, however remote. But to answer your question, I believe Rose was a good officer. The rest of us, the Newfoundland officers, I mean, we had a good opinion of him. The men did too, I believe, the other ranks."

"We're still not sure when Rose moved to the island, or why."

"I don't know when that was, not exactly. It was quite a long time ago - late twenties, early thirties, I believe."

"Greene said he had a business here. Something to do with wood."

"Yes. He was in the timber business. Exports, I believe. He was some sort of agent. I don't know how large his company is, or was, but he obviously did well enough. I think it's possible he also had some private means, and he might have owned property here. You'll want to look into that. He wasn't wealthy, I don't think, not like some of the established families here in the city, but it's obvious he was well off. The house alone says that. But, the fact is, I didn't have a lot of contact with Rose after he moved here."

"Not even at Regimental gatherings?"

"We have an annual dinner and booze-up, and I think Rose attended one or two, but he wasn't a regular, not like me."

"Isn't that a bit unusual? For an old army man?"

"Unusual, but not unheard of. Some of the old hands have no use for the attachment, and would prefer to forget the whole bloody business, and God knows there's a lot to forget. It's not my way, but I can understand it. That having been said, I believe Rose stayed in touch with some of the men he served with. Albert Dancey is one, and he might be your best bet. I see Albert from time to time, and he's one of the regulars at the dinners. Lawrence Rivers also served with Rose, but I haven't seen him lately. I'm not sure Laurie's very well, in fact."

"That's the Lawrence Rivers of Rivers & Sons?"

"Yes. It's the family business. Fish. Laurie's grandfather started it up almost a century ago, down on the south coast, originally, but the company headquarters is here in the city now. Dancey also works for the company, and in a fairly senior position. He might even be a partner now."

"The information we have so far is that Rose seemed to keep to himself pretty much. None of his neighbours appear to have known him very well."

"That's my impression, too." McCowan tapped the ash off the end of his cigar. "We haven't released his name yet, have we?"

"No, sir. Colonel Rose has a daughter, and we found a letter that indicates she's going to be here, soon. She's been visiting with friends in Boston, apparently."

"And a cold, unpleasant welcome awaits her. We don't have her address in Boston, I suppose?"

"No, we don't. And we don't know when she's supposed to be here, just that it's likely to be soon. We'll just have to wait until she arrives."

"When she might find a brace of bloody great policeman standing on her father's doorstep. You've alerted them to the possibility?"

"Yes, we have."

"You know, on the question of Rose's qualities as an officer, you could talk to Jack Corrigan about that. Corrigan was over there, for all four years of it, and he would have served under Rose at some point." McCowan sat back in his chair, thinking. "I'm wondering about Rose's wife. I believe they went their separate ways a long time ago, but I don't know if they were divorced or not. She might be living in England somewhere, I suppose."

"One of Rose's neighbours thought she might be dead, that he was a widower." He didn't mention the woman Mary Holden saw Rose with, and he wouldn't until he had more information on her, and her relevance to the investigation, if any.

"Perhaps she is. And if that's the case, this makes the daughter an orphan, doesn't it?"

"Yes," Stride said. "I suppose it does."

Harry Phelan was sitting at his desk going through the collection of papers they'd found in Rose's study. A cigarette was burning in the ashtray at his elbow. He looked around when Stride came into the room.

"Anything useful in that?"

"Not a whole lot," Phelan said. "Most of this stuff is bills for household expenses, along with some business correspondence. He seems to have kept every receipt he ever had. I haven't been through all of it. Nothing much of a personal nature, other than the letter from his daughter, and you've already seen that. Did McCowan have anything useful for us?"

"Not a lot. He knew Rose, but not very well. He remembers him from the war, and he said he was a good officer. He also suggested we talk to Jack Corrigan about him, to get the enlisted man's point of view."

"That could be interesting, given Corrigan's general lack of respect for authority."

"More than likely," Stride said. "McCowan gave me a couple of names, men who served with Rose in the First War, and who've been in touch with him since he moved here. Albert Dancey, and Lawrence Rivers."

"Of Rivers & Sons?"

"You know them?"

"I know who they are. I even met Dancey, some years back, when I was still in uniform, although he probably wouldn't remember me."

"Anything important?"

"Just a fracas among the crew on one of Rivers's fishing boats. We'll be talking to him, I suppose?"

"Yes, and maybe to Rivers too, although McCowan said he thought Rivers might not be very well."

"Did McCowan have any thoughts on what this is about?"

"No, but he asked me if I had any. I told him I thought it looked like an assassination."

"A big word," Phelan said.

"And a big idea."

"Well, we know that whoever did this is very handy with guns," Phelan said. "And when I think of guns, I think about war."

"Go on."

"I'm wondering if this has something to do with the war. The First War, I mean, Rose's war."

"A revenge killing." Stride said. "Someone getting even for something that happened over there, thirty years ago?"

"Maybe. How about you, sir? Has it crossed your mind at all?"

"It has now. But it looks like a very long shot, Harry. Thirty years is a long time to carry a grudge."

"It was a long time ago," Phelan said. "And it's odd, you know. A couple of Kit's uncles, who were in some of the worst of the fighting over there, they talk about the war with, I don't know, a kind of happy reminiscence, if I can put it that way."

"You can put it any way you want, Harry. But I know what you mean. They belong to an exclusive club, the men who survived that war. Any war, for that matter. It's hard for us to imagine what they went through, or relate to it. Neither of us has ever been in a war. We know some of the words, but we don't speak the language."

"Well, that's true enough."

"Did you have any luck with the gunsmiths?"

"No. None of them had even heard of Harrison Rose."

"Which leaves us with no explanation for the box of .38s."

"As Noseworthy said, he might have loaned the gun to someone. When we release Rose's name, someone might come forward." Phelan looked at his watch. "What time is Rose's autopsy?"

"In about thirty minutes."

"That soon?"

"Yes. I called Butcher and he said he wanted to get it done with as soon as possible. Better for him, and better for us."

CHAPTER 6

The autopsy on Harrison Rose at the General Hospital took much longer than either Stride or Butcher had expected it would. For Harry Phelan, autopsies were always a trial, long or short. Butcher had anticipated it would be routine procedure, with the results matching all of their expectations. It was obvious that Rose had been killed by the gunshot to the head. There was no doubt about that. It seemed also obvious, even before Butcher started cutting, that either of the two wounds in the torso would have been sufficient to kill the man. The quantity of blood that Rose had coughed up over his clothing attested to a large amount of damage to his lungs.

After he opened the body and looked at the internal damage, Butcher concluded that was indeed the case. One of the bullets had torn through Rose's diaphragm and caused damage to major blood vessels, starting a bleed that would have been fatal in only a few minutes. The second bullet in Rose's chest tore through both lungs, and also caused major bleeding. That bullet by itself could have accounted for the blood that soaked through Rose's clothing—his shirt, his jacket and the front of his raincoat.

The bullet to the head, as Butcher had earlier surmised, indeed had the look of a *coup de grâce*—by strict definition, "a finishing stroke."

"Rose was very near death before the final shot to the head," Butcher said.

"Would he have lived much longer?"

"Not very much longer. I would measure the time in minutes. And very bad minutes."

"Was he conscious, do you think?"

"It's hard to say, but it's possible he was. Rose was in very good health for a man of his years, very fit, in fact. The lungs, what's left of them, don't show as much damage from tobacco use as I would have expected." He looked at Stride and Phelan. "Not as much damage as any of us is likely to show, I think."

Phelan surprised himself, and the others, by staying in the room when Butcher opened Rose's skull, although he did turn away during the probing that finally produced the fatal bullet. Butcher extracted it and dropped it in the pan that held the other two.

And that was when the autopsy went off course. Even before Butcher washed the traces of blood and tissue from the projectile, and despite the fact that it was distorted from multiple contacts with bone, it was obvious to all three of them that the bullet taken from Rose's brain was different from the others. For one thing, it wasn't the same calibre, it was slightly larger.

"This, I did not expect," Butcher said.

"I'm guessing a .38, Thomas," Stride said. "What do you think?"

"Probably a .38. But let's wait until Noseworthy takes a look at it."

Butcher carried the pan with the three bullets over to the sink and ran water into it, then laid them on a towel. Now cleaned of blood and tissue, the differences were even more obvious.

"This raises any number of questions about what went on in the park last night, Eric."

"Starting with the number of shots I heard," Stride said. "I heard two."

"Possibly the two bullets that hit Rose in the torso?"

"Maybe." Stride picked up the three bullets and looked at them, rolling them around in his hand. He put them back on the towel. "Rose had a half-empty box of .38s in a drawer in his study."

"You mentioned that earlier. But you didn't find a gun to match."

"We found a Webley .455 in an upstairs cupboard, but we didn't find a .38. Just the bullets." He went back to the table and looked down at Rose's body, at the massive destruction of a man who had been alive and well less than twenty-four hours before. "I'm trying to think what might have gone on last night. So, let's suppose that Rose did own a .38. And let's suppose he had it with him last night when he went out for his walk."

"Had it with him?" Butcher said. "You think he went out armed?"

"He could have. Try this on for size. I heard two shots, but Rose was hit three times, and one of the bullets that hit him is different from the other two. We know that the 9 mm was a semi-automatic. The shell cases with ejection marks tell us that. And one of the characteristics of a semi is that it can be easily fitted with a silencer. I know, because I've used one." He shrugged. "It was a long time ago, and a long way from here."

"You're suggesting that the two shots you heard weren't from the 9 mm?"

"That is what I'm suggesting. We think Rose probably owned a .38, but we didn't find it in his house. Just the bullets. So let's suppose Rose was armed last night, and when he was shot he was able to pull out his gun and get off two shots of his own."

"I think you said the two shots you heard were separated by about twenty or thirty seconds."

"At least that long." He paused and thought about that. "But let's continue to suppose the two shots I heard were fired by Rose. You did say it was possible he was still conscious after he was hit."

"I can't say for sure that he wasn't," Butcher said. "He might have been."

"And able to fire a gun?"

"Who can say what a man is able to do in a situation like that? The body reacts in odd ways to massive stress."

"And one of the things that happens can be a huge jolt of adrenaline," Stride said.

"Yes."

"And with a large jolt of adrenaline, a dying man can do some remarkable things."

"He can. I've heard stories of men fatally wounded in battle who've done incredible things, things you wouldn't believe an injured man could do. In some cases, even a man who wasn't injured."

"And Rose was a soldier," Phelan said.

"Yes, he was." Butcher walked over to where Rose's clothing was laid out on a table. His raincoat was suspended from a hanger on the wall. "Everything you've said is possible, Eric. Rose might have been armed, and he might have been able to pull out his weapon and fire a couple of shots. None of it's impossible."

"You're thinking about something else, Thomas. What is it?"

"Something that's been puzzling me since I got to looking at all this." He indicated Rose's raincoat. "There's a lot of blood on the front of the coat, and I'm quite sure that blood is Rose's own. Shot through the lungs like that, he would have coughed up a lot of blood. But there's a stain on the lower part of the coat that isn't consistent with the rest of it."

"You're thinking that blood might be from the man who shot him?"

"It might be. Try this on. Rose goes down with two bullets in his torso. The man who shot him steps closer to see if he's dead, or to finish the job from close range. And here I'll add that there were powder burns and tattooing on Rose's scalp, and that indicates a shot fired from very close range. So, when the shooter comes close enough, Rose fires two shots, and one of them hits him, and he bleeds onto Rose's coat. I can check the blood types, and see if they're different."

"No, that doesn't work," Stride said. "Not the bit about Rose getting off two shots at his killer. The final shot had to have been fired by the killer, using Rose's own gun. The .38."

"You're right," Butcher said. "My mistake."

"Rose might have gotten off one shot," Phelan said, "and hit the man who shot him, but then he's done. He drops his gun, the shooter picks it up and finishes him off with a shot to the head."

"That fits better," Stride said. "There was a thirty-second gap between the shots I heard. But why Rose's gun, I wonder? Why not his own?"

"He might have dropped his when he was shot," Butcher said. "Assuming he was shot. I'll do the blood tests, and then we'll have a better idea."

Stride looked at the collection of clothing on the table. His gaze came to rest on the leather gloves Rose was wearing when he was shot. He remembered seeing them when he placed his own raincoat over Rose's body to shield him from the rain.

"We'll take Rose's gloves over to Noseworthy as well, along with the bullets, and have him test them for gunshot residue. If Rose did fire a gun last night, there could be some residue on the leather."

"There might be, but it was raining very hard last night, Eric. Any residue might have been washed off. But, you're right. If he finds even a small amount, it would help you piece the picture together."

"If Rose did get off a couple of shots," Phelan said, "we might have a wounded man out there someplace."

"It obviously wasn't an immediately fatal wound," Butcher said. "Perhaps not even a really serious one, or you would have found him already. It also appears he was in sufficient control of his faculties to take Rose's gun away with him when he left the scene."

"But if he's wounded badly enough, he'll need medical attention at some point."

"It's unlikely he'll go to a hospital. They'd be required to report a gunshot injury. And no reputable doctor will treat a gunshot victim without calling the police."

"What about a disreputable doctor?" Phelan said.

"That's another story. Disreputable doctors are like the wise virgins. They don't advertise, and they go about with care."

"I don't think there are any unwise virgins, Thomas. Or not very many."

"Point taken."

They left the autopsy room and went down the corridor to Butcher's office.

"Did Jack McCowan suggest anyone you should talk to about Rose?" Butcher asked.

"A couple of names. Albert Dancey and Lawrence Rivers. They were with Rose in the Regiment thirty years ago. McCowan says they're probably friends of his. And they're both living here in St. John's."

"Dancey and Rivers." Butcher leaned against the edge of his desk.

"You know them?"

"I will go so far as to say, 'yes,' I do know them. And one small step further. They're both patients of mine. That isn't just coincidence. I first met them in France when we were all of us with the Regiment. When they came to me after I set up my practice here, I remembered who they were, and where we'd first met."

"So you've been their doctor for more than twenty-five years."

"I suppose it has been that long. It seems not so long ago, really, only the blink of an eye." Butcher shook his head. "Well, two blinks, perhaps."

"But you can't say any more about either of them."

"No, I can't. Neither wink, nor nod, nor anxious refusal. The doctor-patient relationship is confidential."

"But we could be looking for someone who knew Rose as long as Dancey and Rivers did," Stride said.

"It's possible. Are you thinking that his murder might have something to do with his time in the Great War?"

"Harry and I were talking about that before we came down here. But the war was a long time ago, Thomas, almost thirty years."

"A very long time," Butcher said. "But memories can be long, and for those who survived that war, there's a lot to remember."

CHAPTER 7

Stride dropped Phelan at Fort Townshend with the leather gloves and the three bullets, and then he drove east out of the city towards Outer Cove and the small farmhouse where Jack Corrigan lived. He'd considered bringing McCowan up to date on the findings of the autopsy, but that wouldn't have got him any closer to understanding why Rose had been killed. Talking to Corrigan might. If nothing else, it would give him a clearer picture of Rose's time in the war, and his qualities as an officer. It wasn't that he thought McCowan's opinion was wrong, but he knew from his own time as a uniformed policeman that the man at ground level would have a different perspective.

Not far from the city proper, the pavement ended and he was driving on a gravel road. He'd been out this way in the spring, not long after a road crew had been by with a grader, and the road was smooth enough, hardpan scraped free of the larger stones that could rip a hole in the engine's base pan, or tear an exhaust system to shreds. Today, though, the road was coated with mud, and the potholes that had been filled in earlier were reasserting their command. The rain continued to fall. He slowed the MG down to twenty miles per hour, steering around the larger holes, and hoped for the best. He glanced at his watch. He still wanted to try for an interview with Albert Dancey, and he thought he had time.

Jack Corrigan lived by himself on a plot of land that had once supported an entire family. But the productivity of the land had long since declined, and Corrigan rented part of his holding to a neighbour. As far as Stride could see, the main crop now was hay for feeding livestock. He'd noticed some dairy cows and dray horses grazing in fields in the area. It was the remoteness and privacy of the place that had attracted Corrigan, and that had remained unchanged since he bought it. Eventually, Stride thought, the city would expand eastward, and someone would build on the open fields. That wouldn't please Corrigan at all, but by then he would be retired from the Force, and probably living someplace else, far away from the encroaching city.

He pulled into Corrigan's laneway and parked behind his battered red pickup truck. By the time Stride stepped out of the car, Corrigan was standing in the doorway of his house, wearing the same set of bib overalls and short rubber boots he'd worn the last time Stride was here. This time, though, he wore a heavy plaid shirt, the sleeves cut off at the elbow. Corrigan was shorter than Stride by four inches, but was probably twenty pounds heavier. His hair was red and his complexion florid, qualities that went well with his Irish lineage.

"I'm supposed to be off with the flu, sir, but what I'm actually doing is starting to put down my supply of ale for the winter. I'll be back on my beat tomorrow morning, but there'll be a couple more flu attacks over the next week or two, and then it'll be done. I still have a dozen bottles left over from the last batch, if you're interested."

Stride shook his head.

"Strictly business today, I'm afraid."

"Well, it's a long fuckin' drive from Fort Townshend with the rain pelting down. So, it has to be something pretty big."

Corrigan stepped aside and pushed the door open wider so Stride could enter. Two of the half-dozen cats Stride had seen on his last visit were sitting on the rug near Corrigan's upright piano, and two more were lying on chairs. The place hadn't changed since the last time Stride was here. Corrigan's house was comfortable enough, even if most of the furniture was second-hand, including the piano. Corrigan had told him once that he was planning on taking lessons someday. He wondered now if he had, but that was a subject for another occasion.

"Harrison Rose was shot and killed last night, Jack. Early this morning, actually."

"Colonel Rose." Corrigan frowned and closed the door. He picked a cat off one of the chairs so Stride could sit. He sat on a chair opposite him. He nodded his head slowly. "How did that come to happen, sir? Or do you know yet?"

"We don't know, and now it's looking more complicated than it did a few hours ago. It was complicated enough then. I've just come from the autopsy at the General."

"Something unexpected turned up?"

"Yes, it did." He went through a description of the shooting, and the results of the autopsy. "It's looking as though Rose was armed when he went out for his walk last night. That's the only way it makes sense that there were two guns involved. Do you know of any reason why Rose would go around armed with a pistol?"

Corrigan shook his head.

"Colonel Rose lived here for going on fifteen, twenty years, and as far as I know, he was a respected businessman. If he had some reason to carry a gun with him when he went out for a walk, I don't know what it could be. Mind you, I haven't seen him in a while."

"You did see him after he moved here, though?"

"We bumped into each other now and then, but we weren't friends." Corrigan sat back in his chair and started rolling a cigarette. "Colonel Rose—Captain Rose when I first met him—was an officer, and I never made it past corporal." He smiled. "I was promoted to sergeant a couple of times, and every time I went up, I got promoted back down to corporal right afterwards. Even made it all the way back to private one time. My military career pretty much matches my career as a policeman, up and down the ladder, lickety-split. Something to do with my personality, I think."

"You first met Rose in Gallipoli, is that right?"

"On Suvla Plain, October of 1915. We'd already been there for a while before Rose joined up with us."

"McCowan said he was with the Regiment going on two years, until sometime in 1917."

"And so he was." Corrigan sat forward again. "Are you thinking he was killed because of something that happened back during the war?"

"I'm looking at all the possibilities."

"It's been a long time, sir, going on thirty years. And to be honest, I can't think of anything the Colonel done back then that would inspire anyone to go after him. As far as I was concerned, Rose was a good officer. That's not to say that someone else mightn't have had a different opinion of him."

"Tell me what you know about him, Jack. He was my neighbour, but I didn't know him at all. And now I'm trying to get a picture of the man."

"I'll do my best, sir." Corrigan sat back and stretched his legs out. "We'd been on Suvla Plain since September, most of us. Latecomers, we were. We got there just about the time the high command decided that Gallipoli was a fuckin' disaster and that we should get the hell out of there while we still could. The Allies had took a shitload of casualties by then, with the Aussies and the Kiwis taking the worst of it." He shook his head. "You have to wonder what goes through people's minds when they sign up for a war in a godforsaken place like Gallipoli, especially coming from someplace like Australia or New Zealand. Well, I should talk. I signed up here in St. John's in September of '14 and never stopped for a moment to think that it was very fuckin' unlikely the Hun would come piling ashore on Cape Race.

"Rose joined us just in time to help us think about getting the hell out of Gallipoli. They called it a brilliant retreat, and it was probably the only real victory in the entire campaign." Corrigan closed his eyes for a moment, organizing his thoughts. "First off, I'll say that some of us had our doubts about Captain Rose when he first joined us. For the most part, we had our own officers, Newfoundlanders, I mean. It makes a difference when they're your own people. Rose, now, he wasn't much to look at, just a little fella, about as tall as two jam jars. And some of us wondered about that, whether he might try too hard to impress us, to make up for his lack of size. But that wasn't a problem, as it turned out. He was no-nonsense from the start, and he wouldn't ask any of us to do something that he wouldn't do himself."

"That's high praise, Jack."

"I'll tell you a story. It happened not long after Rose joined us on the Plain. But you have to know what it was like out there. By the time we got to Gallipoli, the campaign was a stalemate, the Turks in their trenches and us in ours, staring at each other across no man's land. Horrible fuckin' place, no man's land. Unburied corpses from both sides, rotting in the sun, feeding flies. You wouldn't believe the flies, sir. Mealtimes was bloody awful. It was a fight to see who would get the food first, you or the fuckin' flies.

"And they weren't just a nuisance. They carried diseases with them, from the dead to the living. It was almost like a punishment for still being alive. By October, when Captain Rose got there, a third of our men was sick, shitting their guts out, dysentery and enteric, and worse. The lucky ones got invalided out. The really lucky ones were so sick after Gallipoli they missed the first day of the Somme in July the next year."

"A mixed blessing."

"Apart from the bloody flies, and the weather, and the diseases, we had the Turkish snipers to deal with, never mind their artillery. Not long after Rose got there, the orders come down that we were to go out and take a Turkish position on a knoll not far from our own trench. Abdul liked to set up there every evening, and then in the morning go back to his own trench. Our orders was to go out there and take it over. There was six of us, including Captain Rose. It was just before sundown when we headed out. We reckoned we had an hour before the Turks would move out of their own trench to set up on the knoll for the evening."

"Six of you."

"Myself, Cecil Cake, Laurie Rivers, Gabriel Hobbs and Curtis Rowe. Captain Rose was in the lead, with Cec behind him. I brought up the rear, and Rivers was a few yards ahead of me. We all had rifles, including Captain Rose, the Lee-Enfield .303, with full ten-round magazine and bayonets fixed."

"Even Rose?"

"Usually an officer only had a sidearm, and that was usually the Webley Mark V. But we all had Webleys on this patrol. We improvised a lot out there. And anyway, Rose having a rifle was a plus for us. He was a marksman, one of the best in the army, we'd heard. We were at the knoll after only a few minutes fast walking, and that gives you an idea how handy we were to each other out there. When we got near, Rose halted us and he was the one who went on ahead to scout the position."

"Unusual for an officer to do that."

"It was. The routine was to send one or two of the men ahead to do the scouting. And Rose doing it, that worried me a bit, because I was afraid he might start playing the hero, do something brave and get us all killed. But it turned out all right. In a minute or two he was giving us the signal to move onto the knoll, and we went up there and set up our positions. And then we waited." Corrigan leaned forward. "That was the worst part, waiting for something to happen. I was almost grateful when the artillery started up, first from their side, and then the answer back from ours. We could hear the shells passing overhead, but we weren't worried, because no one was taking aim at us.

"I was set up as forward observer, so I was the first one to see the Turks coming up from their line. There was four of them, single-file. It was one of the few times I got to see Abdul close-up. Rose assigned one of us to each of the Turks. Hobbs, Rowe, Cec and Rose himself would do the shooting, with Rose taking the last man in the line. Rivers and me, we'd provide backup. And we was under orders to use as few bullets as possible. We'd need the ammunition for the counterattack we knew would come later.

"The first Turk in the line was just a little fella, and he had a neat little moustache. I can still see him, his picture's there, just behind my eyelids. The Turk at the rear of the line, he was a good foot taller than the man in front, and he had a set of handlebars under his nose, like a lot of them did. He was Captain Rose's man. Taking out the last man in the line first was standard. It gave us a little space before the others in the line would know just what was happening.

"Rose waited until they were about twenty yards out, and then he took out the fella with the handlebars, perfect shot, right through the pump. So what we'd heard about Rose being a crack shot was no more than the truth. Up to that point, everything went like fuckin' clockwork. And then it didn't."

"Something went wrong."

"Wrong enough. I heard three more shots after Rose's, very quick, but one of them sounded like a dud. Two more of the Turks went down, one of them dead, but the other one was only wounded. Captain Rose finished him off with a head shot, but the fourth Turk, Hobbs's man, the little fella in front, he made it to cover behind some big rocks. And right away there was a single shot from down by those rocks and the next thing we knew Curtis Rowe was rolling down the near side of the knoll. From the way he was going, arms and legs flapping, I was pretty sure he was dead."

"There was a dud shot?"

"It was the round that Hobbs got off on the lead man. He said he didn't think the slug went anywhere close to the Turk. That's all it took, one dud round, and we end up losing one of our own. Then the next thing I know, Captain Rose has his Webley in his fist, and he's telling the four of us that's left to put covering fire on the rocks down at the bottom of the knoll, keep the last Turk pinned down. And then he was gone."

"And that wasn't usual, either."

"It wasn't. An officer isn't supposed to do that sort of thing. Mind you, no one was arguing with him. I think Hobbs might have gone after the Turk, because that was his man. Anyway, we kept a stream of fire going at the pile of rocks and a minute later we heard three shots, and then Rose himself was coming back up the hill."

"Rowe was dead?"

"Yes. The Captain sent Cec down to take a look. He gave us the thumbs-down, and then he took off back to our own line for reinforcements and a stretcher party. There was a counterattack just as dark was coming down. But we had the position well secured by then, and we beat them off. We took some casualties, and so did the Turks, including two more dead. And the fact is, we held that position for the rest of the time we were there on Suvla Plain. Abdul never managed to take it back."

"So Rose did well."

"He did, sir. And, there was something else."

"Yes?"

"Rose could see that Hobbs was grieved about Rowe getting killed. He blamed himself. The Captain told him it was just bad luck, no way to tell when a round's a dud until you let it go, but that didn't do it for Hobbs. Looking down the hill, we could see the flies starting to gather over the body. Those fuckers could smell out a body only minutes after the last breath went out of it. Hobbs wanted to bring Rowe back up the hill, so he wouldn't be alone down there, feeding the bloody flies. That's not the sort of thing you'd do in a situation like that, take any unnecessary chances, with the Turks only pissing distance away. You focus on the living. But Rose surprised us. He give the order to Hobbs and Laurie Rivers to get down the hill and bring Rowe back up there with us. And I liked the way he said it. He said it was the decent thing to do."

"I'm impressed."

"Rose never pulled any of that upper-class shit with us, none that I ever saw. Some of the officers, the limeys especially, you'd almost want to shoot them first and salute the corpse. But I thought Captain Rose was all right. From that point of view."

"There was another point of view?"

Corrigan smiled.

"I don't think you've ever been in the service, sir."

"No, although there were times during the last war that I wanted to be."

"I can understand that. The reason I ask is that a lot of people who've never worn the uniform have a notion about the military that isn't really in tune with reality, if I can put it that way."

"You can put it anyway you want, Jack. You were there."

"The powers that be like to encourage the notion that when you put a man into a uniform, he gets turned into a kind of overgrown Boy Scout, brimful with good thoughts and high ideals. And that is a part of it. But, make no mistake, sir, an army's main purpose is to break things and kill people. You spend hours learning to fire a rifle, and more hours learning how to shove a bayonet into some poor fucker, then get it out quick so you can shove it into another poor fucker. It's not a boy's adventure story. Not enough people understand that, including some of them that sit in high places. Especially the ones who've only read about war."

"What are you saying, Jack?"

"What I'm saying is that Captain Rose was a good man for the place he was at. Going down that hill to take out that Turk wasn't something he did just because he had to."

"He did it because he wanted to?"

"He had a look on him when he come back up the hill afterwards. I'm not passing judgement, you understand. When you're up against it, the way we was over there, people like Captain Rose is handy to have around."

"Tell me, Jack, did the other men you knew in the Regiment feel the same way about Harrison Rose that you did?"

Corrigan lit another cigarette and dropped the match in an ashtray.

"It was a long war, sir. I can only speak for myself, and the fact is, that one patrol in Gallipoli was the nearest I come to Rose in a combat situation. I saw action other times in other places, but with other officers giving the orders. Some of the other lads might have different stories to tell. You'll have to ask them."

"McCowan gave me two names, Albert Dancey and Lawrence Rivers. You mentioned Rivers in your story, also Cecil Cake and Hobbs. Would it be worth my while to talk to any of them?"

"You can forget Hobbs. He was killed in France, four days after Beaumont Hamel. The Hun dropped a Jack Johnson on top of him. Must have had his name on it because no one else got as much as a scratch. Laurie Rivers might be worth talking to, though, if you catch him on one of his good days."

"One of his good days?"

"He gets untidy with the bottle, is what I hear."

"I'd only heard that he wasn't well."

Corrigan smiled and shrugged.

"The fact is, though, when Rivers can walk a string-line, and I hear that's three days out of four, him and Albert Dancey run a successful business. They ran into a rough patch about fifteen years ago, I heard, but they come out of it all right. I think you'll find both of them knew Captain Rose pretty well."

"What about Cecil Cake? Is he around?"

"Cec is another story altogether." Corrigan took a moment. "There was five of us who were pals, almost from the time we enlisted in 1914. Myself, Albert Dancey, Laurie Rivers and the Cake brothers."

"He has a brother?"

"Had a brother." Corrigan took another moment. One of his cats took his silence as a cue to jump into his lap. Corrigan scratched it behind the ear. "Daniel Cake was killed at Gueudecourt in October of '16, and Cec almost bought the farm the same day. At first Daniel was listed as missing, but a week later they found his body in a shell crater."

"But Cecil Cake survived the war?"

"And more or less in one piece, although the wound he took at Gueudecourt the day Daniel was killed was pretty bad. We thought he'd be invalided home, but he was back with us about two months later."

"Where is he now?"

"Here in St. John's, in the west end. But he's not from here originally, not from St. John's. He's from down your part of the country, south coast, near St. Lawrence. Cec wandered around for quite a while after the war was over, I heard, couldn't seem to settle down. I think he might have blamed himself for Daniel getting killed, even though it made no sense that he should have. They were in different companies. The brass thought it was better that way, keeping brothers separated, I mean."

"Where did Cake go after the war? Do you know?"

"To Ireland, Laurie Rivers told me. An odd place for a good Protestant to go, but there was a lot of Irishmen in the British Army in the First War, in spite of the situation back home. And there was an Irish regiment in Gallipoli that was stationed just alongside us. Cec made friends with some of them, and after the war he took up on an invitation and went off to Ireland for a while. Three or four years, so I heard, maybe more."

"He worked there?"

"Tending sheep is what Rivers told me. Strange job for a man who started fishing with his father and brother when he was only nine years old, but that's apparently where he went."

"They were friends, Rivers and Cake?"

"Close friends for a good part of the war. An odd sort of friendship, because Rivers come from a well-off family, and Cecil Cake's family was poor as field mice. But they hit it off when they met in '14, and it stayed that way through most of the war."

"They had a falling-out?"

"Not really, but after Gueudecourt Cec kept to himself more and more. But you have to remember the times. I don't know that anyone who went over in '14 come out the same way five years later, the few of us who lasted the course. I know I didn't." Corrigan laughed. "Some say I was a better man coming out than going in, but opinion is mixed on that."

"From what you've said, I take it you didn't stay in close touch with the others, after the war, after you came home."

Corrigan nodded.

"That's true enough. I don't stay in close touch with any of them, but I hear things about them from time to time. Rivers and Dancey are in business together, of course. Cec is another story. I don't know if he stays in touch with anyone." Corrigan frowned and stubbed his cigarette in the ashtray. "For me, not staying in touch with people is nothing unusual. I'm not a hermit, but I like my own company. Not so different from yourself, sir, or so I hear."

"You're right," Stride said. "Not so different from myself. I appreciate your doing this, Jack. It gives me a better picture of Rose."

"Pleased to help, sir. But you might want to talk to the others, as well. I don't know about Cec, but Dancey and Rivers would probably talk to you. Not that they'd have any choice, given the situation."

"I will be talking to them. In fact, I'm going to try and see Dancey this afternoon. But I wanted to talk to you first."

He stood up. One of Corrigan's cats jumped into the chair he'd vacated. Another cat walked over and wrapped itself around his ankles. Stride bent down and picked it up. He stroked it under the chin. "You had a good half-dozen last time I was here."

"I probably picked up a couple more lately. I think the word's gone out that

I'm a soft touch."

"Your secret's safe with me, Jack."

"I'd appreciate that, sir. Wouldn't be good for my reputation if word of that got back to Fort Townshend."

CHAPTER 8

Albert Dancey looked with patient disdain at his trembling left hand. He clamped his right on top of it, holding it still. The tremor was always worse in the afternoon, and it was now just past four o'clock. It would be worse still later in the evening. He eased his hands off the top of his desk and placed them on his left thigh, the right still holding the left in place. If Dancey's visitor had noticed the shaking, he didn't indicate that he had.

His meeting with Edgar Holloway would soon be over and Dancey would be able to relax. He glanced at the clock, strategically placed on the office wall over his visitor's left shoulder. In five minutes, Louise Woods, his secretary, would interrupt the meeting to tell him that he had an important long-distance call from Boston. It was a plausible lie, a device for ending meetings with windy clients. Holloway was one of those, a decent man on the whole, but with a tendency to go on about things that didn't matter.

Then to Dancey's surprise, Holloway suddenly looked at his watch and began putting his papers back into his briefcase.

"I'm afraid I have to run, Albert. I didn't realize how late it was. But I think we've discussed everything we need to."

"Yes, I believe so." Fully ten minutes ago, Dancey said silently to himself.

He bore Holloway no ill will. In fact he liked the man. In better circumstances, and with time in hand for both of them, he would have invited Holloway to stay and have a drink and a chat. Lately, though, Dancey found social situations something of a trial, and he tried to avoid alcohol, which tended to make his tremor worse.

Dancey stood up and came around to the front of the desk. He slid the bothersome left hand—it was always the left that started shaking first—into his jacket pocket, and extended his right. The handshake carried all the way to the office door. Dancey wasn't a tall man, but his bearing and posture gave one the impression of height. He was handsome, with dark brown hair fading to grey, but still thick and full.

"I'm sorry Laurie wasn't able to make it to the meeting," Holloway said. "I hope it's nothing serious."

"Nothing that a few days rest won't fix," Dancey said. "I'll tell Laurie you were asking about him."

"Please do. And give him my best."

"I'll do that." Dancey stood in the open doorway and watched until Holloway had exited the outer office.

He started back to his desk, then turned and went back out. Louise was sitting at her typewriter, poring through an address book. A sheet of letter paper was positioned in the Underwood. She looked up at him.

"And I didn't even have to phone you," she said. "Mr. Holloway was a good boy for once."

"Yes, he was." Dancey looked at his watch. "Has Mr. Rivers called?"

"They both called. Mr. Lawrence called at three-thirty, and Mr. Charles about ten minutes after that."

"Did he say anything? Laurie?"

"Just that he hoped he'd see you later, as you'd agreed. I'll put a call through, if you want."

"No, that's all right. I'll be seeing him later on. I'll be seeing both of them, for that matter. We're having supper together. Laurie and I. I'm not sure about Charlie." He touched her shoulder with his left hand, just to see. It had stopped shaking, at least for the moment.

"Is it bad, this time?" She looked up at him. The address book lay in her lap, closed now. She wasn't referring to his tremor. That was something they'd agreed not to talk about, a reality they acknowledged in silence. It was Lawrence Rivers she meant.

"Not so bad," Dancey said. "Charlie says it's one of his minor bouts. I expect he'll be back in the office in a day or two, maybe even tomorrow. Did he have anything to say? Charlie?"

She shook her head. "He said he would see you tomorrow morning, around ten, if he doesn't see you tonight. I've written it into your agenda."

"No other calls?"

"No, that's it," she said. "Can I get you anything before I leave?" She caught the question in his expression. Normally she worked until six. "You've forgotten, haven't you?"

Dancey nodded, smiling. "I appear to have."

"I'm leaving early because it's my niece's birthday. My sister Anna's youngest. She was six yesterday, but the party's today."

"I remember now. You have a good time." Dancey tried to imagine himself among a throng of small children, the noisy chaos of it all.

"I will," Louise said. "And I'll bring you a piece of cake tomorrow. You can have it with your morning tea."

"I'll look forward to it."

Back in his office, with the door to the outer office closed, Dancey massaged his left hand with his right, working the fingers back and forth, commanding the reluctant nerves and muscles to behave. When he was alone, he would often squeeze a soft rubber ball in an attempt to keep the hand and finger muscles toned. Tom Butcher had suggested he do that. He said it might help, might even delay the inevitable downslide, if only by a little.

It was the future that sometimes worried Dancey, to the extent that he allowed anything to worry him. Worry was something he'd learned to put aside during his time in the war, in Gallipoli, and the other places he'd been, where so much had been lost, and—paradoxically—so much gained.

He gathered up the papers on his desk and went through them one final time before placing them in the appropriate file folders. That done, he placed the folders on the front of his desk for Louise to gather later for filing, the last thing she would do before she left for her niece's birthday party.

Louise Woods was one of those middle-aged single women, part of a minority, Dancey believed, who took a warm proprietary pleasure in a sibling's children, but who appeared to have decided at some point that marriage and children were not something they wanted, however much they admired, even extolled, the traditional arrangement. He believed that Louise would have married, had the right man come along at the right time. But she belonged to that generation whose prospects for marriage were dimmed by the Great War, their hopes for a future family buried with the hundreds of young Newfoundland men whose bodies lay in graves on foreign soil. And, sadly, in too many cases, those graves held bodies, or parts of bodies, whose identities were not known with any certainty.

Albert Dancey had been married once, before he went off to war in 1914, one of a minority in the Regiment, most of whom were very young men, not yet married. Virgins, some of them almost certainly, near-boys for whom the war itself was a kind of exotic romance. And for too many of them a fatal attraction.

Albert Dancey's marriage had ended while he was in France, their next posting after Suvla Plain in Gallipoli. There, a letter, more than a month old, finally reached him in April of 1916, at the billet at Louvencourt, the Regiment's next-to-last stop before going into the line at the Somme. The letter was from his father and it told him that his wife had died. The old man hadn't told him the cause of her death, and it was likely he didn't know. Years later, Dancey learned that his wife had died in childbirth. At the time of her death he had been away from home, all of that time overseas, for going on two years.

There was a knock at his door and Louise came into the office.

"I'm becoming as forgetful as you are, Albert. You had another call while Mr. Holloway was here. It was Jack McCowan."

"Did he leave a message?"

"He said you'd probably be getting a call from one of his men. An Inspector Stride."

"I know the name. Did he say why Inspector Stride would be calling me?"

"No, he didn't." She hesitated. "I asked him if I should interrupt your meeting so you could take his call, but he said that wouldn't be necessary."

"Then I'll have to wait until I hear from him."

"You could phone Mr. McCowan yourself and ask."

"I'm just as happy to wait until the inspector calls me."

"There were police all around Bannerman Park this morning," Louise said. "It was on the news, although they didn't say what it was all about."

"Yes, I heard that. Well, if that's the reason for Inspector Stride's call, I imagine I'll find out about it as soon as I need to."

She looked at him, as surprised as she always was that things didn't seem to bother him the way they did other people, or herself for that matter. She thought his equanimity came from his experiences in the war, a sense that if he could walk back from that horror in one piece, and with his sanity intact, then even the more alarming events of day-to-day life were almost beneath his consideration.

"You're having supper with Mr. Lawrence tonight?" Dancey nodded. "I hope you'll behave yourselves. You don't want to start him off again."

Lawrence Rivers's drinking problem wasn't supposed to be general knowledge, but a half-secret held by a select few. In fact, that only meant that it wasn't openly talked about. It was in the nature of half-secrets that they inevitably trickled out, seeping through tiny fissures in the imperfect shroud of supposed confidentiality.

"It won't be a problem," Dancey said. But he could see that his easy assurance didn't have much effect. Such assurances almost never played well with Louise. "I know how to deal with Laurie."

"I'll hold you to that, Albert. And I'll expect you to look after yourself too."

That voiced expectation was as close as she would come to mentioning his tremor. He stood up and went over to her.

"I'm nagging, aren't I?" She touched his cheek. "I'm sorry, Albert."

"No need to be sorry. I don't mind."

"Yes, you do. But you're always the gentleman." She kissed him then, on the cheek, a quick movement, almost furtive, followed by a glance towards the office door. She'd left it open. "You will take care, though?" He smiled. "I'll put these files away, and then I'm gone."

"My best to Anna," Dancey said. "And her daughter. I forget her name."

"It's Louise. Anna named her after me."

"And I managed to forget even that. I really am falling apart."

"We're all falling apart, Albert." She gathered up the files from his desk and started for the door. "I'll remember your cake for tomorrow. That much I think I can promise."

Dancey waited until Louise had left, closing the outer office door behind her. He shut his office door and walked over to a cabinet on the far wall, near the window. He pulled back the sheer curtain and looked through the window, waiting there until he saw her come out of the building. She stood at the curb until there was a break in the traffic, and then she trotted quickly across the street, her long, still-dark hair bouncing on the shoulders of her raincoat. Over the past year she'd let her hair grow long, because he'd asked her to, and she had done it because she was as happy to please him as he was to please her, a mutual pleasure that had surprised them both in the beginning, and still did sometimes. He continued to watch as she made her way along Water Street, going west, walking with her usual rapid stride, holding the package with her niece's birthday present close to her chest, her umbrella held under her right arm like a swagger stick. Several times she nodded and spoke to people she knew. He watched until she was out of sight.

He let the curtain fall back in place and opened the door of the cabinet. He took out a bottle of Canadian whisky and poured a small amount into a crystal glass. The glass, one of a set of four he had brought back with him to Newfoundland from London early in 1919, was an indulgence for Dancey. In most matters he was a pragmatic man who lived his life almost without decoration, and his office reflected that, the plain and solid wood furniture complementing his personality. A *functional man* was the term Louise used to describe him, almost from the day she first made his acquaintance, now more than twenty years ago. But she hadn't told him about that until much later, when they had become close. He confided to her that the purchase of the crystal glasses after the war—only three of them left now—seemed an appropriate gesture, a celebration of being alive, of still being whole.

A drink this early in the day was unusual for him. In partial compensation, he added double the amount of soda from a siphon and sat down at his desk. He massaged his hand again, and finally tasted his drink. He sat back and allowed the warmth of the whisky to ease through him. Sooner or later the alcohol would feed into his tremor. It might even disrupt his sleep later. He didn't care. Just now he wanted a drink.

He thought about the evening ahead, his supper with Lawrence Rivers. Rivers's drinking had started the previous Thursday and continued on through the weekend, getting a bit worse each day, reaching the usual climax on Saturday night. Dancey thought that he was probably past the worst of it now, and was on an upswing. And on the whole, it had been one of his less serious bouts.

He looked at the clock again, wondering when he would hear from McCowan's Inspector Stride. He hoped it would be sooner rather than later.

Then, almost as a fulfilment of his wish, there was a knock at his door. He crossed the office and pulled the door open.

"I thought I'd find someone in the outer office. My name's Eric Stride. I'm with the Constabulary."

The two men shook hands and Dancey stepped aside to usher him into the room.

"I've been expecting you." He gestured towards the chair recently vacated by Edgar Holloway. "Jack McCowan rang earlier and said you'd be calling me."

"I wondered if he would. He was the one who give me your name."

"I assumed as much. McCowan and I go back a long way."

"He mentioned that. Did he tell you what I wanted to talk to you about?"

"No, but I didn't actually speak with him. I was in a meeting when he called. My secretary took the message."

"I need to ask you some questions about Harrison Rose. I believe you're acquainted with him?"

"Yes, of course. I met Harry Rose about the same time I met Jack McCowan, in fact, although I haven't known him for as long. I suppose that sounds contradictory, but there was a long period when I'd completely lost touch with Harry. Has he done something to attract the attention of the Constabulary?" Dancey's smile seemed genuine. "I have some difficulty imagining that."

There didn't seem to be anything but a mildly amused curiosity in Dancey's expression, but Stride wasn't sure. He paused for a moment longer, filling the small gap by taking out his notebook and uncapping his pen.

"I'm sorry," Dancey said. "Here I am having a drink, and I haven't offered you one."

Stride looked at the crystal glass on Dancey's desk blotter. His first impulse was to accept, even if he was on duty. He looked across the office to where the soda siphon was standing on a shelf. He worked a compromise with himself.

"I'd enjoy a glass of soda," he said. "Anything stronger would be against regulations."

Dancey went over to the cabinet and took down another crystal glass.

"I don't know if your district inspector would be proud of you or not. I can't remember the last time Jack McCowan turned down a drink."

"I can't remember the last time I did," Stride said. He took the glass that Dancey held out for him and drank off a third of it. He placed the glass on the edge of the desk.

"So, what's Harry Rose been up to that's caught your attention?"

There still seemed nothing in Dancey's expression other than curiosity. Stride gave it to him straight.

"Mr. Rose is dead."

He left it at that, watching to see how Dancey dealt with it. But he only picked up his glass and briefly stared into it before taking a small sip.

"I imagine, then, that explains the police presence around Bannerman Park this morning? I know Harry lived nearby."

Stride nodded.

"How did it happen? Harry's death? I'm assuming he didn't die of natural causes."

"He was shot," Stride said. "Late last night, in the park. Actually, early this morning, about twelve-thirty."

"I suppose it was murder?"

"Yes."

"I see. And Jack McCowan suggested you talk to me because Harry Rose and I knew each other." He gave Stride a frank look. "Or was there some other reason?"

"Such as?"

"That he thought I might have had something to do with it?"

"Did you?"

"Of course not."

The answer was quick and firm.

"Was there any reason why he might have thought you had something to do with it?"

"Harry Rose and I had our differences over the years, apart from our time in the war together. Business matters. But we remained friends, on and off. I hope that's a satisfactory answer."

"For the moment," Stride said. "I'll ask the obvious question next."

"Do I know of anyone who might have wanted him dead?" Dancey shook his head. "No, I don't. It's not something I've had any reason to think about for a long time."

"But you did, once? Think about that?"

"Harry Rose was an infantry officer in a war that was infamous for the number of men killed, and for the sometimes dubious command decisions that caused a lot of those deaths. I imagine you've thought about that already?"

"Yes. The point's been made often enough."

"As well it should have been. That war was an orchestrated slaughter, probably unique in history. Even the last one doesn't compare with it. The difference with the First War was that massed armies were routinely marched into the line of each other's fire. In retrospect, it's almost impossible to believe that such things ever took place."

Stride took in Dancey's calm demeanour and wondered how the man could have come through it all and still appear to be unaffected, even normal.

"Was Harrison Rose a good officer?"

Dancey didn't answer right away. He placed his left hand on the desk by his glass and covered it with his right. There was another suggestion of the shaking Stride thought he'd seen earlier. It added to his sense that Dancey had moved about the office with deliberate care, and he wondered now if the shaking was an indication of a medical condition, something he strove to keep under control.

"I think you're really asking me if any of the men who served under Harry might have had a reason to want him dead. For the sins of flawed leadership."

"The points are related."

"They are. But the fact is, Harry Rose was a good officer. At least for the time we were in the Regiment together, and that's the only part of his service I know anything about. But that said, men did die under his command, and as a result of orders that he gave. In battle, particularly the kinds of battles we were involved in, even good decisions cost men their lives, and caused other men serious injuries. All of that was inevitable. It was the price of leadership in the field."

"You're saying that none of the men under Rose's command would have a reason to want him dead?"

"No. What I'm saying is that none of those men should have thought they had a reason for wanting him dead."

"Not quite the same thing."

"No, it isn't. What a man thinks, and what he should think, don't always coincide. Emotions—fear, anger, grief—can overwhelm even the best of men. I saw it often enough in France, and elsewhere. But that was all a long time ago, Inspector. I have some difficulty imagining it has any relevance to the present situation."

"Probably not," Stride said. "Harrison Rose seems to have been a rather private man. McCowan told me he didn't often attend Regimental dinners."

"No, he didn't. Harry Rose did seem to keep pretty much to himself after he moved to St. John's."

"Was he always that way, or was that something that came about after he came here?"

"I didn't know him well enough to know what he might have been like before he moved here. You have to remember that the time I knew him before he came to Newfoundland was something less than two years. Actually, closer to a year and a half. Also, Harry was an officer, and I was other ranks. When I first knew him, I was a corporal. Officers and other ranks didn't have a lot of informal contact with each other."

Stride looked around Dancey's office, at the plain but good-quality furniture. The one nod in the direction of personal indulgence was a large framed photograph of a much younger Albert Dancey in his regimental uniform, a sergeant by then, with three chevrons on his sleeve. Stride knew that the Rivers company was very successful. Dancey himself looked the part of the prosperous businessman.

"I know what you're thinking," Dancey said. "Why didn't I have a commission?" Stride nodded. "I didn't qualify for one, not back in 1914 when I enlisted. I come from a very modest background, Inspector. All of this," he kept his hands on the desk and gestured with his head, "came about after the war when I joined the Rivers company. I worked my way up."

"I see." Stride made another note in his book. "Why did Harrison Rose leave the Regiment?"

"He'd been promoted, first to major, then to lieutenant-colonel, and when that happened, the promotion to colonel, he went on to a different sector of the war. But don't ask me where, because I don't know."

"You didn't see him after that?"

"Not until he moved here to St. John's."

"And when was that?"

"I believe it was in 1930. In the summer, I think. By then, I'd been working here for ten years. I ran into Harry at a business function. At the time, I didn't even know he'd moved here."

"That's when you became friends?"

"We had a natural connection because of our time in the war, and then there were our business interests." Dancey smiled. "Men of business tend to have things in common, even when we aren't active in the same areas. Harry and I weren't close friends, but we got along. Most of the time."

"What can you tell me about Rose's business?"

"Harry was an agent, someone who greased the gears, if you will, for sales of wood—timber—to overseas markets. England for the most part, but elsewhere too. As far as I know, he did well, and no doubt he helped other people make money too."

"Jack McCowan suggested that Rose, or his family, might have owned property here in Newfoundland."

"Harry did for sure. But I don't believe it was family property."

"He acquired it after he moved here?"

"Yes."

"Was there family money?"

"I don't know if there was or not. There was some chat in the Regiment that Harry came from a moneyed background. Many of the British officers did come from money, and property, especially early on, when it was thought the war would be a picnic, and over by Christmas of '14. But I really know nothing about his family. Perhaps they did have money. Harry didn't exactly arrive here in St. John's with holes in his shoes, and his trousers held up by a length of rope."

Stride looked over his notes, then back at Dancey.

"One more question, if I may. Do you have any information on Rose after he left the Regiment? Before he came here?"

"No, I don't."

"So, you don't know if he stayed in the army, or moved back into civilian life?"

"I don't have any information on that at all. He was career army to start with, so it's likely he wore the uniform for some time after November 1918." Dancey paused a moment. "Actually, I did ask him once, in a roundabout sort of way, but he didn't answer me."

"He avoided the question?"

"I'm not sure. We were only making casual conversation at the time, and either we were interrupted, or he changed the subject."

"Did you know very much about Mr. Rose's personal life?"

"Not much. Harry wasn't very social. But you know that already. I'm not either, for that matter. Why?"

"Just a general question. The more we know about Mr. Rose, the better we can investigate his death. McCowan suggested that I might want to talk to Lawrence Rivers." Stride looked for a reaction from Dancey to the suggestion, but there wasn't one. "But he also said that Mr. Rivers might not be very well. Can you advise me?"

"McCowan's right, Laurie Rivers hasn't been well recently. And to be honest, I doubt he can tell you much more than I have about Harry Rose."

"I see." Stride picked his words. "Is Mr. Rivers's problem serious?"

"Serious enough, but I expect he'll be around for a few years yet. It's in the nature of a chronic condition that flares up from time to time."

"Would it be an imposition for me to speak with him, do you think?"

"Probably not. I'm having supper with him tonight, and I'll tell him about our conversation, and say that you'll be calling on him tomorrow. Would that be satisfactory?"

"That will be fine."

Stride closed his notebook and screwed the cap back onto his pen. He picked up his glass and drank off the last of the soda water. He stood up.

"I appreciate your cooperation, Mr. Dancey, and giving me your time."

"My pleasure, Inspector Stride. Well, not really a pleasure, I suppose, given the circumstances."

CHAPTER 9

Stride stood on the sidewalk in front of the building that housed the offices of the Rivers company for a moment, and then spent the next few minutes in the shelter of a doorway watching people walk by and traffic make its way along Water Street. It was going on for five now, an hour from closing time for the stores and businesses that lined the street. The rain had slackened a bit, enough that most people were walking with their umbrellas furled. But the sky was still dark and threatening, and he knew the rain could start up again without warning. He'd left his umbrella in the MG. He took a final look at the sky and started down the street, moving quickly. He made it to the MG just as the skies opened up again.

The huge drops of rain hit the blacktop like machine-gun fire, and all along the street, both sides, thickets of black umbrellas suddenly appeared. The few people who had challenged the weather gods without protection were running for cover, coat lapels pulled tightly around their throats with one hand, hats held in place with the other.

Sitting inside the MG, Stride listened to the staccato beat of the rain on the canvas top. He started the motor and set the wipers working to clear the windscreen, but it was pointless. The rain came down so hard and fast that the tiny wiper blades could do nothing useful. On top of that, his breath had condensed on the glass, enclosing him in a cocoon of metal and glass, isolated from the world outside. There wasn't much he could do but wait until the rain slackened enough so that the wipers could cope.

Then the passenger door was suddenly pulled open and Dianne Borg's slender frame slipped into the seat beside him. Stride hadn't seen her in several days. It was usually that way when her husband, a captain in the United States Army, was in St. John's. Their time together was mostly limited to those occasions when Martin Borg was away from Fort Pepperrell, visiting at one or another of the bases maintained in Newfoundland and Labrador by the American military.

Dianne slid her furled umbrella between her seat and the door and brushed a strand of wet blonde hair away from her face. Then she leaned across the gap and kissed him on the cheek.

"No one will notice," she said. "Everyone out there's preoccupied with not drowning. I can't remember when I've seen it rain this hard."

"Commonly called a deluge," Stride said. "What are you doing out and about in this?"

"I had to deliver some papers to one of the Mercantile Association's member companies. It's the sort of thing they have me do from time to time. It reminds me, and them, that I am, after all is said and done, a female working in a man's field."

In fact, in the three years she'd been with the Association, Dianne had established herself as an invaluable keeper of their records on Newfoundland companies, able to find needed information more quickly than anyone other than her immediate supervisor, Bertie Prim, and even giving Prim a run for it some of the time. She leaned towards Stride again and gripped his hand.

"Anyway, I'm glad I've run into you. I have some news. I was going to ring you this evening and talk about it, but now maybe I won't have to."

"Good news, or bad?"

"That depends on your point of view." She dropped his hand, moved away, and drew a circle in the condensation on the side window. "The fact is, I'm not sure myself."

"Something to do with Marty?"

"Of course it's to do with Marty." She added two dots to the circle for eyes, and then a tick mark under them for a nose. "He's put in for a transfer. And as he's been at Pepperrell for going on three years now, he'll probably get one. He has a better-than-good record, and anyway, he's up for promotion. He'll probably be transferred to a larger base. Maybe even to Washington."

"To the Pentagon?"

"The magic word has been dropped into the conversation once or twice." She added a line to the circle for the mouth, turning it up at the corners in a kind of reluctant smile. Then she stroked her fingers across the window and wiped most of her creation away. She turned to him. "What do you think about all of that?"

He didn't have a ready reply. Her words were still bouncing around inside his head. If Marty Borg was transferred out of Newfoundland, everything between Stride and Dianne would change. It was complicated enough already, and he wasn't sure that her husband's leaving would make things simpler. From his point of view, it might be the opposite.

"I'm sorry," she said then. "I fall into your car out of nowhere—I was going to say 'out of the blue,' but that would be silly—and I drop a large hot rock into your lap."

"You did take me by surprise."

"And I did it twice in less than two minutes. We should probably talk about it later, when you've had some time to think, to sort it out." She looked straight ahead through the clouded window. The rain continued to pound down on top of the little car. People and vehicles moved past, vague shapes through the veil of condensation. "The talk in the office is that there was a shooting last night in Bannerman Park. That's not far from your place."

"There was a shooting, and it was close to my place. We have one man dead."

"Can you tell me who it is? Or is it hush-hush until the next-of-kin thing's been done?"

"We haven't been able to contact the next of kin yet, but it won't be a secret much longer, assuming it still is. The dead man is Harrison Rose. He lives— lived—down the street from me."

"Harrison Rose?" Her tone told him she knew the name. "Well, you know I won't say anything to anyone, not even to people at the office."

"I don't think it will take long for the word to get out. We've had two policemen stationed at Rose's house since early this morning. That's almost like hanging out a sign."

He wiped condensation from the windscreen again. The rain had slowed now, the fury of the downpour abated. He started the motor and turned on the wipers.

"I imagine you have to get back to Fort Townshend?"

"Yes. I was at the autopsy earlier this afternoon. There's a lot going on just now."

"Complications?"

"A lot of complications."

"Which you can't tell me about, I suppose."

Stride shook his head.

"I have to check in and see what's happened over the last couple of hours. I'll drop you back at your office."

She took a moment before replying. She was making marks on the side window again, but only random squiggles this time.

"Marty's mentioned divorce." She looked at him. Stride didn't say anything. "Nothing very definite. That's not Marty's way. Ever since I've known him, he edges into things slowly, like going for a swim in the North Atlantic." She slumped in her seat, expressionless. It was one of the few times he had seen her deflated. Divorce was a word almost never spoken in Newfoundland. Married people stayed together, no matter how bad things were. As a native Newfoundlander, Dianne knew as much about that as Stride did, maybe more. "Of course, we'd have it done in the States. It's almost impossible here. Well, you know that."

She pulled her shoulders back and ran her fingers through her hair, sorting it out, rearranging it after the rain.

"You can drive me back to the office. I will call you later, though."

He nodded and pulled away from the curb, heading for Duckworth Street and the Newfoundland Mercantile Association where Dianne worked, a woman doing a man's job, as she put it. But she was good at what she did, and there weren't many businesses in St. John's—or Newfoundland for that matter—that she didn't know at least something about. He was tempted to ask her if she knew anything about Harrison Rose's business affairs, or could find out for him, but it didn't seem appropriate. Not just now, not with what was going on between them, this sudden change in their situation.

When they reached the office building, he pulled the MG up to the curb. Dianne opened the door to get out, but then closed it. They looked at each other. Stride wondered if she was going to start talking about Marty again.

"I can pull Harrison Rose's file and see if there's anything in it that might be useful for you. I could also speak to Bertie Prim about it. If there's anything worth talking about, he'll have it right there at his pudgy fingertips. Would you like me to do that?"

"Yes, I would. It appears Rose was an agent of some kind. Timber exports."

"I think that was it. I'll see what I can find for you."

"Anything at all will help. We don't know as much as we'd like to about Harrison Rose at this point."

"And you need to know more." And now she was smiling again, her tone light. All together again. "We'll have so much to talk about when I do ring later on."

He shouldn't have been surprised that she would offer to help, even in the present situation. It was a part of her character. Her "busy-bee quality," she called it.

She touched his cheek, then opened the door again and stepped out onto the sidewalk.

Stride decided to drive back to Fort Townshend by way of Circular Road. He needed to get back to the office and see what Noseworthy might have come up with—the three bullets, Rose's leather gloves. But his talk with Dianne had unsettled him, started his head spinning. He took the detour to give himself a few extra minutes to calm down.

He was also thinking about Rose's daughter, wondering when she'd turn up. He dug into his memory for the name. Catherine Darnell. He assumed that meant she was married, but it might also mean that she'd taken her mother's name after Rose and his wife had gone their separate ways. He drove down Rennie's Mill and turned right onto Circular Road. The park was no longer populated with police officers, but the marker flags were still in place and a single patrolman was standing watch. The few pedestrians in the area were keeping their distance. Noseworthy had apparently decided that the search for evidence wasn't finished yet. Stride wondered if they'd found another 9 mm shell case. Assuming the semi-automatic had actually been fired a third time, something that he doubted now, given the results of the autopsy.

He drove on to Rose's house. A patrolman was on the veranda, walking slowly back and forth, swinging his arms to fight the tedium. He stopped when he saw the MG pull into the driveway and came down as far as the bottom step, but quickly moved back under the protection of the porch. It was still raining hard. Stride ran from the car to the veranda.

"Anything to report?" He thought the constable's name was Adey.

"Nothing at all, sir. Quiet as can be."

"There's a possibility that Rose's daughter might be in town, or if she isn't here now, she might be soon."

"Sergeant Phelan told us about that when we were getting ready to come down here. Wouldn't be a very nice way to get the news, would it, just arrive here and find someone like me standing on the doorstep?"

"Nothing personal, Adey, but, no, it wouldn't. What did Sergeant Phelan say to do if she does show up here?"

"He said we should just tell her the news straight out. No point trying to pretend her father had an accident or nothing. She wouldn't believe that, not with two coppers standing guard over the house. And that's assuming she wouldn't have read about the shooting in the paper already, or heard it from a taxi driver on the way here."

"What time did Noseworthy finish up?"

"About three hours ago. He went back and forth between the house and the park a couple of times."

"Did he mention finding a third shell case?"

"No, sir, not to me he didn't." Adey paused. "Tom Kennedy was with him when he was here at the house. Has he been assigned to the case?"

"Kennedy?" Stride shook his head. "No. It's on a volunteer basis, at least for now."

"Volunteer." Adey's expression told Stride all he needed to know about his opinion of volunteering for extra work. "Noseworthy said he might be back later on, depending. Anyway, we're supposed to stay here until we're relieved. They'll send a new crew along around six, just about an hour from now." He looked at Stride. "Can I ask you another question, sir?"

"Yes."

"There's a story going around that this Rose fella was hooked up with the British government somehow. Is that true?"

"If he was, it's news to me. What have you heard?"

"Just that the Governor's office rang the Chief early on this afternoon. The word is they want regular written reports on the investigation. They put one together at Fort Townshend and Hynes delivered it to Government House. He stopped by here on his way back to pass the word along." Cyril Hynes was a policeman nearing retirement, and his main duty now was as a driver, ferrying officers and documents around the city. Adey gave Stride a cautious look. "I guess you haven't been back to Fort Townshend since all that started up?"

"No, I haven't. Sergeant Phelan knows about this?"

"I don't know if he does or not, sir. Hynes didn't say. And I haven't seen Sergeant Phelan since we come down here this afternoon."

"Do you know who put the report together?"

"Hynes said it was Noseworthy and District Inspector McCowan. I expect you'll hear about it soon as you get back there."

"I expect so." Stride stepped off the veranda, and then went back. "Who are you on with?" He nodded his head towards the back of the house.

"Bob Morgan, sir."

"He's heard about this too, I suppose?"

"Yes, sir. You know how Hynes likes to tell stories."

"Yes, I do," Stride said. "I might have a word with him later about that."

Now Adey had his cautious look on again. Stride left him to deal with that on his own.

Stride found Phelan in their shared office, sipping a cup of hot tea, the steam curling up around his face. When Stride got closer, he thought he detected something else in the brew.

"Rum," Phelan said. He inclined his head towards the drawer where they kept a bottle of overproof Demerara for emergencies. "I'm worried the cold's getting worse. I know the rum won't help, but I can pretend."

"I don't blame you," Stride said. He pushed the office door halfway closed and took the bottle from the back section of the drawer. Phelan took a mug from the side drawer of his own desk and passed it across. "Remind me to bring in another bottle someday soon. This one's seriously damaged." He poured out a small quantity and lit a cigarette. "Bring me up to date, Harry. What about the bullets?"

"It's just as Butcher thought. Two 9 mm slugs and a .38. And it's not just the difference in calibre. The composition is different too. The .38 has a brass coating, and that matches the box of .38s we found in Rose's desk. The 9 mm bullets are solid lead, and both came from the same weapon."

"And the gloves?"

"That's a bit trickier. They caught a lot of rain last night, and most of the nitrate residue was washed away."

"But there was some?"

"Just a little. Noseworthy says it's not enough to go to court with, but it's his opinion there's just enough there to think that Rose probably did fire a pistol last night."

"What about the blood typing that Butcher was going to do?"

"We're still waiting to hear from him on that. Noseworthy tried to reach him, but he wasn't available. He's probably somewhere between the hospital and his surgery."

"Where is Noseworthy, by the way? I thought he'd still be here."

"He was until about twenty minutes ago. But he had Hynes drive him to Buckmaster's Field. He called around and found someone with the Canadian army who's going to lend him a metal detector. Actually, it's a mine detector, but they think it should do the job."

"He still thinks it's worth looking for the third 9 mm shell case?"

"He doesn't really, but it's a possible loose end, and he doesn't like loose ends any more than we do."

"He's going to look for it today?"

"That's the plan, rain or no rain. His army contact is going along with him."

"Ah, Eric, you're back." Jack McCowan was standing in the doorway. "Harry's told me things have changed a bit since this morning."

"Yes, they have, sir." He pushed the mug with the rum towards the back of his desk. "A lot more went on in the park last night than we originally thought. It's more than likely Harrison Rose was armed, and it might have been him who got off the two shots I heard."

"So I gather." McCowan moved into the room and looked at the mugs that Phelan and Stride were drinking from. "You know, you could offer a fellow a drink. I could damn well use one. The Rose murder, especially with Government

House taking an interest, has got the Chief agitated. That's reason enough for a drink. Anytime they get the wind up over there about a police matter, it's his neck that's potentially on the block. Harry's brought you up to speed on all of that, I suppose?"

"It was the next thing on my list, sir."

Phelan opened his desk drawer and took out the spare mug they kept for visitors.

"I don't know that it means very much, their being interested," McCowan said. "It's natural enough that they'd want to be kept in the picture on this, especially with it happening just next door. But tell me, where you think we are with it now?"

"I had a talk with Jack Corrigan earlier, and then I went to see Albert Dancey."

"You've been busy. I know Corrigan's been off for a few days. Officially he's a bit under the weather. But I happen to know he's putting down his store of ale for the winter."

"He was well along with it when I got there, sir."

"I'm pleased to hear it. Did Corrigan or Dancey give you anything useful?"

"With Corrigan it was pretty straightforward. He told me what he remembered about Rose from the war. His one close experience with him in combat was on a night patrol on Suvla Plain."

"I remember that," McCowan said. "We lost a man on that patrol. A chap named Rowe, I think his name was."

"Curtis Rowe," Stride said. "Corrigan told me that Rose did very well that night. And on the whole he thought Rose was a good officer. A brave man, and decent as well, where his own men were concerned."

"And Dancey?"

"He said much the same thing, that Rose was a good officer. At least for the time that he knew him over there. Although I'm not sure Dancey told me everything he might have."

"Is that based on anything specific, or is it just a feeling you have?"

"Just a feeling. He also told me that he and Rose had some kind of a business relationship, although he didn't go into any detail."

"I'd like to be able to enlighten you about their business history, but I really don't know anything about it. It's obvious they've both done well over the years, although there was a time in the early thirties, during the Depression, when things were touch and go with the Rivers company. It was the same with a lot of the local firms. Laurie Rivers's health situation has been a problem, of course, but they seem to be able to accommodate that."

"Corrigan told me something about that. Rivers's health problem, I mean."

"Did he?" McCowan frowned and drank off the rum that was left. "I'm always surprised at how much Corrigan seems to know about people in this town. I suppose he told you that Rivers's problem is bottle related?"

"Yes, he did."

"Fair enough. It doesn't hurt to know that. It might even help if you decide to interview him." McCowan looked at his watch. "I have to run away in a minute, for a meeting downtown. Is there anything else I need to know before I go?"

"I think we've given you most of it, sir."

"Then we can leave it at that for now." McCowan gave the mug back to Phelan. "Bloody good rum. Just what I needed. You'll keep me posted."

"Yes, sir." They listened until they heard the door to McCowan's office close. "I think I've had about all I can deal with for today, Harry, so let's finish up. You got into Rose's office all right? The court order came through?"

"Yes, it did. Rose seems to have run a respectable operation, a one-man show. Well, one man and one woman."

"One woman?"

"He had an assistant. Her name's Barbara Drodge. Mrs. Norman Drodge, to be accurate."

"And there's a Mr. Drodge?"

"Yes, there is. The address is on Merrymeeting Road. I ran the description you got from Mary Holden past the hotel manager. Mrs. Drodge might be Rose's lady friend."

"That's not enough to go on. We'll follow it up tomorrow."

"Rose's business files are in the evidence room, along with the personal stuff we gathered from his house. Noseworthy and I gave them a quick look, but nothing jumped out at us. On the business side, there's a lot of correspondence about wood, contracts, invoices—just what you'd expect. It was all enough to remind me why I decided not to go into business."

"So, what do you think this Government House business is all about, Harry? When I was there this morning, the fellow I talked to, Gilbert, said he only wanted an occasional update. Is this something we need to worry about?"

"I think we can probably let the Chief worry about it for now. He likes worrying."

"And likes to share that with McCowan. It will keep them both happy."

"McCowan might have it right, sir, that they're interested because it happened next door. Rose being ex-British Army probably had something to do with it, too."

"You weren't involved in writing the report that went down there? Just

Noseworthy and McCowan?"

"I was out when the call came in. But I don't think it was anything special. Just a summary of what we know, and what we don't."

"But you've read it?"

"Yes. The typist did three carbons. One for McCowan, one for the file, and the third one for us. They gave them only the basic facts, but they left out the part about Rose maybe carrying a gun and wounding his killer. I asked Noseworthy about that and he said it was McCowan's decision. We're still not really sure what happened last night, so why bring it up?"

"We can tell them later. Who was it at Government House who actually requested the reports? Was it Rodney Gilbert?"

"No, it wasn't him. Noseworthy said it was someone named Barnes Wilson."

"The name's vaguely familiar. So, who's Barnes Wilson when he's at home?"

"I only have the name, sir. McCowan referred to him as Major Wilson, so I'm guessing he's British Army."

"Or ex-army. Do we know anything about him?"

"McCowan said that he'd met him once or twice, but he doesn't know much about him. He's probably a new boy."

"There've been staff changes there since the war. New priorities, new people." Stride dug into his shirt pocket for his cigarettes. He offered one to Phelan, but Harry shook his head.

"My throat's sore. If this cold follows the usual pattern, I might have one more day of feeling like hell, and then I'll be back to normal, more or less."

"I recommend more rum this evening," Stride said. He added another ounce to his mug, and held up the bottle. Phelan shook his head again. Stride lit his cigarette and sat back in his chair.

His mind was wandering away from the case now, drifting back to what Dianne had said about her husband Marty's possible transfer back to the States, the possible divorce. Make that a probable divorce. Marty Borg might be a gradualist, as Dianne had said, but most of the Americans Stride knew, and there'd been many over the years, weren't chary about making tough decisions. And divorce, just as Dianne said, wasn't the same issue for Americans as it was for Newfoundlanders. They lived in a different world.

He reflected on the memory of when he had met Dianne, and almost his first thought then was, why did she have to be married? But now, months later, when it looked like her marriage might end, his take on it was more equivocal than he'd thought it would be. He was uncomfortable, and his discomfort fed into his uncertainty. It must have showed.

"A penny?" Phelan said. "Two pennies?"

"A handful of bloody sovereigns," Stride replied.

"Something to do with the case, or something really important?"

Stride shook his head. He wasn't ready to bring Harry up to date on the latest turn in his personal life. He would, sooner or later, but not now. They were good friends, Stride and Phelan, but for a reason that he couldn't really explain, he was more inclined to talk to Harry's wife about his travails. In a way, Kitty Phelan had become the big sister he'd never had, a sounding board for whatever personal misery he was going through at the moment. Kitty was also someone who wouldn't take any nonsense from him, who would tell him what she thought, what she instinctively knew he needed to hear.

"I was off somewhere else," he said, finally. "And now I'll park all that and get back to the less important issues of death, life and bloody murder."

"There is something else, sir. With the Government House thing, and McCowan's stopping by, it almost slipped my mind. Crotty came by with some information."

Constable Bernard Crotty was the officer in charge of the Constabulary's files.

"On the case?"

"Maybe. He doesn't know if it's relevant or not, but you know Bern. Nothing slips past him without he makes a file reference. He remembered there was an altercation in Bannerman Park last spring. Last week of May. Maybe you remember it?"

"I remember hearing something about it, but we were busy with the Taylor case. It was some kind of a brawl that landed one of the celebrants in hospital?"

"With a concussion and a ruptured spleen," Phelan said. "It was pretty serious, I think."

"Why does Bern think that might have something to do with the Rose shooting? I don't remember that there were any arrests in the case. Did I miss something?"

"I don't think so. He brought it up because of the location."

"Whose case was it?"

"Cobb's."

"Andy Cobb." Stride shook his head. "Did he find anything worth chasing down? I don't remember that he did."

"Bern thinks there was more to it than Cobb put into his report. Just reading between the lines, he said. He suggested I have a talk with him and see if there's anything to it."

"And?"

"I went looking for him, but he was out."

"Out, or gone home early?"

"I'll give him the benefit of the doubt and say he was out on an inquiry."

"You're more charitable than I am, Harry."

"It's my Catholic upbringing, sir. Makes me want to see only the best in people."

"Which explains why you became a policeman."

"That must have been it."

Stride drank off the last of his rum and stood up.

"You can chase after Cobb tomorrow and see if he has anything useful to tell us. Can I drop you off home?"

"I won't say no, sir." Phelan drained his mug and stood up.

CHAPTER 10

Albert Dancey stood on the front step of Lawrence Rivers's house on Forest Road, waiting for someone to answer the doorbell. When no one appeared after a minute, he pushed the button a second time and took a step back to look through the front-room window. Then he heard footsteps inside and Charles Rivers opened the door.

"You're a bit late, I think," Charlie said. "Laurie was expecting you a good half hour ago, Albert."

"I was held up at the office." Dancey looked into the front room, then down the long hallway.

"He's in the back, in the study. We both were. And I'm sorry you were kept waiting. I wasn't sure the bell had rung. Normally, Martha would have answered, but she's busy in the kitchen preparing dinner."

"How is Laurie?"

"He's more or less sober, Albert, if that's what you're asking."

"That is what I'm asking."

"Actually, it's more sober than less. He asked for a drink about an hour ago, and I made him a very mild one."

Dancey nodded. He took off his raincoat and gave it to Rivers.

"He didn't complain about that?"

"Not a bit. And I can happily report he's been nursing it ever so gently. Nothing to worry about, I think. He's well into his wind-down phase."

"That is a relief."

"It wasn't so bad, this time. And the time before that wasn't too bad, either. I don't think that means he's turned a new page in his life, but maybe we can hope for a new paragraph." Rivers led the way down the hall, past the large dining room and the smaller living room. "And how are you doing?"

"I'm doing all right." Dancey pushed his left hand into his jacket pocket. "Nothing to complain about, really. I spent an hour with Edgar Holloway this afternoon. We've finally completed the contract on the new plant."

"That's what kept you late?"

"No. Something else came up."

"I thought the contract with Holloway was already complete. A week ago."

"There's complete, and then there's Edgar's complete. He's wedded to the slow and gradual approach."

"Yes, I know he is." Charlie grinned. "You know, it's sometimes occurred to me that if he takes half as long to complete his business in bed as he does in the office, his wife must be permanently cross-eyed with pleasure."

"If she is, I haven't noticed."

"Modesty, probably."

"Was there something you wanted to talk to me about, Charlie? Louise said you called."

"Nothing very important, just some bother about a salt order gone astray. If I'd been in the office today, instead of playing watchdog here with Laurie, I would have dealt with it myself. I'll be in tomorrow, and I'll look after it then."

Lawrence Rivers looked up from the newspaper he was reading and raised his glass in greeting. Dancey was pleased to see that it was still more than half full. The Rivers brothers looked more like father and son than siblings. There were fifteen years between them, and where Charlie was tall and slender, Lawrence was shorter and more heavily built, sliding into fleshy middle age.

"Make yourself a drink, Bert," Lawrence Rivers said. "Assuming you feel equal to the challenge."

"I think I can manage a mild one."

"I'll get it for you," Charlie said. "Canadian whisky, isn't it?"

"With soda. Easy on the whisky, Charlie, and generous with the soda. Anything interesting in the paper, Laurie?"

"Yes, there is." He folded the newspaper and gave it to Dancey. "There was a shooting on Circular Road last night."

"I heard something about that on the radio," Charlie said. "They didn't give any names, but they said the coroner was at the scene. That usually means someone's dead." He gave Dancey his drink. "Have you heard anything about it, Albert?"

Dancey sat in a chair close to Rivers, their knees almost touching.

"Yes, quite a lot, in fact." He took a sip of his drink and placed the glass on an end table. He looked at Rivers. "It's Harry Rose, Laurie. He was killed last night."

Lawrence Rivers stared at Dancey. He raised his glass to drink, then changed his mind and placed it on the end table beside Dancey's. His expression, cheerful when Dancey had come into the room, was sombre now.

"Harrison Rose?" Charlie Rivers closed the door of the liquor cabinet. He walked across the study and leaned against the desk. "That's a shocker."

"You said you've heard quite a lot about it, Bert," Rivers said. "Have the police been in touch with you?"

"Yes, they have. I was interviewed by an Inspector Stride. He's one of Jack McCowan's men. In fact, it was McCowan who put him on to me."

"Well, that's no surprise," Rivers said. "What sort of questions did he ask you?"

"General things, for the most part. They don't know a lot about Rose at the moment, except for the obvious. They're just starting to build a file."

"That tells me they don't have any suspects in the case."

"They don't. They're looking for a possible motive. We ended up talking a lot about the war. One of the things Stride asked was whether I thought Rose was a good officer. I said he was."

"And they're wondering, I suppose, if someone from the Regiment might have killed him?"

"I'm not sure they're actually thinking that, but it's an obvious starting point."

"They'll be damned busy, then, won't they?" Charlie said. "There must be hundreds of men from the Regiment living in St. John's, or in the area. Thousands, probably. And it's almost thirty years after the fact. It looks like a near-futile approach to me."

"It might be, but there's a certain logic to it, I suppose. And as I said, they have to start somewhere. But Stride is also interested in Rose's business affairs."

"Well, I suppose he would be," Rivers said. "Did McCowan suggest Stride should talk to anyone else? To me, perhaps?"

"He has your name. I told him I'd be talking with you this evening."

"So, I can expect to see him sometime soon."

"I imagine so. Are you up to it, Laurie?"

"I think so. But I won't really know until it happens, will I?"

"At which time, it will be too late to do anything about it."

"Don't worry about me, Bert, I'm fine." Lawrence Rivers looked at his brother. "You can step in and support me whenever you feel like it, Charlie."

"He'll be fine, Albert."

"He'll probably be talking to Jack Corrigan at some point," Dancey said. "He's right there, working out of Fort Townshend."

"I'm surprised he hasn't talked to him already," Rivers said.

"He might have, for all I know."

"I'm just wondering," Charlie said. "Were you a suspect, Albert? I mean, if he really was thinking along the lines that someone from the Regiment killed Rose, then you must have been on his list." He looked at his brother. "And you, too, Laurie, I suppose. Assuming he has a list."

"He didn't have a list, as such," Dancey said. "But the possibility did come up."

"That you were a suspect?"

"Yes."

"Amazing. They really are reaching, aren't they?" Charlie Rivers laughed. "And knowing you as I do, Albert, I dare say you asked him about that, straight out."

"Yes, I did."

"The frontal assault. Did it work?"

"Better than it ever did in France," Dancey said.

"No casualties?"

"Nothing worse than a flesh wound, as far as I can judge. And even that wasn't serious."

"Did Cecil Cake's name come up?" Rivers said.

Dancey shook his head.

"No, it didn't. But if he talks to Jack Corrigan about this, Cec's name might well come up."

Rivers sighed and shook his head.

"I hope he doesn't get on to Cec. If the police come calling, God only knows what he might say. Or do."

"It's a bit of a worry," Dancey said.

"Cecil Cake." Charlie sat on the arm of an easy chair and looked at his brother. "The fellow who lives in the west end? He's a friend of yours isn't he, Laurie?"

"We were close friends once," Rivers said. "But things aren't the same now. They haven't been for years."

"I remember him," Charlie said. "He's the fellow with the head injury."

"Yes."

"I met him about a year ago," Charlie said. "I think I told you about it. He just appeared one day, wanting to see you, Laurie. Odd little fellow, I thought. He was wearing an old army coat that looked like it dated back to the Great War."

"Yes, that was him," Rivers said. "And you did tell me about it. One of the few things that's predictable about Cec is his unpredictability. And that coat does date back to the last war. He brought it home with him."

Charlie stood up and smoothed the creases from his jacket.

"Well, I'm off. I'm meeting some friends for dinner downtown."

"At the hotel?"

"No. It's a private function. Home cooking. The food's better and the wine flows a lot more freely."

"Anyone I know?"

"I don't know if you know him or not, Laurie. It's a fellow I met a while back. His name's Barnes Wilson. He's at Government House, but he also rents a flat in town. He fancies himself as something of a chef, and in fact he can sling together a damn fine meal when he's in the mood. Which I hope he is tonight."

"Barnes Wilson," Dancey said. "British Army, isn't he? A major?"

"Yes. He's Governor Macdonald's aide-de-camp. Which is one of the reasons he prefers to dine in, in private, and with the drapes pulled. He swears the abstemious Welshman has spies all over the city, reporting back to him on anyone in his retinue seen taking a drink in public. A fellow could develop a complex."

"I think everyone at Government House has a complex," Dancey said. "It's almost a requirement for a position there."

"That's probably not too far off the mark," Charlie said. "But Wilson's all right. He's an interesting fellow, in fact. He's been posted in any number of places over the years. He has stories to tell, and he enjoys telling them." Charlie took a gold cigarette case from his pocket and filled it from a box on the desk. "Martha said your dinner would be ready about six-thirty. Tonight it's veal, and it looks very good. I almost wish I was staying for dinner with you."

"But not quite."

"No, not quite. Which reminds me. I said I'd give Wilson a ring before I came over, to see if he needs me to bring anything." He pushed the door open. "You two behave yourselves. I've asked Martha to give me a full report later on."

"We'll try and make it interesting for you, Charlie."

"Well, don't make it too interesting." He closed the door behind him.

Dancey waited a few moments until he was certain Charlie had left for good.

"This Wilson fellow that Charlie's having dinner with. We've met him, Laurie, a couple of times. He came to the Regimental dinner last year, representing the Governor, and to a few other functions. Tall fellow, dark hair, just going grey around the edges? About our age, I think, maybe a few years younger."

"Yes, I believe I remember him." Rivers laughed. "To the extent that I can remember anything from that particular evening." He looked at his glass and pushed it a few inches farther away from him.

"Have you heard from Agnes?" Dancey asked. Mention of the Regimental dinner, which had coincided with one of Rivers's bad times, had brought a small cloud into the study. "She's in London still?"

"Yes, I did hear from her. But she's in Edinburgh now. Or was when she wrote me. She's visiting the Castle, of course, where our lot were stationed before we went off to the Dardanelles. I asked her to take a picture of the commemorative plaque. She'll be home in another week. No, that's not right. She'll be leaving Southampton in a week, then home six days after that."

"You'll be glad to have her back," Dancey said.

"I miss her when she's not here, although when she is we're at sixes and sevens as often as not. But it's been that way for going on thirty years."

"You need her, Laurie, and she's good for you."

"Well, I can't seem to manage on my own for very long these days."

"I'm surprised you didn't go with her. It might have done you some good to get away. Done you both good."

"I did think about it," Rivers said.

"You haven't been across the water since, when? In 1930, I think it was? And I don't believe Agnes went with you that time."

"It was 1931, and you're right, I did go on my own." Rivers held up his glass. "This, by the way, is 90 percent ginger ale. And it's not awful."

"The worst is past?"

"Yes. Charlie probably told you all about it on the way in."

"He suggested that things are getting better, on the whole."

"Charlie's an optimist. He's had to be, putting up with me all these years. If we were of an age, I think he'd probably have got fed up years ago, and moved out. But the age gap—it's almost fifteen years, you know—it makes a difference. We're more like father and son than brothers."

"Or uncle and nephew."

"One or the other," Rivers said. "And I know I've told you this before, Bert. Charlie's been good to me, all things considered. And he's also more interested in the business than he was." He caught Dancey's reaction. "You don't think so?"

"It's not really for me to say, Laurie."

"Of course it is. This isn't just a family company any longer. You're as much a part of it now as we are."

"Yes, but it still has the family name attached, and in most people's minds it's still the Rivers company. And I don't mind that, Laurie. But I'm not convinced yet that Charlie has the real business sense to take over from either of us. Personally, I like Charlie, I always have. But he's not really a businessman."

"You still think he's a romantic, I suppose."

"He has a lot of the romantic in him, yes. And there's nothing wrong with that. But if you try and bend him into a copy of yourself, or your father—or even of me—you'll be doing a disservice to both of you. And I don't think it'll work."

"There's a lot of truth in what you say, Bert. But I do think he's happier in the situation than he was. His service in the militia during the war did a lot for him. He wanted to go overseas, you know, and that surprised and pleased me in about equal amounts. He didn't see the war in quite the innocent way we did thirty-odd years ago, but he was keen enough to put on the uniform. He would have gone, too, if his eyesight hadn't excluded him."

"Yes, I know. I remember he was very disappointed at first. He thought he'd let the side down. I think he wanted to follow in your footsteps."

"That was part of it, but he handled it well in the end. God knows I made an effort to tell him that war isn't a bloody game, and that it isn't an adventure, either. I was never sure that I'd got through to him, but perhaps I did in the end."

"Is he still resentful of your relative positions in the company?"

"I don't think he is. And that's something that cheers me." He looked at his glass but folded his hands in his lap. "And sometimes I do need cheering. But, let's leave all that for now."

"That suits me." Dancey picked up his drink. "And to change the subject a bit, when's the last time you spoke to Cec? I haven't in ages, and just now I'm feeling a bit guilty about it."

"I know that feeling," Rivers said. He picked up his glass. "It's been a while for me, too. But he's so bloody hard to talk to when we do get together. That head wound did some serious and permanent damage."

"Not much doubt about it. And it might even be getting worse. That and losing Daniel. But he's doing all right, isn't he? Financially, I mean."

"He seems to be." Rivers picked up his drink and looked towards the fireplace. "The last time I spoke to him, I asked him if he needed any money, and he said no."

"That might just be his pride talking."

"I don't think so," Rivers said.

"But he didn't tell you what he's doing for money? How he supports himself? I don't know that he's had a job in a long time."

"I really do think he's all right, Bert."

"Be honest with me, Laurie. Are you giving him money?"

"No." Rivers shifted in his chair. "I did offer him money once, some years back, but he refused. I'm supposing that hasn't changed."

"He must be getting money from somewhere, though."

"I suppose he must," Rivers said.

The door to the dining room opened and Martha Handrigan spoke to them.

"Dinner will be on the table in five minutes, Mr. Rivers." She nodded to Dancey. "Will I open that bottle of wine you put out?"

"What do you think, Bert? Dare we risk it?"

"I'd like a glass of wine with the veal," Dancey said. "Tell you what, Laurie. I'll keep an eye on you, and you'll keep an eye on me."

"And I'll keep an eye on both of you," Martha said. "Five minutes."

CHAPTER 11

Stride drove the MG into the garage at the back of his house and locked the door. He held his umbrella over his head, walked around to the front of the house, and up onto the veranda. He shook the water off the umbrella, furled it, and opened the front door. When he came around the turn in the stairs, halfway to the third floor, he stopped. A woman was sitting on the steps near the door of his flat, knees primly together, her back against the wall. A furled umbrella was propped against the wall on the other side. She was smiling.

Stride hadn't seen Rita Fleming since the Taylor case in the spring. He hadn't thought it likely he would see her again, except possibly to arrest her for plying her trade as a prostitute, a term he knew she hated. He'd never thought that was a real possibility. Rita Fleming had long since moved beyond soliciting clients in public. He heard about her from time to time, and he knew she had a select clientele, none of whom was likely to lodge a complaint against her.

"You should lock your downstairs door, Inspector. You can never tell who might come calling. "

"I take your point." Stride continued on up the stairs, unlocked his door and stood to the side so she could come in. She unbuttoned her coat and turned so that Stride could slip it off her shoulders. While he hung it in the closet, she walked slowly around his living room. She stopped in front of one of his paintings, a watercolour, then moved on to his other paintings. She picked up the occasional object, looked at it, then put it back again. After a minute she turned to him, half-smiling.

"You know, you're allowed to ask what the hell it is I think I'm doing here."

"All right. What the hell are you doing here?"

"That's better." She sat on the arm of the chesterfield. "I'm here because I need to talk to you about something."

"Which is?"

"Take a guess. Take three guesses, if you feel like it."

"Something to do with the shooting last night?"

"You're a clever man. I'm not surprised they made you inspector."

"Actually, I made it entirely on good looks and boyish charm. But that's another story, for another time."

"I'll have to think about that. The 'another time' bit, I mean. I'm a busy girl."

"So I've heard. You have something to tell me about the shootings?"

"Yes." She stood up and started circling the room again. "But you know, a drink would make it easier to talk."

"It usually does. What would you like?"

"Scotch and water, no ice, and easy on the water. I've had a tough day."

He took his time making the drinks, strong for her, as she'd requested, but weak for himself. He watched her while he made the drinks. She was walking around the living room again.

She'd changed somehow since he'd last seen her. He decided it was her clothing, more tasteful than he remembered—less flashy, more mature. A lot of change in only four months. Stride had found Rita Fleming attractive the first time he'd met her, and, if anything, she was even more attractive now. A little under average height, she had a trim figure, slightly boyish even, and she looked younger than her actual age, which was twenty-six. Her hair was light brown, short and stylishly cut. Her presence here in his flat was something he'd never anticipated, and he was, if not actually uncomfortable, then on his guard.

She sipped her drink. Then she sat on the arm of the chesterfield again and looked at the floor between her feet, her shoulders slumped, her expression clouded.

"So, what do you know about the shooting?" Stride asked, breaking the silence.

"For one thing, I know the man who was killed."

"How do you know who was killed? We haven't released the name yet."

"I have friends who tell me things, friends of mine you don't know. And friends of mine you do know, but who haven't told you that they know me. You'd be surprised."

"I suppose I might be," Stride said.

"I knew by late this morning that it was Harry Rose who was shot."

"*Harry* Rose?"

"He was 'Harry' to people who were close to him."

"And you were close to him?"

"Closer than some," she said. "For a while, anyway."

"Go on."

"Harry was one of my clients."

"For a while."

"Yes.

"But there was more to it than that?"

"Yes." She looked thoughtful. "He was more than just a client."

"And how long have you known him?"

"For about a year and a half."

"You saw him regularly?"

"Pretty regularly. A couple of times a month. For as long as I did see him."

"And for how long was that?"

"For about six months after we first met."

"He was a client for the six months?"

"Yes."

"And then he wasn't any longer."

"And then he wasn't," she said.

"You met with him at his house?"

"Sometimes at his place, more often at mine."

"I see." He looked at her closely for a moment. His first thought was that Rita Fleming might have been the woman Mary Holden saw with Rose, but she didn't fit the description. Her hair was short, but it wasn't curly. And she was too young. "You didn't come here tonight just to tell me you'd had Harrison Rose as a client. There's some other reason."

"Yes. One reason is that I want to help if I can. I liked him. Maybe I can tell you something about him that you don't know, and it will help you find whoever did this." She paused. "And another reason is that I'm a little bit scared. Whoever killed Harry might want to kill me too."

The answer surprised him. He thought she did look worried but he wasn't sure. He was wondering if there was something else going on with her.

"Why would anyone want to do that?" Stride asked.

"I don't know why they'd want to do that. If you can tell me why Harry was killed, I'd have a better idea, and maybe I could stop worrying about it. Do you know why he was killed?"

"No, we don't."

"Oh, Christ." She started walking again, moving around the room. Then she stopped pacing and looked at him. "You really don't know why they killed him?"

Stride shook his head.

"No, we don't. So maybe something you can tell me about him might help, if you really were close to him. You have the advantage on me there."

"You and Harry were neighbours," she said.

"We only lived on the same street. All I knew about him was his name." He gestured towards the chesterfield. "Please sit down. You're making me nervous."

"You're nervous? How do you think I feel?"

"Nervous?" He laughed, but it sounded wrong. "All right, I understand that. Someone you knew well has been shot to death. It's a nervous business. So, sit down and we'll talk about it. We'll see if we can help each other."

She sat on the chesterfield and leaned back against the cushions, but after only a moment she leaned forward, her elbows on her knees. For a moment he thought she would start crying, but she seemed only to be gathering herself. He wasn't sure how much of this was performance, and how much really was fear.

"Start by telling me about your relationship with Harrison Rose. How did you meet him? Someone introduced you?"

"No. I met him by accident. I like to walk. Usually I walk early in the morning, before breakfast, but sometimes I'll take a walk at night. That's when I ran into him. He said hello, I said hello, and we ended up walking together for a while. We seemed to get along. It was that simple. That almost never happens, not for me, not in my business. And not for him, either, as it turned out. Plus, when I met him, he was lonely."

"So you gave him your number."

"He asked for my number. He also asked what I did for a living, and I told him."

"Just like that."

"Just like that. I don't pretend things with people. I gave that up a long time ago. Along with some other things."

"And he didn't mind?"

"He didn't mind. He called me the next day. And that's how it started. We got together a couple of times a month. Well, I already told you that."

"But it wasn't just business."

"No, it wasn't. We ended up having a kind of friendship. And it was nice." She turned away from him, so that he couldn't see her face. "You'll understand that's not a word I get to use a lot."

"So, how much did you know about him?" She stiffened at the question, a reflex reaction, ingrained after years in her business. Talking about clients wasn't something she would normally do. "Look, it's why you're here, isn't it? To tell me things about him? You help me, and maybe that will help us find out who killed Colonel Rose." He threw Rose's rank into it to see how she'd react. "You did know that he was a colonel in the army?"

"Of course."

"Did he talk about that? His time in the army, and in the war?"

"Not very much. Sometimes he'd mention it, but when he did it was about places he'd been, or sometimes about the men he'd served with. But he didn't really talk about the war. I think it was something that bothered him."

"Did he say why?"

"No. But he had bad memories, and sometimes he didn't sleep well." She caught Stride's expression. "I don't often sleep with clients. Harry was an exception. We did spend the night together sometimes."

"At his place?"

"A couple of times at his place, a couple of times at mine. And we went away together a few times." She picked up her glass. "Well, we didn't actually go away together. We met outside the city and then spent time together. Three or four days, usually."

"Where did you meet?"

"Why do you want to know that?"

"Someone might have seen you. We might be able to follow that up."

"Like the person who killed him."

"Yes."

"I don't think that's likely. Harry had a cabin outside the city, back in the woods. He said it was in the back of beyond, and it was. There wasn't anyone else nearby. We were always alone there. It was nice, very quiet." She looked almost wistful, showing a softer side of her than he'd seen before, and not one he ever expected to see. "One time I asked him if he would leave me the cabin in his will. He said he would. Of course, I was only joking, and he knew I was."

"You know he had a daughter?"

"He told me that, but he never talked about her much. I know her name's Catherine, and that she lives in England, in London, I think. I don't think they were very close."

"And his wife?"

"They were divorced, years ago. He told me she died, but that was a few years later. I don't know exactly how long ago."

"Did his daughter ever visit him here?"

"Not while we were together. But I think she came once, back before the war. Losing her father will be hard for her, even if they weren't close." She picked up her drink again. "I know about that. My father died two years ago. He was in the war, too, Harry Rose's war, in France. He didn't like to talk about it either." She looked at him. "Do you have a cigarette? I forgot mine at home, and I really need one right now."

He gave her one and held out his lighter.

"When Rose slept badly, what was it about? Did he tell you?"

"No, other than to say that he often had bad dreams, nightmares. Sometimes he would wake me up with his shouting. And a couple of times when I woke up in the night I found him sitting in the bedroom, in a chair, in the dark, wide awake."

"And he never said what it was about?"

"He said it had to do with the war. But that's all he would say. It was the same with my father. He never talked about it, either. When I was growing up, I'd sometimes hear him walking around downstairs in the middle of the night. And some mornings we'd find him asleep in the rocking chair, in the kitchen by the stove. My mother told me, told all of us, not to ask him any questions about it, and we didn't."

"When was the last time you saw Rose? You gave me the impression it was a while ago, that you weren't seeing him any longer."

"Harry stopped being a client a year ago, but we stayed in touch from time to time. I last saw him about six months ago. But only to say hello, how are you."

"Why did he stop seeing you? Something went wrong?"

"Not something. Someone. And when she came into the picture, I went out." She shrugged. "I was sorry about that. I liked Harry, and he was nice to me. But that's life. My life. I'm not really in the happily-ever-after business."

"It must have hurt," Stride said. She looked at him but she didn't reply. "Who is she? Do you know her name?"

"Her name's Barbara Drodge. I suppose you already know about her?"

"We knew that a Barbara Drodge worked for him."

"But you didn't know they were involved."

"No. Are you certain they were involved?"

"I'm pretty sure they were. So, I've told you something you didn't know?"

"More or less," Stride said. "Is that the real reason you came here tonight? To tell me about Barbara Drodge?"

She didn't answer right away.

"Maybe," she said, at last. "It's something I thought you'd probably like to know."

"And a way of getting a bit of your own back, maybe? If you knew her name, you probably also knew she was married."

She looked at him and sighed.

"You're just so damned smart. I might have known you'd catch on to me."

"It's one of the few things I do well," he said. "And I don't mind. You've given me some useful information."

"You think her husband might have been the one to shoot Harry?"

"I have no idea. I'll have to ask him. Do you know anything about him, about her marriage?"

"No. I don't even know what her husband looks like. I've never seen him. And I've seen her only once or twice. From a distance."

"But you know what she looks like."

"Of course. It's one of the things a woman does when she gets passed over. We want to see what the opposition looks like. I'm not so different from everyone else."

"Fair enough."

The telephone rang then. The sudden sharp sound startled them both.

He excused himself and went to the kitchen to pick up the phone. It was Dianne. He'd forgotten she'd said she would call.

"There's someone there," she said. "I can tell from your voice."

"Yes, there is. It's someone who knew Harrison Rose."

"So, this isn't a good time to talk about things, is it?"

"Not really, no."

"Can I call back later?"

"Yes, but it might be better if I called you."

"No, don't do that. I'm expecting Marty back in a little while. If you call when he's here, that will just start a row."

"All right. Call me back in, say, thirty minutes. I think we'll be finished by then."

"You're sure?"

"No, I'm not sure." He spoke more quickly than he'd intended, impatience showing through. Dianne picked up on it at once.

"Jesus, Eric, I—Look, never mind. I'll call back in a half hour, if I can."

"All right." He saw that Rita Fleming was looking at him, probably reading his mood, also something of the situation. "I'm sorry. It's been a long day."

She didn't reply right away, but he could hear her breathing across the telephone line.

"It's all right," she said after a moment. "We're both of us on edge. I'll call back later, and we'll talk if we can. And if we can't, then we'll talk some other time, tomorrow maybe?"

"We can leave it at that for now." He started to say again that he was sorry, but it was something he said too easily, too often.

Dianne spoke again, her tone, and her emotions, back under control.

"Look, since you're working on the case, I'll give you some information I got at the office on Harrison Rose."

"Yes?"

"He had a very good business here in Newfoundland. He set it up in late 1930. Well, December of 1930 was when he registered with us. His office is in the Newfoundland Hotel. Most of his business activity was directed across the water, to England."

"Even during the war?"

"Yes. The demand for timber stayed high, so he was in good shape when the war ended. England is in very bad shape, of course, almost bankrupt. Some of the local companies who depend on English markets aren't doing all that well. But Rose was doing better than most."

"Well, he was living a very good life. Is it possible he had another source of income?"

"The feeling around here is that he might have. Which immediately suggests family money. Opinion is divided on whether he had any to draw on. Some say no, and some say yes, but I think the yeses have it."

"Based on what?"

"Based on his background. Here, and before he left England."

"Go on."

"Well, we know he was an army officer, and he was a lieutenant-colonel. That's a decent rank, but army pay isn't really all that generous, and neither are the pensions. A lot of retired officers from the British Army, even ones with a fairly high rank, like Rose, have to scramble to make a living. Especially the ones still living in England. And Rose retired from the army long before the last war. His pension can't have been very large. But he arrived here with enough money to buy a large house on Circular Road, and then have it renovated. He also had enough money to buy a good business, one that was already well established."

"He paid cash for all of that?"

"Apparently he did. And he wasn't just a chinless wonder with family money to throw around. He managed his business well, and he made money, even through the dirty thirties, it appears."

"None of that would have set a precedent," Stride said. "Having family money, I mean."

"Not really. Having family money, or owning land in the colonies, or both, is still fairly common for a certain class of Brits, even now, in the waning days of Empire."

"How much of what you've told me is based on hard fact, and how much on guesswork?"

"Some of what I told you is based on fact—the house, the business purchase. The family-money part, that's speculation, but from people who know whereof they speak. And I'll add that Harrison Rose knew there was talk that he had family money. He never denied it."

"That helps a lot," Stride said. "Thank you."

"You're welcome." She laughed. "It's easy to talk about business matters, isn't it? The word *divorce* almost never gets spoken."

"That is an advantage."

"And there's something else I meant to tell you."

"Yes?"

"Rose's business was pretty much a one-man show. Most of his office assistance was part-time, but recently, for most of the past year in fact, he's had someone working for him. A woman named Barbara Drodge."

"Actually, we knew that. Also about his office being at the Newfoundland Hotel. Harry Phelan was there this afternoon."

"So, things are progressing."

"We've made some progress, but we've a long way to go."

"I expect you have. We'll talk again tomorrow, probably?"

"Probably."

He hung up the phone. He saw that Rita Fleming was still watching him from the living room. There was a smile playing at the corners of her mouth. He wondered how many times she'd listened to her clients—as she called them—struggling through awkward conversations with wives and girlfriends while she was in the room.

"That had to be a woman. Your girlfriend?"

"You have a good ear."

"I've developed one over the years." She tilted her head to the side. "I don't know what to call you now. Inspector Stride seems too formal, but I'm not sure Eric is proper, either. Someone might overhear that sometime, and they'd think we're friends. And then where would you be?"

"God only knows. But I'm trying to imagine who would overhear."

"Probably no one. So, Eric is all right?"

"Yes, Eric's all right."

She gave him a look that lasted a moment too long for comfort, for either of them. Again there was the sense of attraction, heightened by the developing complications with Dianne. Rita picked up her glass and drained it.

"I think I should be on my way." She stood up. "Look, I'm sorry about the grand performance. I really was ticked off when Harry Rose dropped me. And you're right, it did hurt. Being hurt's not something I allow myself. If I did, I'd go crazy. And going crazy's not part of any plan I'm working on."

"We're only human," Stride said. Brilliantly. "I don't think you have anything to worry about, but if you want, I can drive you home."

"No, don't do that. And, you're right, I don't think anyone is going to come after me. Why would they? And you don't want anyone to see us driving around together. People might talk."

"People always talk."

"Your girlfriend wouldn't like it if she was to find out." She corrected herself. "Were to find out. I've been working on my grammar. That's something Harry was trying to do for me. He was very proper, you know, very correct." She laughed. "Well, in most things."

She stood up and they moved towards the door.

"You're sure you don't want a ride?"

"Yes, I am sure," she said. "But if you hear gunshots, please come running."

He took her coat from the closet and helped her on with it.

"There is one other thing," she said. "I almost forgot. Does the name 'Crozier' mean anything to you?" she said.

"Crozier?" He thought about that, then shook his head. "I've heard the name before, but it doesn't mean anything special. He's someone Rose knew?"

"It's one of the names he said once or twice, on a couple of those nights when he couldn't sleep. I remembered it because it's a name I'd never heard before. Or since, for that matter."

"And it was just the name he said? Nothing else?"

"I asked him who this Crozier was, but all he would say was that it was someone he served with once."

She finished buttoning her coat, knotted the belt around her waist, and turned the collar up. She picked up her umbrella.

"You and your girlfriend? It sounded like you're having some problems."

"You could say that."

"Big problems?"

"Big enough. She's married." And the instant the words were out there, he wondered why he'd said them.

"That is a problem, and I speak from experience. I hope her husband doesn't come gunning for you."

"We'll hope not."

"I'll keep my fingers crossed." She opened the door and stepped out onto the landing. "And if I think of anything else, I'll be in touch. Eric." She smiled. "God, that sounds so strange."

He watched as she went carefully down the stairs, one hand on the railing, her high heels clacking on the linoleum. When she got to the bottom, she pulled the door open, turned and waved. Through the open door, he could see that it was raining again.

CHAPTER 12

Charlie Rivers pulled the cork from a bottle of burgundy, unwound it from the corkscrew and gave it to Barnes Wilson. Wilson sniffed it, then held it close to his ear and rolled it between his fingers. He claimed that the texture and smell of the cork could tell him things he needed to know about the quality of the wine in the bottle. Charlie thought it was a load of codswallop, but he always went along with it.

Wilson, with his diplomatic and other connections, routinely acquired items that the average person could only dream about. If, in fact, the average person even knew that such things as fine burgundy, cognac, caviar and smoked oysters actually existed. George Orwell had it just about right: some people really are more equal than others. And if Britain was all but bankrupt and sliding steadily down the tubes, some of her sons and daughters were doing very well, especially in some far-distant colonies and dominions, where life could often be much better than it was at home.

Wilson reached down three wine glasses from the kitchen cupboard and placed them on the counter. Wilson's flat was small, but comfortable, everything neatly organized in four small rooms. As an army officer with experience in the field, he knew how to make do with accommodations of limited size.

"You can put those on the table, Charlie. Unless you want some wine now. Or would you rather have a whisky?"

"I'll have some wine, I think." He picked up a glass from the counter, but his arm brushed against Wilson's shoulder, and he pulled back, dropping the glass. It shattered on the floor.

"Damn. I am sorry about that, Barnes. Mother always said I'd grow up to be awkward and clumsy."

"No great harm done," Wilson said. "Wine glasses are one thing I have in large supply. I just thank God it wasn't the burgundy that hit the deck. It's an especially good bottle, and good bottles are not that easily come by, not in this corner of the world."

"I'll clean this up. Do you have a broom and dustpan?"

"In that cupboard, there," Wilson said. He took down another glass and placed it on the counter.

"Did either of you see or hear any of what went on in Bannerman Park last night?" Charlie asked. He put the broken glass in the dustbin.

Rodney Gilbert looked up from his glass of whisky.

"I heard the shots, Charlie. Barnes didn't, but I did. Two shots, and I made note of the time, which was helpful when Inspector Stride stopped by this morning to talk to me. I gather there was some question about the number."

"Really?" Charlie asked. "Did Stride think there were more than two shots, or fewer?"

"He said he heard two as well, but as Colonel Rose was hit three times, that seemed to settle the issue."

"My brother served with Harrison Rose in the Great War," Charlie said. "For almost two years, first in the Dardanelles, and later on in France."

"I wondered about that," Wilson said. "I knew your brother was in the war, in the British Army. But the Newfoundlanders were in a separate regiment, with their own officers, weren't they?"

"Yes, we had our own regiment in the British Army, and most of our officers were Newfoundlanders. But the more senior ones were usually English. Rose was one of those."

"Did you ever meet him, Charlie?" Wilson asked. "I think you said you did."

"Once or twice. Laurie introduced us at a business gathering, back before the war. The most recent one, I mean. We were thinking of expanding our business into wood products of various kinds, and Rose was already well established there. Laurie and Albert Dancey had some discussions with him about that, but in the end, nothing happened. They couldn't come to an agreement on terms. But don't ask me for details. I wasn't involved."

"No?"

"No, I think Albert and my brother are waiting until I'm all grown up before they give me that kind of responsibility."

"That sounds a little bitter, Charlie." Wilson looked at him.

"Does it? It must have slipped out when I wasn't paying attention." Charlie sipped his wine. "You knew Rose, Barnes, and pretty well, I think?"

"Pretty well."

"Did you meet him before he came to Newfoundland, or afterwards?" Gilbert asked.

"Both, actually." Wilson opened the oven door and pulled out the middle rack. A roast of beef was sizzling in a pan. He probed it with a fork and looked at the juices that flowed from the meat. He basted it using a long-handled spoon. "Fifteen minutes, gentlemen, and then we can eat." Wilson placed the bottle of wine on a silver caddy in the centre of the dining table. He looked at Rivers. "How is that, by the way? Acceptable?"

"It meets my needs," Charlie said. "Did the cork tell you good things about it?"

"I have so much to teach you, Charlie, I almost don't know where to begin."

"We were talking about Harrison Rose," Gilbert said.

"Yes, we were," Wilson said. "The first time I met Harry Rose was after the war, the Great War, that is, in 1920." He picked up his glass of whisky, and sat in an armchair, draping one long leg over an arm. "For my sins, I'd been posted to Ireland, to Dublin. Harry Rose was already there. Happily, I was more or less safely squirrelled away in Dublin Castle, shuffling bits of paper, trying to make sense of the intelligence we were getting on the IRA."

"It was a very rough go, Ireland, from everything I've read and heard about it," Gilbert said. "And I'm damned happy I missed it all."

"It was a damned rough go," Wilson said. "One went about very carefully, if one was in uniform, which I was some of the time. I wore mufti whenever I could, a lot of us did. It was safer that way."

"Was Rose still in uniform when he was in Dublin?"

Wilson looked at Gilbert for a moment before replying, choosing his words.

"Yes, he was, and he was right in the thick of it. And some of it was bloody awful. Our side took a lot of casualties. One of those was a friend of Harry's, the fellow who'd been his batman from the war, a chap named Hawthorne. He was killed. They'd been together for a long time, Rose and Hawthorne, since before the start of the Great War. Rose took Hawthorne's death very hard. His marriage had gone south at about the same time, and that made it even worse."

"It must have seemed like his life was falling apart," Gilbert said.

"Yes, I think that probably was the case. Mind you, I didn't know him all that well back then. I got to know him better after I ran into him here, in St. John's."

"That name is familiar," Charlie said. "Hawthorne, I mean. I think my brother must have mentioned him once or twice. Basil Hawthorne, wasn't it?"

"Yes, that was his name." Wilson picked up the whisky bottle and looked at Gilbert. "Can I top you up, old man?"

"Just a trickle. I'm saving myself for the burgundy. It won't do at all if I'm staggering when I get back to Government House. The dour Welshman will frown at me for days and days, and mutter imprecations in his native tongue."

"Basil Hawthorne was a decent sort," Wilson said, picking up the thread again. "We actually worked together at the Castle, Basil and I."

"Shuffling papers together, while Rose was out fighting the rebels?"

"More or less. Hawthorne had a desk job, same as I did. He wasn't supposed to be out in harm's way. But he was careless sometimes, especially when he'd had a few, and was more concerned with chasing a bit of skirt than looking out for himself. A great skirt chaser, Basil was. But he paid for it in the end. An IRA assassination squad got him one evening when he was coming back from one of his assignations. I can only hope it was worth it."

"At least he went out with a bang, not a whimper," Gilbert said.

"That's very bad, Rod."

"Perhaps I'll do better with some burgundy and roast beef inside me."

"Harrison Rose wasn't the paper-shuffling type, though, was he?" Charlie asked.

"Not at all. He was always happy to be in the thick of it. A desk job would have driven him mad. At least back then it would have. Some men are like that, and Harry Rose, I believe, was one of them, a warrior at heart. At least that was the impression he gave me."

"He was in the thick of it here, too, in a way," Charlie said. Gilbert looked across the room at him. "It happened before you arrived here, Rod. And it's a good story. I take it you haven't told him about it, Barnes?"

"No, I haven't. And, you're right, it's not a bad story."

"Well, get on with it," Gilbert said.

"I'll just give you the short version. Harry Rose and I had been at a party, and that in itself was unusual. Harry wasn't really the social type, but as I thought it was going to be one of the better parties, I persuaded him to come along with me, and he was quite happy in the end that he'd come. We didn't get stinko, exactly, but we were feeling no pain, and a very good time was had by all. Anyway, Harry and I finally extricated ourselves from the gathering and waddled on home. Wisely, neither of us had a car that night." Wilson raised an index finger. "No, I tell a lie. Harry did drive us over in his car, but he left it there, to go back and pick it up the next day. It wasn't all that far to walk, anyway, and the weather was decent. While we were walking back home, taking a shortcut through Bannerman Park, we were set upon by three oafs who looked, and smelled, like they'd had even more to drink than we had. And decidedly inferior stuff at that. I suppose they thought we'd be easy marks, two middle-aged chaps alone in the park late at night, and Harry using a cane to get around."

"But you surprised them," Charlie said.

"Yes, we did. They just hadn't reckoned with the fact that we both were trained soldiers, even if we were a year or two past our prime. They also couldn't know that Harry Rose carried his cane just for show, a very proper English gentleman, if you will. As things turned out, we beat the living hell out of them. One of them, I found out later, was very badly hurt, and he spent a couple of weeks in the hospital. Later on still, I heard that he'd damn near died."

"I don't remember hearing anything about that," Gilbert said. "Did the police get involved?"

"Yes, they did. There was a uniformed constable, a young fellow, and a detective chap in plainclothes, who was about as old as we were. We were both interviewed by the detective. The constable took care of the oafs. Well, the two of them that weren't quite at death's door. Nothing came of it in the end. Harry didn't want to press charges, and for that matter, I didn't either. That whole business of going to court, and perhaps being interviewed by newspaper people. Harry would have hated that. The Governor wouldn't have liked it much, either, if I'd got my name in the papers. The fact that I'd been drinking would have made it even worse. But in the end, the detective fellow agreed to keep it all hush-hush, tuck it under the sod in the park, so to speak. I know the three oafs were happy about that, even if they were licking their wounds and wondering what the hell had happened to them."

"It's not a bad story," Gilbert said. "Is there a longer and more colourful version?"

"In fact there is, but I need to be primed with a lot more bubbly than I've had so far this evening." Wilson looked at his watch. "Well, it's time to eat, I think. Charlie, I'm putting you in charge of the gravy, as usual. And, Rod, you're on vegetable patrol. So, let's have at it. I'm bloody starving."

Albert Dancey parked his car two doors down from the bungalow where Louise Woods lived. He sat in the car for a few minutes, watching to see if anyone was out on the street. He exercised more care when he visited Louise than she thought was necessary. She'd told him more than once that she wasn't as concerned about her reputation, whatever that was, as he appeared to be. If she had a gentleman caller, even late at night, and someone happened to notice, that was all right with her. Even if his car stayed on the street all night, it wasn't something that concerned her. The people in her life who mattered to her already knew about her and Albert. The rest, the casual observers, they didn't count. She didn't mind being talked about, just as she equally didn't mind *not* being talked about. But he waited just the same. It was his way. Louise even thought it had a certain charm.

Her car, a pre-war Austin coupe, was parked in the driveway. There was a light on in the living room, and another showing from a side window near the back of the house that he knew was her bedroom. He walked to the front step, still looking around him, unlocked the door, and let himself in. He had phoned ahead to tell her he would stop by on his way home from Rivers's house.

Louise was standing in the hallway when he came in. She was wearing a dark blue dressing gown and matching slippers. The lamp behind the armchair where she liked to sit and read was turned on. A book lay on the end table by the chair, her place marked by a soft leather bookmark, frilled at the end. A glass, half filled with milk, stood beside the book.

She helped him off with his coat and hat, and put them both in the closet. She stood his umbrella, still furled, in the corner by the door.

"You look tired, Albert. You should probably be home in bed."

"I am tired. This day has been too long, and too involved."

"I imagine it's too late for a drink, but I think you want one anyway."

"It is too late, and it's a bad idea, but I will have one."

He wiped his feet on the mat a second time, and went into the living room. While she made his drink, he picked up her book and opened it to the page that was marked, read a few sentences, then turned it back to front and read the title. It was Maugham's *The Painted Veil*. Dancey almost never read fiction, and he was only vaguely aware of who Somerset Maugham was. English, he thought, but he wasn't certain even of that much. It was one of many differences between them, his disinterest in reading, and her abiding passion for it. But, somehow, in a contrarian way, their differences didn't hold them apart, they provided binding points. If he didn't read, he was always pleased to listen to her talk about whichever book she was enthusiastic about at the moment.

She gave him his drink and they sat side by side on the chesterfield.

"You and Mr. Lawrence behaved yourselves tonight?"

"We did. A drink before dinner, very mild, and a glass of wine each with the roast veal."

"Good for you. Both of you."

"If this hits me harder than I think it will," he held up the glass, "I'll spend the night."

"I was hoping you would anyway."

"Then, perhaps I'll do that, regardless."

Dancey held the glass in both hands, stretched his legs out and let his head fall back against the plush material of the chesterfield. He closed his eyes for a moment. Louise touched his cheek with her fingertips.

"I think I know why you're here, Albert. It's about Harry Rose, isn't it?"

"Yes." He turned to look at her. "The news was on the radio, I suppose?" He sat upright and sipped his drink.

"I don't know if it was on the radio or not. I didn't turn it on. I was at Anna's until almost nine. On my way home, I drove down Circular Road, just to see if anything was going on in the park still. There wasn't, but there were two policemen at Harry's house, one on the veranda, and the other walking down the laneway towards the back of the house. That told me all I needed to know. Well, almost everything. I didn't want to get the news from the radio. I was about to phone you when you rang me."

"Inspector Stride arrived a little while after you left this afternoon. He was with me for quite a while, asking me questions about Harry Rose. He told me the basics of it. Harry was shot sometime late last night, in the park. While he was out walking, apparently. That's why the park was cordoned off this morning."

"God, Harry and his late-night walks." She looked at him. "Barbara Drodge wasn't involved, was she? Or Norman?"

"Stride didn't mention their names. It's possible he doesn't know about either of them, or didn't when he spoke with me. But he'll find out about them sooner or later." He sipped his drink. "Sooner, I expect."

"You said Harry was shot in the park. Was it robbery? Or was it something else?"

"I don't know if it was robbery or not. Stride didn't volunteer the information, and I didn't ask."

"The house wasn't broken into?"

"I don't know that either. But with the police standing guard over the place, that suggests it's a crime scene. Whatever it is, there's no point speculating about it." He paused. "I suppose I could give Jack McCowan a ring tomorrow morning and ask him what's going on. What went on."

"Is that wise? And, anyway, would he tell you anything about an investigation that's in progress?"

"That's a good point. He might not. And the fact is, Inspector Stride asked me flat out if I had anything to do with it."

"Did he?"

"Yes. And he also took his time getting around to his reason for coming to see me. It was obvious he was looking for some indication that I already knew about it."

"That was a bit dramatic, wasn't it?"

"I suppose it's one of the things they do. By the time he arrived at the office, half the people in town must have known what went on."

"That's an exaggeration, Albert. I expect a lot of people might have wondered if something had happened to Harry Rose, given all the police activity in the area, and the article in the paper, but it would all be guesswork. And if guesses were gold, everyone would be rich."

"Did your sister say anything about it? Anna?"

"Anna?" Louise smiled and shook her head. "Anna had twelve six-year-olds racing around her house, playing Pin the Tail on the Donkey, and spilling cake and juice on the rugs. World War Three could have started and she would neither have noticed nor cared."

"I suppose not."

"You talked to Mr. Lawrence about Harry?"

"Yes. We talked about it for a while. Charlie was there too."

"For supper?"

"No. He went out a few minutes after I arrived. But we all talked about it for a while."

"And?"

"Nothing very much. Laurie was upset, of course, but I expected that."

"It won't start him off again, will it?"

"I don't know. I hope not, but what will happen, will happen. We'll know in the morning." He looked at her. "And how do you feel?"

"A bit numb. I've been trying not to think about it, about him, and waiting for you to get here."

"And reading." He looked across the room at the table where her book lay.

"Reading is my avenue of escape, my refuge."

"I know."

"I still don't know how I feel, Albert. It will take me a while to sort it out. I feel sad, of course, but there's also a sense of relief. I hope that doesn't sound too cold, but it's part of it, and you might as well know it. He always seemed to be there in the background, even if our thing was ages ago."

"I understand." Dancey looked into his glass and then drank a little. Louise always referred to her relationship with Harrison Rose as "our thing." On the rare occasion when she did refer to it.

"Do you?" She looked at him, wondering what he was thinking about it all, and knowing that he would tell her when he was ready. "Yes, I suppose you do."

"It reminds me of some of the things that went on over there, in the war. Men died—friends, some of them. And sometimes, when a man had been badly wounded, limbs blown off, there was a sense of relief when he died, that it was over and done with, that he was out of it now. Sometimes they were even helped along, because that was the best way to handle it."

"Helped along?"

"Never mind. I shouldn't have said that. And I won't say anything more about it. It might upset you."

"Yes, it might." She squeezed his arm. "Finish your drink, Albert, and let's go to bed. It's been a long day."

CHAPTER 13

Stride was restless after Rita Fleming left. He'd stood at his living room window watching her walk along Circular Road until she was out of sight. Her presence in his flat had unsettled him more than he could have imagined. And it had annoyed him too. More correctly, it was his reaction to her being in his flat that had annoyed him. He poured himself another drink and thought about it for a few more minutes. Then he pushed it all aside, and turned his mind back to the investigation.

He sat at his desk and brought his notes on the case up to date. He considered the possibility that Barbara Drodge really was involved with Harrison Rose, and all that that might mean. He thought it over, and decided to drive to the Drodge house on Merrymeeting Road. He took his old raincoat from the closet and went down to the garage and the MG. He started the motor and sat there for a minute while it warmed up, thinking about what he might say to Barbara Drodge and her husband, if he found them at home.

He drove through the dark and mostly deserted streets, taking his time, still thinking about how he would approach this. Their house was on the north side of Merrymeeting, not far from the intersection with Mayor Avenue. It was a small two-storey, brown with white trim. There was no front yard to speak of, and the path from the street to the house was short. It was still early, not yet ten o'clock, and most of the houses on the street had lights showing through their front windows. The Drodge house, though, was completely dark.

He parked the MG two doors past the house, opened his umbrella as he stepped out of the car, and walked back to the front door. He pushed the button on the doorbell, and listened to the sound echoing through the house. It sounded hollow, and he wasn't surprised when there was no response. He rang the bell again, holding it longer this time. He stepped back from the landing and looked up at the windows on the second floor. Then he walked around to the back of the house and into the small yard. He tried the back door and found it locked too.

He went back to the MG and stood beside it, looking at the house. He was halfway relieved that no one had been home, but that relief was transient. He needed to talk to the Drodges and get this part of the inquiry settled, one way or another.

Someone in the house next door had taken notice of his visit and was standing at the front window looking at him through a gap in the curtains. Stride took his cue from that and walked to the neighbour's front door. By the time he got there, the door was open. A short, thick-bodied man was standing just inside, his right hand on the door. He turned on the overhead light, looking Stride over carefully. He didn't speak.

"I'm looking for your neighbours," Stride said. He took his badge from his pocket and showed it to the man. "Mr. and Mrs. Drodge. I need to speak to them."

"You're from the police?"

"My name is Inspector Stride. And you are?"

"Janes. Robert Janes."

"Do you know the Drodges, Mr. Janes?"

"Yes, of course," Janes said. "They're neighbours." He stepped back and pulled the door open wide. "You'd best come on in, sir. It's not much of a night to be standing outside."

"Thank you." Stride stepped into the hallway. The living room was on his left. A tall, angular woman with greying hair was standing by the mantel, her hands clasped close to her chest, her expression holding questions. Stride wiped his feet on the mat and stepped into the room. The woman didn't move any closer to him, but a tentative welcoming smile had slightly softened her expression. She was taller than Stride by a good three inches, which made her almost a foot taller than her husband.

"My wife," Janes said. "Shirley."

"My pleasure," Stride said. Her smile widened a little more.

"Have they done something?" Janes said. "Norman and Barbara?"

"I don't know, Mr. Janes. But their name has come up in an inquiry we're making, and I need to talk to them. They might be able to assist us."

"Have a seat, Inspector." Janes pointed to a ladderback chair to the right of the mantel. "You mentioned an inquiry. What's that all about?"

"I'm not at liberty to say, Mr. Janes. Not at this point. All I'm able to tell you is that I need to speak with Mr. Drodge, or Mrs. Drodge. I tried their house, but there's no one home. Do you know where they are?"

Shirley Janes started to answer, but her husband held up his hand.

"I saw Norman yesterday morning on his way to work."

"What time was that?"

"Eight-thirty. He usually starts work at nine, same as I do. He gave me a drive downtown. He often does when he's in town. Otherwise I walk. I don't own a car."

"Like you did this morning," Shirley Janes said, and her husband turned to look at her. "Oh, don't try and shush me, Robert. There's two of us here in the room, and I can speak as clearly as you can. Norman Drodge is a shipwright, Inspector. He has his own business downtown, but he travels a lot, around the bay."

"He's away now?"

"I suppose he is," Shirley Janes said. She looked at her husband. "Did he say anything to you yesterday, Robert?"

"No, he didn't. But that's not unusual. You see, Inspector, he might get a call during the day, and then he's off somewhere, sometimes for a day or two. It depends on the size of the job, and where it is. One time, last year, he was gone for the better part of a week. Here on the Monday, and then he was off and we didn't see him again until the Saturday."

"But you don't know if that's what's happening now, that he's off on a job around the bay?"

"I don't know it," Janes said, "but that's probably the case."

"And Mrs. Drodge?"

Neither of them replied, they only glanced at each other. Shirley Janes's tentative smile was back again. She looked at her feet. Robert Janes rubbed the stubble on his chin and looked at a picture of a fishing schooner hanging on the wall opposite. It was Shirley Janes who finally spoke.

"Barbara and Norman have been having problems for a while. Trouble in the marriage." Her husband looked at her, and Stride thought he might interrupt her, shush her again, but there was only relief in his expression that she was handling this part of it. "Robert thinks it's because they don't have any children, but I don't believe that. We don't have any children, and we've gotten along very well for going on twenty-three years. And I don't think having children can somehow make bad marriages work. Just the opposite is likely to be the case."

"Does Mrs. Drodge live with her husband?"

"Not for a while, she hasn't. She moved just over a year ago. She's been living with her brother while she and Norman try and work things out." Robert Janes made a grunting noise, and his wife glanced at him. "Robert thinks she did the wrong thing, moving out like that."

"How the hell can you hope to settle something if you almost never see each other, and don't talk to each other? That's what I'd like to know."

"It's a difficult situation," Shirley Janes said. "And who can say if she did the right thing or the wrong thing? But that was the decision she made, and for all we know, Norman might have agreed with her. He might even have been the one who made the decision. And we don't know that they don't talk to each other, Robert. Perhaps they do talk."

"You say she's living with her brother?"

"Yes. His name is Avery Garland. He lives on Monkstown Road. Mr. Garland isn't married, and I think he and his sister are quite close."

"A bloody old woman is what he is," Janes said.

"That's not fair, Robert." Her smile was still there, but it was tight now, and her eyes were hard. "Mr. Garland is different from you, and different from me, too, for that matter, but there's no call for that kind of language." She looked at Stride again, and her expression softened once more. "Mr. Garland inherited his father's insurance and real estate business. He does very well at it."

"I know the name," Stride said.

"The inquiry you're carrying out, Inspector." Shirley Janes gave him an even look. "Does it have anything to do with the shooting last night? In Bannerman Park?"

"I'm afraid I can't answer that question, Mrs. Janes. But I'd be interested to know why you asked."

"Robert heard that the man who was shot was Mr. Rose. Harrison Rose. And we know that he's the man Barbara has been working for, for most of the past year."

Robert Janes shifted in his chair, but he didn't say anything. He was looking at the picture of the schooner again. His wife's expression had softened again. She was looking into the fireplace, which was set for lighting, with small pieces of coal on top of wood splits, and crumpled newspapers under that. They hadn't lit the fire, in spite of the rain. It was warm enough in the room without it.

Stride waited to see if either of them would say anything else, but they had both retreated into silent introspection. He thought he knew what they were thinking about, but decided not to ask. St. John's was a very conservative society, and people didn't talk easily about marriages that were in trouble. And Shirley Janes's comment about people being advised to have children to mend a broken marriage was all too true. It was the standard remedy, liberally applied, and God only knew how many lives it ultimately blighted, parents and children both.

Stride stood up and Robert Janes stood with him. His wife remained seated, gave him a thin smile, and went back to looking into the unlit fireplace.

"We don't always agree on everything, the wife and I," Janes said when they were out of the room. "And she might be right about Norman and Barbara."

"In what way, Mr. Janes?"

"It might be true that it was as much his decision as hers that she move out for a while. He didn't seem all that upset that she did go and live with her brother. Maybe I shouldn't even be saying this to you now. I don't want you to think less of Norman, if you know what I mean. Especially if it's true about Mr. Rose being shot."

Janes looked at Stride, as if hoping he would confirm the rumour Janes had heard.

"I can't comment on Harrison Rose, Mr. Janes. And I'll keep an open mind on Norman Drodge. Until I have the opportunity to meet him, I won't form any opinion."

"I appreciate that," Janes said.

He opened the door and Stride stepped outside. He looked up at the sky, and then opened his umbrella.

CHAPTER 14

Patsy Codner rolled over on the bed and propped herself up on one elbow. She prodded her boyfriend and affected a sultry pout, something she'd seen Lauren Bacall do in a movie. She thought it was very sexy, and she'd practiced in front of a mirror until she felt she had it just right. She wasn't sure it was working this morning, though, because Tom Kennedy only gave her a brief glance and leaned across her to take his package of cigarettes from the bedside table.

"I don't think I want to go to work this morning," Patsy said. She made another effort to capture his attention, plucking the cigarette from his lips and holding it at arm's length so that he couldn't reach it without sitting up. "We could stay here all morning and just have fun. I'll phone in and say I have the curse really bad this month. That always works with our supervisor. It's not something the old cow ever wants to talk about, so she just takes our word for it."

"You could use that excuse too often," Kennedy said. "For all you know she's been taking notes, and she knows your cycle as well as you do yourself."

"I never thought of that." Patsy looked perplexed for a moment, but then she shrugged it away. "I don't care, I'll try it anyway."

"It's your life."

"And I'm free, white and twenty-one." She took the cigarette from him again. "So, how about it, handsome, you want to spend the morning here with me? You're not on duty until six, are you?"

"I'm not on duty at all for the next few days. I had some leave coming, and I'm taking it now."

"You didn't tell me that."

"Yes, I did. Just now." He took the cigarette back. "But I'm going in anyway, and see if Stride has anything for me to do on the case he's working on. You can call me later on, this afternoon maybe."

"I'm not supposed to make calls from work. Or even get them. Which is pretty funny, working for the phone company." She laughed. "So, what case is that? That guy who got shot in the park Monday night?"

"Yes, that one."

"What's he like, your Inspector Stride? I've seen him driving around town in his sports car sometimes. He's not half bad-looking. For an old guy, I mean. Maybe I should give him a call. He'd probably like to spend the morning with me." She poked him. "Having fun."

"Maybe he would. And he's not that old. Plus, he has a reputation."

"A reputation? With women?"

"No, with men." She stared at him. Then she caught his expression, and she poked him again. "The word going around is that he's having an affair with a married woman."

"Go on. A married woman? Are you sure?"

"No, I'm not sure, but that's the story, and I wouldn't put it past him. As a matter of fact I wouldn't put anything past him. He isn't your standard police inspector."

"I think I like that. Do you know who she is?"

"I don't know her name, but the story is she's married to a Yank, one of the officers at Fort Pepperrell. It's been going on for a while." Kennedy gave her the cigarette again, and he leaned back against the brass rails of the bedstead, his hands behind his head. "You know, when I grow up, I think I'd like to be like that. Drive a sports car, live in a big house, have affairs with married women. Give the finger to anyone I don't like."

"I bet you would. And where would I fit in?"

"I don't know. Where would you like to fit in?"

"Somewhere better than this, for sure."

She was renting a single room in a house in the centre of the city, on Carter's Hill, one of a dozen people who'd rented it in the last two years. It was small, the wallpaper was faded and coming loose in the corners, and the ceiling plaster was cracked. A two-burner hotplate sat on a table on the far side of the room. One of the burners was broken. The bathroom was down the hall, and she shared it with everyone else on the floor, although just now there was only one other tenant. But tenants came and went. She never knew when a strange face might turn up at just the wrong moment. It made going to the bathroom an adventure, and not a happy one.

"A big house on Circular Road would work for you, I suppose?"

"It would work very nicely." Patsy drew on the cigarette and gave it back to him. "What's she like? Stride's girlfriend?"

"She looks really good. She's blonde, and she's younger than he is. I saw them together one time, in his car, one night near his house."

"She's not as young as I am, is she?"

"No. She's actually really old, maybe thirty, even."

"Then maybe he would like to spend some time with me? Older men like younger women. And some of us like older men."

"You like older men, I suppose?"

"Sure, I do." She laughed and ran her hand across his chest. "But younger men are better. Over the long haul." She laughed again and ran her hand down over his stomach. Kennedy took hold of her wrist and pulled her hand back from under the sheet. She affected her pout again, but he ignored it.

"I can't imagine being that old," she said. "Can you imagine being thirty?"

"I haven't thought about it," Kennedy said. "But if I did think about it, it wouldn't bother me. Not ever getting old, now, the thought of that would really bother me."

"Why would that bother you? Not getting old? I don't want to get old, not ever, so not getting old wouldn't bother me a bit."

Kennedy looked at her and smiled.

"You don't want to get old, not ever?"

"No, I don't."

"Well, there is a way to arrange that," he said. "You die. And if you do that, you'll stay the same age forever, for all eternity."

Patsy stared at him, her expression puckered with concern.

"That's not funny, Tommy. I don't like it when you talk like that."

"It's all right," he said. "I was only joking. And someday I will be thirty, and I don't think it will change anything very much. Except I'll be a bit older, and a whole lot wiser."

"That's better," she said. She snuggled closer to him. "And what do you expect to be doing when you're thirty? Will you still be a policeman? Like your hero, Inspector Stride?"

"He's not my hero."

"I thought he was. You said you wanted to be him when you grew up."

"It was a figure of speech," Kennedy said. "Actually, I don't even like him all that much. He's standoffish, and some of the guys at the station say he's a prick; he acts like he's better and smarter than all of them." Kennedy laughed. "And he probably is, for that matter. But it doesn't bother me much. And he has things that I want someday, the sports car and the house. And the money everyone says he has."

"So, how did he get so rich? The car, the big house, and all? Not from being a policeman."

"There's a story about that too. They say that Stride has a past."

"Everyone has a past."

"I mean a *Past*. With a capital 'P.' Stride was a rum-runner, back in the thirties. That's the story I heard."

"Go on. You're joking."

"Apparently it's true. They say he worked with a guy, a Frenchman from St. Pierre off the south coast, and they ran booze into the States during Prohibition. The word is he made a lot of money. But then he gave it up, the rum-running, salted his money away and became a policeman."

"I don't believe it," she said. But Kennedy could see that the idea of it appealed to her. "So that's what you're going to do to get rich, and turn into Inspector Stride? Become a rum-runner?"

"The rum-running business isn't what it used to be," Kennedy said. He looked at her and shook his head. There were times when he wondered if she knew anything at all about the world outside the room she rented on Carter's Hill, and the switchboard she worked at with the phone company. And of course, the pleasures they shared in and out of bed. "They don't have Prohibition any more. When they repealed the law, all the wind went out of rum-running and bootlegging. The story is that Stride got out just at the right time."

"He's a smart guy, then."

"They didn't make him an inspector because he's stupid." Then he laughed. "But we've got one or two on the Force who could fit that picture."

"So, if rum-running isn't any good, how are you going to get rich, and buy that sports car, and the big house, and have tons of money to spend on me?"

"I'm still thinking about that. And I guess I'll have to think about it some more still." He was silent for a moment. "But I'll figure it out. There are ways."

"Well, when you get it all figured out, you'll let me know?"

"I'll do that. You'll be the second person to know about it."

"And who'll be the first?" She pulled away and looked at him.

"I will. Who else?"

"Well, that's all right, then." She stroked his chest again, but she still didn't seem to be getting the reaction she wanted. "I suppose I'm going to work after all, aren't I?"

Kennedy took his watch off the night table and saw that it was still early, they still had time. And now he was in the mood. Talking about money and getting ahead had that effect on him. He took a final draw on the cigarette and butted it in the ashtray. Then he slid down in the bed and pulled her towards him, his hands moving on her breasts.

"Not just yet, you aren't," he said.

"Well, maybe I'm not in the mood any more." But even as she said the words, his hands moved from her breasts and down over her stomach. She felt her breath catch in her throat.

"Then I'll just have to try a little harder, won't I?"

"Yes, you will," she said. But the words got lost in the soft space between his neck and his shoulder as he pulled her closer still, and then moved over her.

On the second floor of a rooming house on Empire Avenue, a day labourer named Evan Pugh pulled shut the door of his room and locked it. He looked down at the floor, only dimly lit by a single low-wattage bulb in a fixture high on the wall near the top of the stairs. The dark streaks of dirt he'd noticed the previous morning and evening were still there. He stared at the floor for a long moment, then looked up and down the hallway. Well, it had been raining a lot, and someone obviously hadn't bothered to wipe his feet when he came in Monday night. Pugh thought about it for a few moments. He was annoyed at the situation because he was a fastidious man himself, who respected other people's sensibilities, and he believed everyone should feel the same way. He remembered then that the house's caretaker, Michael Duggan, was due to clean the place later that morning. He'd last been in on Monday, two mornings ago. Duggan's routine was that he came by every other day, so he wouldn't have seen this mess yet.

Pugh thought about it for a moment longer, then unlocked the door of his room and went back inside. He sat at the table by the window and printed a note for Duggan, asking him to take care of the mess on the second floor. Pugh thought that Duggan was a decent enough fellow, someone who took a degree of pride in his work, so he phrased his note carefully, making certain not to offend the man. He read the note through a second time, satisfied that he'd done it well enough, that Duggan wouldn't take it as criticism of his work. He would take the note downstairs and tack it onto the notice board in the kitchen on his way out.

He went back into the hallway, looked one more time at the dark mess on the floor, and on the stairs too, and then walked quickly down to the first floor. Writing the note had put him a bit behind his time, and he didn't want to be late for work. Jobs were in shorter supply now than they'd been during the war, and a fellow who came in late could find that someone else had taken his place and his pay packet for the day.

CHAPTER 15

That morning Stride and McCowan arrived at the entrance of Fort Townshend almost at the same time, McCowan on foot from his apartment on site, near the headquarters building, and Stride driving into the parking area from Bonaventure Avenue. As an unmarried senior officer, McCowan merited one of the apartments the police department had available. He stood under his umbrella and waited until Stride had parked the MG. They walked together to the door.

"There've been some developments since yesterday, sir."

"You were busy last night, were you? Out and about?"

"I was out for a while, but I also had a visitor at my place."

"Someone with something pertinent to say about the Rose case?"

"Yes."

"Well, let's get inside out of this bloody rain, and you can tell me about it." McCowan pulled the door open and followed Stride into the building. "You can start by telling me who your visitor was."

"A young woman we met during the Taylor case last spring. Rita Fleming."

"Rita Fleming?" McCowan gave Stride a look. "The tart? And she knew something about Harry Rose?" He managed to look almost offended at the notion. "You're not about to tell me that she knew him professionally, are you?"

"Semi-professionally," Stride said.

"Semi-professionally? And what the hell does that mean?"

"It means he paid her for her services, but they also got to know each other quite well."

"She said that? And you believed her?"

"Yes, sir, I did believe her."

"Well, I'll trust your judgement, Eric, although I will say I'm more than a bit surprised. So what did she have for you?"

"A couple of things. Does the name 'Crozier' mean anything to you, sir?"

"In connection with Harry Rose?"

"His name came up in a conversation she had with him, but Rose didn't tell her who Crozier was. Only that it was someone he'd served with."

"Someone named Crozier, who had some sort of connection with Harry Rose and his time in the war. You know, the name does ring a bell, but there was no one in our Regiment named Crozier. I'm certain of that much. I don't think the name even exists here in Newfoundland." McCowan led the way towards his office.

"Perhaps it was someone Rose served with after he left the Regiment," Stride said. "Or before he joined you in Gallipoli."

"It's possible, I suppose. Well, I still don't know who it is. I'll give it some thought. What else did she tell you?"

"She said that Rose was having a relationship with a woman, one that started fairly recently."

"Was he, now? You continue to surprise me, Eric. It seems there was a lot more to Harry Rose than met the eye." McCowan made a grunting sound. "Or a lot less. Who is she, this woman he was involved with?"

"Her name's Barbara Drodge."

"The woman Phelan told me about yesterday? The one who worked for him?"

"Yes." Stride looked into their office as they went down the corridor to McCowan's, but Phelan wasn't in yet.

"And Rita Fleming knew about her?"

"Apparently she did."

"She's married, isn't she? This Barbara Drodge?" McCowan opened the door to his office and turned on the light.

"Yes, sir, she is."

"Well, if you're satisfied the information is accurate and reliable, then it's possible we have someone with a motive for killing Harry Rose." McCowan turned on his desk light and pulled his chair back from his desk. "But I'll state my misgivings at the outset. If cuckolded husbands were as prone to murder as popular fiction would lead us to believe, there'd be rioting in the streets, and we'd be knee-deep in corpses two days out of four. You'll follow it up, of course, but let's not blunder down the garden path with this." He sat down and arranged some items on his desk blotter. "And you say you went out last night? To call on the Drodges, I suppose?"

"Yes, sir." Stride summarized his trip to the Drodge house on Merrymeeting, and his conversation with Robert and Shirley Janes.

"So, Mrs. Drodge has been living with her brother for about a year now?" McCowan said.

"His name's Avery Garland," Stride said, "and he lives on Monkstown Road."

"The insurance fellow."

"Yes, that's him."

"I know the name," McCowan said. "I've even met him once or twice. I knew his father. And the husband? He's still living on Merrymeeting?"

"He appears to be. Janes told me that Drodge is a shipwright. He has his own business, and he travels a good deal."

"Around the bay, I suppose."

"Which might be where he is now."

"Assuming he isn't the one who shot Harry Rose, and that he's not on the run."

"There is that possibility, sir."

"But whether he's running, or simply away on business, you might have a problem finding him. At least anytime soon."

"That's possible, too. We'll check with his shop first."

"You and Phelan together, this time. If Norman Drodge did kill Harry Rose, he won't roll out the welcome mat for either of you."

"Understood, sir."

"Is there anything else?"

"No, that's about it."

"I'll add a bit to all that. I had some activity last night, too. This fellow at Government House, Barnes Wilson, Macdonald's ADC. He phoned me at home, just before supper. That was a bit of a surprise. I didn't expect to hear from him again, at least not so soon."

"Is this something that's going to complicate the investigation?"

"I hope not, but I'm always cautious when the people down at Government House get involved, especially when it's someone that close to the Governor. The gist of Wilson's call was that he would personally be looking after the file on Harrison Rose."

"They have a file?" Stride said. "Well, I suppose I'm not surprised."

"These days, almost everyone seems to have a file established in his honour, if honour it be. But what interested me was Wilson's tone, that little dingle of anxiety that one picks up on. Nothing to hang my hat on, but enough to capture my interest."

"I take it you've met Major Wilson?"

"I have met him, but I won't claim to know him. He was at the Regimental dinner last year, subbing for the Governor. Macdonald doesn't do well in situations like that. He's of those righteous teetotallers, and a damned wet blanket, if you want the truth of it. But he has the wit to realize it, at least some of the time, and stay away from affairs like Regimental dinners, or at least leave early. Wilson and I shook hands, exchanged a few words. But I had other people I wanted to see that night, so we didn't talk for very long."

"I understand Wilson's new at Government House." Stride said.

"I think he's been there for about a year. I have to wonder sometimes if being sent over here is an opportunity for one of those boffins, or if it's a punishment." McCowan smiled. "Anyway, after he rang off, I made a couple of calls to see if anyone could give me some information on him. It turns out he's been doing military attaché stuff for most of his career. He was in the First War, briefly, and he was even wounded. But for most of his career he's been riding a desk, pushing paper. Paris, Dublin, Washington, Ottawa—even Berlin for a spell in the thirties."

"He's well travelled."

"So it seems. That might mean he's a valuable property—or it could be that he's someone who doesn't do well anywhere, and they keep moving him along. And perhaps that's why he's over here now, his last stop before going out to pasture. I think he's about the right age for retirement. Although, now that I think about it, I believe he asked for the posting here. I assume he had his reasons. But it might all turn out to be a case of an enthusiastic functionary doing a bit of overtime bum-nuzzling. In the meantime, we'll try and keep him happy."

"Should we interview him, do you think?"

"I don't think so. You have enough on your plate just now, and, anyway, they're a twitchy lot down there at Government House. You've already talked to that other fellow, haven't you? Wilson's superior?"

"Rodney Gilbert."

"Yes, him. I don't imagine there's anything Wilson can tell you that Gilbert hasn't already. It's even possible that Gilbert's directing the show, whatever he said to you yesterday." McCowan took a cigar from his humidor. "Noseworthy said Tom Kennedy's been working with you on the case."

"Yes, he has, on a voluntary basis. He was on patrol on Military Road when Rose was shot, and he got to the scene just after I did. In fact, he thought I was the one who shot Rose. He came close to whacking me with his nightstick."

"Did he, now?" McCowan said. "Well, nothing personal, but good for him. He seems like a half-decent prospect, on the whole. What's your opinion of him?"

Stride picked his words.

"Well, I think he's bright enough, sir. And he seems enthusiastic."

"Damning him with faint praise, are you?"

"Not exactly, sir."

"Well, I'll trust your judgement on him, too," McCowan said. "He comes from decent stock, at any rate. I knew his father, Mike Kennedy. He was over there the same time I was."

"France?"

"Gallipoli. He was wounded there, quite badly, and he was invalided out to England. From there he came on home. Which in a way was good luck for him. He wasn't around for the slaughter at Beaumont Hamel. But he had a hard enough time as it was. His right leg was all but useless. It would have been worse if it had been his arm that was damaged. Mike was a carpenter before the war, and a damn fine one. He got back into it after he came home, even hoped his two boys would follow him into the trade. But he was never able to do better than part-time work. On top of his war injury, he contracted tuberculosis while he was in hospital in England. The compensation he got from the government wouldn't have kept a small dog. The family had a damned hard go of it."

"Is he still alive?"

"No, he passed on just before the last war, and his wife wasn't long in following him. I think she was just worn out. So there's just Kennedy, now, by himself."

"You said he had a brother?"

"Yes, there was a brother. And he had a sister too. She's married and living in the States somewhere. The brother—John, I think his name was—he was a year or two older than Kennedy, I believe, but he was killed during the last war. Royal Navy, convoy duty."

"Very hard on Kennedy, all of that."

"I imagine it was. But he seems to be doing well enough, in spite of it." McCowan looked at his notepad. "Harry told me yesterday that Cobb's coming around to see you this morning, something about a brawl in Bannerman Park last spring. He thinks it might be related to the Rose shooting."

"It was actually Bernard Crotty who brought the file forward. He thought there was more to it than Andy Cobb put in his report."

"That doesn't surprise me. If there's a corner ripe for cutting, Andy Cobb will slice right through it. You know, he's been on the Force even longer than I have. He's looking forward to his retirement with almost as much interest and enthusiasm as I am."

"Your retirement, sir?"

"Not mine, his. Andy was a good enough copper in his day, but that day is about done." McCowan struck a match on the underside of his desk and fired up his cigar. He looked at Stride through the cloud of tobacco smoke. "Said without prejudice, mostly. And the comment doesn't leave this office."

"Which comment was that, sir?"

"I see you understand," McCowan said. "You know, Eric, it's not often I have a personal interest in a case. But this time I do, even if Harry Rose wasn't actually a friend. Keep me posted on anything and everything."

"Yes, sir."

McCowan picked up a file and opened it. Stride was almost out the door when he spoke again.

"Crozier," he said. "I just remembered. There was a Colonel Crozier at the Somme. The Royal Irish Rifles, I believe it was. I knew the name rang a bell. I suppose Rose must have served with him someplace, after he left our Regiment."

CHAPTER 16

Harry Phelan was in the office, smoking a cigarette and drinking a mug of hot tea. He looked much better than he had the previous evening, when Stride had driven him home.

"You appear to have made a rapid recovery," Stride said.

"Kit gave me a large dose of her grandmother's cold cure. Sulphur, molasses, rum and some secret ingredient she wouldn't identify, but it tastes like an old sock. Then she shovelled me off to bed very early in the evening, all by my lonesome. And when I woke up this morning, I felt about 95 percent better."

"The theory being that if you treat a cold badly enough, it will vacate the premises."

"I think that's the guiding principle."

"I had a long chat with McCowan on the way in." Stride sat down and lit a cigarette, then went through their conversation. "He's going to see if he can come up with anything on this Crozier."

"And you got the name from Rita Fleming?"

"I imagine you remember her."

"Not likely to forget Rita Fleming, sir, even in a weakened state."

"She came to my place last night. Voluntarily. She and Harrison Rose had a kind of relationship going for a couple of years."

"That's topside of interesting."

"It's not anything I would have expected, but she seemed genuinely attached to Rose. She was very annoyed when he dropped her for Barbara Drodge."

"You don't suppose she shot him, do you?"

Stride laughed.

"I don't think so. Norman Drodge is a better bet, although McCowan doesn't think much of it."

"Still, if he's missing just now, it's at least suggestive."

"That's a good word for it. We'll take a run down to his shop when we're done here. It's on Water, near Prescott. I called before I left home, but there was no answer."

"Might have been too early."

"Possibly, although Drodge's neighbour, Robert Janes, said he normally goes in at eight-thirty. In the meantime, we can talk to Cobb. Did you manage to track him down this morning?"

"Yes, I did. He said he'd stop by here, just about now." Phelan looked towards the door. "And here he is."

In his prime, Andy Cobb had been taller than Stride, but age had shortened him enough that now the two men were almost exactly at eye level. Cobb was also hampered, and oddly diminished, by a large belly that overwhelmed the wide leather belt that held up his trousers with the assistance of bright red suspenders. He shuffled into the office, his hands buried in the trouser pockets. A rattle of coins came through the fabric on the left side. He had a file folder under his left arm.

"Morning, gentlemen." Cobb gave Stride a brief glance. He got along well enough with Phelan—everyone did—but Cobb and Stride hadn't liked each other from their first meeting, and the situation had improved only a little in the intervening years.

"Bernard Crotty said the fracas in the park you looked into last spring might be related to the shootings Monday night, Andy. Do you think there's anything in that?"

"Bern mentioned that to me this morning," Cobb said. He patted the file folder. "It was quite the scramble, all right, but I doubt it has anything to do with your case."

"Give us some of the details," Stride said. "We'll decide whether it has any relevance, Andy."

Cobb gave Stride a look, and then he shrugged. He dug his right hand into his pocket and pulled out a stick of chewing gum. He took his time unwrapping it, then popped the rolled-up stick into his mouth and chewed thoughtfully for a moment, working it around his dentures.

"There was five of them involved altogether. The three hard cases, the ones who started it, was David Squire, Ferris Dalton and John Smith. Squire goes by the nickname 'Dub.'"

"I've heard the name," Stride said. "Dalton's, too."

"Not surprised you have. They've both been in trouble before, and often. Smith, too, although he's only got the one item on his sheet."

"They're friends?"

"Squire and Dalton are, and they go back a long way. The word is they first met when they was in the Pen together."

"And Smith?"

"I think Smith was a third wheel that night." Cobb opened the file and ran his eye over it. He gave it to Phelan. "Anyway, all three of them was looking pretty sad when I got to the park. Young Tommy Kennedy was the one found them there. That's been his beat for the past six months. I got into it because we had a call from a house on Military Road that there was a rumpus in the park." He looked at Stride. "I hear he's been working with you on your case? Kennedy?"

"He volunteered to help out."

"Doesn't really surprise me, I suppose. I think Tommy's got ambitions." Cobb planted his right cheek on the edge of Phelan's desk. "Anyway, to get back to the Bannerman Park thing, Squire and Dalton was treated for cuts and bruises, and Squire had a couple of busted ribs that they taped up for him. Them two they sent on home. The third bucko, Smith, he was in pretty bad shape. He had a concussion and a busted spleen. Him they kept in the hospital for the better part of three weeks, I heard."

"And the others who were involved? The ones whose names didn't make it into your report?"

"Crotty told you about that, I suppose?"

"He might have. But I think he was guessing."

"Well, he guessed right," Cobb said. "There were two others involved. Your dead man, Harrison Rose, was one of them, and the other was a friend of his, a fella named Barnes Wilson."

"Barnes Wilson?" Stride glanced at Phelan, then back at Cobb. "Why didn't their names make it into your report?"

"Because they didn't want them in there. And as they was the injured parties, it was up to them to press charges, if any was going to be pressed. And they didn't want to do that."

"But it was the other three that wound up in hospital. Squire, Dalton and Smith."

"God's judgement, I call it," Cobb said. "They was the ones who started it, and they got hell beat out of them for their troubles."

"All right, Andy, why don't you just give us the whole story on this?"

"Well, the way it looks to me is that the three buckos, Squire, Dalton and Smith, they saw Rose and his friend Wilson walking through the park late at night, and decided to jump them, and then found they'd made a poor choice."

"A poor choice?"

Cobb grinned.

"I'm thinking what it was probably all about was that they thought they were jumping a couple of old pansies on their way home from a do, taking a wander through Bannerman Park, and they decided to give them a whacking, just for the fun of it. You know it happens sometimes, same as I do."

"They didn't say that, though."

"Course not. But reading between the lines, I think that's what it was. You won't find me shedding tears for any queers who get their asses kicked; they make me sick to my gut, if you want the truth of it. But Rose and Wilson, they weren't queer, and they also knew how to take care of themselves. Must've come as a bit of a shock to the three buckos. I only wish I'd been there to see it. They're a royal pain in the ass, Squire and Dalton, especially. A bad use of air and living space, the both of them."

"Who made the decision not to press charges? Rose or Wilson?"

"It was fifty-fifty. Neither one of them wanted the thing to go any further. Rose said there was no real harm done, not to him, and he didn't want to pursue it. He said it wasn't worth the bother for him. Having to go to court and all, and having to answer questions from some smartass defence lawyer looking to get his name in the paper."

"Rose said that?"

"No, I said that, just now. But it's pretty much what Rose said to me at the time. I just added a bit of flavour."

"And Wilson?"

"The same thing. He didn't want the bother of it either. Plus, he's an aide to the Governor, and Government House don't like to find its people in newspaper stories, especially not in a situation like that. Another part of the deal was that Rose and Wilson had both been pulling at the bottle that night, same as the other three. You could see some reporter making something out of that, probably a front-page story: 'Drunken brawl in Bannerman Park involving respectable businessman and Governor's aide.' No, that wouldn't play well at all. Especially not with Macdonald sitting in the Governor's chair."

"But now Harrison Rose is dead, and all bets are off," Stride said. "The question being, did your three buckos have something to do with that? Squire, Dalton and Smith?"

"Them three? I don't think so. And, anyway, Squire and Dalton have been tucked away in the Pen the last two months. Breaking and entering. They'll be there for the better part of a year, and good riddance to them."

"And Smith?"

"Even less likely, in my opinion."

"He was the one most badly hurt, though."

"That's true enough. But, like I said, I think he was the third wheel that night, likely just along for the ride, in the wrong place at the wrong time." Cobb shifted his position on Phelan's desk and waggled his right foot to jog the circulation. "And then there's the artillery Noseworthy says was used on your client. A 9 mm? That's not the sort of cannon you'd expect someone like Smith to be carrying around. I doubt he'd know which end to grab on to. I won't say he's a complete idiot, but if he was a bulb, you'd need three of him to light up a breadbox."

"We should probably talk to Smith, anyway. Do you know where we can find him?"

"His address is in the report. If he's not there, you might find him slinging coal down at Harvey's Wharf. It's where he was working in the spring, and chances are, he's there again. Either that, or he's back teaching at the College." Cobb laughed at his own joke and stood up. He shoved his hands back into his trouser pockets, and the jingling of the coins started up again. "Happy hunting, gentlemen. And if you have any more questions for me, feel free."

"I have to wonder if it's worth the time and effort," Phelan said when the sound of Cobb's rattling pocket change had faded away.

"It probably isn't, but we can't take the chance. We'll look for Smith later today. I'm also interested in the fact that Wilson was involved in that affair. Wilson and Rose were more or less of an age, both of them English and both of them army men. I suppose it's natural enough that they would be friends. But I've never been a great fan of coincidence."

"You think we should talk to him?"

"I asked McCowan about that, but he said not to, not yet. But he's on the list for future consideration. Right now we need to try and find Norman Drodge, and after that, his wife and her brother."

"We should go see Noseworthy first, sir. He looked in while you were with McCowan."

"Does he have something for us?" Phelan shook his head. "We'll go see him, anyway. I want to talk to him before we take off."

"I think I'll get myself a metal detector some day," Noseworthy said. "Assuming they ever sell them to the general public."

"This is the stuff you found?" Stride picked up a small cardboard box. It held a collection of items: coins, keys, buttons and an assortment of small metal objects.

"There was a lot of noise in the area," Noseworthy said.

"Noise?"

"Bits of metal everywhere, nails and roofing tacks for the most part. Every hit with the detector gives a ping. You get too much of it, and it's like a shooting gallery." Noseworthy dumped the contents of the box onto a large sheet of paper. "There's any number of nails from the temporary buildings from the war that they pulled down last spring. The crew they had working there raked up most of it, but a lot of the nails and other bits of metal got walked into the ground. Fortunately, the area we were most interested in, where you found Rose's body, that wasn't too heavily contaminated."

"But you didn't find anything pertinent to the case?"

"I don't think any of this counts as evidence, sir. A lot of coins, and some of them are pretty old. A handful of keys—and some of those are old too."

Stride picked up two of the coins.

"You don't suppose any of these are valuable, do you?"

"I don't think so. Some of them are foreign, American mostly, but there's English, Spanish and Portuguese in there too. Someone could probably use all this to put together a kind of social history of the war years. A lot of foreigners rolling around on the grass in the park after dark, doing God-knows-what."

"I think God probably did know what they were doing," Phelan said.

"Out-breeding makes for a more robust population," Stride said. "So, no great reward for an hour's toil in the rain?"

"No, but interesting all the same. The foreign coins, those I'll eventually give to my nephew. He's started a collection." Noseworthy moved a few of the items around on the sheet, lining them up. "Those square nails are interesting, and they're very old. We found quite a few of them, and I think they probably predate the wartime buildings. I have a friend at the College who's interested in things like that. I'll ask him if he wants them. And there's some metal buttons that someone is probably still looking for."

"Buttons are in the same category as lost keys and odd socks," Stride said. "Somewhere in the universe there's a repository full of them, and we'll never find it because the socks muffle the sounds of the buttons and keys rattling against each other."

He followed Noseworthy's example and arranged the buttons in two neat rows: there was a dozen of them, large and small. He picked up one that had a caribou-head insignia and looked at it, turning it back and forth.

"Military," Noseworthy said. "Which only confirms my belief that Bannerman Park hosted any number of uniformed types and their partners in close-encounter engagements of the nicest kind." He took the button from Stride. "This one's local, though, probably from the Newfoundland Regiment or the Militia. So, we can score one for our side, although our soldier boy probably caught hell from his sergeant next day if he turned up for parade with a button missing."

"A small price to pay for his pleasure, I suppose." Stride took the button from Noseworthy and looked at it again. He put it back on the sheet. "When you get a chance, Kevin, itemize this stuff, except for the things that are obviously junk. We can go over it all later and see if there's anything there. And there's something else I want you to do, and that's look into Rose's finances a bit more closely. I think you have some contacts at the tax office?"

"I know a tame one I can talk to. What I can tell you right now, though, is that Rose didn't keep a large balance in any of his bank accounts, and he had three altogether. That's not really unusual for the well off. They prefer to have their money out there working for them, instead of lying fallow in a bank generating income for someone else. Bank accounts are for unimaginative and stodgy folk, people like me and Harry."

"I can tell you that my bank account isn't generating much income for anyone," Phelan said. "And I still think it's possible Rose had family money from the old country that he used to set himself up with here. Although part of me has to wonder about that."

"You're not about to say something unpatriotic, are you, Harry?" Noseworthy looked at the rain sheeting across the window. "Like, why in hell would anyone with family money choose this place to live, when he could be well-to-do somewhere else?"

"You've read my mind," Phelan said.

"Cheeky of me to do that, but it wasn't exactly fine print," Noseworthy said. He looked at Stride. "There's something else we might want to think about, sir. I couldn't find Rose's passport. It wasn't in the house, it wasn't in the safe in his office at the hotel, and it wasn't in his safe deposit box at the bank."

"Do you suppose there's a safe somewhere in his house?" Stride asked.

"If there is, it's awfully well hidden. Kennedy and I did a thorough search of the place yesterday, every room, every closet, including down in the cellar."

"And speak of the devil," Phelan said. Tom Kennedy was standing in the doorway. "You're up bright and early, Kennedy."

"I don't seem to need much sleep, Sergeant. So I came on in to see if you or Inspector Stride might have something for me to do."

"I'm glad you did," Stride said. "We're about to head downtown. One of the things we're going to do is talk to one of the people you trucked down to the General Hospital last spring. From Bannerman Park."

"Yes, sir?"

"You worked with Inspector Cobb that evening. Did you know that Colonel

Rose was one of the men involved in the brawl that night?"

"Colonel Rose? No, sir, I didn't know that. There were two gentlemen involved, but I didn't know their names. Inspector Cobb arrived at the scene about the same time I did, and he took their names and interviewed them. I looked after the three toughs who started the fight." Kennedy grinned. "Although they weren't so tough by the time we found them. They were in pretty bad shape, actually." He moved into the room and leaned against a file cabinet. "You say Colonel Rose was one of the two gentlemen involved?"

"He was, but I'm not surprised you didn't know his name. He didn't want it known that he was involved in a brawl."

"I suppose I can't blame him for that. But do you think it had something to do with the shooting?"

"Probably not. Two of the lads involved, Squire and Dalton, they're back in the Pen. It's the third one, Smith, who's still out and about. He's the one we're looking for. We need to talk to him before we close the book on that part of it. In the meantime, you can give Mr. Noseworthy a hand here. He can probably find something for you to do."

CHAPTER 17

Norman Drodge's business was on the south side of Water Street, east of Prescott. There was a light on inside, and the door was open. At first glance, the shop looked too small for the kind of work Drodge did, until Stride and Phelan went inside, and saw that the place opened up and ran all the way back to the waterfront. The shop was well organized, with all the complicated gear that went with ships and boats neatly arranged on the walls and shelves. There was no one in sight, and no bell over the door to alert anyone that someone had come into the shop. But only a moment later, an older man with long white hair appeared from the back. Stride guessed there was some kind of electronic signal attached to the door. The man was too old to be Norman Drodge, Stride thought, but then he didn't know how old Drodge might be.

"Can I help you, gentlemen?" The accent was thick, and it wasn't local. Stride placed it somewhere in New England, Boston possibly. The man had to be around sixty years old, but he moved with an ease that told Stride he was fit and able. He gave the two detectives a quick once-over and went behind the counter.

"We're looking for Mr. Drodge. Have you seen him today?"

"Not today, I haven't. Nor yesterday, either. As far as I know, he's still in Harbour Grace. Maybe I can help you? My name's Lear. Eli Lear." He leaned on the counter and looked them over again. "But if you two are in the boat business, I'll lose the bet I just made with myself."

"Actually, we're with the Constabulary," Stride said. "I'm Inspector Stride, and this is Sergeant Phelan."

"In which case, I win my bet. I'll buy myself a beer at the end of the day, to celebrate."

"We'd like to talk to Mr. Drodge in connection with an inquiry we're carrying out."

"That would be the Rose case, I suppose. It was on the news, this morning, if you're wondering how I know."

"You probably heard the same piece I did," Stride said, "although the name hasn't been officially released."

"I guessed as much. Intelligent speculation on the part of a news writer, I imagine. Not much stays secret in this town for long, not when a fairly prominent citizen gets himself killed, and there are policemen all over the neighbourhood, and two stationed at his house. I suppose you think Norman might have had something to do with it? Things being what they were, I mean?"

"How were things?" Stride said.

"You're not going to pretend you don't know, are you? I hate it when cops do that sort of thing."

"Would I be off base if I thought you've had some experience with the police?"

"I've had more than most. I even used to be one, although that was a while ago, and of course, not here. Boston, if you're wondering, back before the war." He laughed. "The last one, not the First. That one I was a part of."

"What can you tell us about Norman Drodge and Harrison Rose, Mr. Lear?"

Lear dipped two fingers into the pocket of his plaid shirt and extracted a cigarette. He struck a match on the countertop.

"To the best of my knowledge, Norm Drodge never even met Harrison Rose."

"But he knew that his wife was involved with Rose?" Phelan said.

"He surely did know about that."

"And what did he think about it?"

"Not a whole hell of a lot. And by that I mean that he didn't think much about it at all. Norm and Barbara have been on the outs for a long time, for a lot longer than she and Rose knew each other. In a way, Norm was actually relieved when he found out they were involved."

"Relieved?" Stride said.

"You'd have to know Norm to understand. Let me just say that Norman Drodge has never wanted for female companionship. I wasn't living here when he and Barbara got married, but if I was, and if I knew him as well then as I've gotten to know him since, I would have clocked him with a pipe wrench before he left for the church, just to get his attention. I can't imagine what he was thinking."

"You're saying that Mr. Drodge has been unfaithful to his wife?" Stride said.

Lear smiled.

"That doesn't begin to capture the flavour of it, or of him. Norm Drodge is a special case, not one of a kind, but close. He's the sort of man people write songs about. He has the knack for meeting people, female people most especially, even in the smallest of outports. There's a lot of travel involved in this business, and you go where the work is. Norm likes to travel around, always has – by car, boat and train. And you know, I've always had a kind of admiration for men like him, even with my conservative Boston upbringing."

"You don't think that Mr. Drodge would have been angry enough to want Harrison Rose dead?"

"Not even mildly incapacitated, I don't think."

"We'd still like to talk with Mr. Drodge," Stride said. "Do you know when he'll be back in town?"

"Tomorrow, maybe. At least that was the original plan. By now, though, he might have heard about Rose getting shot, and that could bring him back here sooner than he'd planned. In spite of all that's gone on, from his side and hers, he'd be concerned about Barbara, and how she's doing. I know it sounds odd, but in a way, they still care about each other." Lear tapped ash from his cigarette onto the floor behind the counter. "I suppose you've talked to her already?"

"Not yet, we haven't."

"No? Well, do you even know where to find her? She hasn't lived with Norm for the better part of a year."

"We understand she's at her brother's house," Stride said. "Avery Garland's?"

"That's probably where she'll be." Lear leaned against the shelving behind the counter. "I also suppose you're not going to drop the idea that Norm was the one who popped Harrison Rose, even if the jealous-husband motive doesn't have any real weight in the circumstances?"

"We'll take it into consideration, but we won't close the book on him just yet."

"As you wish. But I can tell you, honestly, that I don't believe Norm had anything to do with this, even if he had been in town when it happened. To start with, he isn't the jealous type, and anyway, he's known about Rose and Barbara for going on a year now. You're looking for someone a lot different than Norm Drodge."

"And you're basing that on what?"

"On what I've heard about the case from a friend who works down at the General. He told me Rose took two in the chest, and a curtain-closer in the side of the head. Did my friend have that right?"

"Pretty much," Stride said. "Go on."

"In Boston, we have situations and circumstances that you just don't see in this part of the world. We have gangs down there, and gangs have their own way of dealing with people they don't like, or even with people they do like but need to get rid of. One of the things they'll do is set up an ambush and take their man out, pretty much the way Rose was taken out. And as often as not, the game ends with their man taking a bullet in the brain. It's very effective, a very low rate of failure. I know whereof I speak. I saw it more than a few times when I wore the cop suit."

"You're suggesting that this was some kind of a gang killing?"

"That would truly surprise me. Unless Harrison Rose had some big-city contacts, and I don't know that he did. But that's your department, not mine. No, what I'm suggesting is that this is like a gang killing. An ambush, an assassination, carried out by someone who knew what he was doing, and who might have done it before. That was my first thought when I heard what happened to Harrison Rose. I'd even hazard a guess that you might have thought the same thing. The Norm Drodges of this world don't do things like that. It just isn't in their repertoire. It takes a special type."

"That was fast," Avery Garland said. He stepped back into the vestibule of his house and pulled the door open for Stride and Phelan. "I called you people not five minutes ago. How did you get here so quickly?"

"We started early," Stride said. Garland looked confused by the response, but Stride didn't bother to explain.

He walked to the door of Garland's living room. A woman was sitting on the chesterfield, her feet tucked under her. She wore a dark red dressing gown belted at the waist. She had short, dark hair. Stride found himself agreeing with Mary Holden's assessment of Harrison Rose's lady friend. Barbara Drodge was indeed pretty. Or she would have been if her face was not so pale, and her eyes not so red from recent crying. She gave Stride a brief glance, then returned her focus to a pot of red geraniums sitting on the coffee table in front of her.

Stride guessed she was in her late thirties, a lot younger than Harrison Rose. He found himself thinking about the differences between her and Rita Fleming, both of them attractive, but in very different ways. Barbara Drodge was much the more mature of the two. She was also taller than Rita Fleming, which made her taller than Harrison Rose by several inches.

"Mrs. Drodge?" The woman looked at Stride again. "My name is Inspector Stride. This gentleman is my partner, Sergeant Phelan. We're sorry to have to impose on you at a time like this, but we need to ask you some questions about Harrison Rose."

Barbara Drodge nodded, but didn't say anything. She went back to looking at the geraniums.

"Please take a seat," Garland said. "I know Barbara will do her best to help you. We've already talked this over. That's why I phoned Fort Townshend just now."

"You could have phoned us earlier," Stride said. He took the chair closest to Barbara Drodge and dropped his hat on the carpet by his feet. "As soon as you knew what had happened. Why the delay?"

"We don't have a good reason. Other than the fact that Barbara was very upset. And she really doesn't know anything about this, why it happened."

"I can understand that. But we've learned that Mrs. Drodge was involved in a relationship with Mr. Rose, in addition to working for him. The fact that she has a husband raises the possibility that he might have been involved. She must have known that. Both of you must have known that."

Garland looked uncomfortable.

"I don't know how you know that, about Barbara and Mr. Rose, but, yes, it's true. They were having a ... relationship." The word seemed to stick in his throat. Stride recalled Robert Janes's comment about Garland. It seemed to fit. Garland looked across the room at his sister, but she continued to stare at the flowers. "But it wasn't all one-sided, you know. Norman Drodge will never qualify for sainthood."

"We already know some things about Mr. Drodge," Stride said. "What we need to know now mostly concerns Mr. Rose. When did you last see him, Mrs. Drodge?"

Barbara Drodge took a deep breath and shifted her position on the chesterfield, pushing herself more upright than she'd been.

"Monday night. The last time I saw Harry was Monday night, about ten o'clock."

"You were with him that evening?"

"I was with him all day." She glanced at her brother. "I was at Harry's place on Sunday, and I spent the night there." Another glance in her brother's direction. "Avery didn't like it when I spent the night with Harry. In fact, he didn't like any part of it, my being involved with him. So, we'll get that out of the way right now. All right, Avery?"

Garland didn't respond, but his face was flushed. Whether that was anger or embarrassment, Stride couldn't tell.

"All right. You were with Mr. Rose all day Monday, first at the office in the Newfoundland Hotel, and then at his house."

"Yes. As I said, I left him around ten o'clock that night. There were some things I needed to do here, and anyway, Harry liked to be alone a lot of the time. It was unusual for us to spend more than two nights together in a row."

"Did Mr. Rose say anything to suggest that he might be meeting someone later Monday night, or that someone might be planning to visit him?"

"No, he didn't. He had some work he wanted to attend to. He said it would take him about an hour. And after that, he planned to go out for his walk."

"Was that a regular thing, a walk late at night?"

"Every night that I knew him he went for a long walk. It was his routine. I really can't think of a single night that he didn't take a walk, no matter what the weather. Rain, snow, hot or cold, it didn't matter."

"Can you think of anything that might have happened in the previous week that was different?"

"In what way different?" she asked.

"Unusual telephone calls, letters, strangers walking near his house. Anything at all that seemed out of the ordinary."

Barbara Drodge shook her head.

"I can't think of anything. I took most of the telephone calls at the office. That was part of my job. Harry hated the telephone. He called it the invention of the devil. Half the time he didn't bother to answer. When I asked him about that once, he said he didn't want to answer because there might be someone on the other end."

"Were there any business problems recently? Clients who might have been angry with Mr. Rose? Conflicts of any kind?"

"Nothing that stands out, no. It was a normal week, like all of our weeks at the office. The business wasn't contentious or controversial. Harry was an agent – he arranged contracts; he brought sellers and buyers together. He was good at it, and that made money for people."

"And for himself."

"Of course for himself. He wasn't a charity, he was a businessman."

"Did he always work alone? Apart from yourself, I mean?"

"Yes, he did most of his work alone. Before I started working with him, and that was about a year ago, he had people working for him part-time."

"Did his business increase in volume? Is that why he decided he needed a person full-time?"

"No. I started with him part-time, but we got on well." She treated her brother to a smile, and it had the intended effect. Garland's discomfort level rose accordingly. "And then we got on very well, and I started working for him full-time."

"That's when you got involved with Mr. Rose?"

"Involved. Such a foolish word." She looked at Stride and didn't mask her impatience. "Yes, that's when we got involved."

"There weren't any problems with the business that you were aware of?"

"Not really. The business wasn't that complicated, not most of the time."

"And when it was complicated?"

"When it was complicated, and sometimes it was, it usually involved financing."

"Were they serious problems?"

"They were never allowed to become serious. When there were issues about finance, Harry would call his financial manager, Mr. Madigan, and things would get settled quickly. Mr. Madigan was also his lawyer."

"That's Brendan Madigan?" Stride asked.

"Yes. Do you know him?"

"I've met him," Stride said. "The financing issues. Were they ever a problem?"

"Not really, no. Mr. Madigan is probably the best financial manager in the city, and Harry had worked with him for a long time. I think for as long as he lived here."

"That is a long time," Stride said. "Since 1930, I believe?"

"That's when Harry started up his business here. Bought the business here, I mean. Of course, I didn't know him then." She looked at her brother. "Avery did, though."

Stride shifted his attention to Garland.

"You knew Mr. Rose from back then, Mr. Garland?"

"Yes. I met him soon after he moved here." Garland closed his eyes for a moment. "September of 1930. That's when Rose moved here from England."

"Was your contact with him personal, or was it business?"

"Business. I'm in insurance and real estate." Garland looked at his sister. "Our father started the business years ago, and I inherited it when he died. There's only the two of us, Barbara and me."

"You sold Mr. Rose the house on Circular Road?"

"Yes, and we also wrote up the insurance policy on the place. I say 'we,' because my—our—father was still alive at the time. I also arranged for the people who did the renovations on the house before he moved in. The place was a little rundown, and Mr. Rose wanted a lot of work done."

"We noticed that when we went through the place." Stride turned his attention back to Barbara Drodge. "So, there wasn't anything in the days leading up to Monday night that stand out in your mind as being unusual?"

"No, nothing at all," she said.

"And you can't think of anyone who would want to harm Mr. Rose?"

"No. Actually, when I heard what had happened, I wondered if it was a robbery. But I haven't heard that robbery was involved."

"There was no indication of robbery," Stride said. "Tell me, have you talked to Mr. Drodge since this happened?"

"Yes, I have. He phoned here earlier today."

"Where is he?"

"He's in Harbour Grace. He's been there since Monday morning. He has clients there."

"He drove there?"

"Not exactly, no. He drove to Portugal Cove, and took the boat across Conception Bay."

"The ferry?"

"No. He has his own boat moored there. It's part of the business. When the weather's even halfway decent, it's a lot easier to get about on the water than on land."

"I understand," Stride said. "And he called here because he'd heard about the shooting?"

"Yes. It was on the radio this morning. There, as well as here." She looked at her brother for a moment, then back at Stride. "There are some things of mine at Harry's place. Just some clothes, and a few personal items. Will I be able to get them?"

"In a few days. But if it's something urgent, we can get you in there sooner."

"No, there's nothing urgent. And to tell the truth, I'm not all that anxious to go there. But the sooner the better, I suppose."

"I have another question, Mrs. Drodge. Did Mr. Rose have any unusual habits? Particularly when he went out for a walk late at night?"

She hesitated long enough for Stride to know that there was something, and that she probably knew what he was asking. He thought she was about to reply, but her brother spoke first.

"Tell him, Barbara. Chances are he already knows, anyway."

"Mrs. Drodge?"

"Harry had a pistol," she said. "A revolver. He always carried it with him at night, when he went out for his walk."

"He carried a revolver? Did he tell you why he did that?"

"He said it was something he'd gotten into the habit of doing, years ago, and he just felt more comfortable when he had it with him."

"Years ago? When was that, during the war? Or afterwards?"

"I don't know. He didn't say."

"And you believed what he told you?" Stride said.

"No." She looked at her brother. "No, I didn't believe him, and neither did

Avery. Harry said it was nothing to worry about, but I didn't believe that, either. So, at first I did worry about it, and I wondered what it was that was going on, what he might be afraid of. No, that's not the right word. Harry wasn't really afraid of anything. But he was obviously concerned about something. After a while, though, I just forgot about it, or at least I didn't think about it any more, because nothing ever happened."

"Until Monday night," Garland said.

"Do you happen to know what kind of gun it was? The calibre, the make?"

"I don't know anything about guns." Barbara Drodge looked at her brother again. "Avery probably knows."

"It was a Webley," Garland said. "A Webley .38. It's the model they made after the First War, to replace the .455, so Harry told me. He had one of those also, the .455, I mean. That was the one he had with him during the war. But it was the .38 he carried with him when he went out for his walks."

CHAPTER 18

At the rooming house on Empire Avenue, Michael Duggan chewed thoughtfully on the last piece of the bologna sandwich that was his breakfast, then washed it down with a mouthful of lukewarm tea. He placed the tea mug on the table and picked up his pipe. The clock on the wall told him it was going on for ten-thirty, past time to get to it. He read through the note that Evan Pugh had tacked on the notice board for him, then looked at the list of roomers that the building's owner had left.

John Ross Buckle owned three rooming houses: two on Empire Avenue and one over on McKay Street in the west end. It was the house on McKay that was Duggan's biggest bother. Part of his compensation for his labour was a room supplied by Buckle at half price in one of the houses on Empire. But he was responsible for maintenance at all three, and it was a long haul on foot to McKay Street. Happily for him, he didn't have to do all of the houses every day.

There were six rooms for rent in the one house on Empire, and seven in the other, and it was a hell of a job looking after it all. People came and went, and the ones who moved on after only a few days, chasing jobs here and there, often were not what Duggan would call fastidious—Evan Pugh was an exception—and sometimes they were downright disrespectful of other people's property. When that happened, Duggan was left with the responsibility to clean up after them and make repairs where necessary. But it was a living, better than a government handout.

Duggan got his pipe fired up, drained the last of the tea from his mug and picked up the list again. Four of the six rooms at the house were still occupied, and two had come empty that morning. Duggan knew that the two men who'd lived here for a week were long gone—up early and on their way to God knows where. Wherever they could find work, he guessed. He'd met them both, Duggan had, talked to them, and while they seemed like decent enough fellas, you could never be sure. You couldn't tell a book from its cover was what his father had liked to say. And he'd said it often enough, even though the old man had never actually learned to read or write.

Duggan put off looking at the mess on the stairs and the second floor that Pugh was on about. He went first to the two empty rooms on the ground floor, opened the doors. and looked inside, giving them a quick once-over. The rooms were in decent shape: nothing broken that he could see, and nothing stolen, not that John Ross Buckle put anything of much value into the rooms, for fear it would be trucked away. Light bulbs were the most popular items to walk away with, but when Duggan flicked the switches in the two rooms, the lights came on. Score one for honesty and good will.

He went next to the occupied rooms, one after the other, tapping on the doors, then opening them and looking inside when there was no response. A fella had to be careful that there was no one home before he opened a door in a rooming house. Twice he'd had a huge shock, and saw things, interrupted things, that he'd rather not have known went on, much less seen taking place. That was, he supposed, what they called an occupational hazard. But the three rooms he tried were empty, and he would go through them later and take care of anything that needed taking care of.

He was on the second floor now, and the dirt that Pugh had left the note about was obvious enough. Duggan stood on the landing and looked down the hallway. The trail of dirt went all the way along, down to the fourth room, the last one, situated at the side of the house. The stuff looked like mud, but in the dim light from the single bulb, he couldn't be sure. Well, it had been raining a lot, and roomers weren't famous for wiping their feet. He went down the hall and tapped on the door, but there was no response from inside.

He took hold of the doorknob, then quickly pulled his hand away, because it didn't feel right. There was something on the knob. He stepped back and looked at it, then at his hand. Whatever it was, it was dark coloured and unpleasant looking, something like the material on the stairs and the floor. But at least it was dry. He sniffed at his hand, relieved that it wasn't what he was afraid it might be. If it had been that, it would have ruined his day entirely, might even have brought his breakfast back into view. Hard work, Michael Duggan could deal with. Ill-mannered, even rowdy roomers, he could deal with. Filth, he could not deal with, not well enough. He had what his mother, smiling at the notion, had called a delicate constitution.

Duggan knocked on the door again, louder this time, and when there was still no answer, he pulled a cleaning rag from his back pocket, wrapped it around the knob and tried the door. It wasn't locked. The room was dark, the blind pulled all the way down to the sill. And that, he thought, was odd. Even odder, and much less pleasant, was an odour, a warm and sickly sweet odour that crept into his nostrils. After a moment's indecision, and fighting a feeling of nausea, he stepped into the room and ran his hand along the wall until he found the light switch. He saw that there was more of the same dark material on the bare wood floor of the room that he'd seen on the floor outside and on the doorknob, a lot of it. And now he had a truly sick feeling in his stomach that he knew exactly what it was.

He pushed the door open wide and stepped inside the room, and his discomfort grew even stronger. When finally he was able to make himself look towards the bed behind the door in the corner of the room, the sick feeling, bolstered by the foul odour, overwhelmed him. He staggered sideways and backwards, and crashed into a chest of drawers, knocking it off balance. The collision sent a water jug toppling to the floor, where it broke into a dozen pieces. As Duggan watched, the spilled water ran across the stained and dirty floor, liquefying the brown material, turning it back into something like the viscous and vital fluid it once had been.

CHAPTER 19

Stride angled the MG over to the curb at the head of the lane that led from Water Street down to Harvey's Wharf and turned off the motor. From where they were sitting, he and Harry could see a horse-drawn cart backed into the coal shed. The driver stood beside it, out of the rain, and watched while a tall, raw-boned man shovelled coal into the cart from a large pile just inside the shed's entrance.

"Do you suppose that's John Smith?" Stride said.

"From the description and the picture we have on file, it could be him, sir."

Stride focused on the man shovelling the coal, his smooth rhythm, the way he somehow made it look easy. And maybe it was easy for him, after years of hard manual labour. The shovel he used had at least twice the capacity of any shovel Stride had ever held. If this really was John Smith, Stride wondered how drunk he would have had to be on the night he went up against Harrison Rose and Barnes Wilson, to come out a distant second. It should have been no contest.

"Do you think it's worth it, Harry? The more we learn about Harrison Rose, the less I think someone like Smith could have had anything to do with his murder."

"I don't mind doing it, sir. It's a loose end that needs tying up, and you never know, Smith might have something useful to tell us about Rose and Wilson."

"I admire your optimism. I'll leave it with you. I want to have a talk with Lawrence Rivers. The company's offices aren't far from here."

"Will I make my own way back to the Fort when I'm done here, or will I wait for you?"

They both looked at the rain pounding down on the bonnet of the MG and onto the blacktop of Water Street.

"It's up to you, Harry. It might take me longer to talk to Rivers than for you to finish with Smith. But I'll come by here when I'm done. If you get tired waiting for me, you can shank's-mare it back to the Fort, and we'll catch up later."

"Fair enough," Phelan said. He gripped his umbrella and opened the door of the car.

As he drove the several blocks along Water to the building that housed Rivers & Sons, Stride thought about Rivers's drinking problem. McCowan had suggested that wasn't necessarily a bad thing from Stride's point of view, and it could work to his advantage. Rivers might be careless with words, and that could provide a counterpoint to the interview with Albert Dancey. Dancey had been as careful with his answers to Stride's questions as he had been with his movements about the office.

When Stride came into the outer office, he was greeted by a pleasant-looking woman in her early fifties. Her brown hair was longer than was fashionable, hanging free, and showed no sign of the brutal ministrations of a hairdresser, and the kind of treatment that often gave a woman's hair the look and texture of cast iron. She turned towards the door and smiled a greeting.

"Can I help you?"

"I hope so. I'd like to see Mr. Rivers, if he's in." He remembered that there were two Rivers brothers. "Mr. Lawrence Rivers, that is."

"Well, you might be in luck, Mr. —?"

"Stride. Eric Stride."

"That would be Inspector Stride, wouldn't it?" Stride thought her smile tightened when she said his name, but he wasn't sure. "District Inspector McCowan phoned Mr. Dancey about you yesterday."

"Yes he did."

"You arrived after I'd left for the day, otherwise we would have met already." She picked up the intercom phone and pressed a button. While she waited for a response, she put her hand over the mouthpiece and smiled at him again. "We had this installed just a few weeks ago. It's such a convenience." Then she looked away. "Mr. Rivers? There's a gentleman here from the Constabulary and he'd like to speak with you." She nodded her head. "Yes, it is. All right, I'll send him in."

"I'm not interrupting anything?"

"If you were, Mr. Rivers would have said so. In fact, I think he was expecting you. Please, just go on in."

Lawrence Rivers moved out from behind his desk when Stride came into the office and extended his hand. Rivers was a tall man with an erect posture, and he looked fit and healthy. Not what Stride would have expected for someone who had a serious drinking problem. The only sign of that was a tired look, as though he might not have slept well for a few nights. His complexion was a bit florid, but his hair colour and skin tone suggested that might have been his natural appearance.

"Albert Dancey told me about your visit yesterday." He gestured towards a chair in front of the desk. There was a cigarette burning in an ashtray near Rivers's right hand. He picked it up, took a final draw, then put it out.

"So you've already spoken with Mr. Dancey about my visit?"

"Yes, I have. At supper last night." Rivers put his package of cigarettes into a side drawer of his desk. "That was a terrible thing to have happened to Harry Rose. I'll be happy to assist you any way I can, Inspector Stride, but I'll start by saying that I don't know anything about this affair, other than what I've heard on the news, and from Albert."

"We're still trying to learn as much as we can about Mr. Rose: his background, even his time in the war. And especially after the war, before he moved here to St. John's."

"I understand. Past being prologue, that sort of thing."

Stride nodded.

"We can start with the war, if you like," Stride said, "and go on from there. Mr. Dancey said he thought that Harrison Rose was a good officer, and I'm wondering if you have the same opinion. I believe you and Mr. Dancey were together for much of the war."

"Yes, we were. Albert and I joined up at the same time, September of 1914, and we were together until 1917." Rivers hesitated then, glancing towards the window before going on. "Yes, I'd agree with Albert that Harry Rose was a good officer."

"What happened in 1917 to separate you and Mr. Dancey?"

"Albert was captured in France, in a place called Sailly-Saillisel. That was in January 1917."

"I've never heard of Sailly-Saillisel," Stride said.

"It's not one of the better known places we were posted, and we were there for only three days. We'd relieved the Lancashire Fusiliers. It wasn't a big show, Sailly-Saillisel, but we were under attack by the Germans almost all the time we were there, artillery and gas both."

"Mr. Dancey didn't mention having been captured. How did it happen?"

"It was during a trench raid. It didn't go well, and I didn't see Albert again until after the war. In fact, I thought he was probably dead. Trench raids were brutal affairs, hand-to-hand fighting of the worst kind. *Medieval* is the term that best describes it. Sometimes raiders who were captured were summarily executed. I'm not surprised Albert didn't mention it to you. He doesn't like to talk about it. After his capture, he was sent with a lot of other prisoners to work in the coal mines in Westphalia. It was basically slave labour, and he was very lucky to survive to the end of the war. There were a lot of Russian prisoners working alongside him in the mines, and many of them died. What saved Albert was the Red Cross parcels he received from time to time. The Russians, poor beggars, didn't have that benefit. Albert shared what he could afford to, but it didn't help them very much."

"I thought that trench raids were only ordered before a major push, to get some idea of the enemy's defences. That doesn't seem to have been the situation at Sailly-Saillisel."

"That's true, but raids could be ordered for any number of reasons."

"Who was it gave the order for that particular raid?"

"Those decisions came about in different ways. Sometimes they came from quite high up, from senior officers, often far removed from the action. For example, we carried out two trench raids in our sector just before the big push at the Somme in July 1916. Those were ordered by the high command."

"Who then ignored the information the raiders brought back, that the German defences were mostly unaffected by the artillery bombardment."

"That's true, too." Rivers affected a wry smile. "I see you do know something about the war."

"A little," Stride said. "But where did the order come from for the raid at Sailly-Saillisel?"

"That was made at the battalion level."

"Was Colonel Rose involved in that order?"

"Yes, he was." Rivers leaned forward. "And I think I know where you're taking this. You're trying to make a case that Harry Rose was somehow responsible for Albert's being taken prisoner."

"Actually, I'm not. I'm only asking questions, Mr. Rivers."

Rivers looked at Stride for a long moment. He retrieved his cigarettes from the drawer.

"I'm sorry," he said. "I shouldn't have said that. Please go on."

"You stayed with the Regiment after Mr. Dancey was captured?"

"I did, except for two months in May of 1918, when I was ill and I was taken out of the line."

"And by that time, Harrison Rose had moved on to another command?"

"Yes, long since. Harry left us in 1917, in May, after he'd been promoted to colonel. I didn't see him again until he turned up here in St. John's. That was in 1930."

There was another pause and Stride decided to follow up on the hesitation that Rivers had shown earlier.

"And did something happen after Mr. Dancey was captured? Something that might have gone against his view of Colonel Rose's performance as an officer?"

"Yes, there was something. And it might have become an issue if Rose had stayed with the Regiment, but after he left it was mostly forgotten. And if he was still alive, I wouldn't be talking about it now."

Rivers paused to light his cigarette. He broke the spent match in half and dropped the pieces in the ashtray.

"Perhaps you've heard of a place called Ville Ste-Lucille?"

"I have heard of it," Stride said. "There was an engagement there involving a dozen or so men of the Newfoundland Regiment, and a few others from a different regiment. They held off a much larger force of Germans for the better part of a day."

"That's more or less what happened. It was in April 1917, and the action there was part of what was later called the Battle of Arras. It wasn't as big as the push at the Somme, but it was big enough. By the time it was over, we'd taken more casualties than at any other time since Beaumont Hamel."

"You were at Ville Ste-Lucille?"

"Yes. The fight there was one of those things that often happened in a major battle, with heavy enemy artillery and small-arms fire, units disorganized, communications lost because of cut telephone wires, runners killed by snipers. In a situation like the one at Ville Ste-Lucille, disaster is often just one bad decision away."

"But that didn't happen."

"No, it didn't. It was even a victory of sorts. And since you know the name of the place, you probably also know that every man there who survived the day was decorated. The Military Cross for the two officers, the Military Medal for the other ranks."

Rivers looked across the desk at Stride through a haze of smoke from his cigarette and, it seemed, across a space of thirty years. He seemed different now, more energized, secure for however short a time in a memory that was probably the singular point of his life.

"We'd established a secondary command post at Ville Ste-Lucille, one of several that day. There was a church with a tall spire in the village, and that gave us an observation post. The problem with an observation post, though, is that it comes under heavy artillery and mortar fire, and the enemy wants to take it as badly as the defenders want to keep it."

"Colonel Rose was in command of the position?"

"Yes, although he was a major then. The officer originally in command of the position was a lieutenant-colonel, but he'd been killed earlier in the fighting. There was a lot of reorganizing going on, most of it on the run. One of the problems we had that day was that the creeping barrage we'd been promised for the initial assault wasn't heavy enough, or sustained long enough, so most of the German machine guns were still operational, and their artillery was trained on our positions. We had some companies that were all but wiped out, and the men who weren't killed or wounded were fighting alone, or in small groups, sometimes only two or three men together. A few hours after it all started, there was just me and three others left from my platoon, fighting our way towards the village, and not even knowing for certain that we still held the place."

Rivers paused again, looking at the smoke rising from the tip of his cigarette.

"It's almost impossible to explain what it was like out there. The area had been fought over for days, and it had seen engagements before that. The landscape was churned up beyond recognition by artillery fire. It was easy to get lost, and you often didn't know if you were going towards your own lines or towards the enemy's. Men would sometimes think they were home safe only to be shot down because they'd gone the wrong way and were at the enemy's trench."

"Or were shot by their own side by mistake."

"That happened, too. What we did have in our favour at Ville Ste-Lucille was that we could see the church spire. But, as I said, even that wasn't a certainty until we actually got there. By then, there were only two of us, myself and a fellow named Rankin, and he was killed an hour later by a German sniper.

"But getting to Ville Ste-Lucille wasn't the end of it. It wasn't even the beginning of the end. By mid-morning, when Rankin and myself got there, the word had come through with a runner that we had to hold the village, no matter what, because if we lost it and the Germans set up a defensive perimeter, it would take God knows how many thousands of men to take it back again. There were twenty-two of us there still able to fight. We'd collected all the weapons and ammunition we could find. We took them from dead men, and from men too badly wounded to use them. Some of those men were our friends, and they needed help, but we couldn't help them. We had to focus on holding the position."

Rivers paused again and closed his eyes for a moment.

"We had one advantage. The Germans didn't know how few of us there were in the village. The fact that their artillery continued to pound the place told us that they probably thought we were there in force."

"It had to be taking a toll, though. The artillery."

"When we counted heads at eleven that morning, we had twenty-two men. An hour later, we were down to an even dozen. The Germans were dropping both high-explosive and shrapnel on the village. Harry Rose made a quick reconnaissance by climbing halfway up the church tower. From there he could see the Germans, a lot of them, dropping into the same jumping-off trench we'd used ourselves earlier that morning. It was obvious they were assembling for an attack.

"When he came down from the tower, Harry made what some of us thought was a mad decision. He'd picked out a spot halfway between the tower and the trench where the Germans were assembling. There was a well-banked hedge there, and Rose thought it was a defendable position, our best hope to hold off an attack. The problem was, we had to run across a hundred yards of open ground to get to it. Most of us wanted to stay at the church and make our stand there, but Harry said the contour of the land was all wrong for that, that we'd be chewed up by artillery and trench mortars, never mind the small-arms fire, and that we'd have no hope of holding off a frontal assault. So he gave us the order, and we followed him across those hundred yards of open ground, firing as we went. When we got to the hedge, there were only nine of us left. We'd lost three more men on the way.

"In the end, though, he was right, and we held that position for four hours. The Germans still didn't know there were only a few of us there. We rationed our ammunition, every so often letting off rounds of concentrated fire, to make it look like there was the better part of a company holding the position. We had one Lewis gun, and that was a big help. Harry Rose did more shooting than anyone, and he was by far the best shot in the group. I think we killed upwards of forty Germans in the first two hours, and Harry himself probably accounted for thirty of those. He had us concentrate on the scouts the Germans sent out, so they never found out that there was only a handful of us at the position. If they'd known, they could have taken us out easily enough with a concerted frontal assault."

Rivers crushed his cigarette in the ashtray.

"Reinforcements finally arrived in mid-afternoon and the position was secured. We saved a lot of lives that day. But we also lost a lot of our own men, Newfoundlanders and British both. And I can tell you that there were more heroes that day than the nine of us who walked out of Ville Ste-Lucille in mid-afternoon."

There was near silence in the office now, with only the sound of traffic passing below on the wet pavement of Water Street. Stride waited to see if Rivers would add anything to his story. When he didn't, he asked his question.

"Did something else happen that day? You started off by saying that something did."

Rivers looked across the desk at Stride, nodding his head slowly.

"Yes, something did happen. I've never been really sure what it was about, beyond the fact that the whole day, like so many other days in the war, year after year, was a mad affair, bloody insanity. I don't think any of us thought we'd survive to see the end of it. And when you see men dying all around you, it has an effect. You start off with friends to the right and the left of you, in front of you and behind, and then they start falling away, some of them wounded, some of them killed. And some of them blown to pieces, not men at all any more, just fragments, pieces of meat and bone."

"What happened?"

Rivers pursed his lips as though preparing to whistle, but no sound came out. And then, after a minute, he spoke again.

"The thing that I'll tell you about, it happened after most of the fighting was done that day, when we had reinforcements coming in to relieve us. With the turn in the tide of the battle, there were some Germans who'd surrendered—they were with a Bavarian regiment—men caught between their own lines and ours. We'd taken prisoners before, lots of them, and for the most part we treated them well, following the rules.

"Just about then, one of our men, a corporal from the Essex Regiment who'd been with us at the hedge, he gave a shout and said there were some Germans approaching our position. There were two of them, about fifty yards away. I shouldered my rifle and put one up the pipe just in case, but it looked to me like they were surrendering. I was just turning to my right towards the fellow from the Essex to say that it looked like we'd have two more Bavarians for supper, when I heard three shots, rapid-fire, and when I looked back, the two Germans were down, and they weren't moving. The shots had come from my left. When I looked to see who had fired, it was Major Rose."

"You're sure it was him?"

"There was still smoke coming from his Enfield, and he was racking in another round, and looking straight at the two men on the ground, ready to drive another one home if he needed to. No, there was no doubt that it was Harry Rose who'd shot them."

"Is it possible he saw something you didn't? Perhaps they weren't about to surrender."

"I don't think they had any thought of attacking our position. They'd have been mad to even think about it, although madness was something you ran into out there." Rivers nodded his head as if agreeing with himself. "And there was something else. When he was satisfied the two Germans were dead, Harry turned and looked at me. There was something in his expression just at that moment that I hadn't seen before. And I can see it still."

"Something you hadn't seen before?"

"Not with him, although I'd seen it with some others, and more than once. It was something I think you see only in wartime. I can't really describe it."

"Did you speak to Rose about what happened?"

"No, not then, and not ever." Rivers shook his head and went silent again. He took out another cigarette and lit it, and again he broke the spent match into two pieces.

"Did you say anything about this to Mr. Dancey? After the war, I mean."

Rivers shook his head.

"No. The truth of it is, I didn't know what to say about it, so I didn't say anything. I put it in the same place I put a lot of the things I saw in the war, and I left it there. Until now."

"And later? After Rose had moved to St. John's and you met him again?"

Rivers lifted his hands in a gesture of resignation.

"I didn't speak about it to anyone until today. And now I almost wish I hadn't said anything. I can't explain what it was happened that day in Ville Ste-Lucille, and maybe I should have left it there, part of the dead past."

"Except that you said yourself, just a few minutes ago, that past is prologue."

"Yes, I know it can be. But I can't imagine that two dead Germans from thirty years ago had anything to do with Harry Rose's murder."

"Maybe they don't," Stride said. "But they had something to do with Harrison Rose. What do you know about him in the time between his leaving the Regiment and his arriving here in St. John's?"

"I don't know anything about what might have happened to Rose after he left the Regiment in 1917, or what he might have been involved in. When he went away, I didn't think I'd see him again."

Stride thought about his next question. He wasn't sure how well Rivers was handling the interview, but he seemed all right, and even appeared to be waiting for the next question.

"I understand there were five of you in the Regiment who were especially close during the war." Stride wasn't sure, but he thought that Rivers might have stiffened slightly. "Yourself, Mr. Dancey, Jack Corrigan, and the Cake brothers, Daniel and Cecil."

"I suppose Jack Corrigan must have told you that. Yes, we were all friends. You probably know that Daniel Cake is dead, killed at Gueudecourt."

"Yes. Have the four of you stayed in touch over the years since? You and Mr. Dancey have, obviously."

"I'm wondering why you ask, what it has to do with your investigation. It's been a long time since the war, going on thirty years now. A great deal's happened since then."

"It's in the line of background information. I've spoken with Jack Corrigan, and with Mr. Dancey, and now yourself. I'm wondering if it might be worth my while to speak with Cecil Cake, if he could add anything to the picture we're trying to build up. It's part of the routine. The more we know about the victim in a case like this, the better our chances of working through to a solution. Corrigan seemed to think it might be useful to talk to Cake. I'm interested in what you think about that. You and Cake were close friends during the war. I understand he lives here, in the west end?"

"He does live in the west end, but I haven't seen him in a while. I really can't give you any advice on that."

"Would Cake have stayed in touch with Colonel Rose?"

Rivers shook his head.

"I don't know that he did."

"Corrigan told me that Cake was seriously wounded, badly enough that it was thought he would be invalided home. But he wasn't."

"I don't know why they let him rejoin the Regiment, except that he wanted to, and he passed the physical. As manpower was always an issue, he was taken back. He was a fierce warrior, Cec, so in one way, we were glad to have him back with us. And as it turned out, he was all right, at least in the sense that he acquitted himself well."

"But?"

"He wasn't the same man he'd been. He was withdrawn, if I can put it that way." Rivers stubbed his cigarette in the ashtray. "Daniel's death had something to do with that. In addition to the head injury."

"I understand Cake didn't come back home after the war ended, that he went off to Ireland for a time."

"Yes, he did."

"Tending sheep is what Jack Corrigan told me."

"Yes, sheep. That was a surprise. I had assumed he'd come back home after the war and return to fishing with his father. It's what he'd done before he enlisted. Most of the men I knew over there, they wanted nothing more than to get back to a normal life, the kind of life they'd had before the war. But I know that some men found it hard to come back, impossible even. They were changed by the experience, and they needed to do something different. I think Cecil Cake was one of those." He shook his head. "Looking after sheep in Ireland. Well, perhaps it does make some sense, after all."

CHAPTER 20

John Smith dug into the pile of soft coal and heaved shovelfuls into the red cart. As each shovelful landed in the box, the horse's head jerked up. It almost seemed that the animal was keeping count, doing a dismal calculation of the weight of the load it would have to haul over the streets and hills of the city. The driver leaned against one of the tall wheels of the cart, smoking a pipe, alternating his gaze between the heap of coal on the shed floor and the growing pile in the cart.

Phelan stood under his umbrella and watched until the driver signalled to Smith that he had as full a load as he needed. He climbed up onto the seat and started the horse on its way, out into the afternoon rain. As the cart moved past him, the driver gave Phelan and his umbrella a brief glance, then twitched the leather reins on the horse's back and made a clucking sound in his throat. The animal increased its pace to a slow trot and the cart moved on up the incline towards Water Street.

Smith dropped his shovel onto the pile of coal and lit a half-smoked cigarette. He leaned against one of the thick beams that supported the roof of the shed. Smith had the leathery, half-emaciated look of a man who'd never done anything but hard physical work all his life, and had only more of the same to look forward to. Phelan put Smith's age somewhere between twenty and thirty. In five years the upper estimate would probably be ten years higher.

When Smith saw Phelan coming towards him, he stood a little straighter and shot a glance at his cigarette as though afraid he'd be reprimanded for taking a break.

"John Smith?" Phelan stepped under the cover of the shed. "My name's Phelan. I'm with the Constabulary. I need to ask you some questions about an incident in Bannerman Park last May."

Smith looked at his cigarette and took another drag. He leaned back against the beam.

"I already answered some questions about that," he said. "The night it happened, when I was in the hospital."

"I have different questions," Phelan said.

Smith looked around him, up and down the road that ran between the wharf and Water Street, and then back into the coal shed, where three more labourers were watching the encounter, standing close together, leaning on their shovels.

Phelan stepped closer to Smith, close enough that he could smell the sweat that soaked through his shirt and ran down his arms. He looked around the shed and saw a bench against the far wall. "Let's go over there and sit down, Mr. Smith."

Smith dropped the butt of his cigarette on the floor of the shed and stepped on it. He hitched up his dungarees and walked over to the bench. He sat down, his feet spread wide apart, his elbows on his knees. He took off his cap and held it in both hands, swinging it back and forth in a small arc. He didn't say anything. He didn't look at Phelan.

"You heard about the shooting Monday night, in Bannerman Park?"

"I heard something about that. Why?"

"The man who was killed was one of the men you and your friends jumped in the park last spring."

Phelan watched for Smith's reaction, but all he saw was an expression of dazed confusion. It took Smith almost a minute to put together a response.

"I wasn't anywhere near Bannerman Park Monday night. I has people who'll back me up on that."

"Their names?" Phelan took out his notebook and wrote down the three names Smith gave him. "Do these people live with you?"

"Yes, sir."

"The same place you were living last spring?"

"Yes, sir, the place on Calver Avenue."

"You understand I'll be checking this out."

Smith nodded and dug into the top pocket of his dungarees, then patted the side pockets. Phelan took out his cigarettes and offered the package.

"The affair in Bannerman Park last spring. What happened that night? How did it start?"

"It wasn't me started it. It was Dalton and Squire."

"But you were with them.".

"Yes, sir, I was."

"Tell me what happened."

"The three of us was drinking together that night."

"The whole night? The fight in the park happened very late, sometime after midnight."

"I was by myself most of the night. I run into Dub and Ferris later on, when I was down on the corner of Duckworth and Prescott." He looked at Phelan and managed a thin smile. "I had a bottle of gin, Dutch gin. I run into a fella I knew who was off a ship. He sold me the bottle for a half-dollar."

"That's where Dalton and Squire found you?"

"Yes, sir. I knew the two of them from the one time I was in the Pen. We was never friends, though. I just knew who they was, that's all."

"What time did they come along?"

"It was getting on for midnight, I suppose. I don't own a watch, but I know it was late. We all had a couple of pulls at my bottle, finished it up, and then we headed for home."

"But you ended up in Bannerman Park. Why?"

"The three of us lived up that way. I was living on Calver Avenue, and I think Dub and Ferris lived not too far away from my place."

"So you were just going on home? You weren't heading for the park?"

"No, sir, no one said nothing about going to the park. It was just along the way, that's all. We went on up Prescott, up to Military Road."

"And then you went into the park?"

Smith thought about that, sorting his memory of the night four months ago.

"Later on, we did."

"Later on?"

"I knows we went on up Prescott to Military. When we got there, Ferris took a mickey of rum out of his back pocket, and we sat down on the curb on Rawlins Cross, and passed that back and forth. We hung around there for a spell, and then Dub said we better get off the street or we might get arrested. Dub said he seen a cop on the beat farther down the street."

"And that's when you went into the park."

"Yes, sir. We sat down under a tree and passed Ferris's bottle around." Smith made a face. "Rum and gin don't mix too good, and after a while I started to feel sick." He ran a hand through his hair. "All I wanted to do then was get on home and get some sleep. I had to work the next day. Them two didn't, but I did."

"But you didn't do that."

"I started to, but then Ferris said something to Dub, and the next thing I know, Dub has me by the arm, and the three of us is following along behind these two old guys in the park."

"Two old guys?"

"They looked old, in their fifties, I guess. And I remember thinking they looked like Mutt and Jeff, one of them tall, and the other one short. The short one, he had a cane."

"And those were the men you had the fight with?"

"Yes, sir."

"Did you know who they were?"

"I never seen them before."

"And Dalton and Squire?"

"I don't think so."

"So, how did it start?"

"I don't remember, exactly. One minute the three of us is walking along behind the two of them, and I'm wondering what it's all about, and then Dub and Ferris, they jumped on ahead of me, and Dub give one of the guys a shove, the little fella. He almost fell down, but he kept a hold of his cane. Then Ferris, he grabs the other one, the tall fella, by the coat collar and swings him around in a circle, and he does fall down."

"What were you doing then?"

"I was just standing there and wondering what the hell is going on. And all I'm thinking about is that we're going to get in trouble. Then Dub, he's got the little fella by the collar and he shoves him right at me."

"And that's when you started to fight?"

"I didn't start fighting. All I did was try and shove the guy away from me, because I didn't want nothing to do with it. But I guess he thought I was going to hit him, because he lets me have one in the gut with his stick, and another one on the side of the head. He near half-killed me. I tried to get away from him, and he hit me again. By now I'm not worried about going to jail, I'm worried this little bugger is going to kill me. He hit me a couple more times, and I fell down."

"And what about Squire and Dalton?"

"I don't know. They was fighting with the tall guy, and then the little fella went to help him out. I remember hearing Dub yelling, and Ferris too, so I knew they was getting some of the same I got."

"Did you go and help them?"

"I suppose I must have. All I really wanted to do was get the hell out of there, but Dub and Ferris, they was taking a licking, and I figured I better go give them a hand. But by then it was all fucked up. There wasn't no way out of it. And those two old buggers, they was kicking the shit out of us. After a while, I saw Dub and Ferris lying on the ground, and then the one with the cane, he comes after me again. He clocks me another one across the side of the head with his stick, and then he shoves the end of it into my gut, hard, two or three times. It felt like I was split in two. I fell down again, and then I was throwing up, and rolling around in it."

"And then?"

Smith shrugged.

"Then it's over. I'm lying on the ground thinking I'm probably going to die, I hurt so much, and I can see that Dalton and Squire are still down. And the tall guy, he's got his arms wrapped around the little fella, holding on to him."

"He was hurt? The smaller man?"

"No, sir, he wasn't hurt." Smith pulled on his cigarette and exhaled the smoke in a long stream. "I think the bigger one was trying to keep the little fella away from us."

"Keep him away from you?"

"Yes, sir. I think he would have killed the three of us if the tall fella hadn't took a hold of him. I think he would've beat us to death. He damn near killed me as it was."

Phelan looked closely at Smith. He could see he wasn't making it up. His face was contorted with remembered pain.

"And then the police got involved?"

"I don't know exactly when the cops got there. I think I might have passed out for a while; I don't remember."

"And the two men you attacked, they were still there?"

"Yes, sir, they was still there."

"And the policemen. Were they in uniform, or plainclothes?"

"One of each. The first cop who come, he was in uniform. But the other one, the one dressed like you, he was there just about the same time. Then the ambulance was there, and they put me on a stretcher. And then we was at the hospital."

"Were the two men at the hospital as well?"

"No, sir. Just me and Dalton and Squire, and the cop in the uniform." Smith closed his eyes for a moment. "No, that's not right. At first there was just the one cop at the hospital, the one in the uniform. The other cop, the older one, he come in later. The one without the uniform."

"So, why did it start? What was it all about?"

"Dub said the two old guys was queers, and we could have some fun with them, smack them around a bit, maybe even get some money out of them. Dub said queers couldn't fight, didn't know how, and didn't have no guts anyway." Smith shook his head and pulled on his cigarette. "He's a fuckin' genius, Dub is."

"And you have no idea who the two men were."

"No, sir. I don't have a fuckin' clue who they were. I never saw them before, and I hope to Christ I never see them again." He dropped the butt of his cigarette on the floor, ground it under the sole of his boot, and looked at Phelan. "You said one of them's dead now. Is that true?"

"Yes, it's true."

"Which one?"

"The man with the cane. The smaller one."

"They must of took him by surprise, then. No fuckin' way he'd go down without a fight."

"That's what we think," Phelan said.

"And you think it had something to do with that night in the park?"

"We don't know if it did or not."

"Well, I told you I didn't have nothing to do with it. You talk to those guys I give you the names of. They'll tell you I wasn't nowhere near Bannerman Park Monday night. You ask them about that. They'll tell you."

Phelan nodded and stood up. He looked through the wide double door that led outside. It was still raining. He picked up his umbrella and started towards the doorway. Then he turned back.

"How are you feeling, by the way? From the surgery, I mean?"

"I'm back shovelling fuckin' coal for a living, so I suppose I must be all right."

"I suppose so," Phelan said.

"Do me a favour, will you?"

"If I can."

"If you talk to Squire and Dalton about all this, don't tell them you was talking to me. If you do, they're likely to come after me when they gets out of jail."

"Why would they do that?"

"Because that's the way they are. And two on one is their idea of a fair fight."

CHAPTER 21

Constable Billy Dickson hung up the phone and finished making a note in his book. He went over what he'd written, then signalled for another officer to stand in for him at the reception desk for a few minutes. He went down the hall and knocked on District Inspector McCowan's office door.

"A body at a rooming house on Empire?" McCowan sat back in his chair. "And this Duggan thinks the fellow was shot?"

"Yes, sir. And he said there was a lot of blood, on the floor of the room, and on the stairs and the hallway leading to the room. He thinks the man's been there for a while. Long enough that he's started to turn."

"Lovely." McCowan thought about it for a minute. "This might be connected to the Rose murder. But you say Stride and Phelan are out somewhere?"

"Yes, sir, they went out about an hour ago. Noseworthy might know where they are. They were with him just before they left."

McCowan nodded and picked up his phone. Noseworthy arrived in his office in less than a minute.

"I'm not sure where they are, sir," Noseworthy said. "I think Sergeant Phelan was planning to go down to Harvey's Wharf at some point. Inspector Stride probably went to the Rivers company to interview Lawrence Rivers. I suppose it's possible he might still be there."

"I'll put in a call for him," McCowan said. "In the meantime, we need to get a crew over to the house on Empire and start the investigation." He looked at Dickson. "Who's available?"

"There's only Inspector Cobb, sir. Deckard and Batty are out on an inquiry, and Phil Dick called in sick this morning."

"Then, it will have to be you and Cobb, Noseworthy. Get hold of him, Dickson, and have him come see me." McCowan waited until Dickson left the office. "I'll depend on you to keep an eye on Cobb, Noseworthy. You know the situation. Stride and Cobb can hardly stand each other, never mind working together. And my faith in Andy Cobb has gone down in the last few years. But that sentiment's between you, me and the gatepost. Understood?"

"Understood, sir."

"Get to it, then. And you'll let me know if anything unusual turns up."

McCowan made some notes on his pad. Then he picked up the phone and told the operator to connect him with Rivers & Sons.

After Stride left Lawrence Rivers's office he sat in the MG for a minute, thinking about what Rivers had told him about Ville Ste-Lucille, about Harrison Rose killing the two Germans who were trying to surrender. The way Rivers described it, it sounded as though Rose might have had some kind of breakdown following the defence of the village against the attacking Germans. Rivers had said that Rose shot thirty Germans that afternoon, not counting the two who were trying to surrender. He wondered about the effect that might have had on the man, and whether the repercussions had continued after he'd retired from the army. It was something he needed to talk to Thomas Butcher about.

He started the motor and drove to the laneway that led down to Harvey's Wharf. Phelan wasn't anywhere in sight, and now there were two horse-drawn carts pulled into the coal shed. The man he thought was John Smith was heaving coal into one of them, moving with the same practised rhythm as before. Stride decided that Phelan had gone on back to Fort Townshend on foot. Harry didn't mind walking, even in the rain. He said it helped keep his weight down, a continuing struggle after he'd embraced matrimony, and second helpings at dinner.

Stride drove west along Water Street until he came to a Constabulary call box. He wanted to be sure that Tom Butcher was in and would have some time to talk to him about Harrison Rose. He looked at his watch. It was close to noon. Before calling Butcher, he put in a call to Fort Townshend. A minute later he was on his way to the rooming house on Empire Avenue.

"Almost exactly in the centre of the forehead," Butcher said. He took the bottle of menthol gel from his bag again and placed a bit more under his nose. "He also has a bullet wound in his right thigh, and that's where the blood came from. The head wound's bled hardly at all."

"It was obviously immediately fatal," Stride said.

"Just so."

Butcher stepped away from the bed and went out into the hall. Stride followed behind him. Kevin Noseworthy was sitting on an equipment satchel at the far end of the hallway, waiting to get the go-ahead to do the room. Andy Cobb was standing in the hallway alongside Noseworthy, leaning against the wall, chewing on a wad of gum and smoking a cigarette. If Cobb was annoyed that Stride had now taken command of the investigation, he didn't show it. Stride thought that Cobb had totted up the pluses and minuses, and was happy enough to let Stride deal with it.

It wasn't a pleasant situation. The windows of the room appeared to have been shut for a long while, and the room was warm and damp, near-ideal conditions for the accelerated decomposition of a body. The dead man was well on the turn, the odour not quite overwhelming, but getting there.

Harry Phelan was downstairs. He'd arrived a few minutes before Stride had. Stride knew that Harry would stay downstairs. The scene in the bedroom was far beyond anything he was capable of dealing with. Butcher had enough on his hands with the departed, without having to deal with a pale and unhappy detective sergeant teetering on the brink of collapse.

"I think Noseworthy's right," Butcher said. "This probably is the man who shot Harry Rose. If the bullet in his leg matches any of the three I took from Rose, that will confirm it. He's also been dead for going on two days, so the timing is about right."

"It all seems to fit," Stride said. He looked back towards the room, and then pushed some of the menthol he'd put on his lip inside his nostrils. The odour was starting to get to him, and he wondered how much longer he would be able to stand it. "The thing that doesn't fit is why someone didn't hear the shot and call it in sooner." He saw that Butcher was smiling at him, and then the answer was there. "Unless he was shot with the same 9 mm that was used on Rose."

"With silencer attached," Butcher said.

"So it does fit."

"I'll send Noseworthy in to take his snaps," Butcher said. "And then we'll have him moved. I'll drive along to the General behind the van and get the bullets out right away. I expect my findings will be the same as with Harry Rose, except in reverse."

"A .38 in the leg, and a 9 mm in the head."

"Just so," Butcher said again.

Harry Phelan and Michael Duggan sat across from each other at the kitchen table. Stride wasn't sure which of them looked worse. Now that the bedroom door had been opened, the odour of putrefaction had crept through the house and invaded the kitchen, even if it was nowhere near as oppressive and enveloping as it was upstairs. Stride wondered how Noseworthy was making out, even though he had a stomach that he routinely described as being made of cast iron. He lit a cigarette in an effort to kill the smell. Not for the first time he wondered why humans, in death, should smell so awful.

Harry had his notebook open on the table, and it was obvious he'd been busy.

"Our man's name is Robert Benton," Phelan said. "We can hope Noseworthy finds some documentation when he goes through the stuff in the room. How is he doing, by the way?"

"As best he can. It's pretty grim up there."

Kevin Noseworthy walked into the room, carrying his camera case, and pulling a fresh trail of odour behind him.

"I've taken all the pictures I need to, sir. When they get the body out of there, and we can air the place out a bit, I'll go back up and collect anything that looks relevant. But did I hear Harry say that our man's name is Benton?"

"Yes, why?"

"I don't think Benton's a local name. I know more than a little about family names, and I've never seen that one in St. John's, or even on the island. And to that I'll add what I could stand to look at upstairs. Our man's clothing, I mean. It's not local, either. To me it has the look of the old country. England, maybe." Noseworthy looked at Duggan. "When did Benton move in here?"

Duggan took a notebook from his hip pocket and turned a half-dozen pages.

"Ten days ago, sir. He paid the rent for two weeks in advance. That's not the usual way things are done here. A week in advance is unusual, never mind two. Mr. Buckle was more than pleased." He looked towards the upstairs and shook his head. "He won't be when he sees this mess. The room he gave him, around there to the side, that's one of the nicer ones. Or it used to be." Duggan tucked the notebook back in his pocket. He looked at Noseworthy, then at Stride. "But I'll tell you something for free, sir. I don't know if the fellow's name was Benton or no, but I can tell you he wasn't English. Not from the way he talked. From his accent, I'd say he was Irish. Thick as peat, it was."

"You're sure of that, Mr. Duggan? His being Irish?"

"I'd bet money on it. I was over in Ireland, in Dublin, right after the war, on leave from the navy, and I was there for the better part of two weeks. My family comes from over that way, and I took the opportunity to pay a visit to the old country, courtesy of His Royal Majesty. Because God only knows it will be a long while before I can scrape together the coin for a trip across the water on my own. Yes, sir, he was Irish, and no mistake about it."

The front door opened and two large policemen wearing oilskins came into the house carrying a stretcher. One of them came into the kitchen and looked hopefully at Stride, and then at Noseworthy. He made a face as the smell of death reached him from upstairs. Noseworthy took a bottle of menthol gel from his pocket and gave it to him.

"Our friend upstairs is not at his best right now. Liberal applications are recommended. And when you're finished doing that, follow along behind me. I'll show you exactly where to go."

Andy Cobb came into the kitchen. He leaned against the counter.

"Looks like this one's yours, for sure, Eric, and you're welcome to it. I'll stick around and help out, if you like, but if you'd rather I didn't, I'll go on back to Fort Townshend. Your choice."

"Most of what's about to happen next is Noseworthy's department, Andy, but I'd like you to stay on. I think Kevin can probably find something for all of us to do." He looked at Duggan. "We'll want to go through all the rooms in the house, Mr. Duggan, including the basement. We can't exclude the possibility that Mr. Benton might have spread himself around."

"I can give you a hand with that," Duggan said. "As far as I know, Benton had only the one bag when he got here, and it was still there in his room when I found him this morning. But I'm only here one day out of two. I have no idea what he might have been up to when I wasn't around."

There was the sound of heavy and careful footsteps on the stairs. Phelan stood up, opened the kitchen door and stepped outside into the back yard, moving as far away from the body as he could. He stayed there until the stretcher was loaded into the van and the motor started. He came back into the kitchen just as the van was moving down the street.

"You're safe, now," Stride said. "Our client's on his way to the General."

"But his memory lingers on," Phelan said. "Let's get the windows and doors open. We need some fresh air in this place if we're going to spend the next couple of hours here."

The scene at the St. John's Airport at Torbay had been one of barely controlled chaos for two days. Fog had rolled in from the Atlantic like an invading force, even before the rains had started, and it had waged a mostly successful campaign against airline schedules. Flights that made it to the airport at Gander, 125 miles northwest of St. John's, from points in North America, or from overseas, were stalled on the runways, waiting for the weather to clear. Which it did, from time to time, teasing the flight controllers, the aircrews and the passengers, with occasional glimpses of blue sky, only to close in again soon afterwards. It was like an elaborate game of hide-and-seek: now you see me, now you don't. But a few planes did make it into St. John's that day, wildly off schedule, but landing safely nonetheless.

Catherine Darnell's flight had left Boston the previous afternoon, Tuesday, and her itinerary placed her in Halifax for the night, where she visited with friends. Before she left Boston, though, she'd placed a call to her father in St. John's, and after a half-hour delay, the operator made the connection. They talked for just under three minutes—Harrison Rose was strict about wasted words on trunk calls—and she brought him up to date on her time in Boston, and told him she'd be in St. John's on Tuesday. He told her that getting into St. John's might be a challenge because of the weather system that had settled in. She said she would come anyway, and take her chances.

Now, safely on the ground, if a day late, and standing in the terminal building at Torbay, she searched for her father among the throngs of people awaiting the arrival of passengers. She looked at the watch pinned to the lapel of her suit coat. It was just past three. After a few minutes, she decided that he'd probably already been there and gone. She looked for a telephone to call him at home. But there were few phones available for use by the public, and those had long line-ups, queues of weary and irritated people waiting their turn. She stood in one of the lines for a few minutes, found that it moved hardly at all, and gave it up.

She decided to look for a taxi to take her into the city. When she stepped outside the terminal, she found that the situation with ground transportation was almost as chaotic as the one in the air. An assortment of cars and small trucks competed for space in front of the terminal building. There were few taxis, and those few seemed filled almost to overflowing with passengers and baggage, the drivers seeking desperately to egress from the turmoil to the Torbay Road beyond. People ran through the rain, to and from the terminal building and the parked vehicles. It halfway reminded her of the frantic wartime conditions in London during the Blitz.

Catherine stepped back into the terminal building, dragging her two suitcases with her, wishing someone would design wheels for them. A glance in the direction of the telephones told her that the queues were at least as crowded as before. She took a deep breath and thought about what to do next. She closed her eyes and imagined that her father would magically appear and whisk her off to the house on Circular Road. The absurdity of the thought, and of her situation, made her smile. She wasn't the sort of person to become unravelled by inconvenience and bother, and her sense of humour almost never abandoned her.

She settled finally for a cigarette, certain that something positive would happen soon. It was what her mother had called her Micawber reflex. Catherine Darnell was an optimist by choice, and her resident optimism was buttressed by the fact that she was well dressed, slender and attractive. She understood the advantages those qualities gave her, and she was comfortable with that. She had learned early on in her life to take advantage of a situation, anytime she could.

It took only two more minutes for her fortunes to change.

"Do you need a taxi, Miss?"

The voice was gravelly from decades of tobacco smoking, and it had the thick accent of the St. John's near-Irish. That was something she remembered from her last visit to the city, even though it was almost ten years ago. She turned and gave the voice's owner her best smile, and he gave her one in return. It didn't matter to her, and certainly not to him, that his smile was compromised by the complete absence of teeth in what she could see of his upper jaw. He had a kind face, and he was paying attention to her. Those were the things that mattered.

"Yes, I do need a taxi," she said. "I'd almost given up any hope of finding one."

"Well, you got one now, Miss." The toothless smile broadened. The movement recast his face into a cascade of lines and creases, so that it resembled a parchment of very old soft leather on which stories could probably be read, if one had the time and the interest. The man bent over, picked up her bags and nodded his head towards the exit door. "You follow after me, Miss, and if you has an umbrella, you'd best get it out. It's raining like to beat hell out there."

She followed him through the door and they came to a halt under the cover of the building's wide eave. The driver was right about the rain. It was coming down harder now. It probably could have challenged hell's inferno.

"Now, you wait right here, Miss, and I'll get me vehicle and be right back. Don't you go away, now."

"Not to worry," she said. "I won't go anywhere without you."

The driver smiled again, and stepped out into the rain. He lumbered to the far side of the road with a gait that was halfway between a run and a stagger, pulling his coat collar up and his cap down as he went. She watched him climb into a black car, start the motor and set the wipers working. In only a moment he was back, working the vehicle in and out, nudging others out of the way and finally pulling up close enough to the door that she didn't need her umbrella after all. A minute later she was in the back seat, her bags were in the trunk, and the driver was behind the wheel again, smiling at her over the back of the front seat.

"Now, where can I take you, Miss?"

She gave him the address of her father's house on Circular Road.

The driver nodded, shifted the car into gear and started off towards the Torbay Road. But after less than a minute, when they were still on the road leading to the highway, one in a long line of vehicles, he braked the taxi to a stop. He turned and once more he looked at her over the back of the seat. This time he wasn't smiling.

"Can you give me that address, again, Miss?"

She was puzzled that the warm and friendly smile was there no longer. She gave him the address a second time, speaking the words slowly and with care.

The driver seemed at a loss as to what he should say next. For a long moment he stared through the window on the passenger side of the car, at the rain streaming down the glass, at the continuing turmoil near the terminal building. Then he turned back to her.

"I don't suppose your name would be Rose, now, would it?"

"It used to be," she said. "It's my father's name."

"And that would be Colonel Rose?"

"Yes, it would. Colonel Rose is my father. Is something wrong?"

The driver looked at her again, the creases in his face reconfigured to an expression replete with sadness and concern.

"Yes, Miss, there is something wrong. And I'm as sorry as I can be to have to be the one to tell you about it."

CHAPTER 22

Thomas Butcher was partway through the post-mortem on the man they knew as Robert Benton when Stride arrived at the autopsy room in the basement of the General Hospital. It was just past four in the afternoon. The smell of decay was still there, but not nearly as strong as it had been in the room on Empire. But Stride placed a liberal quantity of menthol gel under his nose anyway.

Butcher laid his scalpel on the table and looked across the room at Stride.

"Noseworthy got the bullets all right?"

"He's looking at them now. I left instructions with Harry to call me here when he's done."

"I have some additional information for you," Butcher said. "I've finished the blood work on the stain on Rose's raincoat. It was B-positive."

"Rose's blood type was O-positive. You've done Benton's?"

"Yes. It's B-positive, also. That's not conclusive, of course, but it's strongly suggestive."

Stride stood by the table across from Butcher. The man he was looking at appeared to be in his mid-fifties, but he looked older in death than he probably would have in life. And it seemed that his life had been marked by a great deal of violence even before he had come to St. John's. There were deep scars on his left thigh, and also on the left shoulder and chest area.

"What do you make of those, Thomas? They look like war wounds to me."

"They almost certainly are war injuries. I think our man was probably a veteran of the Great War. The age is about right, and I saw a lot of injuries like these when I was in France, looking after men from the Western Front."

"These are shrapnel wounds, I suppose?"

"No, these injuries were caused by shell fragments," Butcher said.

"I didn't know there was a difference."

"Most people don't. Nowadays the terms are used more or less interchangeably. Shrapnel is actually something like a musket ball, or grapeshot, packed into an artillery shell. A shell fragment is what you get when a high-explosive shell blows apart. The fragments are often larger, and because they're irregular in shape, they can cause a lot more damage. The word *shrapnel*, by the way, is from a Lieutenant Henry Shrapnel, the man who invented it. He was an Englishman like myself, except he was in the business of tearing bodies apart, and I was in the business of trying to put them back together again. Shrapnel was eventually made a general —a reward, one assumes, for his gift to a grateful nation."

"And you made it all the way to major."

"Enough said."

"The leg wound?"

"It's consistent with a .38 calibre bullet, but we'll wait for Noseworthy's opinion on that. It was serious enough, and it obviously bled a great deal. You've already seen that from the amount of blood in the house on Empire. It would have slowed him down considerably. It might even have killed him eventually."

"Would he have needed help getting back there, do you think? From the park?"

"It's hard to say. I've seen men walk away from battle with wounds much worse than this, although our friend here was some years past his prime. I'll go so far as to say that he probably could have made it back to the rooming house on his own."

"But not necessarily alone."

"You're thinking he had an accomplice."

"At the moment I can't come up with a better explanation for his being dead. He didn't shoot himself in the forehead."

"I was about to say something like that, myself," Butcher said. "Drawing on my great experience with violent death, you understand."

"Understood."

"Seriously, though," Butcher said, "I'd be almost willing to consider suicide as a possibility, but the gun would have been there in the room with the body, and it wasn't. The possibility that he had an accomplice has a lot of merit. It might be a case of said accomplice deciding that Benton, with his leg injury, had become a serious liability, a threat to his own safety."

"So, he shot him."

"Yes. And it's possible the accomplice might have left the country already. Staying here only increases the likelihood of his being apprehended. The two of them might have booked passage out of here for the day after they planned to kill

Rose. If I was in the assassination business, it's what I'd have done. Do the job, and get out right away."

"Unless the accomplice is local," Stride said. He looked at the body again, trying to imagine the sequence of events, Benton being shot in the head at point-blank range by a man who might have been his friend once. "Time of death?"

"It's even harder to be precise in this case than it usually is, because of the temperature and humidity in the room. But I'd say he was killed sometime Tuesday morning. We know that he was alive at about twelve-thirty that morning, because that was when he shot Rose in the park. Assuming Noseworthy's ballistics analysis confirms that."

"He should have completed that by now," Stride said.

"You can use the telephone in my office, Eric. I have more to do here. But before you go, there's one more thing I want to show you."

"Yes?" Stride moved closer to the table.

"Our Mr. Benton was not a well man." Butcher picked up the scalpel again and indicated one of several parts of the liver that he'd dissected, separating the layers of tissue. "These are tumours, and they're almost certainly malignant. Cancer. I won't know for certain until I've done the cytology, but I've seen enough of these over the years to be 95 percent sure that's what we're dealing with."

"Was he terminally ill?"

"Yes, he was. The malignancy's well disseminated through the liver. I doubt he had more than six months to live, and probably less than that." He laid the scalpel on the table again and stepped back.

"Would he have known he was that ill, do you think?"

"I expect he would have. The malignancy is far enough along that he would have been unwell, even in some degree of pain. Discomfort, certainly. Still, people are very good at pretending that everything's fine. Denial's part of our nature."

"It's one of my better developed skills," Stride said.

He went down the corridor to Butcher's office and gave the operator the number for Fort Townshend. After a minute, Phelan came on the line.

"Your timing's right on the mark," Phelan said. "Noseworthy's just finished doing the comparison. The bullets match up, and just as Butcher said, in reverse order from what we found with Rose."

"A .38 in the leg, and a 9 mm in the head."

"Yes. How did things go with the autopsy?"

"Some interesting items. For one thing, it looks like Benton was a war veteran, probably from the First War, Butcher thinks."

"So he might have served with Rose at some point," Phelan said.

"That has to be a possibility," Stride said. "And if he really is Irish, that would tie in with Crozier. McCowan said there was a Colonel Crozier who commanded a battalion of the Royal Irish Rifles at the Somme. There could be a connection there. And there's something else. Benton was probably dying of liver cancer, and Butcher thinks he probably knew that he was."

"So, killing Rose might have had some added significance for him. Do you think?"

"I'd agree with that," Stride said. "If Benton had some personal reason for wanting Rose dead, knowing that he was terminally ill himself would be a really strong motivator to get it done. And then there's the blood work. That probably was Benton's blood on Rose's raincoat. At least it's the same type, B-positive."

"So things are coming together," Phelan said.

"They're starting to. And I have some information on Rose from Lawrence Rivers that's of interest."

"And I have a couple of things from John Smith," Phelan said.

"Christ, I'd all but forgotten about him. You're not going to tell me that he was involved in Rose's murder, are you?"

"No, I don't think so, although I have a little more work to do on that still. He did tell me a couple of things that were interesting, but they can wait until we get together back here."

"Which shouldn't be too long from now." Butcher came into the office as Stride dropped the phone back onto its cradle. "All done?"

"No, but all the significant stuff's finished. I'll do the rest of it later. Any word from Noseworthy?"

"Yes. The bullets match up."

"So there's no longer any doubt that Benton is the man who killed Rose."

"Or was at least involved in it," Stride said. "We still don't know who fired the fatal shot."

"Or why he used Rose's .38, instead of the 9 mm."

"That, too," Stride said.

"Did I hear you say you'd spoken to Lawrence Rivers about the case?"

"Yes, I did speak to him. This morning. I also had a long talk with Jack Corrigan yesterday, and he told me about serving with Rose in Gallipoli."

"Did something happen there might have a bearing on the case?"

"Yes, something did happen, but I'm not sure how it might relate to the case. Corrigan told me about a patrol he went on with Rose and some other men, a half-dozen altogether. Rose was in command of the patrol, and the fact is his performance was first-rate. He put himself at risk rather than detail some of his men to go after a Turkish soldier who had already killed one of their number."

"That's unusual," Butcher said. "An officer is supposed to lead and command, not place himself in harm's way, if he can avoid it. There's a fine line between an heroic action and a foolhardy one. Did Rivers have anything useful to tell you?"

"Yes, he did."

"How was he, by the way?"

"He seemed fine. Albert Dancey said Rivers had been ill lately, but Jack Corrigan told me that Rivers has a drinking problem. 'Untidy with the bottle,' is the phrase Jack used."

"Yes, I'm aware of that. It's been going on for as long as I've known him. Laurie's drinking started during the latter stages of the war. It was common enough in the trenches, particularly among some of the officers, but the other ranks did their fair share as well." Butcher looked at his watch. "I have some time in hand. Tell me what you're thinking about, and I'll see if I can add anything more to what you have."

"You know that one of the approaches we're taking with the investigation is the possibility that Rose was killed by someone who served with him in the war."

"Or someone who had a relative or friend who did, and who's now exacted a kind of revenge by proxy? Did you put that question to either Dancey or Rivers?"

"Not directly, no, but Dancey volunteered an opinion along those lines. What he said was that some of the men might have come away from the war with a sense that Rose was responsible for deaths and injuries, even if he wasn't really."

"Guilt by circumstance. Orders are given, orders are obeyed, and men are killed or wounded in the process. The logic of association is as obvious as it's flawed."

"And now we have Benton involved. If it turns out that he is in fact Irish, his involvement could have something to do with Rose's time in the war. Rose had some kind of relationship with a Colonel Crozier who commanded a battalion of the Royal Irish Rifles at the Somme."

"So he and Rose might have served together after Rose left the Newfoundland Regiment."

"Lawrence Rivers also told me about an incident at Ville Ste-Lucille."

"I'm familiar with the engagement. But I didn't know there was an 'incident' at Ville Ste-Lucille."

"Rivers said that at the end of the day, after reinforcements had arrived to relieve them, Rose shot and killed two Germans who were trying to surrender."

"I hadn't heard about that," Butcher said.

Stride went through his notes, point by point. When he was done, Butcher sat back in his chair and closed his eyes. It was a minute before he spoke.

"That's disturbing, but it might have been a case of exhaustion, a temporary loss of control on Rose's part. When I was over there, I heard of cases of summary execution of Germans who'd surrendered, or were about to. And, obviously, their side did the same. Sometimes it was a matter of the heat of battle being carried beyond the end of the engagement, and the inability of some of the men involved to turn it off, if you will. And you have to remember that Harry Rose killed as many as thirty men that day at Ville Ste-Lucille. Try and imagine having killed thirty men at relatively close range, over the space of four hours."

"It was what he had to do, to protect himself and his men. And it was what he was trained for."

"All of that's true. But it also runs counter to what most men are willing or able to do, no matter how well they're trained, or how strong their motivation." Butcher opened his cigarette case, extracted a cigarette and tapped it against the side of the case. "There's some work going on right now, mainly in the States, looking at the performance of soldiers in the recent war. Some of the information I've seen indicates that only a minority were willing to fire their weapons at the enemy, even when their own lives were at risk."

"A minority?"

"The figure I've heard is 15 to 20 percent. I don't know that the figures are accurate, and it's possible they won't stand up to scrutiny over time. But they are in accord with some of what I observed in the Great War. And, if true, it goes against what we're led to believe. It's very possible that in many men, perhaps in most, there's an aversion to taking another man's life, no matter what the situation."

"But some men do kill, and with … I'm looking for a word."

"Facility," Butcher said. "Yes, some do seem very capable in that department. Some men even like it."

"Jack Corrigan suggested something like that, from his experience in Gallipoli. One of the Turks Rose killed on that patrol was at much closer range than the Germans at Ville Ste-Lucille. Face to face, almost."

"Then it's possible that Harry Rose did find it easier to kill than most men. I really can't comment. I didn't know him well enough, or know enough about him, to form an opinion." Butcher finally lit the cigarette he was holding. "What Corrigan told you about Rose and the patrol in Gallipoli suggests a man who was brave in battle, but who was also sensitive to the feelings of the men under his command. I'm thinking of the incident with Rowe's body."

"I think I'd agree with that," Stride said.

"But his killing of the two Germans at Ville Ste-Lucille does seem very different. We can speculate that the action there pushed him past his breaking point, and might even have set him on the road to some kind of breakdown. But we don't know that, and even assuming that is the case, where can you go with this? In terms of the investigation, I mean? Does it really get you anywhere?"

"I don't know. There might have been similar incidents after that. Maybe worse ones."

"And you're suggesting that if even more erratic behaviour followed, he might have made poor command decisions later on, and those decisions might be linked to his murder by some second or third party the decisions affected?"

"Something like that," Stride said. "And now we have this Robert Benton. Even if he is Irish, I suppose it's possible he fought under Rose at some point, after he left the Newfoundland Regiment. His being involved only reinforces my feeling that Rose's murder has something to do with the war."

"I understand that. So, hold on to the feeling, Eric, but take care that it doesn't hijack your investigation."

"I'll hope I'm not wandering off in the wrong direction."

"I think the murder of a complex man requires a complex approach." Butcher smiled. "Was that vague enough?"

"Just about."

"What you need, obviously, is more information on Rose's war record, especially after the incident at Ville Ste-Lucille. You've contacted the War Department in London?"

"Yes, but we haven't had anything back from them yet. And there's someone else I'm interested in. Cecil Cake. Has either Dancey or Rivers ever mentioned him to you?"

"The name's familiar. Remind me who he is."

"He was a close friend of Rivers's during the war. They enlisted together in 1914, and they were over there together for most of it."

"Didn't he have a brother who was also in the Regiment, and who was killed?"

"Yes, at Gueudecourt. His name was Daniel."

"That connects the dots for me. Yes, I remember the name. Rivers mentioned him to me once or twice. Why are you asking about him?"

"Cake himself was wounded at Gueudecourt, a serious head injury."

"And you're wondering if the injury left him with some kind of a deficit, perhaps even mentally unbalanced?"

"Not a very original thought, is it?"

"No, but it's also not something you'd want to disregard totally. Where's Cake living now?"

"He's here in St. John's."

"Have you interviewed him?"

"Not yet, no."

"I sense some reluctance, Eric, and I can understand that. Cake's had a history of instability since his head wound. Your comments have made that clear enough. And it's possible he might react badly to an interview."

"But that isn't reason enough not to interview him, is it?"

"You've answered your own question. Interviewing Cake might be intrusive, and along the lines of a fishing expedition, but it's a necessary part of the process." Butcher smiled. "As if I needed to tell you that."

"I will get to it, and sooner rather than later." He stood up. "I have to get on back to the Fort. And I know you have things to do as well."

"Yes, I do." Butcher said. He walked with Stride into the hallway. "This woman that you told me Rose was involved with. I take it you're satisfied that her husband had nothing to do with the murder?"

"He didn't. Drodge was in Harbour Grace, on the other side of Conception Bay, when Rose was shot. Noseworthy talked to the client he'd gone to see, and we have confirmation."

"It helps, though, that Mrs. Drodge was able to confirm that Rose probably was armed when he went out Monday night."

"Yes, it does," Stride said. "But the question remains why."

CHAPTER 23

Y ou had a call while you were out, Inspector." Constable Dickson handed
Stride a phone message when he arrived back at Fort Townshend. It was
twenty past five. "A Mrs. Darnell called from the Newfoundland Hotel
about ten minutes ago, asking for the officer in charge of the Harrison Rose case.
I rang you at the General, but Dr. Butcher said you'd left already."

"That would be Catherine Darnell," Stride said. "She's Harrison Rose's
daughter."

"I knew the name sounded familiar, sir, but I didn't make the connection.
And she didn't say who she was."

"We were expecting her here sometime soon." He looked at the note, then
folded the paper and put it in his shirt pocket. "Is Harry here?"

"No, sir. He went out twenty minutes ago. He said he was going to talk to
some people whose names he got from John Smith."

"I'll probably be going out again myself in a couple of minutes, to talk to
Mrs. Darnell. If Harry's not back by then, tell him I'll catch up with him later."

Catherine Darnell walked to the window and pulled back the curtain. Her room
gave her a good view of the harbour and Signal Hill. She stood there for a minute,
looking through the water-streaked glass at the rain that seemed to sweep down
from the Southside Hills to engulf the city, and at the slow late-afternoon crawl of
traffic on the streets below. Harrison Rose had told his daughter that the weather
in Newfoundland was often inclement, a description she now thought was too
diplomatic by half. But she'd lived much of her life in London, and she was used
to bad weather. In fact, she rather liked the rain, taking pleasure in the anonymity
it layered on people and things.

She sat in one of the two armchairs the room provided and thought about the hours and days ahead. She was tired from her trip and really wanted nothing more now than to be alone. She wasn't looking forward to dealing with the funeral rituals that she would have to organize. She especially didn't relish playing the role of grieving daughter, making polite conversation with people she didn't know.

Not that she wasn't upset, even saddened, about what had happened. The sadness had surprised her a little, though. When the news of her father's death was delivered to her in the taxi, the driver staring at her over the back of his seat, his own features wreathed in something like grief, she almost burst into tears, the unfamiliar emotion sweeping over her without warning. What had surprised her most was the first thought that assailed her when he gave her the news. It wasn't grief for having lost her father. The sadness came because she realized then, with a sense of terrible finality, that now she would never have one.

She took her cigarettes and lighter from her handbag. She wanted a drink to go with the cigarette. She'd brought a bottle of gin with her from Boston, but it was in her large suitcase, wrapped in layers of lingerie to deflect the attentions of customs agents. And just now she lacked the energy to dig it out.

She smoked her cigarette and tried to empty her mind of everything related to her father and the manner of his death. She knew she'd hear from the police in due course, probably sooner rather than later. She'd phoned them—and how very colonial that the headquarters should be a called a fort—and asked that the officer in charge of the investigation call her at the hotel.

She butted her half-smoked cigarette in the ashtray and thought about taking a bath, but she'd noticed that there was no phone in the bathroom, and dragging herself out of the tub to answer the expected call wasn't something she wanted to do.

Then the telephone rang.

"Mrs. Darnell?" It was a man's voice, vaguely accented, which gave her the impression that its owner had made an effort, was still making an effort, to hide his origins.

"This is Mrs. Darnell. Who is speaking, please?"

"My name is Eric Stride. I'm with the Constabulary."

"Yes, of course. I left a message there a little while ago. You're the officer in charge of the investigation?"

"Yes, I am. I need to meet with you, but if you've just got in, it might not be convenient to do that right now. If you like, we can meet later, when you're more settled. Even tomorrow would be all right."

"To be honest, I'd be just as happy to meet with you as soon as possible. All I know about things at the moment is what the taxi driver told me on the way in from the airport. He said my father had been shot. Did he get that right?"

"Yes, he did. And I'm sorry."

"We drove past my father's house. There was a policeman standing guard there. Is that really necessary? I thought my father was shot in the park nearby, not in the house."

"It's a routine precaution. We can't be certain that whoever killed your father might not break into the house at some point."

"I see."

"I'll need to ask you some questions about your father."

"I understand. Well, I'll do my best to answer them."

"Thank you. I appreciate that. I know this isn't easy for you. I'll come down to the hotel, whenever it's convenient for you."

"Can you give me a half hour to freshen up a little? With the weather delays, it was a much longer flight than I'd expected."

"Please take as long as you need."

"Thirty minutes will be fine. I'm in room 614."

"Yes, I know. The switchboard operator gave me your room number."

"They shouldn't do that," she said. "Give out hotel-room numbers, I mean. Some of the hotels in London and in the States have a policy of not doing that now."

"I think it's a good idea," Stride said. "But we always seem to lag a bit behind things here in St. John's."

"I suppose so. By the way, will you be alone, or will you have someone with you? For the interview, I mean?"

"I'll be alone."

"All right. Thirty minutes, then."

She sat on the bed and looked at the phone for a minute after she'd hung up, then went back to the table by the window, and took a ring of keys from her handbag. She unlocked her suitcases, picked up the largest one and placed it on the bed. She had a moment of unease as she opened it, worried that the bottle of gin might have broken during the flight. Most of her clothes were in there, and she could imagine the bother of having everything washed and cleaned, including the suitcase itself. But when she opened it there was no odour of gin, only the faint bouquet of lavender, a holdover from when her mother had last used the suitcase for a trip to France, years ago, before the war. She took out the bottle and peeled off the layers of lingerie, folding each item and placing it in the top drawer of the bureau.

She went into the bathroom and poured two ounces of gin into a glass, and added half that amount of water. She closed her eyes as the alcohol burned its way into her system. Then she went back into the bedroom and quickly emptied both suitcases, distributing the items between the bureau, the closet and the bathroom.

She opened a small bottle of scent, dabbed some onto the palm of her hand and applied it to her neck and behind her ears. The traces that remained on her palms she distributed over the backs of her hands and her wrists. It probably wouldn't completely hide the smell of gin, but it would help.

Stride took off his wet mackintosh in the hotel lobby and shook the rain from it. He started for the elevators, and then took a detour in the direction of the dining room when he saw someone he knew. After twenty-five years with the Constabulary, Sid Purchase had traded in his uniform, nightstick and handcuffs for a tailored black suit and a diffident table manner in the hotel's dining room.

It was convenient, and sometimes useful, having a former policeman working at the Newfoundland Hotel, the largest and busiest hotel in the city. Purchase had maintained his interest in police work, and from time to time he passed along bits of information to his former colleagues at Fort Townshend, about some of the people who stayed at the hotel, or who visited there.

"Is it business or pleasure today, Eric?" Purchase took a quick look over his shoulder into the dining room, and satisfied that his services weren't needed at that moment, moved a few paces away from the entrance.

"Harrison Rose's daughter has just checked into the hotel. She flew in today from Boston. Via Halifax."

"Long flight, I hear, with the weather delays."

"That seems to be the story."

"She was in Boston when her dad took the bullet in the head?"

"I think so."

"Rose was from England, so I heard. His daughter's English as well, or is she an American now?"

"As far as I know she's still English. We have a London address for her from her father's address book."

"And her name would be Rose?"

"No, it's Darnell," Stride said. "Catherine Darnell."

Purchase wrote the name in a notebook he'd taken from an inside pocket of his jacket.

"Is there a Mr. Darnell in the picture, or is the lady travelling solo?"

"If there's a Mr. Darnell, I haven't heard about him. At least not yet."

"Room number?"

"Six-fourteen," Stride said. Purchase wrote that down too.

"I'll keep my ears and eyes open, Eric. If anything at all presents itself, I'll let you know. Or Harry, if you're not around."

"I'll appreciate that, Sid."

"No trouble at all. I like to stay in touch with things. A fella like me can take just so much peace and quiet. Not that I'm complaining, you understand. This is about as good a situation as a retired copper could hope to have." He smoothed his lapels. "A nice suit, no outside work in bad weather and fine leftovers for supper. I'm even putting on weight."

"It looks good on you, Sid."

"I'll pretend to believe you. And I'll add that a big hotel can be a lively spot for a fella like me. I could write a book."

"Just make sure you change the names," Stride said.

"Bloody right." Purchase took a half-step back and glanced into the restaurant. "Duty calls, Eric. Some of the patrons are getting that anxious, feed-me look."

"I'll stand if that's all right with you," Catherine Darnell said. She leaned against the wall by the window looking out at the Narrows. "I've spent so much time sitting today, I'm almost paralyzed."

Stride took a chair by the table and opened his notebook. Catherine Darnell didn't look very much like her late father. She was taller than Harrison Rose by a good four inches, and where Rose's hair and colouring were fair, almost Nordic, his daughter was a brunette. Her complexion was darker than he'd expected, even taking the time of year into consideration. He guessed that she took after her mother. He also noticed that she wasn't wearing a wedding ring, no rings at all, in fact.

"My visit here was planned for a while," she said. "After I visited with my friends in the Boston area."

"We knew that, actually. We found the letter you wrote to your father about your travel plans."

"Really?" She seemed surprised. "Well, I suppose that's the sort of thing that happens in a situation like this. Almost nothing's private any longer. Can I have it back? The letter?"

"Yes, but we'll have to wait until our investigation is concluded."

"That almost suggests that I'm on your list of suspects," she said. "Am I?"

"We don't actually have a list of suspects."

"And that doesn't actually answer my question. Do you think I had something to do with my father's death?"

"Did you?"

There was a moment of silence between them, and then she laughed.

"I suppose I asked for that. Please forgive my reaction. This isn't an easy situation for me."

"I understand. And I meant it when I said we don't have a list of suspects."

"That doesn't sound very encouraging. From my point of view, I mean. But I'll stop being silly now, and let you get on with it."

"I was about to ask if you've been here before. In St. John's?"

"Once, a long time ago," she said.

"Before the war."

"In 1936, just after the Prince of Wales gave up the throne for Mrs. Simpson, 'the woman he loved.' It was all so dramatic. My father had been living here in Newfoundland for some time by then."

"Since 1930?"

"Yes. After he moved here, he rented a house for a few months until he had some renovations done to the place on Circular Road."

"You stayed with him on that visit? At the house on Circular?"

"For part of the time, yes. But it turned out that we didn't get along very well. That wasn't a great surprise to either of us. After two days of getting on each other's nerves, I decamped to a hotel."

"Here?"

"No, it was one of the smaller hotels. Devon something."

"Devon Manor."

"Yes, that's the name. And it was very nice. I think genteel is the word I would use to describe it. Are they still in business?"

"No, it's been sold. It's a private residence now."

"Very fortunate for someone."

"I think so," Stride said. "One of the things we're interested in is why your father moved here from England."

"I'm not surprised." She smiled as she looked through the window at the rain. It was sheeting down now and washing across the glass as though being sprayed from a high-pressure hose. "I'm sorry if that sounded harsh, I didn't mean it to. But even my Boston friends expressed some surprise at his choice."

"It's all right. We don't have any illusions about our climate. It can be a challenge."

"I'm sure it can also be very nice, sometimes."

"At least ten days in any given year," Stride said. "In fact, we've just come off a heat wave of sorts. Two weeks of hot, dry weather. This is the first rain we've had in a while."

"I'd actually heard that. But as to why my father moved here, I'm afraid I can't really enlighten you very much. You see, we were often out of touch, and that was a long-term thing. Family strife. Well, I've already alluded to that, haven't I? Daddy moved here during one of our glacial periods."

"I'm sorry."

"There's no need to be, but thank you for the sentiment."

"I take it your mother never lived here with him?"

"No, she didn't. My parents separated not long after the war. The First War, I mean. I should have mentioned that. They eventually divorced."

"You knew that your father served with the Newfoundland Regiment for a time during the war?"

"Yes, I knew that. I'd always supposed that was one of the reasons he moved here."

"One of the things we don't know about your father is what he did after the war. Can you help us with that?"

"It isn't a great secret," she said. "Although I'm not sure he would have talked about it very much afterwards. He was in Ireland."

"During the Troubles?"

"Yes."

"With the army?"

"Not exactly. He was with the Auxiliaries. They were a division of the RIC, the Royal Irish Constabulary. Do you know anything about them?"

"Some." It took Stride a moment to register what she'd said, and to realize the possible implications for the investigation. The likelihood that Robert Benton was Irish. And the possibility that the IRA might be involved in Rose's murder. "The Auxiliaries didn't exactly cover themselves with glory in Ireland."

"That's an understatement, and then some. The Auxiliaries developed a reputation for extreme brutality. You've probably heard about some of their reprisal raids, against mostly innocent people."

"Yes, I have. The burning of the town of Cork was one."

"That was infamous. The Auxiliaries and the police set fire to the commercial centre of the town, and then they prevented the fire brigade from operating. They also shot innocent people in the street. The government, the British Government, I mean, claimed that the citizens of Cork themselves were responsible, but a commission of inquiry found that it was the Auxiliaries who'd started the fires."

"I knew about that," Stride said. "The British government tried to suppress the report, but it got out just the same."

"That's not to say there weren't some good men in the Auxiliaries. Some of them were fine and decent officers from the First War, and at least two of them wore the Victoria Cross. But there were a lot of bad men too, some of them, I've heard, no more than brutes. In the end, their commanding officer, General Crozier, resigned his position as head of the Auxiliaries because he could no longer support what was going on."

"General Crozier?"

"Yes. You know the name?"

"It came up earlier, but I didn't know the context until now. What was your father's part in all that? Do you know anything about his time there?"

"You mean, do I know if he was one of the bad men?"

"Or one of the good ones. Do you know?"

"No, I don't. He never told me anything about it. I don't even know what his rank was. But he was there, and he was one of them. Just how much he'd taken part in was one of a number of things I wanted to talk with him about on this trip." She looked towards the window for a moment. "But now it won't happen, something else that won't ever be resolved. But I can tell you that the Ireland posting was a major reason for the breakdown of my parents' marriage. My mother was very much opposed to his going there."

"Why?"

"She just thought it was wrong. My mother was anything but a typical army wife. Too independent by half was the way she would have described herself."

"Would have? Your mother is dead?"

"Yes, she died three years ago. I should also mention that my husband is dead, too. He was killed in the war. He was a pilot, coastal patrol. Anyway, my mother was years ahead of her time, probably even by a generation. She was opposed to the whole idea of Empire, and she especially disliked British actions in Ireland. But Daddy went anyway, and his batman went with him, although he was with the army, not the Auxiliaries. His name was Basil Hawthorne. Has that name come up too?"

"No. But there's a picture of your father in his house, from Gallipoli, standing beside a soldier."

"I know that picture, and that was Basil. They were friends as well as being comrades in arms. Although I have to say, it was one of those peculiar English master-servant friendships."

"They parted company after their time in Ireland?"

"Basil is dead. He was killed in Dublin, murdered by the IRA, my father told me."

"I see." He made a note in his book. "You mentioned Empire. Was that why your father went to Ireland? To help protect British interests there?"

"I'm not sure why he went. I was very young then, just a small child."

"Do you know why he was with the Auxiliaries, rather than the army?"

"No, not really. I think it might have been because his regiment wasn't slated to go to Ireland."

"His batman went, though, and he was still in the army."

"I've wondered about that. He might have asked to be transferred there, because my father went. As I said, he and Basil were friends, after a fashion. But to answer your question, I don't know why Daddy joined the Auxiliaries. Perhaps because they were more involved in the fighting than the army was. My mother once told me that Daddy had a need for that sort of thing, to be close to the danger. I find it so hard to believe that anyone would really want that, but perhaps he did."

"Interesting." He couldn't think of anything else to say.

"Whatever his reasons for going, it pretty much wrecked what was left of the marriage. I have a memory of loud voices, and doors slamming. But in the end, he went off to Ireland, and my mother set up house in London for the two of us. There was family money—my mother's family, I mean. And that was fortunate, because it meant we could manage well without him."

"And that was the end of the marriage?"

"Almost. There was one attempt to reconcile, but it didn't work. He came to stay with us one time in the London flat, when I was about four, the year before I started school. But nothing important had changed. Nothing had been resolved. The doors kept slamming and the voices were just as loud."

"He was in Ireland, still?"

"Yes."

"You said your mother had family money. Did your father, as well?"

She shook her head.

"His family did once, generations ago, but he had no money to speak of. Well born, but almost penniless. I've sometimes wondered if that was one of the reasons he married my mother. An army officer wasn't paid a lot, and it was almost essential to have some family money to bolster the salary, especially at the more senior levels. The social obligations of an officer grew with his rank. Someone told me once that it actually cost money to be an officer back then. It might even be true."

"Do you know when your father left Ireland?"

"I know that the Auxiliaries were disbanded in 1922. I think he left about that time, but I'm not sure of the actual date."

"That leaves an eight-year gap between the time he left Ireland and his coming here to St. John's. Do you know what he was doing during that time?"

"I know he was in England for most of it. He moved around quite a lot. I have some letters and postcards he sent me. It was one of the things I wanted to talk about when we got together."

"Did you bring them with you? The letters and cards?"

"No. They're in a box in my flat in London." She looked at him. "Does what I've told you about my father's being in Ireland during the rebellion mean something? You seemed to have a reaction when I mentioned it."

"It might."

"You're thinking the IRA might have been involved in this? In my father's death? A revenge killing for what he did in Ireland years ago?"

"It's something we'll have to think about now. And the fact that a large number of Newfoundlanders have Irish ancestry, especially here in St. John's."

"Then, perhaps he was involved in some of the awful things the Auxiliaries were responsible for." She looked through the window for a moment. "I wonder if he would have talked to me about any of it. I didn't get a strong feeling that he would have. But no try, no succeed." She smiled. "That was a phrase my mother liked to use, although I'm not sure she tried very hard with her husband." She moved away from the window and went to the bureau and pulled the second drawer open. "I'm going to make myself a drink. I've already had one, and now I'm going to have another. Would you like one? I have only gin, and there's only water to mix it with."

"Not while I'm on duty," Stride said. "Another time, perhaps." And immediately wondered why he'd said that.

"Perhaps." She poured some gin into her glass and stepped into the bathroom to add water. "You probably know quite a lot about my father now, from your investigation. Can you tell me anything about his life here?" She looked at him over the top of her glass. "Was he alone? I know he lived alone, and that he seemed to prefer it that way. But did he have anyone? A companion?"

"Yes, he did. He was involved with a woman."

"Involved? That has an unpleasant sound to it."

"I didn't intend it that way. She's married, but separated from her husband."

"I see. And do you suspect him, the husband?"

"No. He was out of town when your father was killed."

"My father and the married woman. I wonder if I'll have an opportunity to meet her. Although, to be honest, I'm not sure that I want to." She looked at him. "Well, this will sound contradictory, I know, but what is her name? This woman?"

"Drodge. Barbara Drodge."

"I don't know why I asked that. But for some reason, I just needed to know." She went back to looking through the window again.

"Perhaps we should continue this another time, Mrs. Darnell, after you've had a chance to rest. You've had a long day."

"Yes, it has been a long day. My wheels are slipping off the rails a bit, and the gin isn't helping." She moved towards the door. "You can call me in the morning, if you like. I'm an early riser, up before seven, usually."

"It will be a little later than that, I think." He stood up and picked up his hat and coat. She walked with him to the door.

After Stride left, she carried her drink to the window and looked down at the street below. A few minutes later, he came out of the hotel and sprinted across Cavendish Square through the rain to the MG.

His owning an English sports car intrigued her. She thought there might be more to him than she would have expected in a policeman toiling away in a backwater of Britain's crumbling Empire. It also didn't hurt that he was an attractive man, tall and very fit. She continued watching until the little car pulled out of the parking area on Cavendish Square and moved south in the direction of Duckworth Street.

CHAPTER 24

Constable Jack Corrigan was standing in the doorway of a hardware store on Water Street, smoking a cigarette while he watched pedestrians and vehicles making their way through the continuing rain. The daily migration home from work had started. Smoking on duty was frowned upon by senior officers, but no one would see him, and anyway, Corrigan didn't care a lot about rules and regulations that had little to do with the actual job of policing. Just the same, he dropped the end of his cigarette on the sidewalk when he saw Stride's MG pull over to the curb across the street. He watched as Stride waited for a break in the traffic and then ran across the street and stepped into the doorway beside him.

"I need some information, Jack. About Cecil Cake."

With the new information Stride had on Harrison Rose, his reservations about interviewing Cake had evaporated.

"Cec? Has his name come up in connection with the case?"

"In a way, it has. You told me Cake was in Ireland after the war. I talked to Lawrence Rivers today, and he confirmed what you said. The thing is, Harrison Rose was in Ireland after the war too."

"Colonel Rose was in Ireland?" Corrigan looked surprised. "I didn't know that. His outfit was transferred there, I suppose, to deal with the rebellion?"

"No, it wasn't, but Rose was involved with the rebellion, all right. He was in Ireland with the Auxiliaries."

"You're sure about that?"

"Yes. I've just come from talking with his daughter."

"The Colonel was with the Auxies? I sure as Christ didn't know that, sir. I couldn't even have imagined it. And are you saying that Cec was a part of that whole business too?"

"I don't know if he was or not. But the coincidence has caught my attention."

"Assuming it is just coincidence," Corrigan said.

"Well, that's the question, isn't it?"

"The story I got from Rivers was that Cec was tending sheep while he was in Ireland," Corrigan said. "He was off up in the hills someplace, miles from anywhere. Well, I already told you that."

"We can hope that was what he was doing there."

"Hope's like the spring ice, sir. It don't always hold a lot of weight." Corrigan looked past Stride out into the street. "Cec is the only one who can tell you what he was doing in Ireland, so you better go ask him. That's assuming he'll want to talk to you about it. For what it's worth, he lives on Eric Street. I suppose you know where that is?"

"In the west end, off Leslie."

"If you can find him at all, sir, that's where he'll be." Corrigan took off his cap and rubbed the back of his neck. He turned away and looked down the street at the slowly moving traffic.

"Is there something else I need to know about Cake before I go out there, Jack?"

"You should be careful, that's all. Keep in mind that Cec was a soldier in the war, and he's still tough as nails. And don't expect too much of him. He's been through a lot, and I don't know that he'll even want to talk to you."

"I'll be as careful as I need to be," Stride said. The two men looked evenly at each other for a long moment, and then Stride stepped out of the doorway and ran back across the street to the MG.

Corrigan watched as the little car pulled away from the curb and joined the stream of traffic heading west. He continued to watch until it disappeared from view.

Eric Street ran in a rough east-west direction between Leslie and Shaw Streets, a block south of Hamilton Avenue. The street's name had intrigued Stride since the first time he'd heard of it. He'd promised himself a dozen times that he would find out where the name came from, but so far he hadn't done that.

Cake's house faced south and his front door opened off a landing that was nine steps up from the street. Stride rang the doorbell three times but there was no answer. Then he heard a voice from the house next door. A short, stout woman with a patterned yellow bandana tied around her head was standing in her front doorway smoking a cigarette.

"He might be out in his backyard," she said. "With his birds. It's where he was a half hour ago."

"Mr. Cake keeps hens?"

"It's pigeons he keeps, and he's even built a house for them. He feeds them, too, so he always has a flock around him. I don't know what he sees in pigeons, I don't. Dirty beasts, if you want my opinion, but they seems to make him happy, the poor man, and that's the main thing. He don't seem to have much else in his life." She tapped ash from the end of her cigarette and looked Stride up and down. "Are you a friend of his? I don't believe I seen you here before."

"No, I'm not a friend of his, but I need to talk to him for a few minutes."

"You're not a salesman, are you?" She stole a look at the MG parked on the street. "Mr. Cake don't give much slack to salesmen. He chased one out of his yard with a shovel last year, and we never saw that fella around here ever again. He's probably still running."

"No, I'm not a salesman."

"You might be all right, then. But you might find he's not the most talkative man in the world, Mr. Cake. And when he does talk, he sometimes don't make a lot of sense, poor man." She tapped the side of her head. "He was in the war, you know, and he wasn't all in one piece when he come back home."

"When was that, when he came home from the war?"

The woman gave him a closer look, his question making her immediately cautious. Stride didn't want to tell her he was a policeman, but he thought she already suspected something like that.

"You'd best ask Mr. Cake when he come home from the war, sir. That's his business, not mine."

And not yours either, was the unspoken trailer.

"He's out in the backyard?"

"That's where he was last time I looked. If he hasn't gone out wandering, that's where he'll be."

"Wandering?"

"Mr. Cake has got the wanders. That's what we calls it where I grew up. He goes out walking, for hours sometimes, night and day, rain or shine, it don't matter."

"Where does he go when he goes out walking? Do you know?"

"I haven't got the faintest idea," the woman said. "That's Mr. Cake's business, too."

With the same unspoken trailer applied.

She took a final drag on her cigarette and threw the butt over the railing. Then, with one more look at Stride and the MG, she went back inside her house and closed the door behind her.

Stride went down the steps to the street, then walked up a narrow laneway to a gate that opened into Cake's backyard.

Cecil Cake's pigeon house was halfway to the fence at the back of his yard. It was six storeys tall and ten feet wide, and the structure was haphazard and uneven. Stride imagined it had probably been added to over the years, as word spread through the feathered community that free room and board could be had behind the green clapboard house on the north side of Eric Street. A covered galvanized pail sat on the ground at one end of the pigeon house, and there were feeding pans nailed at intervals along its length, at three different levels.

Stride wasn't sure if the pigeons were wild or tame, somewhere in between, or both. A dozen bluish purple birds sat on the roof, chattering in a broken chorus. Discussing the persistent bad weather, perhaps, although at the moment, and for a change, it wasn't raining at all.

He stood by the gate and looked around the property. Cecil Cake was nowhere in sight. There was a porch attached to the rear of Cake's house. Stride guessed it had been added on after the main part of the house was completed, an afterthought perhaps, neither the design nor the clapboarding a match for the rest of the place. The yard was nondescript. There was no lawn to speak of, but lawns weren't often an important item for homeowners in St. John's, especially not in this part of the city, where just making do was the main goal. Patches of rough grass competed for living space on the uneven ground with dandelions, plantains and a multitude of other weeds.

He walked over to the pigeon house and looked at the feeding pans. Each pan held a generous quantity of seeds. He scooped up a handful from the nearest pan and allowed the seeds, oats for the most part, to run through his fingers. The seeds were almost dry, and that told him that Cake had been there recently to replenish the supply. A few pigeons waddled across the roof of the pigeon house to the edge closest to him, button-eyes bright, small heads bobbing. He brushed the dust from the seeds off his hands and went to the back door.

The windowless inner door was closed and a screen door fronted that. He pulled at the metal handle but the door did not yield, and then he saw there was a hook-and-eye latch on the inside. Stride rapped on the wooden frame and got no response. He tried again, and again there was only silence. Either Cake had locked the back door and left earlier through the front, or he was still at home, refusing to respond. Corrigan had said Cake might not want to talk to him. Perhaps his not talking to people was the norm.

He stepped away from the door and looked up at the sky. More rain was in the offing and he could see that it might start in earnest any time. He didn't want to be caught in it. He looked towards the pigeon house. It seemed the pigeons were thinking the same thing. Most of the birds had retreated inside the structure. There was no point in him standing there any longer. He left the yard and closed the gate behind him.

He sat in the MG and smoked a cigarette. He wondered how Cake had managed to pay for his house, assuming he actually owned it. Corrigan had told him that Cake came from a fishing family on the south coast. "Poor as field mice" was the way he described them. But that had been a long time ago, more than thirty years now. Just what Cake might have been doing since the war, apart from looking after a flock of sheep in Ireland, he knew nothing about.

He rolled the window down to let the smoke out and to prevent the windshield from being coated with condensation. He looked at Cake's front window, then turned his attention to the house next door. He saw that the woman he'd spoken with was watching him, although she was far enough back from the window that she was only dimly visible.

He looked at Cake's window again. A man was standing there now, looking down at him. A small man with reddish hair, wearing a workman's checked shirt with a green tie, and over that, what looked like a heavy wool sweater. There was something about him—a bearing, an attitude—that held Stride's attention. The two men looked at each other for a minute. Stride opened the door and stepped out of the car, but when he looked again, the man was no longer there. He stood in the street beside the MG and waited to see what would happen, if the man would come to the door of his house. But he didn't.

Stride thought about going back up the steps and ringing the bell, but he already knew that the effort would be pointless. It was more than obvious that Cake wasn't going to talk to him. It might take a court order to make that happen. The notion had little appeal for Stride, but if it came to that, he would do it. He waited another minute, looking up at the house. Then he got back into the MG, started the motor, and moved on down the street.

CHAPTER 25

When Stride got back to Fort Townshend, Constable Dickson intercepted him for the second time that day.

"Constable Noseworthy left you a message, sir."

"He's gone for the day?"

"About ten minutes ago. He wanted you to know he's sent a telegram off to London asking for information on Benton. He said he thought the passport he found in Benton's luggage was genuine, but he wasn't sure about that."

"If past history is anything to go by, it will take at least a couple of days to get any kind of reply, and maybe nothing useful even then. Do you know if Corrigan's still here?"

"He pulled out of here about ten minutes ago, sir. I expect he's halfway home by now."

"I'll catch him tomorrow. Is there anything else?"

"You have a visitor. Alex Greene. The reporter fella. He came in about twenty minutes ago. I told him I didn't know when you'd be back, but he said he'd wait around for a while."

Stride looked at his watch. It was just past six. This time of day could be tricky for Alex Greene. Cocktail hour came earlier for him than for most people, especially if the weather wasn't conducive to outside activity.

"He's sober?"

"As far as I can tell, sir. Unless he's found the bottle yourself and Sergeant Phelan keep in the back of the drawer in your desk."

"If he has, he's a dead man."

"I'll start an arrest report, just to be on the safe side."

"Do that. Is Harry back yet?"

"No, sir. And it's probably just as well that he isn't. Greene's not one of his favourites."

"If he calls back again, tell him I'll wait for him here." He started towards the office when Dickson spoke again.

"I just remembered. Tommy Kennedy was looking for you earlier, sir."

"Did he want something in particular?"

"He was just looking to see if you had anything for him to do, sir. I told him you were at the hotel, talking to Rose's daughter. I think he left right after that."

Stride found Alex Greene sitting in Phelan's chair, his feet resting on the edge of the desk. The one odd thing about that was the fact that he was wearing neither shoes nor socks.

"I know what you're thinking, Eric. Barefoot boy with too much bloody cheek."

"Something like that." He looked towards the window. A pair of argyle socks and two shoelaces were draped over the radiator. A pair of wet brown Oxfords was tucked underneath, the tongues hanging over the toes. "Got caught in the rain, did you?"

"That, and wading through puddles only slightly smaller than Windsor Lake." He looked at the rain sheeting across the window. "I can't remember when it's rained this hard, or this long."

"I hear that a lot these days," Stride said. "What's up, Alex? Are you looking for information on the case, or do you have something for me?"

"A bit of both, actually. Potential tit, for potential tat. How is it going, by the way? The investigation?"

"The way these things often go, except more so this time. A fog of information and circumstance."

"Well, perhaps I can add a little more to the general overcast," Greene said. "Did you know that Harrison Rose's house was vandalized two years ago?"

"I didn't know that. I had Crotty pull everything we had on Rose, and that amounted to nothing at all. Who gave you the information?"

"Persons who've had the odd run-in with your lot, and who therefore prefer to remain anonymous."

"Okay. When did it happen, and what was it all about?"

"The when was May 8, 1945."

"VE Day. The day the war in Europe ended."

"You'll remember there was a whole lot of celebrating going on in the old town that night, mobs of people out and about, bands playing, dancing in the streets, even a few shots fired into the air by make-believe warriors."

"And a hell of a lot of liquid joy going around," Stride said. "I remember it well. Some of us were assigned extra duty to keep things more or less under control. So, what happened, exactly?"

"Two gentlemen of Irish extraction got themselves properly lacquered, went on along to Circular Road, and threw a brick through Colonel Rose's living room window."

"You're sure about this?"

"I have the name of the fellow who repaired the damage. I went around to see him this morning, and he confirmed the story. One of the large panes in the front was broken, glass all over the place."

"What was it all about, Alex?" But even as he put the question, Stride thought he already knew the answer.

"Harrison Rose, it seems, had something of a dodgy career when he left the British Army after the First War. It appears that word eventually leaked out about what he'd been up to in the twenties. Which is another bit of information I have for you."

"I already know what he'd been up to. He was with the Auxiliaries in Ireland. The Auxiliary Division of the Royal Irish Constabulary. ADRIC, if you're partial to acronyms."

"You're a step ahead of me, then," Greene said.

"No, I think we're moving pretty much along parallel lines. We just have different perspectives, different sources."

"I like the way you've put that. Makes us seem like colleagues, almost."

"The right hand washes the left," Stride said. "I found out about Rose being in the Auxiliaries only an hour ago, from his daughter. She's just arrived in town."

"Did she already know about her father being killed, or was that something she learned after she got here?"

"She didn't know until she arrived. A helpful taxi driver gave her the news."

"Painful," Greene said. "Where's she staying? Not at Rose's house, I don't imagine."

"She's at the Newfoundland Hotel."

"Her name's Rose?"

"No, it's Catherine Darnell. But you'll keep that to yourself, and you'll leave her alone until I say it's all right to talk to her. She needs some time to sort things out."

"She was close to her father?"

"Not especially," Stride said. "And in a way that makes it harder for her. One of the reasons she came here was to try and mend fences. Her visit was planned a while ago. But let's get back to Harrison Rose and his time in Ireland. What have you heard?"

"Not much more than what I've told you. And I imagine you've already made the obvious leap in logic about his murder. His getting gunned down late at night in a public park, assassination-style."

"The IRA was the first thing that came to mind when I heard about the Auxiliaries. And there's something else now. We have another body."

"I'd heard there was something going on at a rooming house on Empire," Greene said. "That's where the body was?"

"Yes."

"How much can you tell me about it?"

"Almost nothing at this point. McCowan will make a statement later this evening, or tomorrow morning. We're still sorting through what we have."

"But you think the body is connected with the Rose murder?"

"More than likely."

Greene gave Stride a look.

"All right. He is connected with the Rose murder. He might even be the one who shot Rose. But you'll sit on that too. That's understood?"

"Understood," Greene said. "Your new client wouldn't happen to be Irish, would he?"

"Do you know something you're not telling me, Alex?"

"No, just making an educated guess."

"As it happens, your guess is right, he probably is Irish. But that's one of the things we haven't sorted out yet."

"Either way, it brings us back to the IRA," Greene said. "And while there's a certain logic there, I have to wonder about it."

"Why?"

"The IRA has a fierce reputation, Eric, but the organization isn't anything like what it was twenty-odd years ago."

"You know something about them?"

"More than a little. It's an ongoing interest of mine. I first got on to the IRA when I was at that rich-boys' boarding school in New Hampshire."

"Haleybury."

"One of the masters there was Anglo-Irish, and he'd been working on a history of the IRA since forever. He was something of a dodderer, and I don't think he ever published anything, but he knew a lot about them. He liked to talk about Ireland and the IRA when he had a glass of whisky inside him. That started my interest, and I've kept a file on them since then."

"The long and the short of it being?"

"Just as I said. That the IRA today really isn't what it used to be. It's not even a pale shadow of the crew that took on the British Empire back in the twenties. You probably don't know this, but it was only two years ago that Gerry Boland, Ireland's Justice Minister, declared the IRA to be dead and buried."

"You're right, I didn't know that," Stride said.

"We both know that politicians are almost never 100 percent right about anything except taxation and death, and even there they can make a balls of it. But Boland had it close enough to the truth at the time. Since he read the IRA their last rites, though, they've been reorganizing and rebuilding. And while they've a long way to go to be anything close to their former glory, the way they were in the days of Collins and de Valera, I think we'll see them come roaring back someday. As they see it, there are still hills to climb and scores to be settled."

"Would someone like Harrison Rose be a score they'd like to settle?"

"Because he was in the Auxiliaries?" Greene shrugged. "Maybe. The scene that got played out in Bannerman Park Monday night, that looked a lot like some of what went on in Ireland in the twenties."

"Go on."

"You've heard of Michael Collins, I suppose."

"Of course," Stride said.

"Then you know he was one of the leaders. Among other things, Collins was their organizational genius during the Troubles. And one of the things he did was set up an IRA assassination unit based in Dublin. He called it the 'Squad.' They were also known as Collins's Twelve Apostles, possibly because their speciality was arranging last suppers for selected individuals."

"But that was then, and this is now," Stride said. "Collins is long dead, and if the IRA's all but disappeared as a functional organization, where's the connection with what went on here Monday night?"

"I don't know. The IRA isn't what it used to be, but it's been around for a long time, and not just in Ireland. You probably don't know this either, but the name itself, Irish Republican Army, that was first used in the States, not Ireland. It was coined in the 1800s by a group who called themselves the Irish Republican Brotherhood. They were probably more Irish than the Irish themselves. And that's not unusual. Expatriates are often as not more nationalistic than the folks back home."

"I take your point, Alex. We could be looking at a homegrown IRA man."

"Or woman." Greene said. "We've had Catholics and Protestants beating the hell out of each other for generations here in Newfoundland, playing at fighting the ancient battles over and over again."

"But at least they've stopped trying to kill each other, and that's progress of a sort."

"Progress isn't a straight line," Greene said.

"I suppose not. That affair on VE Day. Who was involved?"

"No one of any real significance. What's important is the likelihood that someone here in St. John's knew about Rose and his background in the Auxiliaries. But for what it's worth, their names are Brendan Tobin and Tom Kelly."

"Brendan Tobin's dead." Harry Phelan was standing in the doorway. He nodded at Greene. "I was there on Beck's Wharf the night they fished him out of the harbour last year. He drank himself stupid one time too often and fell in when there was no one there to pull him back out." He came into the office and leaned against the side of Stride's desk. "And there must be a half-dozen Tom Kellys living in St. John's."

"There probably are," Greene said, "but the Tom Kelly we're interested in has been living on the west coast of the island for the past year. Rumour has it that Tobin's death sobered him up, and he went looking for an honest job. And found one. So he's out of the picture."

"And we're interested in Tobin and Kelly, because?"

"Have a seat, Harry," Stride said. "We've got some new information on Harrison Rose."

"The bloody Auxiliaries," Phelan said, when Stride had brought him up to date. "My old man's Irish, from the old country, and I grew up listening to him and his friends trade stories about the IRA, the Auxies, the Tans and the bloody British. Or trying not to listen."

"A lot of us are tired of it," Greene said. "I know we can't completely rule out the possibility that Rose's murder was a revenge killing. But the fact is that Harrison Rose was just one of two thousand Auxiliaries, and he was twenty-five years and three thousand miles removed from the situation in Ireland in the twenties."

"All of that's true," Phelan said. "And, anyway, there's a much more inviting IRA target living here in the city."

"You've stolen my thunder," Greene said.

"Feel free anytime to tell me what the hell the two of you are talking about," Stride said.

"Do you know the name Hugh Tudor, Eric?"

"Yes. Tudor was the head of the Royal Irish Constabulary during the Troubles. Not a very popular man in Ireland, then or now. Are you telling me Tudor's living here in St. John's?"

"I'm not surprised you didn't know that," Greene said. "Tudor keeps a very low profile. But he's lived in Newfoundland since the mid-twenties. And to say that he's an interesting character would be an understatement. He was one of the more effective British generals in the First War, and he's been a great friend of Churchill's for about as long. After the 1921 agreement between the British and the IRA that finally ended the rebellion, Tudor moved on to Palestine, where he had a position similar to the one he had in Dublin. Director of public safety, or some such title. He was there until 1924, and after that he moved here."

"To St. John's?"

"Not right away. At first he was in Bonavista, working in the fish business. It was after that he moved here to the city. He's living on your street, in fact, in the home of the man he worked for in Bonavista, George Barr. You've probably seen him walking in your neighbourhood, Eric. You just didn't know who he was."

"You knew he was here, Harry?"

"My old man told me about him, years ago, but I parked that information. It didn't really mean anything to me, or more likely, I didn't want it to mean anything."

"Along the same lines as not wanting to hear stories about the IRA and the Troubles."

"Something like that."

"All right, try this on for size," Stride said. "Is it possible that Rose was killed by mistake? That the real target was Tudor?"

"That hadn't occurred to me," Greene said. "It doesn't seem likely, though. Tudor's in his mid-seventies, now, and that makes him about twenty years older than Rose."

"But it's possible Tudor knew Rose from his time in Ireland. He might even have some information on him that would be useful to the investigation."

"You could ask him, although he might not want to talk to you. I wanted to interview him two years ago, the same time I tried to interview Rose, but he refused. He even threatened me with legal action if I used his name in a story."

"If we decide to interview Tudor, he won't be able to refuse to talk to us, not in a murder investigation."

"That's true," Greene said. "But you should probably talk to McCowan first, don't you think? As a matter of protocol?"

"I suppose McCowan knows he's living here?"

"He probably does. He and Tudor would move in some of the same circles. To the extent that Tudor moves about at all."

"What do you think, Harry? Are you up for an interview with a retired General?"

"I'm up for it, sir. If nothing else, it will make a great story to tell to my old man and his friends someday. But Alex might be right. Perhaps we should talk to McCowan first?"

"If we do, he might say no. And I'm not in the mood for being turned down."

The telephone rang then, and Stride picked it up. It was Dianne. He nodded at Greene and Phelan and walked the phone to a corner of the office.

"I was expecting to hear from you, today," Dianne said. "And I haven't."

"I'm sorry, but it's been a busy day."

"I know you're busy, Eric, but I wish you'd at least called."

"I should have done that. I am sorry. Did something happen after we talked last night?"

"Marty and I had another go-round after he came home."

"It was bad?"

"Bad enough," Dianne said. "We need to talk, you and I. I've lived with this situation for about as long as I can stand it. Being in limbo isn't any fun. When can we get together?"

"I'm not sure. I'm going to be tied up here for a while yet, and then I have something else I have to do. That Harry and I have to do." Spreading the blame around. "When will you have some free time?"

"Meaning, is Marty going to be out of town sometime soon? The answer is yes. He's leaving this evening for two days on the west coast. Harmon Field, Stephenville."

"So, I can call you at home tonight?"

"You can call me at home. When you're able. And I'm not being snarky. I know you're really busy."

"Yes, I am. Really."

"Can you tell me how it's going?"

"Other than that it's become even more complicated; not really, no."

"I'll let you go, then. You will call me when you get a chance? Promise?"

"I promise. This evening."

He hung up the phone and for a moment he stared through the window at the rain. Greene and Phelan were pointedly not looking at him. He placed the phone back on his desk.

"Where were we?"

"General Hugh Tudor," Phelan said.

"You're sure you want to be part of this interview, Harry? We might catch hell from McCowan later."

"I wouldn't miss it, sir. A bit of hell is good for the system. That's what Kit says."

Stride turned his attention back to Greene.

"You understand that nothing that we've just talked about leaves this office, Alex?"

"As well as I've ever understood anything," Greene said. "But you will give me an update sometime?"

"I will."

Greene took one of his socks off the radiator, pulled it on, and reached for the second one. "I expect the shoes are still wet, but what the hell. I have to meet someone in about twenty minutes, and I don't want to be late."

"Another party to go to?"

"It might turn out to be that. It often does." Greene laced up his shoes, stood up, and performed a shuffling dance step. He looked at Stride. "Do you think Fred and Ginger would be impressed?"

"I've seen worse."

"I'll take that as a compliment," he said.

"I take it that was John Smith we saw down on Harvey's Wharf?" Stride said when Greene had gone.

"That was him. He didn't have anything to do with Rose's murder, and he didn't know that Rose was one of the men he and his friends jumped in the park last spring. He gave me the names of a couple of people to vouch for his whereabouts Monday night."

"And you've talked to them?"

"That where I was just now. He's definitely not involved. He did tell me one thing about Rose that was interesting, though. It seems that Rose was the one who did most of the damage that night in the park. Smith told me that Wilson had to hold Rose back after the two of them got the upper hand. He said he thought that Rose probably would have killed all three of them if Wilson hadn't taken hold of him."

"Taken hold of him?"

"Wrapped his arms around him, Smith said. And I believed him. That was probably the worst night of Smith's life. He wasn't making it up."

"That's interesting," Stride said. "And it more or less fits with something that Lawrence Rivers told me about Rose."

"Murdering German prisoners," Phelan said, when Stride was finished. "So maybe Rose did something of the same while he was in Ireland. And if he did, this could be a revenge killing. We might not have been as far off the mark as we thought. We just had the wrong war."

"There's someone else we're interested in," Stride said. "Someone who served with Rose in the Great War. Cecil Cake."

"I've heard the name. Isn't he the odd sock who lives in the west end, and keeps a herd of pigeons in his backyard?"

"That's Cake. How did you hear about him? Did I bring him up already?"

"No, you didn't. But one of Kit's uncles knows him. Or knew him from back then. He says Cake's gone around the twist, or nearly. Harmless enough, he said, but who can say for sure? Have you talked to him?"

"I tried to. I went to his house, but he wouldn't answer his door."

"You're sure he was home?"

"I saw him standing in his living room," Stride said. "And he knew that I saw him there."

"That's interesting by itself. Maybe Kit's uncle was right about him. But do we really need to talk to him?"

"I think so. He was in Ireland when Rose was there. What I don't know is if they were in contact then."

"It might be worth finding out," Phelan said.

"I think so." Stride stood up and stretched, then took his coat and hat off the rack. "One thing at a time, though. Let's go and see if General Tudor has anything to tell us about Harrison Rose."

"Should we phone ahead, maybe?" Phelan looked at his watch. "It's almost seven, he might be eating supper."

"No, let's surprise him. If he isn't expecting us, he won't have time to make up stories."

CHAPTER 26

The house on Circular Road where Hugh Tudor lived was at the opposite end of the street from Stride's, but the two houses were so similar in appearance that he wondered if they'd been designed and built by the same man. Stride had to wonder why someone like Tudor, with his background and singular personality, would be living as a guest in another man's house. Perhaps it had to do with money, a mostly distinguished military career bringing more in the nature of honours than financial reward. Or perhaps Tudor and Barr were close friends, as well as colleagues in business.

Stride rang the doorbell and they waited. It was almost a full minute later before the door was opened by a small man wearing a three-piece tweed suit and what looked like a regimental tie. He appeared to be in his mid-seventies. He looked at Stride and Phelan for a few moments without speaking.

"You're from the Constabulary, I think."

"Yes, we are," Stride said. He made the introductions. "You're General Tudor?"

"Yes, I'm Hugh Tudor." Tudor regarded them both for a moment longer and then stepped back, pulling the door open wide.

"I've been halfway expecting a call from you fellows." He closed the door behind them and pointed in the direction of the front room. "But I thought it would be your district inspector, Jack McCowan, who would call, if anyone did." Tudor gestured towards two matching armchairs on the far side of the room. "Does he know you've come to see me?"

"No, sir, he doesn't."

"No?" Tudor raised his eyebrows and the trace of a smile passed across his face. "I assume you're here about this business with Colonel Rose?"

"Yes, we are."

"Can I ask what you might expect me to tell you about him? I've met Colonel Rose on a number of occasions, but I didn't know him very well, in spite of our shared origins."

"We wanted to talk to you about him, sir, because it's recently come to our attention that you might have known him somewhat better twenty-five years ago."

"Go on."

"In Ireland," Stride said. "Dublin, to be specific."

"Thank you. I'm fond of specifics, Inspector Stride. Generalities tend to irritate me. My military rank notwithstanding." Again the fleeting half-smile. "May I ask how you came by that particular piece of information?"

"From a journalist friend who attempted to interview you a couple of years ago. Also from Colonel Rose's daughter. She's just arrived here in St. John's."

"I see. And your journalist friend, that would be Mr. Greene. I remember him. But he couldn't have told you very much about me, other than what's on the public record. In the event, I declined to do the interview he wanted. And before we start, Inspector, I want you to understand that I won't answer any questions I consider to be personally intrusive."

"I understand."

"Thank you. Please go ahead."

"You did know Colonel Rose when you were both in Ireland?"

"Yes, I did. Although you should know that Colonel Rose wasn't under my direct command during his time there. I expect you know that he was a member of the Auxiliaries, and while it's true that I established the Constabulary's Auxiliary Division, that group was under the command of Generals Crozier and Wood."

"General Crozier later resigned from the position, though."

"Yes, he did. We disagreed over certain policies, and I was sorry to accept his resignation. But, as that had nothing to do with Colonel Rose, I will say no more about it. It was a decision taken at a much higher level than that occupied by the Colonel."

"I understand, though, that General Crozier resigned because of actions taken by the Auxiliaries that eventually brought the organization into disrepute."

"There is controversy over some of the actions of the Auxiliaries, and they are well enough documented. There was even a commission of inquiry in Britain. I won't comment on any of it, except to say that, in my opinion, the controversy was political, rather than operational or strategic. And quite frankly, I don't care a hoop in hell about politics. I didn't back then, and I don't now. I was a soldier. I had duties to discharge, and I did that. On the whole, I received the full backing of the government of the day. If you're interested in the politics of that business in

Ireland, you're speaking to the wrong man." Tudor turned away from Stride and Phelan and looked towards the window. After a long moment he turned back. "We've strayed off the topic, and away from the purpose of your visit, Inspector. You came here to ask me about Colonel Rose, I assume with the aim of furthering your investigation into his death. Let's please return to that."

"Are you familiar with the manner in which Colonel Rose was killed?"

"Not with the details, no, because they have not, to my knowledge, been released. What I know is that he was shot near here, in Bannerman Park, while he was out for his evening constitutional."

"We think Colonel Rose was probably assassinated, sir, and the method of his assassination is similar to killings carried out in Ireland by the Irish Republican Army during the rebellion."

"I see." Tudor's expression changed slightly, and once more he looked towards the window. "Do you have any evidence that the IRA was in fact involved, or is that only speculation?"

"Intelligent speculation," Stride said.

"We all of us like to believe our speculations are intelligent, Inspector. That's human nature. But do you have any hard evidence?"

"Not yet." Stride considered telling Tudor about finding Benton's body, but decided not to. "But we have to consider the possibility that the IRA, or someone with IRA sympathies, might have been involved in Colonel Rose's murder." Stride gave Tudor an even look. "I think there's a certain amount of wisdom in that approach."

"Possibly. Is there a message for me in what you've just said?"

"I'll let you decide that for yourself, General. I'll suggest, though, that if Colonel Rose *was* killed because of something he did in Ireland while he was with the Auxiliaries, you might be in danger as well. Your presence in St. John's isn't general knowledge, but some people do know that you're living here."

"And some of those people will be sympathetic to the goals and tactics of the IRA. As it used to be." This time, Tudor's smile was more open, and it had a quality of quiet resignation. "Inspector, I've lived for more than twenty-five years in the knowledge that someone from the IRA, or someone with IRA sympathies, might come looking for me. But if you know anything about me and my career in the army, you'll also know that I've lived with the possibility of imminent and violent death for a large part of my adult life. I've had a number of close calls, and the scars to prove it. If one takes up the trade of soldiering as a profession in a violent world, one accepts that, or one does something else to earn his daily bread."

"But one also wants to avoid a violent death, if possible."

"I have every intention of doing that. If I can. But, to go back to the purpose of your visit, do you have more questions for me about Colonel Rose?"

"Can you give us any information about him, specifically, from his time in Ireland?"

"Not very much, I'm afraid. As I said, he wasn't under my direct command. General Crozier, or General Wood, might have more information, but neither is available to you for questioning. That having been said, though, I do recall one conversation I had with Frank Crozier about Harry Rose."

"Yes?"

"I'll preface my recollection by saying that Ireland was a very rough situation for everyone there, British and Irish alike. Whatever you might think of the record of the Auxiliaries, you have to remember they were fighting a guerrilla war against a determined, and often ruthless enemy. Ambushes were common, and on both sides. The incident I will relate now had to do with a patrol that Colonel Rose was on with a group of his men, some half-dozen of them, I believe. They were ambushed on their way back to headquarters one evening, and only two of them survived, Colonel Rose and another officer, whose name was Knowles. General Crozier told me it was a minor miracle that any of them came out of it alive. It was obviously a very well-planned and well-organized operation."

"I see," Stride said. "Is there anything else?"

"Not that I can think of." Tudor leaned towards Stride and Phelan, and spoke again. "You know, some of those IRA men we fought during the rebellion? We'd trained them in the British Army, for service in the Great War and other conflicts."

"I understand that General Crozier commanded a battalion of the Royal Irish Rifles at the Somme."

"Yes, he did, and with distinction. And there's a lesson there for anyone who has the wisdom to pay attention. Today's ally is potentially tomorrow's enemy. It's been that way through all of history, and no doubt will continue. Which is something the British government is now finding out. The more things change, the more they remain the same." Tudor turned his attention to Phelan. "I take it your family is Irish, Sergeant Phelan? From your name?"

"My parents were born in Ireland, sir. But they've lived here for a long time."

"You were born here, then?"

"Yes, I was."

"And do you consider yourself an Irishman, just the same?"

"Not as much as some," Phelan said. "I've listened to the stories that my father's told me, and friends of his, but for the most part, I prefer to live in the present, not the past."

"I'm pleased to hear it. The line between proud heritage and unwieldy burden can be a fine one." Tudor stood up then, signalling an end to the interview. "I hope this has been of some use to you, Inspector."

"It has, General. Thank you."

The three men moved towards the door together.

"And you say Jack McCowan doesn't know that you've come to talk to me?"

"No, he doesn't."

"You're not strict adherents to protocol, then."

"Only when it's convenient, General."

"Protocol has its merits," Tudor said. "It can be an anchor, but sometimes only a dead weight."

He smiled again, and opened the front door.

CHAPTER 27

S tride hadn't seen her cry before, and her tears unnerved him. He didn't know what to say; he never did in situations like this. Dianne turned her face away from him as soon as the tears started to flow, and he knew that had more to do with her own sense of privacy than anything else. He also knew that she was angry about the tears, not at him necessarily, but more because she was angry about anything that suggested she wasn't in control, that she was vulnerable.

Stride had phoned Dianne after he returned home from the visit with General Tudor. Dianne's husband, Marty Borg, had already left on his flight to Harmon Field on the west coast of the island. Stride's call had caught Dianne stepping out of the bath, and she'd told him it would be a half hour before she could make it to his place. The delay gave him some small relief. Things coming to a head with Dianne in the middle of a murder investigation was the worst kind of timing. But it was a bed he'd made for himself, and if it wasn't comfortable for him to lie in, he couldn't shift the blame to anyone else.

They sat quietly for long minutes in his living room, not quite together and not exactly apart, each too aware of the other's presence in the room. He desperately wanted a cigarette, but he didn't light one. He was afraid she would see it as an indication that he was detached from the situation, impatient even.

And then it was over, almost as quickly as it had started, or appeared to be. Dianne pulled a handkerchief from the sleeve of her blouse and blew her nose. She thumbed the last of the tears from the corners of her eyes, and turned back to face him. He was relieved to see that she didn't seem to be angry.

"Well, that's done," she said. "It's been coming on for two days now. I can't cry at the office, for obvious reasons. And, anyway, if I do, Bertie Prim would become very upset. I did once, last year, and there was just me and Bertie in the room. I think the poor man almost had a coronary. He seemed to take it personally, and blamed himself because he was there. And of course, it had nothing to do with him. It didn't have anything to do with you, either, because you weren't in the picture then." She dabbed at her cheeks again with the handkerchief, removing the last evidence of her tears. "And I can't cry at home because, well, I don't want to, not there, not any more." She crumpled the damp handkerchief and pushed it back into her sleeve. "So I saved it all for you."

"Well, that's fair enough, I suppose."

And right away she let him know it wasn't the right thing to say.

"God, Eric, please don't play the martyr. That only makes it worse. I suppose it is as much your fault as it is mine, if it's anyone's fault. But you don't have to say it."

"Actually, I thought it did need to be said. I am involved in this affair."

The words came out with more flavour than he'd intended. And that had the unexpected effect of making her smile.

"Well, good for you. You drive me mad when you do your Christ-on-the-cross routine, or go silent on me. I like this better." She leaned against him, resting her head on his shoulder. "But I don't much like the word *affair*." She turned her head and looked up at him. "Is that what this is? An affair?"

"That's the kind of question I might try and answer if you held a gun under my chin."

"And probably not even then." She moved away a little so that she was facing him. He thought she might start crying again, but no tears came, and there was a different, more familiar attitude on display now. She confirmed that by coyly smiling at him. "I think crying sets my hormones into some kind of rage. Do you mind?"

"Hardly. I think it's what happens with most people."

"Does it happen to you? Like now?"

"Yes."

She moved closer to him again, her arms around his neck, her mouth on his. He had the pleasant sensation that her lips were fuller and softer for the flow of tears. After a moment, she pulled away and stroked his face, then touched each of his eyelids in turn.

"I might cry again, later. When we get to talking about all that we have to talk about. Will you mind?"

"I'm willing to take the chance."

"I'll bet you are."

She stood up and gripped his hand, then tugged him off the chesterfield. She led him to the bedroom, pulling him along behind her like a reluctant child.

Which captured some of his feeling at that moment, although not very much of it, and not for very long.

They took their time, and there was a deliberateness to their lovemaking that was different than usual, a sense that this might be their last time together for a while. Stride detached a little, focusing a part of his senses on the soft patter of rain on the roof and on the leaves of the trees in the backyard. He had the feeling that Dianne was doing that also. Close, but not too close. Much later, when they were finished, both of them sated, they lay side by side, almost separated, only their fingers touching, his left hand and her right.

Dianne was the first to speak.

"I think if we could bottle some of that, we could probably make a fortune."

Stride turned his head to look at her.

"Let's not do that," he said. "We'll keep it for ourselves, alone." For as long as we can, he thought, but he didn't say that.

He touched her face, tracing the contours with his fingertips. She smiled and then reached across him over the side of the bed to retrieve the sheet that had fallen onto the floor. The bedspread was nowhere in sight and she didn't bother looking for it. It was warm in the room, even with the window open.

Stride rested his head on two pillows propped up against the headboard. Dianne sat in the middle of the bed, the sheet loosely draped over her thighs, drinking water from the glass he normally kept on the bedside table.

"That has to be stale," he said. "It's been there since last night."

"That's all right, I like it that way. My father always had a glass of water on his bedside table, and sometimes in the morning, after he'd gone downstairs for breakfast, I'd go into their bedroom and I'd drink it. It always tasted different from water just out of the tap. For some reason I liked it better that way." She held the glass out for him. "Do you think I'm just a bit odd, maybe?"

"If you would like me to think you're odd, I'll agree with you."

"And you like that, of course."

"Yes."

Stride took the glass from her and drank the little water that was left. Now, all passion spent for the moment, his mind started to drift back towards the investigation, his conversations with Greene, with Harry and with General Tudor. He shook his head to chase the thoughts away and placed the glass on the bedside table. He picked up his cigarettes.

"You can light one for me too," Dianne said.

They smoked in silence for a minute, the ashtray balanced on his abdomen.

"I have some news," she said. "Marty's taking the promotion. Part of the deal is that he'll be transferred to Washington."

"To the Pentagon."

"It is, as they say, a done deal."

"A done deal?"

"Yankee slang. The Americans are working very hard to destroy the English language, and they're making progress, as they do in most things they set their hands to. It kind of catches the spirit of the thing, don't you think?"

"I suppose so. And when does it happen, the done deal?"

"In a week, two at the outside."

"That fast?"

"When the military makes up its mind, they don't waste a lot of time. Target sighted, target within range, target blown to hell." She butted her cigarette in the ashtray. She'd smoked hardly any of it. "You've had a while to think about all this now. So, what do you think? I know it's my decision, really, but to restate the obvious, you are involved."

He started to answer, then pulled on his cigarette as a diversion. He'd been thinking about it since yesterday, when she'd suddenly dropped into his car on Water Street. But he hadn't really got anywhere with it.

"No comment?" she said.

"I don't know what to say, and I don't want to say the wrong thing."

"Just say whatever comes to mind. If it's the wrong thing, I'll let you know, and we'll take it from there. Backwards or forwards, whatever's required."

"That's very reassuring," Stride said. Dianne smiled and poked him with her finger. "But it really is your decision, isn't it?"

"Is it? All mine alone?"

"I think so. And I don't think you should make a decision based on what you feel about me, or about us. You've already decided that you don't want to stay with Marty for the rest of your life, and I think that has to be your starting point. If he was staying here, you wouldn't want to live with him, and you'll want that even less if you leave St. John's and find yourself in a strange place, living among strangers."

"Well, that gets you nicely off the hook, doesn't it?" Her colour had risen again, but there was no sign of tears this time.

"If it does, I don't mind. But was I on a hook?"

"Bad choice of words," she said.

"Mine, or yours?"

"Mine. And I'm sorry. You're right, I'm the one who has to make the decision, and now I'm trying to jiggle it around to make it look like it isn't entirely mine to make. Then, if it goes wrong, I can blame someone else."

"That someone being me?"

"You're the naked man lying next to me."

"I guess that's fair enough." He placed the ashtray on the bedside table and sat up, readjusting the pillows against the headboard. "What has Marty said about it?"

"Marty's a man of few words, always has been. And now he's even more so."

"But he has said something."

"He says a change of venue—he was born to be a bureaucrat—might get us back to where we were before. Well, before you happened."

"So, now we're back to me again." He lit another cigarette. "That's not the way I remember it. When I first met you, you'd come to Herc Parsons's party by yourself, and you told me that was the way things were with you and Marty, a lot of being alone. For both of you."

"You know, I really hate it when you remember things so well."

"I've been told that before."

"And were you without clothes on that occasion too?"

"There was more than one occasion. And the answer is yes, I was." He drew on his cigarette and she reached out and took it from him. "When we met, you and I, I'd been drifting away from Margaret for a while, and she from me. We each had our reasons, and some of those reasons corresponded. And in the middle of all that, you happened. To borrow a phrase."

His mind went back to that night and the feeling he had then, the excitement of meeting someone new, someone who seemed to be interested in him: an occasion full of promise, and all the more exciting for being undefined. But it was different now, months after the fact, the early passions dimmed. They were getting used to each other on a new level, the greater familiarity bringing comfort, but also a degree of unease, and a sense of diminishing potential. It wasn't what he'd anticipated, or wanted, and the sense of loss left him saddened and frustrated.

"Tell me you think it's been good." Dianne reached across him and stubbed the cigarette in the ashtray. She moved closer to him, tugging at his chest hairs. It was an attempt to be playful, but he could sense her uncertainty.

"Yes, it has," he said.

"But maybe not good enough?"

"That's not a fair question."

"I suppose not."

She sat up then, and swung her legs over the side of the bed. He watched her walk away from him until she'd left the room and went down the hall to the bathroom. His throat was dry, but the water glass was empty. He picked it up and went to the kitchen. As he passed by the bathroom, he heard the toilet flush and then the sound of water running into the sink.

When he got back, she was lying on the bed, the sheet pulled up almost to her chin.

"Water?" He held out the glass and sat on the side of the bed.

She took the glass from him and drank.

"You need a glass in the bathroom."

"I think I need a lot of things." He touched her hair, and she tilted her head so that her cheek was against his hand. "Like the ability to know the right thing to say at the right time. Like right now. I haven't been much help to you in this, other than to complicate your situation."

"And your own."

"Yes, but mine less than yours. Whatever you decide, I'll still be here, in this house, at Fort Townshend, doing what I'm doing now."

"Which is another way of saying it's still my decision to make."

"Yes."

"Tell me. Have you ever wanted to be married?"

"I have thought about it," he said.

"That's not really an answer."

"All right. Yes, I have wanted to be married."

"Since we met?"

"Yes."

"And before we met?"

"Yes."

"Was that Margaret? Or someone else?"

"Yes, to both," he said.

"I see." He thought she looked disappointed with his last reply, but he wasn't sure. "But you never asked anyone to marry you?"

"No, I didn't. I was never sure enough about it for that."

"Sure enough of yourself."

"I think that was it."

"And now? Still not sure?"

"Still not sure," he said.

"And if I asked you to marry me?"

"Are you about to?"

"No." She sat forward and the sheet fell away from her breasts. "You might say no, and that would be awful."

"And if I said yes?"

"Just about as awful." She sat back against the headboard, but left the sheet where it was. "One marriage at a time. If I end this one, I won't be quite the same person afterwards." She poked him again with an index finger. "That might bring some new excitement into your life."

"That would probably be the case," he said. "Are you going to end it? Your marriage?"

"Yes."

"When did you decide? Just now?"

"No."

"Then, when?"

"That would be telling."

She stood up and stretched, arms above her head, fingers entwined. She did a half-pirouette, showing off, he thought, but he didn't mind. She began to dress.

"You're going somewhere?"

"Yes."

"Am I going with you?"

"No." She was half-dressed, now, buttoning her blouse, smoothing out the wrinkles. She rummaged in one sleeve and located the handkerchief that she'd tucked in there earlier, folded it and put it back in the sleeve. "I'm going for a walk."

"In the rain."

"Of course, in the rain. There isn't any choice."

"And then you're going home?"

"Yes," she said. "Well, the place where I live."

"Will you call me later?"

She arranged her skirt so that the pleats fell into place.

"Yes, but not right away. Not for a while." She sat on the side of the bed and looked at him. Then she touched his cheek and kissed him. "You're right, it is my decision. It was, all along. If it helps, it wasn't easy. Inevitable and easy aren't the same thing. But I'd made the decision even before I met you that night at the party."

"So all of this has been a distraction?"

"In a way, it has been. It was so good being with you that it was easy—almost easy—to put off making a decision."

"Can I take that as a compliment?"

"You can if you like. But it's mostly a statement of fact. We were a distraction, you and I, and a lot more besides. Just how much more is something that will take some time to sort out, for both of us. Everything's about to change, and we both know that with change, events and outcomes are unpredictable." She stood up and started for the door, then turned back. "That's not an original thought. I think I must have read it somewhere."

And then she was gone.

Stride lay back against the pillows and willed his mind to move away from Dianne and speculations about what might happen next between them. But it didn't happen right away; she was still there with him. She'd made her declaration—he was pretty sure it was a declaration—and she would take it from there. He was beginning to think of himself almost as a passenger now, someone along for the ride. Well, that was what he'd been from the start, really, a passenger. Or a spectator, someone who'd paid a price for admission and who would have to wait to see what would happen next. The spectator image had some appeal, but he was already wondering about the price he'd paid, and would continue to pay in the days ahead.

After a few more minutes, he was able to turn his mind back to the investigation. The IRA's likely involvement was intriguing and frightening in approximately equal amounts. Stride found himself wondering about Tudor's calm take on it, that assassination was just another possibility for violent death in a life already filled to overflowing with violence and death.

He went to the window and leaned on the sill, looking out at the rain. Robert Benton was dead, but there was still the matter of the accomplice. If Rose's assassination had been planned carefully enough, he might have left the island sometime Tuesday, after killing Benton. St. John's was a busy port, ships large and small arriving and departing almost every day. There were also daily flights from the airport—however disrupted now because of the weather—and travel by train across the island, followed by a short ferry ride to the Canadian mainland. It was also possible that the accomplice was local, and had never planned to leave. That possibility only added to the potential threat.

He was tired now, but restless too. Part of him wished Dianne was still there with him, but another part was content that he was alone. He should have been tired. It had been a long day, several long days, and the lovemaking with Dianne had relaxed him. But their conversation had started the adrenaline flowing again and now he was wide awake. He went to the kitchen and poured an ounce of rum into a glass and drank it down in a single swallow. He thought of pouring a second one, but decided that was probably a bad idea. He put the bottle away.

CHAPTER 28

Constable Michael Doyle thought he was about as bored as he'd ever been in his life. It was going on for ten o'clock and it would be another two hours before his relief would come down from Fort Townshend and he could go on home to bed. Stride, with McCowan's approval, had decided to maintain a guard on the Rose house for at least a few more days. McCowan had agreed, but said that with the manpower situation what it was, the guard would be reduced to a single man. Doyle wasn't happy about that, because now he had no one to talk to. He thought he could see the logic in reducing the number to one, though. A single man could be bored senseless even more efficiently than two.

Why anyone had to stand guard on an empty house didn't make much sense to Doyle. The other thing that Doyle couldn't understand was why he had to stand guard duty outside the house. He thought he could do that just as well—better even—from inside the place. There he could at least read a magazine or a newspaper, or even make a pot of tea sometimes, to break the tedium and help keep himself alert. But the word had come down from on high—Adey said it came from the Deputy Chief's office—that the surveillance would be maintained on the outside.

Doyle thought the Deputy Chief had lost touch with the patrolman's life, no longer remembering what it was like to walk a beat or stand guard duty and endure the indignities heaped upon policemen by the North Atlantic climate. Adey, who'd been on the Force for more than five years now, five times as long as Doyle, was sympathetic, but he advised Doyle to keep his opinions of the Deputy Chief to himself. If he planned on making himself a career on the Force, that is.

About the only thing that alleviated the tedium even a little bit was to smoke a cigarette, and even that small diversion palled after a few hours standing around in the dark and the wet. To make things worse, the Deputy Chief had driven by in the afternoon and taken exception to the sight of Adey smoking on the job. So Doyle was told that he could smoke his cigarettes at the back of the house only, and that he would pocket his cigarette butts. Doyle couldn't imagine why that was necessary. As far as he knew, all the evidence that could be gathered had been, and Noseworthy had declared himself done with the place and gone on to other things.

But Adey told him that the Deputy Chief felt that cigarette butts dropped on the ground were unsightly. And because he came from a military background, he believed that things should always be neat and tidy. It was almost a religion with him, Adey said. As if that made any sense. The military, after all, were famous for making messes—killing and maiming people in unpleasant ways, and in large numbers, and generally blowing the bejesus out of everything in sight.

He looked at his watch one more time and was dismayed to find that the minute hand had scarcely moved since the last time he'd looked. He decided that now was a good time for a cigarette. He stepped off the veranda and went down the driveway and out onto the sidewalk in front of the house. He spent a minute looking up and down the street, allowing his gaze to linger for a bit on Bannerman Park, where all this ruckus had started.

Satisfied that no one was approaching from any direction, Doyle turned and trudged down the driveway. When he reached the corner at the back of the house, he took a final look over his shoulder in the direction of Circular, then took out a cigarette and lit it. And just because he felt like it, a small protest against his situation, he flicked the spent match towards the back fence and watched it disappear into a clump of bushes. Let Noseworthy find that sometime and make an issue of it. He turned the corner and moved around the rear of the house, making for the spot under the back steps where there was better protection from the rain.

He didn't quite make it. He was almost at the landing when he thought he heard something from the direction of the garage. He started to turn to look, but he didn't quite manage that either. The last sensation Doyle had was of a loud and heavy sound inside his head, and then he pitched face downwards, unconscious, his left cheek coming to rest on a rain-sodden patch of fall dandelions near the back steps. The cigarette he'd been holding burned for a few moments longer before it was taken over by the surrounding damp and fizzled out.

The General Hospital wasn't far from Circular Road, and the ambulance made it to Harrison Rose's house only a few minutes after Stride put in the call. An intern wearing slightly soiled whites introduced himself as Patrick Flaherty. Stride stood under the back steps of the Rose house and watched while Flaherty tended to Michael Doyle. The good news was that Doyle was still breathing. The bad news was that the head injury was serious, possibly life-threatening. That determination would require a closer examination than Flaherty could make while the man was still lying outdoors in a patch of wet dandelions in the rain.

After another minute, Flaherty pulled the ends of the stethoscope from his ears and stood up. He directed the two stretcher bearers to lift Doyle onto the gurney, get him into the ambulance and strap an oxygen mask over his face.

"Concussion for certain," Flaherty said, "and likely a fractured skull. The part that worries me is that the fracture is near the base of the skull. I'm thinking that a slightly harder blow might have killed him outright."

"You're saying there's a chance he won't make it?"

"There's always a chance for the worst outcome," Flaherty said. "The gag in his mouth didn't help. It's just good luck he didn't choke on it. How did you happen to find him? More good luck?"

"Pretty much," Stride said. "I live up the street, and I went out for a walk. When I saw there wasn't anyone at the front of the house, I came around here to take a look."

"What we don't know is when this happened," Flaherty said. "How long he's been lying here. It won't make any difference to the outcome, but it wouldn't hurt to know."

"Sometime between nine o'clock and fifteen minutes ago," Stride said. "A patrolman came past here just at nine and spoke to him. It was eleven-fifteen when I came by."

"Which also means that you don't know what might have been going on for more than two hours," Flaherty said. Stride looked towards the back door of the house. "If he's been unconscious that long, then his injuries probably are very serious. In any case, we're off. You might want to stop by the hospital at some point and see how he is."

"If I can, I'll do that," Stride said. "You'll be on duty until when?"

"In theory I'm off at midnight, but in this business there's a wide gulf between theory and practice. If I'm not there, ask for Gerry Drover. He'll be relieving me."

Flaherty climbed into the back of the ambulance and pulled the doors shut. The vehicle moved down the driveway and onto the street. Stride lit a cigarette and watched as the ambulance made its way east on Circular. A minute after the tail lights disappeared, the Black Maria came down the street from the opposite direction and pulled into the driveway. Phelan and Noseworthy stepped down from the passenger side of the cab.

"What the hell's been going on here?" Phelan said. "Someone's coshed Doyle and broken into the place?"

"Doyle's been coshed, all right, and he was tied up, hand and foot, and gagged too. But I don't know what else might have gone on. It's obvious someone wanted to get into the house, but I waited until you got here before starting in on that part of it."

"How is Doyle?"

"It's too early to say. Concussion, fractured skull. It might be really serious. We won't know for a while yet." Stride threw his cigarette towards the fence at the back of the house and watched it disappear into the foliage. Then he looked at Noseworthy. "I suppose I should pick that up?"

"I'll make a note of it, sir. You're still smoking *Royal Blends*?"

Stride nodded and led the way to the back door under the landing and tried the knob.

"It's locked. The other doors are, too. I've already checked them."

"Maybe no one went into the house after all," Phelan said.

"We can hope," Stride said.

Stride took a ring of keys from his pocket, copies of the ones Rose had been carrying when he was shot. He found the one that fit, unlocked the door and stepped into the cellar.

"You take the lead, Kevin."

Noseworthy had photographed every room in the house and had put together the dossier on the investigation. He'd have a better sense of what might be out of place now, if anything was. He stopped just inside the door, found the switch, and turned on the lights in the cellar.

"Someone's been in here," he said.

There were small puddles of water on the floor, diminishing in size towards the stairs at the far end of the room.

Noseworthy took his time, moving slowly through the cellar, making a mental inventory, and then leading the way upstairs.

Thirty minutes later, they had gone through every room in the house and they'd found nothing obviously amiss. In several more places they found traces of rainwater on the floor and carpets, upstairs and down. Now they were back in the kitchen. Phelan sat on a chair. Stride and Noseworthy stood by the door that led to the hallway.

"It's obvious someone's been in here," Stride said, "but it doesn't make sense that nothing's been touched. Come on, Kevin. They had to be after something."

"I'm guessing a safe," Phelan said.

"That's the obvious possibility, but we went through this place Tuesday, Kennedy and me, and we didn't find one," said Noseworthy.

"You mentioned that the other day," Stride said. "But let's assume there is a safe in here someplace. There's no point looking in the same places you and Kennedy have already been through. So, where else do we look?"

"For a safe in a place like this, there are the two standard options. A wall safe, or a floor safe. And I'm pretty much ruling out a wall safe. It's not in the study, and there's no safe in any of the closets, or under any of the pictures. I'm certain of that."

"The cellar, then?"

"We looked there, too."

"So that leaves a floor safe," Stride said. "Rose had a lot of renovations done to this place after he bought it. He could have had a floor safe installed then."

"We have the invoices in the evidence room for the work Rose had done here. He had a special file for all that. I didn't really look at it, so I can't say there's nothing about a safe in there."

"So where do we start, Kevin?"

"I think we can forget about the cellar, or at least leave it until last. The floor down there is poured concrete."

Noseworthy butted his cigarette and walked around the kitchen, looking at the corners of the room. Then he did the same in the hallway, in the dining room and the living room.

"Let's start with the upstairs rooms. We have three bedrooms and two bathrooms. I'm guessing the large bathroom, the one off the master bedroom."

The large bathroom had a long counter with a double sink, a bathtub and a separate shower enclosure. The cabinetry was high quality hardwood—oak, Phelan thought.

Noseworthy walked around the room twice, looking at the floor from different angles. Then he pointed to the corner between the toilet and the shower enclosure.

"It could be there. Four of the tiles are just a little bit out of whack with their mates. I think that's because they can be moved. There's also an anomaly in the room underneath this one, less space in it than I think there should be. I noticed that on Tuesday, and wondered if there might be something odd about the room above, but it didn't register then. It should have, but it didn't."

"You're forgiven," Stride said. "You weren't thinking about a floor safe on Tuesday. None of us was."

Noseworthy knelt on the floor beside the toilet. He used his penknife to prise up a corner of one of the tiles, then took hold of it and pulled the four tiles away as a unit. Under that was a square of plywood, a fraction of an inch smaller than the space covered by the tiles. He used the penknife again to lift the plywood. And when he did that, the handle and hinges of a floor safe came into view, recessed just below floor level. The safe didn't have a combination lock. It opened with two keys.

"Whoever installed this thing knew what he was about, sir. It's a damn fine piece of work." He stood up and snapped the penknife closed.

Stride took his handkerchief from his pocket, knelt down, wrapped it around the handle and tried to turn it. The safe was locked.

"This far, and no farther," Noseworthy said. "I suppose we can hope that whoever came in here tonight couldn't find the safe, and didn't open it."

"Call me a pessimist, but I think that's a very long shot," Stride said. "You don't half-kill a policeman and risk being caught in a murder victim's house unless you have a very definite objective."

"If we follow that logic, then whoever whacked Doyle and came in here knew where the safe was, and he also had the keys. This thing is a Chubb, sir, and it's top-of-the-line. It would take half a lifetime to pick those locks, and probably not even then."

"Well, we have to get in there and see if it's been cleaned out. How do we open this thing, Kevin?"

"Without the keys, it will be one hell of a job. And I don't think we have the keys, sir. None of the keys Kennedy found in the bedroom, or any of the ones we took off Rose's body looked like safe keys to me."

Stride took the ring of keys from his pocket again.

"These are copies of all the keys we found?"

"Every last one of them. They open all the doors and closets in this place, but like I said, none of them looks like a key for a safe. But try them anyway, I could be wrong."

Stride knelt down and tried each of the keys in turn. None of them fit. He stood up and stared at the ring of keys, as though hoping to will two of them to change shape and do the job.

"All right. We don't have the keys. And we're thinking that whoever came in here tonight does have them."

"Or has copies."

"And he got them where?"

"I don't know, sir."

"I don't either," Stride said. He walked out of the bathroom into the hallway, stood there for a moment, thinking, then came back in. "Well, it's a certainty that Rose had keys to his own safe. So, where the hell are they?"

"My best guess has to be that he hid them someplace in the house," Noseworthy said. "He probably wouldn't have carried them around with him, for any number of good reasons."

"This is one hell of a big house," Phelan said. "It will be like looking for the needle in the famous hay pile."

"And that's assuming they're still here," Stride said.

"You think someone else knew where they were? Benton's accomplice, maybe?"

"I don't know what to think," Stride said. "The one thing I do know for sure is that we need to get into that safe. The question is, how? Kevin?"

"I have a suggestion. Damien Ryan. He's blown a few safes in his day, and he could probably do the job for us on this one. The good news is he's still in the Pen from his last job."

"Which means we have to pull this thing out of here and take it to an open field someplace and blow it open."

"Or maybe not," Phelan said. "Rose's daughter might have a set of keys, sir. It's possible her father sent her duplicates."

"That's a good thought, Harry." Stride looked at his watch. "It's almost too late to call on her tonight, but I really want to get into that thing, and sooner rather than later. I'm going down to the hotel and talk to her."

"She's had a long and hard day, sir. She might be asleep."

"Then I'll just have to wake her up, won't I?"

"Better you than me."

"It's why they pay me the outrageous salary, Harry."

"In the meantime," Noseworthy said, "I'll get onto the Pen and let them know we might want to pick Ryan up tomorrow morning. Just in case."

The night clerk at the Newfoundland Hotel turned and looked at the bank of keys behind the registration desk, then ran his finger along it until he came to number 614. There were two keys in the slot.

"I'm sorry, Inspector, but it seems that Mrs. Darnell isn't in."

"Do you know what time she went out?" Stride looked at his watch. It was 12:40.

"No, sir, I don't. I only came on at midnight." He smiled. "It's my week in the barrel."

"She hasn't checked out, has she?"

"I don't believe so." He checked the registration file. "No sir, she's still registered. But I really can't tell you any more than that."

Stride walked to the hotel entrance and looked out through the glass onto Cavendish Square, trying to imagine where Catherine Darnell might have gone. He wished now he'd phoned ahead and avoided a fruitless trip. Then he felt a hand on his elbow.

"You're out and about late tonight, Eric." Sid Purchase had quietly come up behind him. He was still wearing his tailored black suit, but his bowtie was undone, the ends dangling down over his shirtfront. The top two buttons of his shirt were also undone, and the delicate bouquet of a good single malt filled the space between them.

"Late nights seem to be the hallmark of this case, Sid."

"I take it you're not down here just for the atmosphere, not this time of night. You're looking for someone?"

"Yes, I am, but the lady appears not to be in."

"That wouldn't be Mrs. Darnell, I don't suppose?"

"Yes, it would. She's not in her room, and the desk clerk couldn't tell me when she went out, never mind where."

"The *when* is just past eight-thirty," Purchase said. "But I could only make a guess about the *where*."

"You saw her go out?"

"She came down to the lobby at eight-thirty, and about five minutes later a car pulled up. In she got, and off she went."

"Well, she's been here before," Stride said. "She probably has friends in the city."

"And fairly upscale friends, at that."

"You know who it was picked her up?"

"A fellow named Wilson. Major Wilson, when he's togged out in his British army uniform for his duties as Macdonald's ADC. I've seen him here from time to time, at various functions, usually trailing behind the Governor."

"Barnes Wilson? Well, I suppose that's not a big surprise. Wilson and Rose knew each other. They might even have been friends."

"You haven't interviewed him yet?"

"McCowan's talked to him. Wilson asked for regular reports on the progress of the investigation."

"I suppose they'd want to keep track of it. How much do you know about him?"

"He's career army, a Great War veteran, and had a lot of diplomatic postings since then. Why?"

"I've always wondered about diplomatic types," Purchase said. "But I should talk. I'm a bit of a diplomat, myself. I wear a natty black suit that isn't all that comfortable, and I make pleasant chat with people over plates of food. All things considered, it's not a bad deal, although some days I think I'd rather be out fishing."

"You're going somewhere with this, Sid?"

"No flies on you," Purchase said. "Your Major Wilson is what our British friends would call a bit of a lad."

"I'm listening."

"Working in a hotel like this, a fella gets to see and hear quite a lot. If he pays attention."

Purchase nodded towards two armchairs on the far side of the lobby, which stood under a not-very-good likeness of King George V flanked by two Irish setters, brilliant in their redness. It was an appropriate setting, Stride thought.

"So, tell me about Major Wilson."

"As I said, the word going about is that he's a bit of a lad." Purchase leaned towards Stride and grinned. "I've always liked that phrase. It has—what's the word? Resonance? It seems the Major's been having it on with a lady of substance here in the city."

"A married lady, you mean?"

"Indeed she is married. Her husband's Arthur Hammond. You know who he is, and you probably also know that he's a good—or bad—thirty years older than his wife."

"He also isn't very well, I've heard."

"No, he isn't. A host of ailments of the kind that grow out of a life lived too well, and for too long."

"He's almost ninety, isn't he?"

"He looks it, and that's the truth, but in fact, he's just the wrong side of eighty."

"Which makes his wife about fifty."

"Forty-nine," Purchase said, "and maybe more than once. But she's a looker, and no mistake. She's taken care of herself. And she also likes to be taken care of."

"I can't imagine that's a problem. Hammond is only slightly less well off than Croesus."

"But it's his money, not hers. And like a lot of rich men, Hammond holds the purse strings very tight. The popular point of view is that he's a cheap sonofabitch."

"That would be inconvenient for Wilson."

"Very inconvenient."

"Is it common knowledge? Their affair?"

"Depends on your definition of common. The affair is being very properly conducted, one of those arrangements that everyone who knows them seems to be aware of, while they pretend nothing's going on at all."

"And Hammond? Does he know about it?"

"There's not much of significance in this town that Arthur Hammond doesn't know about."

"And he doesn't mind?"

"I wouldn't know about that," Purchase said. "It's been ages since he's invited me around to his house for a drink."

"So, how did you hear about it?"

"Wilson and Mrs. Hammond like to rendezvous every so often in one of the top-floor suites. You'd be surprised how much I hear, working here at the hotel. There's not much action of that kind that escapes the notice of the housekeeping staff."

"A suite has to cost a shilling or two." Stride imagined himself and Dianne frolicking in one of the hotel's suites, and smiled at the idea. But the thought reminded him that their frolicking days might be over. Were over, for the time being.

"It does. And the story I've heard is that Major Wilson doesn't like the idea that people might think he's a kept man."

"He pays the freight?"

"Yes, he does. Very gallant of him, no doubt, but the word is that he's living beyond his means. His army salary, even with an overseas allowance, doesn't match his ambitions or his tastes."

"And no family money to ease the burden?" That phrase again, so often applied to apparently affluent British citizens living in Newfoundland.

"Maybe not enough to make up the difference. At least, that's what I've heard. Like I said earlier, Eric, I could write a book."

"I think so." Stride stood up. "If you see or hear anything more about Major Wilson, or Mrs. Darnell, you'll let me know?"

"I will do that."

Purchase got up and moved off in the direction of the elevators. Stride wondered if he was living at the hotel, then realized he couldn't be. Sid Purchase was married, and he owned a house in the city. Stride continued to watch until Purchase disappeared into a waiting elevator and the doors slid shut after him. He wondered if the housekeeping staff could tell stories about Sid Purchase.

He went to the registration desk and asked to use the phone. He gave the operator the number for Rose's house. Phelan picked up the phone on the second ring. Stride told him that the evening was over, and that he and Noseworthy should both go on home. The van was still there, Phelan said, so getting home wouldn't be a problem.

Stride stood on the sidewalk in front of the hotel and spent a minute looking up at the sky. The rain seemed to have stopped for good, and the overcast was starting to fragment. He could see a few stars, and there was even a faint light from the moon spilling out around the edges of the broken clouds. He walked to the MG and slipped into the driver's seat. He sat there for a minute, smoking a cigarette. He wondered if he'd be able to get any sleep tonight. A large tot of rum might help. Sometimes it did.

He'd parked the car on the east side of Cavendish Square, facing west, and he found himself looking at the steeple and bell tower of the Garrison Church, St. Thomas's. It was one of the oldest churches in the city, and unlike most of the others, it was built of wood, the sides clapboarded and painted dark blue. Twice, in 1846 and 1892, it had somehow escaped being destroyed by the two huge fires that had reduced most of the city to cinder and rubble. Looking at the church brought his mind back more sharply to the shooting on Monday night. Phelan had said that Harrison Rose sometimes attended services at St. Thomas's. Stride found himself wondering what Rose might have thought about while he sat through the church services, listening to the hymns, the readings from Holy Scripture, the sermons that discussed morality and love for one's fellow man. And how he would have squared all that with his time in Ireland, never mind the Great War.

He looked at the church for another minute, then started the motor and drove around the square. He headed west along Military Road, driving past the old church, moving in the direction of Government House and home. A short way past the church, he pulled over to the curb, turned off the motor and stepped out of the car. He walked back to St. Thomas's, stood there for a minute looking up at the bell tower, then turned and walked back towards the MG. He stopped there for a moment, then continued along Military until he was beside Bannerman Park. The area was quiet: nobody out walking, only an occasional car driving by. Looking across the park, Stride could see the spot where he'd found Rose's body, and where Tom Kennedy had found him.

He stood there for several minutes, smoking and thinking. Then he walked back to the MG, started the motor, and went on home.

CHAPTER 29

Stride was back at the Newfoundland Hotel early the next morning.

"Yes, I do have keys to my father's safe." Catherine Darnell opened the door of her room so that Stride could come in. "He mailed them to me a few months ago, after I told him I was going to visit him here. They came with some instructions about his estate."

"Is that where he kept his will? In the safe?"

"I think it's where he kept all his personal papers."

"You've seen the safe, I suppose? You know where it is?"

"He showed it to me when I was here last. It's in his bathroom." She smiled. "I thought that was quite funny, so much like that other side of him, the one with the quirky sense of humour, to have his valuables right next to his potty. I think he might have been making a comment on life in general." She sat on the side of the bed and rummaged in her handbag, then took out a ring with five keys on it. "The two matching keys are for the safe. The others open the three outside doors of the house." She looked at Stride. "But can I ask you a question? How did you know my father had a safe? And however did you manage to find it? It was awfully well hidden."

"There was a break-in at the house last night. Well, not a break-in exactly. The officer on guard duty was knocked unconscious and someone went into the house. We guessed he was looking for a safe, so we looked for it. It took us a while to find it."

"Wasn't the house locked?"

"The doors were locked, but whoever knocked our man unconscious must have had keys. There was rainwater on the floor just inside the cellar door, and more in the house, including upstairs."

"I don't understand. How could he have keys?"

"We don't understand it, either, but he must have had."

"And you don't know who it could be?"

"We're guessing it was someone who knew your father, someone he trusted with keys to his house."

"And to the safe as well?"

"That might have been the case. And if he did give someone the keys, and that's the person who broke into the house last night, the safe might be empty now. We won't know until we get inside."

"What about this woman my father was involved with? Mrs. Drodge. You said she worked for him. Would she have had the keys?"

"I don't know whether she does or not. It wasn't an issue until last night."

"Then, it might have been her, or her husband, who attacked your constable and went into the house."

"It wasn't either of them. We've had surveillance on Mrs. Drodge since we learned of her relationship with your father. She's living with her brother. And as of this morning, her husband was still in Harbour Grace."

"I see. I suppose that was unkind of me, to suggest that she'd do such a thing."

"It's a logical thought," Stride said. He considered his next question. "Do you know why your father had a safe in his house, instead of keeping all his valuable papers in his safe deposit box at the bank? It's a very elaborate arrangement. And he did have a second safe in his office."

"It is, as you put it, an elaborate arrangement." She walked to the window and looked out for a few moments. "Well, all of this will probably come out sooner or later, so I might as well tell you now. My father kept a substantial amount of cash on hand, always. It was one of the few things he told me about his affairs. He didn't tell me about Mrs. Drodge, and that doesn't surprise me, but he told me about the safe. He wanted me to know, in case something happened to him. And he said I should keep that to myself, and take the money after he was … gone."

"How much money?"

"I don't know how much, he didn't say. But my impression is that it might have been quite a lot."

"Did anyone else know about this? His lawyer?"

"Mr. Madigan? I don't know. Maybe he did. You'll have to ask him. Daddy said he handled most of his finances for him."

"But?"

"My impression, reading between the lines of the letter he wrote me, is that no one else knew about the cash in his safe. That was between us, I think."

"And what do you make of that? You said he didn't have any family money."

"He didn't. And I don't know what to make of it. Until now, it was all theoretical anyway. My father and I lived very separate lives. He might have had a king's ransom in that safe, for all I knew, or cared. But now it isn't theoretical any longer." She crossed the room and went to the clothes closet. "Shouldn't we be getting over to the house? I'm assuming your people are there, waiting for us?"

"Yes, they are." Stride reached into the closet, took out her coat, and held it for her.

"The policeman who was attacked last night. Is he all right?"

"No, he isn't. He was struck very hard. When I called the hospital this morning, he was still unconscious."

"I'm sorry. You know, I feel responsible, somehow, because it happened at my father's house. But I suppose that's silly of me?"

"I think I understand," Stride said. He pulled the door open.

"I was out earlier," she said. "Before breakfast. I like to take an early morning walk, whenever I can."

"At least the weather's improved."

"Yes, it has. When I got back here last night, I could actually see the moon. It was such a relief." She locked the door and they started down the corridor. "The desk clerk said you were here last night, looking for me."

"It was after we'd located the safe. I came down here to see if you might have the keys."

"And of course you wondered where I was."

"Yes, although it's none of my business, really."

"I would have thought that in a murder investigation, everything would be your business."

"In a way it is. But there's a line between investigation and intrusion."

"That's nicely put. But I think you'd still like to know where I was."

"Only if you want to tell me."

"I was with Major Barnes Wilson. I called him after you left yesterday. He was busy in the early part of the evening, but he picked me up later on and he took me to his flat. I asked him to do that, by the way. It was a relief to get out of the hotel for a while."

"I knew he was acquainted with your father," Stride said. He decided not to mention the brawl in the park.

"I suppose you could almost say he's become a kind of family friend, although last night was the first time I met him. He first met my father in Ireland. Barnes was there too, you know, although in quite a different role. He was posted there with his regiment."

Stride stopped and looked at her.

"Major Wilson was in Ireland when your father was there?" Then he remembered that McCowan had listed Dublin as one of the places Wilson had been posted.

"Yes, he was."

"And he would have known that your father was with the Auxiliaries."

"Yes, of course he would have." She looked at him, puzzled. "He didn't tell you that?"

"I haven't actually talked to him. My district inspector did, but the matter never came up. He never mentioned it."

"Isn't that odd? I would have thought he'd have given you the information right away. Surely it's relevant to the investigation?"

"Yes, it is," Stride said. He worked at keeping his tone even.

"Now I feel doubly awkward about having spent the evening with him. But I'll add that it felt good talking to someone about Daddy, someone who knew him. You can understand that?"

"Yes, of course."

"I was at Major Wilson's place until quite late. But I expect you know that, already."

"It was after midnight when I came to the hotel looking for you."

"Look, I am sorry, really I am. But I had no way of knowing that you'd come looking for me. And this business about Barnes having been in Ireland when my father was there."

"Please don't worry about it. These things happen." They stepped out of the elevator into the lobby. "Tell me some more about Major Wilson. Did he know your father well?"

"Fairly well, although not while they were in Ireland, I don't think. He got to know him much better after he was posted here, to Government House."

"That was just over a year ago, I believe."

"Yes. Daddy first mentioned him in one of his letters about eight months ago. I think he was pleased to know someone on the Governor's staff. He said Barnes might be someone I could contact if anything ever happened to him. Of course, he was thinking about falling ill, or having an accident, something like that." She stopped then, and bowed her head, her eyes closed. She gripped his arm. "I'm sorry. I'm still not used to the idea of it, his being dead, and being killed like that. It comes on me in waves, without warning." She took a deep breath and stood upright again. "Like just then."

They walked out of the hotel and onto Cavendish Square. The sun was shining now, and the few clouds that were rolling in over the Southside Hills were soft and white. It was like being in a different world.

"Why an MG?" She was smiling, now, the car a distraction from the situation she was in. "It seems an unlikely choice for Newfoundland. The roads being what they are, I mean."

"I just liked the look of it, and the idea of it. And one came available from someone I knew in Boston. I couldn't pass up the opportunity. I know a good mechanic, and he modified the suspension for me. I haven't had any real problems with it, not so far, anyway."

"And the fact that probably no one else in the city has one? Was that a part of it?"

"Of course."

"Well, good for you. I think everyone should do something like that, if they can." He held the door open for her and she slid into the seat. "We're going straight to the house, I suppose?"

"Yes. We have to get into the safe. Until we do, we won't really know what we're dealing with."

"I suppose so." She wasn't smiling now. Mention of the safe had dampened her mood again.

He slid behind the wheel and started the motor. He'd left the top down, and the early morning sun had warmed the leather seats. He saw that she was tying a scarf around her hair in preparation for the drive. "I can put the top up if you prefer."

"Certainly not. I love driving in an open car. And what are the odds that I'll get another chance while I'm here?"

"About fifty-fifty." That sounded halfway to an invitation, but she didn't respond. He pulled away from the curb.

Noseworthy and Phelan were standing outside Rose's house, smoking, enjoying the sunshine. Stride made the introductions and they went inside. Catherine Darnell stopped in the vestibule and looked down the hallway, then up the stairs. The house, after only a few days, had taken on an air of abandonment, even something more. Stride felt it, and he was sure the others did too. It was a minute before Catherine spoke.

"I have this awful feeling, like being in a funeral parlour. It's as though I'm here for a viewing." She turned and looked at Stride. "I'm sorry. Can we get on with this, please?"

They started up the stairs, Noseworthy leading the way. When they reached the bathroom, Stride inserted the two keys into the safe. For no reason he could explain, he had a sense that they would not be the right keys, that the safe wouldn't open. But they fitted perfectly, and when he turned the handle, the door opened easily on well-oiled hinges. The safe was empty.

"Well, that answers one question." Stride closed the safe but left it unlocked. Catherine Darnell glanced at him, then moved towards the door.

"I have to get out of here," she said. "Please?"

"We can go down to the living room," Stride said. "Or somewhere else, if you like, but we need to talk some more."

"About the money that isn't there."

"Yes."

Catherine Darnell led the way downstairs to the living room. Stride watched while she spent a minute walking around, settling herself, looking at the pictures on the walls, at the furniture, at a framed picture of herself standing on the mantel.

"Some of this is new since the last time I was here." She spoke more to herself than the others. "But that was more than ten years ago."

She sat on the chesterfield, opened her handbag and took out her cigarettes. Phelan fetched the ashtray from the kitchen and placed it on the coffee table. He held out his lighter.

Stride sat on the arm of the chesterfield.

"There's a general belief among the business community that your father arrived here in St. John's seventeen years ago with a substantial amount of family money, and he used that to purchase this house and his business. He also told you there was money in the safe. But you say there was no family money. Do you have any idea where his money came from?"

"I don't have any idea. I'd assume that any money that was supposed to be in the safe came from his business, money he made after he moved here. I don't know where else it could have come from." She stared at the smoke curling up from her cigarette, then at Stride. "Are you thinking now that the money he originally came here with might have been stolen?"

"That's a possibility we'll have to consider."

"This is very distressing for me, Inspector. It's never occurred to me that my father could be a thief. He was a soldier, an officer, and he served his country well in the war."

She stopped then. Stride wondered if she was thinking the same thing he was, about her father going from courageous and decorated soldier to membership in the Auxiliaries, and all that might have entailed during the brutal conflict in Ireland. Discomfort sat heavy on everyone in the room. Catherine looked at each of them in turn.

"I think I probably know less about all of this than any of you." She stubbed her cigarette and stood up. "I'm sorry, but I really can't stand it here in this house any longer. If you need to ask me more questions, we'll have to go someplace else."

"I think that's all the questions we have at the moment," Stride said. "I'll take you back to your hotel."

"Thank you," she said. "I'd appreciate that."

CHAPTER 30

arry Phelan was standing on the sidewalk in front of Rose's house talking to Constable Adey when Stride got back from dropping Catherine Darnell off at the Newfoundland Hotel. Noseworthy and the Black Maria were nowhere in sight.

"They went on back to Fort Townshend," Phelan said when he was settled in the passenger seat of the MG. "And, by the way, Dickson rang to say there was a phone call for you this morning. It was from Major Wilson. He wants you to call him at Government House."

"Did he say why?"

"Only that it's something to do with the case. That's all he said."

"It's a damned good thing he did call," Stride said. "My next move after picking you up was to go over there and lift him up by the lapels and shake some information out of him."

"Sir?"

"Wilson knew Rose had been in Ireland, also that he was with the Auxiliaries. He was there at the same time. If we'd known that from the start, we might be further ahead than we are."

"Mrs. Darnell told you that?"

"She said that was when Wilson and her father first met."

"Maybe he wants to make amends, set things right?"

"He damn well better." Stride turned off the motor and sat back in his seat. "Give me a cigarette, Harry. I'm going to have to calm down before I go over there and talk to him. Otherwise I'll find myself saying rude things to Major-Bloody-Wilson, and that won't do anyone any good."

"Maybe he wasn't acting on his own, sir. He might be taking orders from someone else."

"Not from Governor Macdonald, I don't think."

"Maybe from that fellow you talked to on Tuesday," Phelan said.

"Rodney Gilbert."

"McCowan said Gilbert is Wilson's superior over there. Gilbert's a senior aide. I think Wilson's job is probably more ceremonial. Gilbert could be giving the orders."

"Assuming that orders are being given by someone. Well, maybe that is what's going on." He turned to look at Phelan. "So you're saying I should give Wilson the benefit of the doubt, and not jump to the conclusion that he's just an imperious prick who doesn't mind screwing around with the colonials?"

"It really goes against my Irish nature to stand up for a British army officer, sir, but that's more or less what I'm suggesting."

"That's very noble of you, Harry."

"We'll keep that to ourselves, sir. I have a reputation to maintain."

"Fair's fair," Stride said. He threw his cigarette into the street and started the motor.

Barnes Wilson was talking on the telephone when Rodney Gilbert tapped on the door of his office at Government House. He nodded at Stride and Phelan, then went back to his conversation. He spoke a few more words into the phone and hung up.

"Barnes, this is Inspector Stride and Sergeant Phelan. I don't believe you've actually met them, have you?"

"No, I haven't." Wilson stood up. "I'm sorry that it's taken so long to make contact with you, Inspector, but it couldn't be helped."

"I could join you, if you'd like," Gilbert said. He gave Wilson a questioning look. He appeared to sense the tension that Stride had carried into the building with him. "I have some time before my meeting downtown."

"No, that's all right, Rod. I'll take it from here. You see, I asked Inspector Stride to stop by."

"If you're sure?"

"Quite sure, thanks. Just close the door behind you, if you will." Wilson indicated two chairs that faced his desk. "Make yourselves comfortable, gentlemen. I expect you have questions for me, and we can proceed that way, if you like."

"We do have some questions, Major Wilson. The first one being why you didn't tell us that Colonel Rose had been in Ireland with the Auxiliaries."

"I knew you'd be asking me that. It's the reason I made my call to Fort Townshend this morning. It's something we need to talk about." Wilson held up his hand to forestall Stride's next question. "I apologize for not giving you the information on Colonel Rose right away, but the fact is, I didn't really have any say in the matter. I'll take a minute to explain. The first thing I want you to know is that this meeting we're having now is very much off the record. I don't actually have permission from Whitehall or the Home Office to talk to you."

"You need permission to talk to us about a murder investigation we're carrying out?"

"I'm afraid I do. And I know it sounds Byzantine, but it's the way things are, at least as they concern Colonel Rose. We're operating on several levels here, Inspector. On your level, you have a murder to deal with. On my level, there's a problematic can of worms that a lot of people would like to keep the lid on, if they can. And that's why I say this meeting's off the record. Rod Gilbert knows that you're here, of course, but he doesn't know what's on the agenda, other than the obvious fact that it's about Rose's murder. In the end, I think you'll find the information I'll give you useful, although there's no guarantee that it will get you any closer to a resolution of your case. Questions?"

"Would you have called us at all if Mrs. Darnell hadn't arrived here yesterday?"

"Not as quickly as I did, no. But once she was here, I knew she'd tell you about her father's having been in the Auxiliaries. And that would have brought you to my doorstep, demanding some answers from me. You were probably on your way here when I called. I suppose she's told you I first knew the Colonel in Dublin, back in the twenties?"

"Yes."

"I was in the army then, of course, just as I am now, and our paths did cross a few times, Rose's and mine. I didn't know him well, and I knew very little about what he was doing there. Him, personally, I mean. I knew all about the Auxies, of course, everyone did. And I probably knew more than most. I worked out of Dublin Castle, and my principal duty was putting together intelligence information on the rebellion, specifically on the IRA. That didn't involve actual time in the field, thank God, but it was dangerous enough. The IRA were dedicated to killing off as many British intelligence people, at all levels, as they could. I lost some good friends in Ireland."

"The information you were processing? It had something to with Harrison Rose?"

"Eventually, it did, yes. A lot of the so-called information I dealt with was useless, and some of it was pure invention—people making things up, brown-nosing for advantage. There's always a lot of that in intelligence work. But there were occasional gems among the dross."

"Such as?"

"One of the gems had to do with a series of bank robberies in Ireland, north and south. We assumed the IRA were responsible. They were always short of weapons and ammunition. Neither was easy to get, and neither was cheap. Even at the height of the rebellion, at the time of the treaty negotiations in London in 1922, the IRA had only a few thousand rifles in their arsenal. They financed their weapons program any way they could. So, when the robberies occurred, we naturally assumed it was the IRA."

"And were they responsible?" Stride thought he already knew where Wilson was going with this.

"For some smaller ones, yes. But there were three very large robberies that netted over a hundred thousand pounds. That was enough money to put the IRA in a position to purchase large quantities of arms on the international market. I can tell you there were a lot of sweaty collars and waistbands in Dublin Castle and Whitehall around that time. But the fact was, nothing much changed on the fighting front. The IRA's weapons situation didn't improve, and there was no intelligence coming in about significantly larger arms purchases on the black market. That was a great relief to us, but it was also a puzzle."

"Until you decided it wasn't the IRA who'd carried out the larger robberies," Stride said.

"Yes, but it took a long while before we twigged onto that. The collective bias was that all the bad things that happened in Ireland in those days, north or south, had to be the work of the IRA. It was the mindset of the time. So there wasn't an objective investigation. But to be fair to ourselves, the robberies had been well set up, and they were carried out with considerable violence, an IRA trademark. In two of them, there were people killed, including three known IRA men, whose bodies were found after the fact. What else were we to think, other than that these were IRA operations?"

"And when did you decide that Colonel Rose was involved in the robberies?"

"I see you're a step ahead of me," Wilson said. "That came a lot later. Early on, a few of the wiser heads suggested the Auxiliaries might have had something to do with the robberies, but no one wanted to think about that. The Auxies had received a lot of bad press, and no one wanted to add to it. General Crozier had resigned his position because he thought they were out of control and a bloody disgrace. Which indeed some of them were. General Tudor stayed firm, of course, because that was his way, unbending and unbendable."

"So the investigation was shelved."

"An investigation never really got started. Not then. A few people were interested, but we all had a lot of other things to do, and for me, a transfer was in the works. The money that was stolen was important, of course, but compared to the sums that had been thrown into the Great War, and into fighting the IRA? It was almost a pittance. The main thing was that the rebellion was over at last, our troops were standing down, and life up there was getting back to something like normal."

"What happened to change that?"

"What happened was that a former Auxiliary, a man named Knowles, was assassinated in a town in Surrey by IRA men. But that was years later, in the late thirties." Wilson paused again and looked at Stride and Phelan. "Is that name familiar to you? Knowles?"

"We talked to General Tudor yesterday. He mentioned the name in connection with Colonel Rose."

"You talked to General Tudor? I knew he was living here, of course, but I'm surprised he would talk to you."

"It was a matter of knocking on his door and telling him that we were policemen. But go on with what you were saying, Major."

"Right. Well, this fellow Knowles, he didn't go easily, and he took two of his killers with him. But one of the IRA men lived long enough to tell his story to an investigator togged out in priest's robes. A deathbed confession. And you can guess what his story was."

"That some of the Auxiliaries had staged the bank robberies back in Ireland."

"Yes."

"Rose was in charge of it? Or Rose and Knowles together?"

"The two of them together, we think. And in the end we believe they made off with all of the money. Split two ways, it would have been enough to set each of them up for life."

"The two of them couldn't have pulled off three major robberies on their own. There had to be others involved."

"Once again, you're ahead of me. Yes, we believe there were four other Auxies involved."

"And they were killed in a supposed IRA ambush," Phelan said. "And later became official casualties of the rebellion."

"Tudor told you about that, too, I suppose."

"Not exactly," Stride said. "But he told us that Rose and Knowles survived an ambush one night that killed all their fellow Auxiliaries. We're able to add two and two and get something close to four."

"Yes, I suppose you are," Wilson said. "And that does seem to have been the case. It would have been easy enough to set up. Four out of six Auxies killed in an ambush by the IRA? That sort of thing really did happen sometimes. And it always played better than the pantomime back then. It got everyone fired up and hungry for revenge. No one even wanted to think about an alternative explanation."

"And the three IRA men they found dead near the scene of the bank robberies," Phelan said. "Who were they? Prisoners that Rose and his friends brought along for the occasion?"

"That seems to have been the case, too."

"This fills in a lot of the blanks," Stride said. "But not all of them. You've known about Colonel Rose and the bank robberies for a long time. But you were here for more than a year, and you didn't do anything about it, or about Rose. He was complicit in the murder of a large number of people. Four of his fellow Auxiliaries, and the three IRA prisoners. You even struck up a friendship with him after you arrived here. I'd like to hear what you have to say about that."

"I'm not sure that I can say anything about it that will satisfy you, or make you feel any better about me. And I understand that. But, the thing is, I had no authority to do anything about Harrison Rose."

"You said you've known about Rose and Knowles since the late thirties."

"Not personally, I didn't. I had half a dozen postings after Dublin, and I'd pretty much forgotten all about Harry Rose by the time this present posting came up. The Knowles murder, that was looked into by others, not by me. The local police, obviously, and then the Home Office. The Foreign Office and the army got involved too. The file went back and forth, the way files do. Harry Rose wasn't even in England by then—he was over here, a prosperous businessman, settled in the community. Newfoundland's a long way from London, Inspector. And you have to remember the times. It was 1938, Hitler was casting his eye over Europe, and another bloody war was in the offing, a war that promised to be even worse than the last one. The file slipped through the cracks. Almost no one had any time for it. There were too many other things going on."

"But you asked for the posting here in St. John's, Major. Why?"

"Yes, I asked for the posting here, and for a damn good reason. I was due for a transfer, and there were two openings available to me. It was here or Palestine. It was no contest. Palestine was a very rough go, even two years ago, when the transfer was in the works, and I knew it was only going to get a lot rougher. You might remember that in July of last year, a gang of Zionist militants, the Irgun, blew up the King David Hotel in Jerusalem. At final count, ninety-one people were dead. Twenty-eight of them were British, and most of them worked for the British Secretariat there. That's where I'd have been working if I'd chosen the Palestine posting. I'm sorry as hell for the people who were killed and injured, and I say a prayer of thanks every night that I wasn't among them."

"So Rose's presence in St. John's was just coincidence?"

"Not entirely. When I was looking at the two postings that were available, Harry Rose's file came to my attention, more or less by chance. My knowing something about him was a useful wedge to get the job here. Whitehall still had a residual interest in Rose, the money that had been stolen in Ireland, and the people who'd been killed, and I used that. Not very honourable of me, but there it is."

"So were you planning to do anything about Rose?"

"As I've told you, I had no authority to do anything, and that's the truth. I asked about it when I was getting ready to move here, and I was given leave to 'look into it.' That's a wonderful bureaucratic term, and it means damn all. So, I looked into it. I contacted Rose, and invited him for a drink. As it turned out, he didn't remember me. But there was no good reason he should have."

"Did you talk about Ireland at all?"

"Not very much. For obvious reasons, he didn't want to. Ireland was a long time ago, in a different lifetime. So we talked about other things."

"And you became friends."

"After a fashion, yes. It turned out that Harry Rose, for all his awful history, was a pleasant fellow, well read, cultured. He'd made a new life for himself here. I'm not even sure he was the same person he'd been twenty-some years ago."

"And you didn't feel like disturbing that."

"As a matter of fact, I didn't. You see, I'd been through something like this before." Wilson stubbed his cigarette in the ashtray. "I'll tell you a story. In the early thirties, I was posted to Berlin, and I can tell you I had some serious quavers about that. Fifteen years earlier, we'd only been interested in slaughtering each other, us and the Germans. But by 1932, all that was a memory, and Berlin turned out to be a very pleasant experience for me. I got along well with my German counterparts, the butchery of the war was pushed aside, and we got on with the day-to-day things that had to be done." He leaned forward. "And I'll make a prediction. Within five years, probably less, we'll be friends with the Germans again. We'll find common ground. The horrors of the battlefields, and the worse horrors of the death camps, all of that will be set aside. It won't be forgotten, but other priorities will take over. I'm told it's already happening, old enemies turning into new friends. It's the way it works. It always has worked that way."

"Thank you for the lecture, Major. I'm sure that all that you've said is true. But you still haven't answered my question."

"About what I intend to do with this? Well, I'll tell you. I'll write a report and send it up the line, where someone at a higher level than mine will make a decision on it. The possibility of real action on Rose's file was never very great, not in my opinion. For all his perfidy, Harry Rose was small beer, something of a relic, an embarrassment from a past the government in London would just as soon forget about."

"He wouldn't have been arrested?"

"Probably not. That would have dredged it all up again, the bloody seven-hundred-year occupation of Ireland, the Troubles, the sorry record of the Auxiliaries, Britain's sometimes cruel Imperial past. We're in the age of democracy now, the Atlantic Charter and all that. No, I expect any report I write on this will be given all due consideration, and then will most likely be filed away. You know how the bureaucracy works. Assemble the facts, study them at length, do as little as possible and hope that no one really notices."

"We know how the bureaucracy works, Major. Not at your level, perhaps, but we do have an idea. And we also know that people make comfortable nests inside it. People like yourself."

"Steady on, Inspector, there's no call to be abusive. I know you're cheesed with me, and with the whole bloody system, and in a way, I don't blame you. And before you bring it up, I know that one of your men was attacked last night, and that he was badly hurt. I'm sorry about that. It's one of the reasons I called Fort Townshend this morning. I didn't want to leave you in the dark on Rose any longer. I might catch hell for talking to you without clearing it with London first, and I'll deal with that. I'm not quite the complete shit you seem to think I am."

Stride couldn't think of anything to say to that. He looked at Phelan and got a resigned shrug in return.

"You're right," he said. "I apologize."

"Accepted. And at least we're all on the same side now. I understand there was a robbery at Rose's house last night, after your man was attacked?"

"You've talked to Mrs. Darnell today?"

"She phoned me just before you arrived," Wilson said. "She told me her father's safe had been cleaned out, and that there might have been a lot of cash in it."

"We're guessing it was some of the money left over from the bank robberies in Ireland."

"It might have been. But it could just as easily have been new money. By all accounts, Rose was a good businessman. He did well here in Newfoundland. That being said, though, the probability is that he started his business here with the money he stole in Ireland. Starting up businesses with stolen money isn't something new, but it's obviously worth taking note of. And you know the old saying, Inspector. Follow the money. It might take you where you want to go."

"Assuming it's possible to do that."

"Yes. But to get back to Rose's murder. I understand you've got the man who shot Rose. Or at least you have his body."

"Yes, we do," Stride said. "His name's Benton, or at least, that's the name on the passport we found in his things."

"Not a very Irish name, is it?"

"No, it isn't, but we think he probably was Irish."

"And using a forged or stolen passport."

"Possibly. We don't know yet."

"And his accomplice? The one who shot him?"

"We don't know anything about him at all," Stride said. "Not a thing."

Wilson unlocked a drawer of his desk and took out a portfolio. He extracted a file, opened it, and found the item he was looking for.

"You might find this interesting, and it's possible that it's relevant to your case. It's the names of the three IRA men who were killed during the bank robberies."

Stride looked over the names.

"There's no one named Benton on this list." He passed the list to Phelan.

"Yes, I know. But Benton might not be your man's real name. A false name to go along with a forged passport?"

"It's possible." Stride took the list back from Phelan, folded it and put it in his jacket pocket. "We can keep this?"

"Yes, you may," Wilson said. "I have more copies."

CHAPTER 31

Noseworthy was sitting at Stride's desk writing a note when Stride and Phelan got back to their office at Fort Townshend.

"Tell me that's good news," Stride said.

"I don't know how good it is, sir," Noseworthy said. He looked at the unfinished note, then crumpled it up and dropped it in the wastebasket. "But it is news, and it's interesting. The late Mr. Benton's name wasn't Benton."

He let the words hang in the air for maximum effect. He liked to do that sort of thing when he had something out of the ordinary to pass along. Stride allowed him his moment.

"So, how do you know this? We can't have heard back from London this quickly."

"No, sir, we haven't had anything from London. But I took Benton's fingerprints when I was at the rooming house on Empire. I thought London might ask for them. If he really was IRA, they might have his prints on file over there. And anyway, I wanted to have them on file here. I ran them through our system, as much for practice as anything, and there they were. His real name is Patrick Whelan."

"Patrick Whelan," Stride said. "How did we come to have his prints on file? Is he local?"

"No, sir, he isn't. He's Irish. Michael Duggan had it right." Noseworthy's smile was triumphant. But then he saw that Stride was becoming impatient with his game. "Our file on Patrick Whelan goes back four years, sir, to May 1943."

"May, 1943," Stride said. "From back during the war."

"Yes, sir," Noseworthy said. "We registered him as an alien, along with three of his countrymen."

"They were on the *Emily Frances*?" Phelan asked.

"Yes, they were," Noseworthy said.

Phelan looked at Stride.

"You probably remember the night, sir. The *Emily Frances* was part of a convoy out of Halifax, she developed engine trouble and fell behind. She was on her way here for repairs when she was torpedoed by a U-boat a mile outside the harbour."

Stride nodded. He did remember the night. A fitful sleeper even in quiet times, he'd been jolted into sudden wakefulness in the early morning by the sound of the explosions that carried all the way into the harbour, echoing off the surrounding hills.

"There were survivors," Stride said. "And I remember that some of them were Irish."

"Eleven survivors altogether," Noseworthy said. "A mixed lot, English, Canadian, American, French. And four Irishmen."

"And Whelan was one of those four?" Stride said. "He matches the photograph we have on file with his fingerprints?"

"Close enough, sir. Whelan really wasn't at his best this morning, and he was also four years older. But the resemblance is there. Specifically, his left earlobe. Part of it is missing."

"What else do we have on him? Anything?"

Noseworthy picked up a file from his desk and gave it to Stride.

"What there is, is in there, sir. Bernard Crotty found it in the Security Division boxes."

The file on the survivors of the *Emily Frances* was similar to hundreds of others that had been generated during the war by the Constabulary's Security Division, when Newfoundland had been turned into something like a fortress on North America's eastern extremity. Thousands of foreign troops and civilians— American, Canadian and British—had streamed into the island to construct and man military bases for the war against Germany. And this file, like all the others, would likely have been forgotten, just one more dossier gathering dust in a document box in the Constabulary file room, destined for the archives a few years down the road. Except that one of the four Irishmen registered in 1943 had now turned up again, shot dead in a rooming house on Empire Avenue.

"Whelan and his three mates were bunking down at the hostel, the Caribou Hut on Water Street," Noseworthy said. "They left the city at different times, though. The other three caught a military flight to Halifax two days after they came ashore here. They had berths waiting for them on a freighter that was being readied for another convoy later that same month."

"Christ," Stride said. "Two days after they're almost killed by a U-boat, they were ready to go back out there again."

"I think merchant seamen were almost a special breed, sir."

"Not much doubt about that," Stride said. "But was there a reason why Whelan stayed on here?"

"I don't know if there was or not. Andy Cobb might have something to tell you about that."

"Cobb?"

"Andy was assigned to keep an eye on Whelan and the other three while they were here, given the situation with Ireland and Germany at the time. It wasn't close surveillance, but Cobb more or less kept tabs on the four of them. There isn't anything much in the file about it, and chances are there wasn't a lot to report. If there had been, I think even Cobb would have made a note of it."

"I didn't actually know this file existed," Stride said. "But I'm not really surprised that Cobb was assigned. Andy always got along better with the head of Security Division than I did. I'm not sure Rex Hayward really trusted me all that much."

The file had two memos between Cobb and Hayward, and a third between Hayward and Basil Redmond, the Commissioner of Security.

"We'll talk to Andy about it," Stride said. "He might remember something that didn't seem relevant at the time, but might be relevant now."

"Like the possibility that Whelan ran into Harrison Rose four years ago, and recognized him," Phelan said.

"It's possible that's just what happened. Does McCowan know about this?"

"I briefed him about it," Noseworthy said. "He's in a meeting downtown for the next couple of hours."

"We have some information for him as well," Stride said. "We had a long talk with Major Wilson before we came back here."

"I knew he'd called you here. I'm assuming he had things to tell you about Rose?"

"A hell of a lot," Stride said. "I'll give you the short version, the words without the music."

"A man of many parts," Noseworthy said, when Stride was finished.

Stride took the list of names Wilson had given them from his pocket. He gave it to Noseworthy.

"You'll see there's a Gerald Whelan on that list."

"So it's possible Whelan's motivation for killing Rose was as much personal as political."

"Maybe even more so," Stride said. He took the list back from Noseworthy. "We'll see what, if anything, Cobb can add to this."

Andy Cobb was just hanging up the phone when Stride and Phelan came up to his desk. He sat back in his chair, feet spread wide apart, his hands clasped over his belly.

Stride sat on a chair beside the desk and took out his cigarettes. He offered one to Cobb, but Cobb shook his head and unwrapped a stick of chewing gum.

"Trying to cut down," he said.

"Any luck with that?"

"Some good, some bad. The good part is I smoke less, the bad is I eat more, and I'm putting on weight." He patted his belly. "The wife keeps on at me about that, just like she's always on at me to stop smoking. Not sure what might make her happy."

Phelan placed the Security Division file on the desk. Cobb picked it up and gave it a quick look.

"Well, they say what goes around comes around. Bern Crotty gave me the heads-up on this when Noseworthy picked up the file. He says the stiff we found on Empire is one of the fellas in here."

"You didn't recognize him at the rooming house?"

"I didn't get that close," Cobb said. "Was I supposed to? It was your case, after all, yours and Harry's. I was just along for the ride."

"But you were assigned to keep an eye on Whelan when he was first here in St. John's, back in 1943?"

"That was four years ago. I trailed around after a lot of people back then, during the war." Cobb picked up the file again. He looked at Whelan's photograph, then scanned the rest of it. "Okay, it's coming back to me now. So what do you think I can do for you on this?"

"We've read the file, Andy, but we'd like you to go through it with us in more detail, maybe flesh it out a bit?"

"You think I might have left something out?"

"I don't know. Did you?"

Cobb gave Stride a look, then he shrugged and went back to the file. He spent a minute or two reading through his memos and his summary report. He closed the file and pushed it in Phelan's direction.

"I'll give you the ten-cent tour. Hayward always got interested when we had Irishmen wandering around the city during the war. Well, you know that already. If Hayward had been Commissioner of Security, they'd have all been locked up the moment they set foot on the island, every last one of them." He glanced at Phelan. "No offence, Harry, but that's the way he felt about it. But if we'd even thought about doing that, there would have been hell to pay. Half the city's Irish, and the Archbishop would've pissed carbolic, never mind the mayor and the council. So would Redmond, for that matter, and him and Hayward was pretty close. So he did the next best thing. He tried to keep an eye on as many of them as he could."

"Did he have some particular reason to think that Whelan or the other three might have posed a risk?"

"Apart from them being Irish?" Cobb smiled. "No, he just wanted someone to keep an eye on them. And that's where I come in."

"It doesn't look like you kept a very close eye on them," Phelan said. "Not from what's in here."

"The first day they were here, I didn't have to. They were tired and beat up, and they scarcely budged from the hostel. They ate and they slept, and that was about it. Then, two days after they got here, three of them left the city on a flight to Halifax. That left the fourth one, Whelan, for me to look after. And that was a relief. Chasing around this town after four sailors isn't what I call light duty. Not over those hills, and especially not that year. It was hotter than the hobs of hell, that May-month."

"Did Whelan do anything interesting while he was here?"

"Not much. He did some shopping. One night he went to a band concert, but he didn't seem to like it much, because he left early. And he went to church. St. Patrick's was his choice, over on Patrick Street. He started off with the Cathedral, but maybe he found that was a bit too grand for his tastes. I don't know, I never asked him. All I know is he went to church a lot—two, three times a day."

"Was there something going on at St. Patrick's that had him coming back so often?"

"I don't think so, but twice I saw him out walking with one of the priests there. His name's Father Feehan, Dermot Feehan before he put on the collar. He's local, but I found out later he'd done his studies at a seminary in Dublin. So, Whelan being Irish, I imagine they found things to talk about."

"They probably did. Anything else, Andy?"

"Nothing that comes to mind," Cobb said. "But maybe Father Feehan can tell you something more about him. He's still there, the last I heard."

St. Patrick's Church was built in the style of Late Gothic Revival, and it had dominated the lower part of Patrick Street since its completion in 1881. The addition of a tall spire and bell tower thirty years later only added to its pre-eminence.

Stride parked the MG across from the church on the west side of the street. A few people were going in and out of the main entrance. Some of them looked to be members of the congregation, but others had probably come just to see the church, to walk up and down the aisles under the vaulted ceilings, looking at the stained glass windows—windows which, ironically, had been imported from England, erstwhile oppressor of the Irish nation and their patron saint.

"I knew Feehan when I was at Holy Cross School," Phelan said. "Just across the street there. And I've met him a couple of times since then." He pointed to a short, red-faced priest sorting books at a table on the far side of the church. "That's him over there."

Father Feehan caught sight of Phelan and Stride when they started down the aisle towards him. He gave Harry a look of tentative recognition and arranged the last few books on the table. He walked towards them.

"It's Sergeant Phelan, I think?"

"Yes, it is, Father. It's been a while."

"And so it has, but you're looking well, Harry. And it's good to see you again." Feehan turned to Stride. "And I believe I've seen you here at St. Patrick's once or twice. But you're not a regular, I don't think."

"My name's Eric Stride, Father. I'm an inspector with the Constabulary. And I'm afraid I'm not a regular anywhere."

"Shopping around, then, are you? Looking for a spot to hang your spiritual hat, so to speak?"

"That's about the size of it."

"And you've found that one size doesn't fit all," Feehan said. "Well, it doesn't do a man any harm to try things on. Sometimes it's the only way to get a proper fit." He looked at Phelan and Stride in turn, a cautious smile on his face. "Now, as I know you're both with the Constabulary, I'm supposing this isn't just a chance visit. You'll be wanting to talk to me about something."

"If you have some time to spare, Father," Stride said.

"I can manage that." He looked across the church where another priest was looking in their direction. "I'll just have to step over there for a moment, Inspector, and tell Father Reagan that I'll meet with him later on. I won't be a moment."

"I hope we're not interrupting something."

"There's always something to interrupt, no matter the time of day. Father Reagan is wanting to discuss church finances with me. In the catalogue of evils, there's purgatory, there's hell, and then there's church finances, more or less in that order. I'll consider it displeasure deferred."

Feehan stepped into the pew and sidled across to the other side of the church. His conversation with Reagan took less than a minute. Then he looked back at Stride and Phelan, and gestured with his hand towards the front of the church, before moving off in that direction. They caught up with him near the altar.

"We can use the office back there." Feehan pointed to a door behind the choir stalls. "That will give us some privacy."

Feehan moved on ahead of them, the hem of his cassock swirling around the heels of his black boots. He walked unevenly, and Stride noticed that the heel and sole of his right boot were thicker than the left. He was also breathing heavily, and a sheen of sweat glistened on the back of his neck.

Feehan waited until Stride and Phelan were seated before taking a swivel chair near the desk. He leaned back in the chair, took off his glasses and laid them on the desk. He massaged the bridge of his nose, then folded his hands in his lap.

"Well, ask me your questions," Feehan said, "and I will answer if I can."

"We need to ask you about someone we believe you knew four years ago. A man named Patrick Whelan."

"Patrick Whelan." Feehan repeated the name, the words just audible. He closed his eyes and his head slumped forward until his chin touched his chest. His lips moved, but Stride couldn't make out what he said.

"Father?"

Feehan looked up.

"As soon as I saw you come into the church I had the feeling that you were here about that business with Harrison Rose. And now you're asking me about Patrick Whelan, and that tells me I was right."

"You know something about this?"

"Not in the way you mean when you ask the question, Inspector. Not in that way."

"What way, then?"

"Give me a moment to collect my thoughts. This has been a difficult few days for me." Feehan took his glasses from the desk, looked through the lenses, and put them on. "I'll start by telling you that I've known for a long while who Harrison Rose was, or more exactly, I knew what he'd been. Mr. Rose was with the Auxiliaries in Ireland, back at the time of the Troubles." Feehan was silent for a moment. He shook his head, and the movement caused a rivulet of sweat to run down the side of his neck. "I was in Dublin then, and I was also there when the Easter Rising took place. I wasn't a part of any of it, you understand; I kept well clear of it all. But, if it matters, or makes any difference to your opinion of me, I was on the side of the Irish, the rebels, and I was on their side for all of the time I was in Ireland. I hated the violence, but that was the choice I made, and I would make the same choice again today."

"Did you know about Colonel Rose from back then?"

"No, not then. I found out about Mr. Rose four years ago."

"When Patrick Whelan was here in St. John's?"

"Yes. It was Patrick Whelan who told me about him."

"How did that come about, Father?"

"It was entirely by accident. Although, in a way, I had a hand in it."

"I'm not sure I follow you."

"Let me try again. After he arrived in St. John's, after his ship was torpedoed, Patrick Whelan came here to St. Patrick's quite often. You'll understand that the man was in very bad shape—wounded, if you will. Not in his body so much, but in his spirit. The night his ship went down, the *Emily Frances*, he escaped death only by the smallest of margins. Just minutes before the torpedoes struck the ship, he'd been down in the engine room, working with his mates. It was pure chance that he went up on deck to get a breath of fresh air. All of the men he was working with died that night. And that was something that weighed heavy on him."

Feehan paused then, and looked at Stride.

"But before I go on, can I ask you a question, Inspector?"

"Of course."

"You must have known that I was acquainted with Patrick Whelan, or you wouldn't be here. How did you know to come and talk to me about him?"

"We have a file on Patrick Whelan back at Fort Townshend. It was established during the war, after the *Emily Frances* was torpedoed."

"Because he was Irish."

"Yes. Ireland was nominally neutral during the war, but there were strong German sympathies among some people in the country. Including in the Irish Government."

"I understand. So Patrick was under surveillance while he was here. As a possible enemy alien."

"Yes."

"And never mind that he was risking his life as a merchant sailor on ships bringing supplies to England."

"Unfortunately, that is the case."

"And was it yourself who was peeping around the corner at me and Patrick Whelan, Inspector?" He looked at Phelan. "Or was it you, Harry?"

"It wasn't either of us, Father," Phelan said. "But it was one of our people."

"I see." Feehan turned away and looked towards the window for a moment. "I just wanted to know, that's all. And now I'll get on with it. One night, there was a band concert in Bannerman Park. You'll recall there were a lot of concerts like that in the days during the war. I persuaded Patrick to go. I told him it would be a good thing, that it would take him out of himself, give him an hour or two of relaxation, something I believed he needed. And so he took my advice, and he went."

"And that was where he saw Harrison Rose," Stride said.

"Yes. Mr. Rose was there at the concert, large as life."

"And Whelan already knew who Rose was?"

"He knew who he was from Rose's time in Ireland during the Troubles, with the Auxiliaries."

"Whelan was with the IRA then?"

"Yes, he was an IRA man. And he knew Harrison Rose as one of the men who captured him, who took him into custody with a dozen of his mates." Feehan paused again. "He also knew him as the man who murdered his brother."

"His brother." Stride glanced at Phelan. "Do you know how that happened?"

"After the lot of them were taken prisoner, and Patrick's brother was one of that group too, Rose and some of his men took three of their number out one night. Patrick's brother was one of the three. Their bodies were found the next day, all three of them shot to death. The official report was that they'd been killed while robbing a bank, but Patrick knew that wasn't true."

"The brother. Was his name Gerald?"

"Yes, it was," Feehan said. "How do you know that?"

Stride took out the list of names. He gave it to Feehan.

"We got this list this morning from an official at Government House, someone who had information on Rose's activities in Ireland. Gerald Whelan's name is there."

"So you're telling me the British Government knew about this all along? And they did nothing about it?"

"It's complicated, Father, but that's more or less the situation. But, tell me, what happened after Whelan saw Rose here in St. John's? Did he speak to him, or try and make contact?"

"No, he didn't." Feehan stared at the backs of his hands for a moment. "He came back to the church to see me that same night. He was very agitated, very upset. Seeing Harrison Rose, and it coming so soon after the tragedy with the *Emily Frances*, the poor man was in a terrible state. It took me a very long time to calm him down, to make him see sense."

"I'm sorry?"

"Patrick wanted to kill Rose that night. It was complicated, because his first reaction when he saw him in the park was fear and disbelief, all mixed up together. He left the park before the concert was over and he came straight back here, to the church. He was afraid at first that Rose would recognize him. But later on, after he'd gathered himself, he wanted to go back to the park, find the man and kill him."

"But you talked him out of it."

"It took a long time. He even asked me for absolution for what he was going to do, but of course I refused him. In the end, I persuaded him that there were terrible things done by both sides in Ireland during the rebellion. Too much blood had already been spilled in that war, and it was past time to let it go."

"Did Whelan try and see Rose again?"

"I can't be sure, but I don't think he did. And anyway, two days later, he had a berth on another ship and he was back at sea."

"Did you hear from him again?"

"Once, only. It was some months later, a letter from Dublin. He wrote to thank me for my kindness to him while he was here in St. John's. He chose his words carefully. I believe he knew that a letter from Ireland would be opened and read by someone in the government here, and that if he mentioned Harrison Rose's name, I'd have had a visit from you people."

"You would have," Phelan said. "But you never heard from him after that?"

"I never did. I wondered if perhaps another of his ships was sunk under him, and that this time he was not so fortunate." Feehan looked at Phelan, and then he turned his attention back to Stride. "And, now, Inspector, are you going to tell me that Patrick Whelan is back here in St. John's, and that he's made good on his threat to kill Harrison Rose? Is that what this visit is about?"

"Yes," Stride said. "That is what it's about."

"You've arrested him? You've got him in custody? Is that what you're going to tell me now?"

Stride shook his head.

"No, Father, we haven't arrested him. Patrick Whelan is dead. We found his body yesterday. We believe he killed Harrison Rose, but he was wounded himself in the attempt. And later on he was killed, probably that same night."

"I don't understand. How was he killed? By one of your people?"

"No. We think he must have had an accomplice. Either he came here with one, or he met up with someone here in the city. Then, when he was wounded during the attack on Rose, his accomplice killed him. Probably because it jeopardized his own safety."

"I've heard of such things happening," Feehan said. "During the Great War, and during the Troubles, too." He sat silent and still, now, his hands clasped in his lap. His eyes were closed tight, and he seemed scarcely to breathe. After a minute he looked up again. "When I heard that Mr. Rose had been killed, Patrick's name came to mind at once. Well, I've already told you that. I wish he had contacted me when he got here, but he didn't. Four years ago, I was able to talk him out of killing Harrison Rose, and I might have been able to do it again, if I'd had the chance. But perhaps that's why he didn't contact me. He didn't want to be talked out of it this time."

"That might be the case," Stride said. "And there's something else. Whelan was ill, terminally ill with cancer. That came out at his autopsy."

"So his killing Harrison Rose was, in a way, almost a last act for him," Feehan said.

"It's possible."

"It's madness," Feehan said. "An obsession with death, all of it. And I've no real faith that it will ever stop. Dear God, Patrick Whelan fought with the British Army against the Germans in the Great War. Then he fought against the British as a member of the IRA. And after that, he fought with the Allies again, this time as a merchant seaman, carrying goods to England. And now, facing his own death, he's committed murder, and he's been murdered himself." Feehan was silent for a minute, looking towards the window. "Do you find fault with anything I've said, Inspector? Have I missed something?"

Stride shook his head.

"No, I don't think you've missed anything, Father."

"And this accomplice you've talked about. Do you know who he is? Do you even have any idea?"

"No, we don't."

"Then, it's not over yet, is it?"

"No, it's not over," Stride said. "Not yet."

CHAPTER 32

Noseworthy was working at one of the tables, catching up on his filing, when Stride and Phelan got back to Fort Townshend. Filing was Noseworthy's least favourite activity, the sort of routine work that he hated, and towards the end of every week, the files tended to pile up. But he always knew where everything was, no matter how disorganized things appeared to an outsider.

"I want to have a look at the files you took from Rose's house," Stride said.

"The personal ones?"

"The information on the renovations he had done."

"You'll find them in one of those two boxes on the table over there, near the window."

"I see this is your filing day. Were you about to start working on them?"

"No, not just yet. Today is mostly for last week's pile. This week's pile I'll probably get to tomorrow." He pulled a new collection towards him. "How did it go with Father Feehan over at St. Patrick's? Anything useful?"

"Not in terms of bringing this thing closer to a conclusion, but we have a better understanding of what was behind it. Rose and his fellow Auxiliaries killed Whelan's brother. He was one of the three IRA men on the list."

"Gerald Whelan."

"And the sequence of events is more or less what we figured. When Whelan was here four years ago, he went to a band concert one night in Bannerman Park."

"And that's where he saw Rose."

"Yes, and everything else seems to have flowed from that. Feehan said Whelan was ready to kill Rose that night, but he talked him out of it."

"Which delayed the event by four years," Noseworthy said. "Until Whelan found out he was dying of cancer, and decided to take Rose with him."

"It might have been something like that."

"I think I can understand it, sir. If I were to find out I had only a few months left, I might want to settle some accounts before I departed the scene."

"You'll give all of us fair warning, I hope."

"It will depend on my mood," Noseworthy said. "And whether I have all my filing done when I get the bad news."

Stride went over to the table by the window and pulled one of the file boxes towards him. He rifled through the collection of files, and when he didn't find what he was looking for, he pulled the second box towards him and went through that. He turned to Noseworthy.

"Kevin, are you sure the files were in these boxes?"

"That's where I put them on Tuesday, sir. When we got back here from Rose's place. I haven't really touched them since then."

"Well, I can't find the ones I'm looking for. The stuff on the renovations."

"Really?" Noseworthy came over to the table and went through each of the boxes. "Well, that's odd. I know they were there two days ago, because I had a quick look through them, just to see what was there."

"But you didn't look at them in detail?"

"No, sir. I only scanned them to see what we might have. All the information on the renovations Rose had done was in there."

"Including the installation of the safe?"

"I suppose so," Noseworthy said. "If the files are anywhere, that's where they should be."

"Then where are they now?"

"I don't know, sir. If those files aren't here, I don't know where they are."

"And you brought them here when? Tuesday?"

"Tuesday afternoon, after we'd finished searching the house. We gave them a quick once-over after we came back here, just to get an idea of what it was we had."

"You and Harry."

"Yes, me and Harry. And Kennedy helped out, too. You remember he was working with us then. He's on leave now."

"Yes, of course," Stride said. He ran his hand across the tops of the boxes again, looking at the filing tabs as they flipped past. "There's a lot of files here still. Have another look, Kevin. Is it only the renovation files that are gone?"

Noseworthy went through the boxes a second time, then stepped back from the table.

"I hadn't got around to actually cataloguing them, sir, but the stuff that's missing had to do with the renovations. I think everything else we brought back is still there." He took out a file, opened it and showed it to Stride. "Here's the receipt for the safe. It shows that Tim Belbin ordered it in from the States." He closed the file and slapped it on the table. "Damn it! I should have looked at these more closely. If I had, we would have known there was a safe in the house."

"Spilt milk," Stride said. "We can't change that." He opened the file again. "This only says that Belbin supplied the safe. He didn't do the installation."

"No, sir, someone else would have done that. That job needed a master carpenter, and I know for a fact that Belbin hasn't ever done carpentry work as complicated as that. He would have hired someone to do it, or recommended someone to Rose."

Stride looked at the boxes again.

"And this room's not locked during the day?"

"Not while I'm in the building, it isn't. The more sensitive material—fingerprint information, photographs, forensic items like the bullets that Butcher took out of Rose and Whelan—that's all locked away in cabinets unless I'm actually working on them. I requisitioned another cabinet two months ago so that I could secure all the material I have in here, but the request is still working its way through the system."

"Like it would," Stride said. "So anyone can come in here during the day."

"Yes, sir. Anyone who works here. But I don't know who would have taken the files, or why."

Stride leaned against the table and stared at the two boxes, thinking. And then he thought he knew what had happened.

"Have you seen Kennedy today?"

"No, sir. I haven't seen him since sometime yesterday. As far as I know, he's still on leave. Why?"

"Because Kennedy's father was a master carpenter. Mike Kennedy. McCowan told me something about him a day or two ago."

"Kennedy's father," Noseworthy said. He looked at Stride, and then at the file boxes. The penny dropped. "Christ. Is that why he was being so helpful?"

"Maybe," Stride said. "But let's not jump to conclusions, not just yet. Do we have anything else that that can tell us something about Rose's household accounts? Cancelled cheques, bank statements, an account book? Anything?"

Phelan walked into the room. He picked up on the tension between Noseworthy and Stride.

"Something's going on?"

"We're missing some of Rose's files," Stride said. "We think Kennedy might have taken them."

"Kennedy?"

"Kennedy's father might have done some of the work on Rose's house."

Stride turned his attention back to Noseworthy.

"Rose had a personal account book, sir, and I think it itemized his expenditures on household items. I saw it when we were looking through the files. I didn't spend any time on it, but I took it out of the file box and locked it away." He went over to a filing cabinet, unlocked it, and took out a hard-covered black book. He placed it on the table and opened it. Stride and Phelan looked over his shoulder while he turned the pages.

"There it is," Stride said. "An entry for Michael Kennedy. Carpentry work."

"There are a half-dozen entries here for Mike Kennedy," Noseworthy said. "Living room, kitchen, bedrooms, bathroom. Kennedy's father did a lot of work for Harrison Rose."

"Tom Kennedy must have known about that," Stride said. "McCowan told me Mike Kennedy wanted both his sons to follow him into the carpentry trade."

"He probably brought Kennedy along with him when he was working on Rose's house," Phelan said. "It's the sort of thing a father would do. My old man used to take me along with him on jobs sometimes."

"There's something else," Noseworthy said. "Kennedy's the one who found the ring of keys in Rose's bedroom when we went through the house Tuesday morning. The keys to the safe could have been among them."

"And you said you haven't seen him since yesterday?"

"No, I haven't. He's been on leave this week. But I know he has a girlfriend. It could be he's with her."

"Do you know who she is, or where she lives?"

"No, I don't, but Dickson probably does. He's the one who told me about her."

"Harry, you and Kevin go and check the barracks. Ask if anyone's seen Kennedy today, or even since yesterday. I'm going to talk to Dickson."

"Her name's Codner," Dickson said. He consulted his notebook. "Patsy Codner. Kennedy told me she rents a room in a house on Carter's Hill. I have the address here in my book. I asked him for it in case I needed to get hold of him when he was playing hooky from the barracks. There's a phone in the house, if you want to call her, although she's probably at work now."

"And where's that?"

"The telephone company. I believe she's a switchboard operator."

"Did Kennedy say anything to you about where he'd be today, Billy?"

"All I know is what he told me yesterday, sir. He said he'd be on leave again today. But I already knew that because it's here in the duty roster. Can I ask what's going on, Inspector? Has Kennedy done something?"

"I don't know yet, but we need to talk to him. If he shows up, or calls in, tell him that I need to see him about the Rose investigation. Tell him that I've asked McCowan to assign him to work with us on the case for a few more days."

Noseworthy and Phelan came into the room.

"He's not in the barracks, sir, and he didn't sleep there last night. No one's seen him since sometime yesterday."

"All right. Harry, you and I will check at the house on Carter's Hill." He turned back to Dickson. "You're all right with this, Billy?"

"Yes, sir, of course. I'll be surprised to hear that Kennedy's done anything wrong, though. He seemed like a decent lad to me. I even knew his father."

"I'll explain it all later. Just bear with us until we get hold of him. And don't say anything to anyone. It's important."

Stride parked the MG at the top of Long's Hill, far enough away from Carter's Hill that it wouldn't be seen from the house where Patsy Codner lived.

"Before we go knocking on doors, Harry, let's think about this for a minute. I see two possibilities. One is that Kennedy thinks he's got away free and clear with this, and he won't be expecting anyone to come looking for him. The other is that he knew he was only buying himself some time by taking those files from the evidence room, and he'll try and make a run for it."

"There's a third possibility, sir."

"That he had nothing to do with this at all," Stride said. "You're right, three possibilities."

"But if he is involved, and he's making a run for it, that will at least tell us what he's all about."

"Small compensation if we don't find him," Stride said. He looked at Phelan. "There's something else you're thinking about?"

"I'm trying to imagine that Kennedy is the accomplice we've been wondering about. I'm having a problem with that."

"So am I, but if he did empty out Rose's safe, he has to be our leading candidate."

"And maybe he is," Phelan said. "He did have the opportunity."

"To kill Whelan."

"If he is the accomplice," Phelan said, "he would have known where Whelan was bunking, and he could have gone there after we packed it in Monday night.

We don't know that he went back to the barracks, or even to his girlfriend's place."

"So he goes to the rooming house, finds that Whelan is wounded, and makes the obvious decision."

"It could have happened that way."

"The part that doesn't add up for me, Harry, is how he made contact with Whelan in the first place, and why. Kennedy wasn't even on the Force when Whelan was here four years ago. Never mind that I don't see him as the type to shoot someone in cold blood. And, anyway, we don't really know that he did anything. So far, everything's circumstantial."

"So it might all be just a merry mix-up."

"The only way to find out for sure is to go and ask him," Stride said. He opened the door and stepped onto the sidewalk. "So, let's go and do that. If he's with his girlfriend, and all they're doing is being together on his day off, we might have our answer."

"We'll have to ask the question very carefully."

"Don't we always?"

Carter's Hill was on the north side of the Waterford Valley, on one of the steepest inclines in the city. Some of the houses seemed at risk of tearing loose from their foundations, to slide inexorably downwards at gathering speed, across New Gower and Water Streets, and into the waters of the harbour. The house where Patsy Codner lived was an aging two-storey clapboarded structure, with faded green paint that was peeling badly.

They went up to the front door, stepping across a gap created by a broken board in the lower step. Stride tried the door but found it was locked. He pressed the button on the doorbell, waited for a minute, and when he got no response, he tried again.

"I don't hear a bell," Phelan said. "Chances are it hasn't worked since Christ was in nursery school."

"It's probably just as well. If Kennedy's in there, it would only let him know that visitors are calling."

"Let's pretend we found the door unlocked," Phelan said. He took a clasp knife from his pocket, opened it, and slid the blade between the jamb and the door. With only a bit of effort the door shifted far enough that the bolt disengaged and it swung open.

They stepped inside, closed the door, and stood in the entranceway, listening. From upstairs came the sound of voices, but the words were indistinct. Stride thought he could hear a man and a woman.

A door opened at the end of the hall and an elderly man poked his head through the opening. Stride raised a finger to his lips and moved quietly down the hall, gesturing with his hand for the man to go back inside his room. Phelan followed behind and the three of them went into the room together. Stride eased the door shut and took his badge from his pocket.

Stride guessed the man was about eighty years old, maybe older. A grey stubble of beard, at least a week's worth, garlanded his face. His sunken mouth and barely visible lips gave testimony to the loss of all his teeth at an early age. His right eye had the milky look of a cataract long since past any hope of repair.

"It's been twenty years or more since I done anything interesting enough to catch the attention of the police," the old man said. "So I'll guess it's not me you're here to see." He raised his eyes towards the ceiling. "I don't know that them two are breaking any laws up there, although they might break that bed one of these days."

"We're looking for a young woman named Patsy Codner," Stride said. "Is she one of the people upstairs?"

"Yes, she is, and a decent-looking bit of gash she is, too. She's up there now with her fella."

"The man who's with her. Is his name Kennedy?"

"I don't know if that's his name or no. But if your man Kennedy's first name is Tommy, then that probably is him. I heard her call it out often enough. Hardly slept a wink the whole bloody night, and I'm deaf in one ear." The old man laughed. "I don't like to lose a night's sleep, because it leaves me all wore out the next day, but all that activity up there brought back some darling memories." He winked at Stride with his one good eye. "I wasn't born this old, you know."

"Is there anyone else living here?"

"Just now, there's three of us here altogether. Me and that young woman upstairs, and a fella named Goobie, but he isn't here right now. Goobie's a salesman, and he's on the road most of the time. Chinaware is what he sells. Cups and saucers, plates and bowls. And fancy pisspots too, I dare say. He loaded up his car three days ago, a big old '36 DeSoto, and lit out for the Southern Shore, down Ferryland way, I think. Said he wouldn't be back for two weeks, and I think he was telling the truth, because I haven't since him since."

"All right, Mr.—"

"It's Peckford. But you just call me Harold, sir. Everyone does."

"All right, Harold. Sergeant Phelan and I are going upstairs to have a word with Mr. Kennedy, if that's who it is up there with Miss Codner. I want you to stay here in your room until we tell you it's all right to come out. You understand that?"

"Sure, I understand, but to tell the God's honest truth, I'd rather tag along and watch what's going on. I suppose I'd just be in the way, though. And if your man Kennedy gets pissed off, like I think he might, he could do me an injury, and I don't bounce too good no more."

Stride offered the old man a smile and opened the door. He looked towards the staircase that led to the second floor and motioned for Phelan to follow him. They started up the stairs, treading on the sides of the steps to minimize the noise.

Once on the landing, they took their positions, just as they'd done a hundred times before, one on each side of the door. Kicking doors in—when it came to that—was one of Harry's specialties, a skill honed to perfection during the war years, when it was necessary sometimes to get quickly into rooms that housed drunken servicemen, or occasionally servicewomen—or sometimes some of each.

There was a buzz of conversation from inside the room, and there was also the sound of activity, although Stride wasn't sure what that was. He motioned to Harry, and then rapped on the door. The conversation inside the room came to a halt and there was almost complete silence, with only faint sounds coming from the street outside.

Stride raised his right index finger to let Harry know that he would try one more time. He rapped again, and as he did so, Harry positioned himself to apply his right foot to the door. Then, a woman's voice came from inside.

"If that's you, Harold, you can just go away. I'm busy right now."

"It's not Harold, Miss Codner. My name is Stride, and I'm looking for your friend, Tom Kennedy. I need to talk to him about some police business."

There was no reply. Stride rapped on the door again.

"I need to talk to you, Kennedy. Open the door, please."

"Tommy's not here." Another soft buzz of whispered conversation from inside the room gave the lie to what she said. "He went out. And I can't open the door now because I'm not dressed. You'll have to come back later."

There was a different sound from inside the room.

"I'm guessing a window," Phelan said.

Stride nodded. Phelan's double-soled brown oxford hit the door panel just under the knob. The door exploded inward and slammed against the wall. Stride stepped into the room, Phelan right behind him.

Tom Kennedy was clambering over the windowsill, only half dressed, his blue uniform shirt unbuttoned. Patsy Codner backed towards a far corner of the room, confused and frightened, alternating glances between Kennedy and the two detectives. She was barefoot and wearing only a white slip.

Two suitcases lay on the bed, both of them open, half filled with clothing. A canvas bag lay on the bed between them, the zipper pulled shut.

Kennedy was all the way through the window now, hanging onto the sill, looking down at the ground, judging the distance.

Stride tapped Phelan on the shoulder and then headed for the door. He went down the stairs three at a time, one hand on the banister for balance. He just missed colliding with Harold Peckford, who was standing at the bottom. He eased the old man out of his way and ran to the front door.

When Stride rounded the corner of the house, Tom Kennedy was climbing the fence at the rear of the property. Stride sprinted to the fence and caught him by his right ankle.

"Give it up, Kennedy, you aren't going anywhere."

"Fuck you," Kennedy said. He kicked at Stride with his free foot.

"No points for originality," Stride said. He gripped Kennedy's ankle in both hands and yanked him off the fence.

Abruptly the situation slipped out of Stride's control. Kennedy surprised him by rolling with the fall and he was on his feet almost at once. He picked up a handful of gravel and stones and threw it at Stride's face. A stone struck him under the right eye, opening a cut. Stride touched the spot, saw blood on his fingers, and felt it trickle down over his cheek.

Kennedy had a piece of wood in his right hand now. It was about three feet long, and solid looking. Worse still, there were two bent nails sticking out of the business end. By reflex, Stride's right hand went to his hip, but he'd left the Colt in the lock box in the MG. Kennedy picked up on the motion and smiled at him. He was circling Stride slowly, his feet well spread, balancing himself. Stride scanned the ground around him, but saw nothing he could use for a weapon.

So he kept moving, maintaining the distance between himself and Kennedy, playing for time. He thought Harry would soon be on the scene, although that could be a mixed blessing. Kennedy would have two targets to play with, and he could do a lot of damage to both of them before they got him under control.

Keeping the distance between them, and moving steadily, Stride slipped his jacket off and wrapped it around his left forearm. It was something he'd learned years ago, a standard defensive move for someone who found himself in a knife fight. This wasn't a knife fight, but it was close enough. The unexpected movement caught Kennedy's attention, and a look of uncertainty crossed the younger man's face. There was a shift in the balance between them now, and to Stride's advantage. He reversed direction and started moving towards Kennedy, a bit at a time, his swathed left arm held out in front of him, inviting a strike, his right hand balled into a fist.

Kennedy's uncertainty in the new situation came across the distance between them, and gave a slight hesitancy to his movements. Stride feinted with his head towards the corner of the house. Kennedy picked up on the movement and turned his head to see if Phelan was on his way. It was the opening Stride needed, and the only one he was likely to get. He thrust forward. Kennedy saw him just in time and the piece of wood came down on Stride's forearm. The jacket absorbed some of the impact, but not all of it, and Stride felt the pain shoot up his arm and into his shoulder.

Kennedy pulled the stick back for a second try, but before he could do that, Stride threw a right cross that caught him flush on the left side of his jaw. The blow staggered Kennedy, but he didn't drop. He stumbled sideways and backwards, struggling to gather himself, the stick still in his hand. He regained his balance and was about to get off another strike against Stride when Harry Phelan appeared behind him.

Phelan caught the end of the stick in his left hand and spun Kennedy off balance again. Then he stepped forward and drove his right knee into Kennedy's groin, catching him exactly between the thighs. Kennedy's face went chalk white and he sank slowly to the ground, coming to rest on his knees. He struggled to draw a breath.

Phelan picked up the stick and tapped the end with the nails against his palm. He looked down at Kennedy.

"We can keep this going for a few minutes more if you're in the mood, Tommy. What do you say? Yes or no?"

Kennedy looked up at him. He cradled his genitals in his cupped hands, his face wreathed with pain. He made no attempt to stand up. He shook his head and sat back on his heels.

Stride unwrapped the suit jacket from his left arm and rolled up his shirt sleeve. A dark bruise was already forming on his forearm and a hard pain was setting in, raking his arm from fingertips to shoulder and across his upper back.

"You've got a nasty cut under your eye, sir. An inch or two higher and he'd have done you a real injury."

Phelan held out the stick. Stride took it from him.

"We'll take it along for evidence," he said. "It might add a year or two onto his sentence." He looked towards the window that Kennedy had climbed out of. The young woman wasn't in sight. "You took care of the girlfriend?"

"Handcuffed to the bedstead," Phelan said. "Unhappy, but secure." Then he laughed. "I opened that zippered bag. It was full of the money from Rose's safe, and there's a lot of it, all in neat little packets of bills secured with rubber bands. I left all of it on the bed just out of Miss Codner's reach. Something for her to think about."

"Fair enough," Stride said. The pain in his arm and shoulder was making his stomach twist. He concentrated on breathing slowly and evenly. "I saw a wall phone on the second floor, next to her room. You can put in a call for the wagon."

"You'll be all right here with Kennedy?"

"I will be when you've handcuffed him." Stride took his handcuffs from his belt pouch and gave them to Phelan. He watched as Harry secured Kennedy's hands behind his back, looping the cuffs through his belt. He moved off towards the house.

Stride looked at the stick again, felt the heft of it. Kennedy was watching him closely, his eyes moving from Stride's face to the stick and back again. The pain in Stride's arm continued to grow, and his stomach took another turn. The temptation was there, all right, but he pushed it away, and only stood over Kennedy, tapping the end of the stick against his pant leg, and looking down at the man on the ground.

CHAPTER 33

The next morning, Stride and Phelan sat across the table from Tom Kennedy in an interview room at the Court House on Duckworth Street. Kennedy was fully dressed in his uniform shirt and trousers, but the clothes were wrinkled, and he was unshaven. The left side of his face was discoloured and swollen, and weariness sat on him like a lead weight.

When Stride looked at him, they locked eyes for a moment, and then Kennedy looked away. He appeared to be interested in his fingernails. Then he took a deep breath and looked up again.

"You've read your statement through, Kennedy, and now I'll summarize. You've known about Harrison Rose's safe since he had it installed seventeen years ago, because you were there for part of the time when your father was doing the carpentry work. After Rose was killed, and you assisted with the routine search of his house, you came across the keys for the safe. You pocketed those, made impressions of the keys to the back door, and turned the rest of the keys over to Mr. Noseworthy. You continued to volunteer to assist with the investigation because that kept you in touch with what we were doing. When the guard on Rose's house was reduced to a single constable, you saw your chance to get in there and empty the safe. You attacked Constable Michael Doyle, rendering him unconscious, after which you bound and gagged him. You entered Mr. Rose's house and emptied the safe. Among other things, including Mr. Rose's passport and will, you took cash in the amount of some $18,000, all of it in used bills of small denomination." Stride paused and looked at Kennedy. "Do you disagree with any part of that?"

"No, sir."

"It's all correct?"

"Yes, sir."

"What part did Patricia Codner play in this affair? Was she involved?"

"No, sir. She didn't have anything to do with it."

"But she was prepared to help you spend the money," Stride said.

"I suppose she was."

"Did she ask you where you got it? And before you answer, I want you to understand that we'll be questioning her later to see if your stories match. She will likely be charged with being an accessory after the fact, but that's a decision for the Crown to make."

"I told her I got the money from Mr. Rose's safe."

"And she considered that to be acceptable?"

"I don't know if she did or not. I didn't ask her."

"Do you want to add anything to that?"

Kennedy shook his head.

"I require a spoken reply to my question."

"No, sir. I don't want to add anything to what you just said."

"You understand you'll be charged with assault, and theft, both of which are major offences. If Constable Doyle should die, and that is still a possibility, you will be charged with murder. That is a capital offence, and you could face the death penalty. You understand that?"

"I didn't mean to hit Doyle that hard. I only wanted to stun him, and then tie him up and gag him. I didn't know he was hurt that bad. That's the truth."

"Duly noted," Stride said. "Now, some further questions. Do you know, or did you know, a man named Patrick Whelan, or a man named Robert Benton?"

Kennedy looked back and forth between Stride and Phelan, and then he shook his head.

"No, sir, I don't know either one of them."

"You're sure about that?"

"I don't know either of those names. There are lots of people named Whelan in the city, and I know some of them, but I don't think I know anyone named Patrick Whelan."

"Are you familiar with an organization known as the Irish Republican Army?"

"The IRA? Sure, I've heard of them. Everyone has. My father used to talk about them, sometimes. And I've seen movies about them. And I know the IRA was suspected of killing Mr. Rose. But that's all I know about it. I never had anything to do with anyone connected with the IRA."

"The night Harrison Rose was killed, when the two shots we both heard were fired, you stated to me, and in your report from that night, that you were on patrol near St. Thomas's Church on Military Road. You further stated, to me, and in your report, that you saw no one on the street that night, except for some cars driving past. Is that correct?"

Kennedy didn't reply at once. He appeared to be thinking about his answer.

"Your hesitation in replying has been noted. Do you wish to change your account of what you saw that night?"

"I saw Rose out walking that night."

"On Military Road?"

"No, not on Military. When I saw him, he was just coming along to Cavendish Square, near the hotel. I was coming out from Forest Road onto King's Bridge. Rose was quite a ways ahead of me, turning the corner onto Military. I think that's the way he always went. Well, anytime I saw him he went that way."

"But you were close enough to him to know who it was?"

"I wasn't very close, but I recognized him. He was walking with his cane, the way he always did, and he had a distinctive way of walking. I knew it was him."

"And when you saw him, he was going west, towards Bannerman Park?"

"He must have been. But he was out of sight by the time I got that far."

"You claimed you hadn't seen him that night. Why?"

Kennedy hesitated again. He turned away from Stride and looked towards the corner of the room. Then he sighed and he seemed to slump in his chair.

"Because I knew who he was. When I got to the park, I mean, and I saw him lying on the ground. I knew it was Rose."

"That was after you almost struck me with your nightstick."

"Yes, sir. But that part was real. I really didn't recognize you, not right away, not until you identified yourself. And you had a pistol in your hand. That's what I was really looking at. I thought you'd probably shot Mr. Rose."

"All right, go on. How did you know it was Rose? Because of the brawl in the park last spring?"

"There was that, but I knew who he was before then."

"Before then?"

"My patrol route was down that way for about six months."

"Before the brawl in the park?"

"Yes. I used to see him sometimes, out walking, or driving by. I knew who he was because I'd been in his house with my father, and Mr. Rose was there sometimes. It was a long time ago, but I remembered being there when my dad built the safe into the floor of the bathroom. You don't forget something like that. When I was a boy, I used to ride my bike around all those neighbourhoods, looking at the big houses and wishing we lived in one of them. Rose's house was the only one I'd ever been in, and I remembered it. Then, when I saw him after the thing in the park, I remembered who he was. The first few times I saw him after that, while I was walking my beat, I said hello to him, but he pretended he didn't know me, never saw me before. Well, he'd seen me before, and I knew he recognized me. I could tell. It really made me angry that he pretended not to know me."

"And when you saw him in the park Monday night, lying on the ground, you pretended you didn't know who he was because you were already thinking about the safe."

"Rose was rich, and if he had a safe hidden away like that, I guessed there was probably a lot of money in it, or at least something really valuable."

"And that's why you volunteered to assist with the investigation. In case an opportunity came up for you to get at the safe."

Kennedy nodded.

"Yes, sir. I guessed that none of you even knew the safe was there. I was with Mr. Noseworthy when he went looking for one, and he never even thought about looking in the bathroom. I didn't really expect to have a chance at it, but I thought it was worth a try. Then, when we were going through the place, I found the ring of keys in the bedroom."

"And you pocketed the ones you thought might be for the safe."

"Yes. I guessed which ones were the keys to the safe, and I was right."

"And the keys for the door?"

"It was later on that I made the impressions of the door keys. While I was working in the evidence room with Noseworthy."

"I'm interested in the timing of the robbery," Stride said. "When Rose's daughter, Mrs. Darnell, arrived in town, you guessed she would tell us about the safe, and your chance to open it would be gone. Am I right about that?"

Kennedy nodded again.

"Yes, sir, that's correct. I knew it was the only chance I had."

"All right. We'll go back to the night Rose was killed. You saw him on Military Road, or heading towards Military Road, and you lied about it. You also said you didn't see anyone else out walking that night. Was that a lie, too? The man we now know was Patrick Whelan was there that night. He's the one we believe shot Harrison Rose. Maybe you saw him? Maybe you even saw him shoot Rose. Did you?"

Kennedy shook his head.

"I didn't see anyone shoot Rose. The part about being down near St. Thomas's when I heard the shots? That part was true. After I saw Rose go around the corner onto Military, I slowed down a bit, in case he stopped or something. I didn't want to take the chance of bumping into him again, and have him pretend he didn't know me."

"And he was alone that night."

"Yes, he was alone."

"And you saw no one else on the street?"

"There were a few other people on the street, but not very many. It was raining, and it was late."

"But you did see some people."

"A few."

"Can you describe them?"

"There were a couple of young guys, coming along Military, but they were going in the opposite direction Rose was, heading down Ordnance Street, towards Water."

"Anyone else?'

"There was a man."

"A man. That's all you can tell me about him?"

"I just know it was a man. He was a long way away from me, almost out of sight when I saw him."

"Where did you see him?"

"He was on Military Road, going west."

"The same direction Rose was walking. But he wasn't walking with Rose?"

"No, he was a little way behind him, and he was on the opposite side of the street. By the time I got around the corner at Cavendish, he was nearly out of sight."

"And Rose was out of sight by then."

"Yes, sir."

"And that's all?"

"Those were the only people I saw. Apart from Rose, I mean."

Stride looked across at Phelan to see if he had any questions to add. But Harry only shook his head.

"Can I ask a question?" Kennedy said.

"Go ahead."

"What's going to happen to Patsy? Miss Codner?"

"She'll likely be charged with being an accessory," Stride said. "That's for the Crown to decide. I think I already told you that."

"The whole thing was my idea, you know. She didn't have anything to do with any of it."

"Maybe not directly, but she knew you'd stolen the money and she didn't do anything about it. And she was willing to help you spend it."

"I never wanted her to get in trouble."

"It's a bit late to think about that now, isn't it?"

"I know it is," Kennedy said. "But I just wanted to mention it."

"A sideshow." Stride lit a cigarette and slid the package across the table to where Phelan was sitting. He touched the dressing under his eye. The cut had taken three stitches. "This whole affair with Rose's safe was a bloody sideshow."

"I think so," Phelan said. He lit a cigarette and slid the package back to Stride.

Stride and Phelan were sitting together in the interview room. Kennedy was back in his cell under the Court House.

"Kennedy isn't the accomplice we've been wondering about, Harry. I'm certain of that. I believed him when he said he didn't know Whelan."

"So did I, sir. He was telling the truth about that. And, anyway, I don't see Kennedy as the type to shoot someone in the forehead. A thief, yes, and an all-around prick, no question. But the man who killed Whelan is someone a lot different from Kennedy."

"Tell me who that is, Harry, and I'll be your friend for life."

"And if I don't?"

Stride laughed.

"I'll be your friend for life anyway."

"Then I have no incentive to tell you who it is. I'll take the secret to my grave."

"I worry that someone might," Stride said. He looked at his watch. "We might as well get on back to the Fort. I'm overdue for a briefing session with McCowan. I won't object if you elect to pass on that."

"I don't mind, sir. He'll be at least halfway pleased with what we've managed so far. We know who shot Rose, and why, and we know who broke into Rose's house. We don't know who shot Whelan, but at least we don't have to worry about him any longer. I figure two out of three's not too bad. We could have done worse."

"I'll hold on to that thought," Stride said.

There was a knock at the door and a constable came into the interview room.

"You've had a call, Inspector, from Fort Townshend. Dickson said to tell you that Mrs. Darnell phoned. She wants to talk to you about something."

"He didn't say what it was?"

"No, sir. Just that she wants to talk to you."

"I'll call her from here. Was she at the hotel?"

The constable shook his head.

"She's at the house on Circular Road. Dickson said she's decided to move into the place."

"That's a surprise. Last time we saw her, she couldn't get out of there fast enough."

"She had to move there sooner or later," Phelan said. "I suppose she thought about it and decided sooner."

Stride used a phone near the Court House entrance. The conversation with Catherine Darnell took only a few minutes. When he was finished, he dropped the phone onto the cradle and went to the doorway where Phelan was standing, looking out into Duckworth Street.

"Anything important, sir?"

"I don't know. She said there was someone in front of her house this morning, just a little while ago, on the opposite side of the street. She said he was just standing there, looking at her living room window. He stood there for quite a while, she said. It worried her."

"I can't say as I blame her," Phelan said. "But she might have to get used to it, at least for a while. A major crime tends to bring out the gawkers and jackasses." He looked at Stride. "Did she say anything else?"

"She gave me a description of the man. I might be reading something into it that I shouldn't, but I'm wondering if it might have been Cecil Cake. The age was about right, and she said he was a small man. Also that he looked odd. Whatever that means."

"He didn't have a flock of pigeons with him, I don't suppose?"

"I think she would have mentioned that."

"You might want to go on over there, sir. She'd probably appreciate it. And you can take the opportunity to bring her up to date on what we know about her father's murder. I can walk on back to the Fort, if you want to go alone."

"You don't mind?"

"It's a grand day, not a rain cloud in sight. I'll enjoy the walk."

"It's probably just as you're suggesting," Catherine Darnell said. "I suppose I'll have to get used to being an object of curiosity. When word gets out that I'm living here now, there could be a steady stream of people coming by."

"There might be," Stride said. They were sitting together on the chesterfield in the living room. "Most people are kind, but some are not."

"I suppose so. And along the same lines, I've had several calls from reporters. One of them was named Alex Greene. He said he knows you."

"Yes, he does. He's a friend of sorts."

"He was very polite, not pushy at all. Some of the others were, and I said I wouldn't talk to them. Do you think it would be all right for me to talk to Mr. Greene?"

"You don't have to talk to anyone, Mrs. Darnell, not if you don't want to. But if you decide to talk to a reporter, Alex is probably your best choice. He's intelligent, and he's honest." Stride smiled. "And I've told him that I'll personally wring his neck if he behaves badly."

"So, he really is a friend."

"Yes, he is. But tell me some more about the man you saw watching your house."

"I'm not sure there's really a lot more to tell. It's not as though he did anything. He didn't. He only stood there looking at the house. He was a small man, about my father's age, I think, and he had reddish hair. He didn't frighten me, that wasn't it, but there was something about him that made me uneasy." She looked at the backs of her hands, then clasped them together. "No, that's not it, that's not the feeling I had. It was more that I felt he must know me from somewhere, although I can't imagine where that might have been. I'm certain I've never seen him before, but at the same time, there was something very familiar about him."

"How long was he there?"

"I don't know for sure, but at least five minutes from the time I first saw him. He might have been there longer than that, because before I saw him, I'd been in the kitchen and out in the yard at the back. I watched him for about five minutes, on and off, and then I went upstairs and put some things away. And when I looked again, he was gone."

"Perhaps he reminded you of someone you know. Or did know once?"

"Yes, I think that might have been it. I know there was something." She stood up and walked to the front window and looked out at the street. Stride wondered if the man might be there again, but when he looked, there was no one. After a minute, she turned back to him. "It was Dunkirk."

"I'm sorry?"

"It just came to me. That's what it reminded me of, what he reminded me of. The men who came back from Dunkirk. I was there in Dover in May of 1940, when the men from Dunkirk were being brought back across the Channel. I was one of the volunteers. You've probably seen the pictures and the newsreels from then. Tens of thousands of exhausted men, wounded men, some of them beaten into the ground by the experience. But a lot of them, most of them, I think, standing tall, not really defeated, and still ready to fight."

"And this man reminded you of them?"

"In a way he did. He even looked like some of them, weary and dishevelled. As much as anything, I think it was the coat he was wearing, an old army greatcoat that looked to be a size too large for him. But there was something else. He had, I don't know, a certain dignity about him. I know it sounds odd, but dignity is the word that comes to mind." She came back to the chesterfield and sat beside Stride again. "Does any of that make any sense?"

"I think so, yes."

"I'm getting the impression that this strikes some kind of a chord with you. Do you think you know who this man is?"

"I might." Stride thought about the description she'd given him. He decided the man she'd seen must have been Cecil Cake. "There's a man who served with your father in the First War. His name has come up a number of times."

"Is he someone who was involved with my father's death?"

"I don't think so." Stride shook his head. "I don't know."

"Barnes Wilson told me that you have the man who killed my father. A man named Benton. Or at least you have his body. Is that true? I haven't seen anything in the papers about it."

"We haven't released anything yet. Benton's real name is Whelan, and there are still things we don't know about him. But we'll have to release something soon, because people are starting to ask questions."

"So, what Barnes said is true?"

"Yes. We think we know what went on the park Monday night, or most of it. But there are still some loose ends."

"Barnes also told me that you don't know who killed the man who shot my father."

"That is one of the loose ends" Stride said. "We think Whelan must have had an accomplice, and that his accomplice killed him."

Catherine looked at Stride.

"Are you thinking now that this man I saw today might be involved in some way?"

"We don't know that he is."

"But you also don't know that he isn't, do you?"

"No, we don't," Stride said.

Phelan was on the phone when Stride got back to the office. He turned when Stride came through the door and held up his hand.

"Right, yes, I have that," he said. "Thanks. I owe you one." He hung up the phone. "That was the city registry. They got back to me a bit quicker than I expected."

"They had something for us?"

"They gave me the information we wanted. Not all of it's official, but they assure me that all of it's correct."

"The long and the short of it being?"

"The house Cake lives in on Eric Street—he doesn't own it. Lawrence Rivers does. He bought it in 1931. It didn't cost him very much because it was sold for unpaid taxes. Quite a few properties were back then, during the Depression."

"And who pays the property taxes? Rivers?"

Phelan nodded.

"The cheques come out of his personal bank account."

"So, Rivers's friendship with Cake didn't come to a complete end during the war."

"Either that, or it got renewed at some point," Phelan said. "The registry doesn't know exactly when Cake started living there, but the census information has him there from 1932 on."

"Which could be about the time he came back to Newfoundland. But that part might not be important, or even relevant to the investigation."

"Do you think it was Cake that Mrs. Darnell saw watching her house this morning?"

"I'm pretty certain it was, Harry. I had only a brief look at him when I went to his house, but the description she gave me matches what I saw. And it feels right, somehow. There's something else. When Mrs. Darnell saw him, he was wearing an old army greatcoat."

"An army greatcoat. You're thinking about the caribou-head button Noseworthy found near the spot where Rose was killed."

"Yes, I am. It's a long shot, Harry, but that doesn't mean it isn't true. Is there any way to tell how old that button is?"

"I asked Noseworthy about that, and he said there really isn't any way to tell. Those things were mass produced, and the design hasn't changed since the First War. Kevin says the button looks old, but that might only mean that it had been on the ground in the park for a couple of weeks, maybe months. Maybe even longer."

"Is he sure about that? Where did he find it?"

Phelan looked past Stride towards the door.

"You can ask him, yourself, sir. He's right there behind you."

"Ask me what?" Noseworthy came into the room and sat on the edge of Phelan's desk.

"That button you found, in the park. The one with the caribou head. Where exactly did you find it?"

"Very close to the spot where you found Rose's body Monday night."

"Was it on the surface, or under the ground?"

"It was near the surface, just in the grass."

"You didn't have to dig it out, then?"

"No, we didn't," Noseworthy said. "And I know what you're getting at. If it had been there for any length of time, it would have been walked into the ground long since, and we would have had to dig it out."

"But you didn't have to do that."

Noseworthy shook his head.

"I should have made note of that at the time, but I didn't. We picked up a lot of stuff that afternoon. It just got lost in the shuffle."

"That's all right," Stride said. "It really wasn't relevant then, but it might be now. You say the button looks old. But there's a possibility it really is old?"

"It's been around for a while, and that's a fact," Noseworthy said.

"From as long ago as the First War?"

"It could be; I can't say. Why?"

"Because it might be important," Stride said. "We've had a development. Let me bring you up to speed." He looked at Phelan. "I want Corrigan involved in this. Have Dickson try and contact him while I talk to Kevin. Corrigan's beat is on Water Street. You might get lucky and find him near a call box."

Noseworthy sat on the edge of Phelan's desk while Stride went through it all.

"I agree with you that it's a long shot, sir, but maybe Cake was there in the park Monday night. Didn't you tell me that Kennedy saw a man walking west on Military Road that night, not too far behind Rose?"

"Yes, he did," Stride said. "For all we know, that man might have been Cake. But it's all just bits and pieces at this point, not even at the level of circumstantial evidence, and we might find we're only chasing rainbows. But I want to know if that's the case." Phelan came back into the office. "Did Dickson manage to get hold of Corrigan?"

"No, he didn't, sir; he wasn't near a call box. I sent Hynes down to Water Street in the van to bring him back here. He's taking a relief constable with him."

CHAPTER 34

Y es, I own the house on Eric Street." Lawrence Rivers closed the door of his office and motioned for Stride and Corrigan to sit. "I bought it years ago."

"In 1931," Stride said. "You bought the house for Cecil Cake?"

"Yes, I bought it for him. And it was in 1931." Rivers sat behind his desk. "Cec wasn't very well at the time, and he needed a place to live."

"I see. Is he well now?"

"Not really, no, but on the whole he's able to manage."

Stride waited for Rivers to go on, but he didn't.

"What else can you tell us about him, Mr. Rivers?"

"Quite a lot, if you're really interested. But I think it's Harry Rose's murder that you're interested in, and whether Cec had anything to do with it. You wouldn't be here, otherwise."

"That is what we're interested in. The reason we're here now is that Cake turned up at Rose's house this morning. He didn't do anything, he only stood across the street looking at the house for a while. Rose's daughter was in the house. She didn't know who Cake was, or why he was there, so she called us."

"But you say he didn't do anything."

"No. He just stood there looking at the house, and then he went away. Why would he do that, Mr. Rivers?"

"I don't know why he'd do something like that. But let me start by saying that if I thought Cec had anything to do with Harry Rose's death, I would have told you about it the day you visited me. Wednesday?"

"Yes, it was Wednesday. We talked about Cake a little bit then."

"Yes, we did. But there's more to tell, and I think I should probably do that now."

"All right. Let's go back to before Cake moved here. One of the things you told me about him was that he'd been in Ireland after the war. That part was correct?"

"He did go to Ireland. He was there for about four years."

"That leaves a long gap until he came to live in St. John's," Stride said. "Do you know if he was involved with the rebellion in Ireland while he was there? The timing would be about right. And I ask that because Harrison Rose was there then, as a member of the Auxiliaries."

"Harry Rose was with the Auxiliaries? I didn't know about that," Rivers said. "But I suppose I'm not really surprised. Harry was a warrior. It's where he would like to be. But to answer your question, as far as I know, Cec wasn't involved in any part of that. All the information I have on him tells me he really was herding sheep when he was in Ireland. He wasn't involved in any of the fighting there."

"And he was there because he met someone from Ireland during the war?"

"There was an Irish regiment posted near us in Gallipoli, on Suvla Plain. Cec made friends with some of the men. We all did. One of them was from a farming family, and he invited Cec to visit when the war ended." Rivers shook his head. "The likelihood that either of them would survive the war wasn't very great, but they both did. And that's where Cec went when the war was over."

"And that's all he did while he was in Ireland? Herd sheep?"

"For the most part. He did other things, too, odd jobs of various kinds. Men like Cecil Cake, coming from his sort of background, they're able to do a lot of different things. He even went back to fishing for a while, working on a boat on the west coast of Ireland. Fishing's what he knew best, of course. It was the life he'd had before the war, the life he was born into."

"But he was away from Newfoundland for a long time after the war. Did he spend all of that time in Ireland?"

"No, he didn't. If things had worked out for him, I think he would have stayed there. From everything I know about it, from what he's told me, and from what I heard from the people who knew him there, he was happy in Ireland. He'd managed to put the horrors of the war mostly behind him."

"Mostly?"

"Almost no one I know has ever managed to put all of that behind him, not completely. It comes out in different ways. For me, it's drinking too damn much. But I think everyone would have a story to tell, if he was willing to." Rivers looked at Corrigan. "I can only talk about my own story."

"Why didn't things work out in Ireland for Cake?"

"It was his health, specifically the head injury from Gueudecourt. At first, it seemed that he'd recovered well enough. He did come back into the line, after all, and he performed well. But later on things got bad again. I've been told that serious head injuries can have consequences later in life, and maybe that's what happened. Or maybe he fell and struck his head, or got into a fight while he was living in Ireland, I don't know. But whatever it was, after a few years things got bad for him. He was in and out of hospital in Ireland, and later on in England, too. Then, in 1931, a mutual acquaintance, someone who'd known both of us in the war, came across Cec in a hospital in England. He wrote to me, and he told me what was going on."

"And you arranged to bring him back home to Newfoundland."

"Actually, I went over to England and collected him. He really wasn't well enough by then to come back on his own."

"And that was in 1931?"

"Yes. I brought him back to St. John's and set him up in the house on Eric Street." Rivers thought for a moment. "And if you're wondering why no one's mentioned any of this to you, I didn't tell anyone about it, not Albert Dancey, not even my wife. It was something strictly between Cec and me."

"And since then you've paid his bills?"

"Yes, I have. I can afford it, and Cec was a good friend for most of the war. We drifted apart a lot after he was injured. Well, I've already told you about that. The injury changed him."

"That and his brother's death."

"That had an effect, too." Rivers looked at Corrigan again. "Jack knows almost as much as about it as I do. He was there."

"It did have an effect," Corrigan said. "I told you about that, sir. He was never the same man after that. The injury, and Daniel's being killed."

Rivers turned to Corrigan.

"I don't think you've seen him very often since he came back to St. John's, Jack."

"No, I haven't, Laurie. I don't see anyone from back then very often. That's one of the things I brought home with me from the war, wanting to be alone." Corrigan looked towards the window for a moment. "I should have tried harder to stay in touch with Cec. With everyone. I should have, but I didn't."

"Cec isn't an easy man to see, Jack. I was closer to him than anyone, and it's hard for me too. And every year it gets a bit harder. He's gone back a lot."

"I don't know what that means," Stride said. "Gone back?"

"Back to the war. It's a touchstone for him, the most important event in his life. It's that way for many of us, but a lot more so for Cec than for me. Or for Jack, here, I expect. It sometimes seems that Cec's memories of the war are all that he has. But in an odd way, it's where he's most comfortable." Rivers took his cigarettes from his desk drawer. He lit one, and as he'd done when Stride was there before, he broke the spent match in half before dropping it in the ashtray. "When I go and visit him, and I try to go every week, he sometimes talks about the war as if it's still going on."

"Has he ever talked about Harrison Rose?"

Rivers tapped his cigarette against the edge of the ashtray and watched the spiral of smoke for a moment.

"Yes, he's talked about Harry Rose sometimes."

"Go on."

"Harry Rose was our commanding officer at Gueudecourt, the day Cec was wounded." He looked at Corrigan again. "The same day Daniel was killed. Sometimes when I'm talking to Cec, it seems that he's back there again, back at Gueudecourt."

"In what way, Laurie?" Corrigan asked.

"He talks about it in the present tense, Jack. He wonders what's happened to Daniel, why he wasn't there at roll call, and how he wants to get a search party together to go and look for him. But, then, the next thing I know he's back in the here and now, talking about the weather, or about his pigeons, something that has nothing to do with the war."

"He drifts in and out," Corrigan said.

"He does."

"Have you seen Cake since Rose was killed, Mr. Rivers?"

"No, I haven't, although I tried. I drove out there twice, but either he wasn't home, or he wasn't answering the bell. That's not unusual, though. Half the time when I go to visit, he won't answer the door. I've found it's best to leave him alone when he's like that, and try again another day."

"I tried to see him two days ago," Stride said. "I know he was home, because I saw him standing in his front room. But he wouldn't open the door for me."

"You're a stranger, Inspector. I'd have been very surprised if he had opened the door for you."

"I did manage to speak to one of his neighbours, though. The lady who lives next door."

"Her name is Mary Comerford," Rivers said. "She's a widow, and she looks after Cec. She cooks for him, cleans his house, shops for him, does his laundry."

"You pay her to do all that?"

"Yes. We've had an arrangement for going on ten years now, since a year or two before the last war."

"One of the things she told me is that Cake has the *wanders*. That's not a term I'm familiar with, but I know what she meant."

"Yes, he goes out walking a lot. When I first heard about it, I was worried he'd get lost, or get into some trouble. But as far as I know, he never has, and he always manages to find his way back home. He keeps to himself and he doesn't bother anyone. Mrs. Comerford told me he goes out mostly at night. Quite late, she said, when the majority of people are in for the evening."

"You knew that Harrison Rose liked to walk late at night too?" Stride said.

"Yes, I knew that. Albert Dancey told me." Rivers paused. He was uncomfortable now. "But it was a long time ago he told me that, and I just didn't think anything about it. Not until now."

"But did Cake know about that? Rose's late-night walks?"

"I don't know. Maybe he did."

"He said something to you about it?"

"One night he said something about being out on patrol with Rose. It was garbled and confused, like a lot of the things he says, and I thought he must have been talking about something that happened during the war." He looked at Corrigan. "Like the patrol we did that evening in Gallipoli, when Curtis Rowe was killed. But now I'm not sure. He might have been talking about something that was going on now, here in St. John's. I don't know." Now he looked at Stride. "Are you thinking that Cec might have had something to do with Harry Rose's death? And before you answer, I'll say that I don't think that's at all likely. Cec thought that Harry was a good officer, and he had a great deal of respect for him. He's said so to me more than once. And I think this notion of his, his going out on patrol with Harry Rose, it was all about doing his duty for an officer he respected."

"We already know who shot Rose," Stride said. "It was an Irishman named Patrick Whelan. Someone who had a reason to want Rose dead, for something that happened in Ireland during the Troubles."

"Is that the man whose body was found in the rooming house? On Empire Avenue? I read about that in the paper, but they didn't give a name."

"Yes, that was Whelan."

"But who killed him? Have you identified anyone?"

"We think Whelan had an accomplice," Stride said. "And we think that's probably who killed him."

He stopped then, and he thought for a moment about what he'd just said. Then he saw that Rivers and Corrigan were both staring at him.

CHAPTER 35

J ack Corrigan looked at the caribou-head button, turning it over in his hand.

They were assembled in the evidence room at Fort Townshend—Stride, Phelan, Noseworthy and Corrigan.

"Noseworthy found it near the spot where Rose was killed," Stride said.

"And you think Cec dropped this in the park?"

"He could have. Rose's daughter told me that when she saw Cake this morning, he was wearing an old army greatcoat."

"I've seen him in that coat," Corrigan said. "It was a long while ago, but it's probably the same one. I don't know where he got it, but there are a lot of coats like that around the city, sir. And a lot of buttons like this one rattling around, too. Hundreds of them, I expect."

He took a last look at the button and gave it back to Stride.

"I know," Stride said. "And I know it doesn't have to mean anything."

Stride looked at the button once more and gave it to Noseworthy to put back in the evidence box. But then he changed his mind and took it back from him. He wrapped it in his handkerchief and put it into his jacket pocket.

"But it also doesn't have to mean nothing, sir. This could be off Cec's coat. From what Laurie Rivers told us, it's possible that Cec was in the park Monday night."

"Then, let's assume that's the case," Stride said. "The question is, where do we go from here?" He looked around the room at the three men. "I'm open to suggestions."

"We've interviewed people with less reason than this," Phelan said. "I don't see that we have much choice."

"Cec isn't one of your ordinary citizens," Corrigan said. "I don't think he's living in the same world as you and me, Harry. As any of us, for that matter. I'm not saying we shouldn't go talk to him, but he is a special case."

"There's also the matter of the two guns," Noseworthy said. "Rose's .38 and Whelan's 9 mm. Someone has them, and if Cake did kill Whelan, then it's more than likely he does have them. And we have to consider the possibility that he might use one of them if strangers show up at his place wanting to ask him questions."

"What do you think, Jack? Would he be less likely to use them if you went out there with me and Harry?"

"It's been a while, sir, but I think he'll still recognize me. But let's put this in some kind of context. If Cec did shoot Whelan, then he might have turned a corner."

"Meaning?"

"That he might not be in the here and now any more." Corrigan raised his hands in a gesture of futility. "But what the hell do I know?"

"What's your best guess, Jack? You, me and Harry, together?"

"Better just you and me, sir. Three of us might be too much of a crowd for him to deal with." He looked at Stride. "Even two might be pushing it, but I think we have to draw the line someplace. This is a murder investigation."

Stride looked at Phelan.

"Harry?"

"What Jack says makes sense to me, sir. If three of us turn up on his doorstep, it could set him off. If you and Jack go together, and Jack takes the lead, I think you'll have a better chance. But maybe some of us should be nearby, in case you need help. Like Kevin says, those two handguns are missing, and Cake might have them."

"What do you think, Jack?"

"I knew Cec pretty well when we were over there together, sir, and more than once I trusted him with my life, same as he did with me. I can't make that claim now. It's been too long, and too much water's gone over the dam. But, tell the truth, sir, I don't like the idea of anyone else being nearby. The more people at or near the scene, the better the chances of a fuck-up. And with fuck-ups, someone usually gets hurt." He looked at Phelan. "No offence, Harry."

"None taken," Phelan said. "But regulations are regulations, sir, and in a situation like this, there has to be support of some kind."

"All right," Stride said. "This is how it will be. Harry, you and Kevin take the van and park on Shaw Street, well out of sight of Cake's house, but within earshot.

Just. Jack and I will go in together. And you don't come anywhere near Cake's place, either of you, unless you actually hear gunfire."

Stride parked the MG near the corner of Shaw and Eric Streets, just out of sight of Cake's house. The van with Phelan and Noseworthy was another fifty yards away.

Stride and Corrigan walked to Cake's house and up the front steps. Stride touched the Colt in its holster, clipped to his belt under his jacket at the back. He left the jacket unbuttoned. He rang the bell but there was no answer, and no sound from inside. He stepped back and looked towards the house next door, half hoping to see Cake's neighbour appear, but she didn't. There was no sign that anyone was home there either.

"He could be in the yard with his pigeons," Stride said. "He spends a lot of time out there."

"I heard he had a flock of pigeons for company," Corrigan said. "Strange choice, was what I thought, when I heard that. But who I am to talk, living out in the back of beyond with a barrelful of fuckin' cats?"

They stood on the landing for another minute, and then Corrigan started down the steps towards the street. Stride followed behind him. As they passed in front of Cake's house, Stride thought he saw a movement behind the curtains. He mentioned that to Corrigan as they went down the narrow laneway into the backyard.

Cake wasn't in the yard. A scattering of pigeons sat on top of the pigeon house, and more were on the ground nearby, pecking at seeds that had fallen from the feeding pans. Then, suddenly, as Stride and Corrigan stood by the gate surveying the scene, a single pigeon flew into the yard from the street behind them, passing barely over their heads, the beating of its wings loud in their ears, startling them both. They watched the bird fly once around the yard before it settled on the roof of the pigeon house.

Stride led the way to Cake's back door. The screen door was closed and locked, as it had been when he was there before. Across the porch, they could see that the door to the house was open. Stride rapped on the wood frame, but still there was no response from inside. Corrigan moved past him, and he tried, rapping even harder on the wood. When he got no reply, he took out a clasp knife and cut a slit in the screen. He slipped the blade through the opening, lifted the hook from the eye and pulled the door open. Stride followed him into the porch and eased the door shut behind him. Corrigan went to the open back door and rapped on the frame, but still there was no sound from within.

The sun had set now, and evening was coming on. But the sky was clear, and it wouldn't be dark outside for a while yet. The kitchen blinds had been pulled, though, and there wasn't much light inside the house.

"Cec, it's Jack Corrigan. If you're in there, then say something. We need to talk to you." He glanced over his shoulder at Stride. "We're only here to talk, Cec, nothing more than that."

There was only silence.

"Playing hard to get," Corrigan said, but his expression was heavier than his tone. He stepped close to the threshold but stopped short of the kitchen. "I know you're in there somewhere, Cec. It's me, Jack Corrigan, who's talking to you. I know it's been a while, but I hope we're still friends."

Stride moved across the porch until he was close behind Corrigan. He could see into the kitchen, and across it to the hallway beyond. Corrigan turned to look at him, nodded, and stepped through the doorway into the kitchen.

Then Stride heard the sound of a revolver being cocked. He saw the barrel of a pistol appear from the right and touch Corrigan's neck just under the chin. Corrigan made himself stand very still, then slowly raised his hands to show Cake that he wasn't carrying a weapon.

"It's Jack Corrigan, Cec. I'm not armed. You can see I'm not." Corrigan raised his arms higher, and then he slowly clasped his hands behind his head. "Tell me what you want me to do, Cec, and I'll do it."

Cake spoke for the first time. His voice was soft, his tone questioning, and Stride could sense the confusion in the man, just as Rivers had described.

"Jack? Jack Corrigan?"

"Yes, Cec, it's Jack Corrigan who's standing next to you. I'm not surprised you didn't recognize me, though. It's pretty dark in here. Why don't we put on a light, and then we can have a smoke and a talk. Just like old times. Why don't we do that?"

Cake continued to hold the pistol steady. The barrel didn't move from Corrigan's neck.

"I didn't see you at roll call this morning, Jack."

"I was out on a patrol, last night, Cec, and it was a late one. You know what that's like. Out all night and not back until dawn. It leaves a man worn out. I even missed breakfast."

Cake didn't reply. He held the pistol steady for a few moments longer, and then he lowered it, easing the hammer back into place. He stepped away from the wall, and into Stride's view. The pistol, Rose's Webley .38, hung down at his side.

"The Colonel's dead, Jack. Colonel Rose is dead."

"That's bad news," Corrigan said. He stepped into the kitchen, close enough to Cake to take the pistol from him, but he made no movement in that direction.

"That's very bad news. How did it happen, Cec?"

Cake shook his head and started walking towards the hallway that led to the front of the house, still holding the Webley. But then he stopped and turned back to Corrigan.

"What did you say, Jack?"

"You said Colonel Rose was dead, Cec, and I asked you how it happened."

"He was shot," Cake said. "They shot him." He stopped by the hall doorway and looked at Corrigan. He rubbed the side of his head as if trying to stir the memory, bring it into focus. "I think we were on patrol, and there was an ambush. I think that was it. I'm not sure, but I think that's what happened."

Cake looked at the Webley in his right hand, and it seemed to Stride that he was surprised to find he was holding it.

"You saw it happen, Cec? You were there?"

"What?" Cake looked at the pistol again. He tapped the barrel against the palm of his hand. Then he looked at Corrigan. He took a half-step towards him, but then he stopped. "What did you say, Jack?"

"I asked if you were there when the Colonel was shot."

"I was there. And it was bad, Jack, it was very bad."

Cake looked at Corrigan, squinting his eyes to get a better focus in the dim light. Then his gaze moved to the doorway where Stride was standing. He raised the pistol again and pulled the hammer back. He took careful aim at Stride's chest.

"It's all right, Cec, he's with me. He's one of ours. It's all right." Corrigan looked towards Stride. Stride could see that he was trying to find the right words to say. "It's Captain Stride. You remember him, Cec. From our time at Pleasantville, before we went over to England."

"I don't remember any Captain Stride," Cake said. The pistol didn't waver. He moved a step closer.

"He's one of ours, Cec. Truly, he is."

"Are you sure, Jack? I don't remember him."

"I'm sure, Cec. I'm sure." Corrigan moved to place himself between Stride and the pistol. "I wouldn't turn my back to him if he wasn't one of ours, would I?"

Cake didn't reply. He continued to look in Stride's direction, shifting his own position to the side so that he could look past Corrigan and keep the pistol trained on Stride's chest.

Stride tried to read something, anything, in Cake's expression, but the only thing he saw there was resolve, a cold determination.

"It really is all right, Cec. He is one of ours, I promise you. Put the gun down.

You don't want to hurt one of our own."

"If you're sure, Jack."

"I'm sure."

Cake took a final look at Stride, then eased the hammer back into place. He let the Webley fall to his side again.

"I could turn on a light, Cec. Would that be all right? We could sit down and have a smoke together. The three of us." He waited. "All right?"

"The snipers watch out for lights," Cake said.

"There are no snipers, here, Cec. We cleaned them out, remember? We went out on patrol and we took over the hill they liked to set up on, and we kept that hill until we left Gallipoli. You remember."

Cake stared at Corrigan. Stride wasn't sure he was buying the story, or if he even knew what Corrigan was talking about.

"I think I remember," Cake said finally. He turned to walk away, but then turned back again. He rubbed his left hand along the side of his head. He looked at Corrigan. "But that was a long time ago, Jack. That was back during the war."

"You're right, Cec, it was a long time ago."

Cake was looking at the Webley now, and once more, Stride had the feeling he wasn't sure why he had it in his hand. He turned and looked at Stride again.

"Who's that, Jack? Is he a friend of yours? I don't think I know him."

"He is a friend of mine, Cec. His name is Stride. We work together."

"Work together ..." Cake's words trailed away.

He walked across the kitchen and placed the Webley on the counter by the stove. There was another handgun on the counter, one with a long barrel. Stride thought it was a Walther 9 mm, a German pistol. He took a second look and saw that the long barrel was actually a silencer. Cake stood by the counter for a minute, looking at the two pistols. He lined them up carefully, side by side, and then he pulled a chair away from the kitchen table and sat down. He rubbed the side of his head again, and this time Stride could see the wound that Corrigan and Rivers had told him about—a deep indentation in the bone, running the length of his head, only partly grown over with hair. Cake traced the scar with his fingertips, from the front of his head to the rear. He sat silently for some moments before turning to look at Corrigan again.

"I get confused sometimes, Jack. I get very confused. It comes and goes."

"That's all right, Cec."

"No, it's not, Jack, it's not all right. It's not all right at all." He looked down at his hands, and then he spread his fingers wide on the surface of the table. "Sometimes I think ..."

But again his words trailed away into silence.

Corrigan moved slowly across the kitchen, and then he sat on a chair across the table from Cake.

"You said you were there when the Colonel was shot, Cec. Can you tell us about that?"

"What?"

"When the Colonel was shot, Cec. Can you tell me about it?"

"I was there, Jack, but I was too far away to stop it, I was too late. I'm not sure why I was there, but I was. I must have been out for a walk, down by the Colonel's house, and I was nearby when it all happened."

"And you saw the man who shot him?"

"I saw a man …" He was silent then, and again he looked at his hands, the fingers still spread on the table. Then he looked up. There was more life in his expression now. "The Colonel got off one of his own, though. And he hit him, Jack. He hit the bugger."

"He hit the man who shot him?"

"He hit him good, Jack. The Colonel was a good shot, one of the best. You remember. You remember the way he took out those Turks on Gallipoli."

"Yes, Cec, I remember."

Cake's expression dimmed. And then he was silent again for a moment.

"But he was hit bad, Jack, he was hit very bad."

"Colonel Rose."

"He was hit very bad. I couldn't leave him like that, Jack. I couldn't. It wouldn't have been right." Cake looked straight at Corrigan, and as Stride watched, tears flowed down his face. The tears dripped off his chin, onto the backs of his hands and onto the table. "I had to do it, Jack. It was the decent thing."

"Do what, Cec?"

"Put him out of his pain. The Colonel would have done it for me, I know he would have. Just like he done it for Daniel. It was the decent thing. You don't let a man suffer. You have to do the decent thing."

Cake was looking at his hands again. He sat very still. The tears continued to flow, but he made no sound. Then he looked up at Corrigan, and the two men regarded each other across the space of Cake's kitchen table. But over a greater distance than that, over decades, and a host of memories that Stride knew almost nothing about and could never really hope to understand. The silence dragged on for what seemed an age, but was only a handful of seconds.

Still standing there by the kitchen door, not really a part of this, Stride was conscious of the bulge the Colt made in his jacket at the back, and he was embarrassed that he'd brought it with him. It didn't belong here, and he didn't really belong here, not in this situation, not with these two men, men years older than he was, of a different generation, men who'd seen, done and endured things that he could scarcely begin to imagine.

"It was that bad, Cec?"

"It was, Jack. I couldn't leave him like that. Not the way he was."

"I don't know that I could have, either. I might have done the same thing."

"You would have, Jack. You would have done the decent thing."

Corrigan stole a quick look at Stride, then turned back to Cake.

"You said Colonel Rose did it for Daniel. How do you know that?"

"He told me, Jack. He told me himself. When I come back from the hospital, after Gueudecourt, the Colonel took me aside and he told me how he found Daniel in a shell hole that day, and how he was almost cut in half, in terrible pain, and he was dying. The Colonel did the decent thing. He told me that. It was a comfort."

The words tumbled out in a torrent, as though it was something that Cake had been wanting to tell someone for a long time, and this was the first chance he'd had. He was leaning forward and staring at Corrigan with an intensity that was almost frightening. And when he was done, he slumped back in his chair and his chin fell on his chest. His hands dropped into his lap. The room was silent.

Corrigan looked tired, Stride thought, more tired and older than he had ever seen him look before. Corrigan got up from his chair, walked around the table and stood behind Cake. He placed his hands on Cake's shoulders and held on to him.

Stride watched them for only a few moments longer, and then he left the kitchen and walked through the porch into Cake's backyard. He stopped just outside the door, long enough to light a cigarette, and then he went over to the pigeon house. With the fading of the light, most of the birds had retreated inside. Stride saw that the feeding pans were almost empty, and because he knew it was unlikely that Cake would be around to tend to his birds again for a long time, if ever, he decided to top up the pans himself.

He took his time, making extra trips between the pail of seeds and the pans, thinking all the while about what he would do when he was finished. He really didn't want to think about it, but he knew that he would have to come up with something, some way to get Cake from his house to the lock-up, or better still, to a hospital, without causing the man more harm than had already been done to him. When the pans were filled with seeds, he dropped the scoop into the pail and replaced the lid.

He went back to the porch to smoke the last of his cigarette. He reached into his pocket and took out the caribou-head button. He looked at it, rolled it around in his hand, then wrapped his handkerchief around it again, and put it back in his pocket. He took a final drag on his cigarette, dropped the butt on the ground and stepped on it. Then he pulled the screen door open and went back inside the house.

EPILOGUE

Catherine Darnell was wearing a red bandana around her head when she opened her front door for Stride.

"You've caught me in the middle of cleaning and straightening," she said. "But I'm better than halfway done for today, and I'm also ready for a cup of tea. The kettle's on. Why don't you join me? I'd appreciate the company."

"Thank you, I will."

He followed her down the hallway to the kitchen, where the kettle was already rumbling to a boil.

"I'd like to be able to offer you something stronger than tea, but tea's all I have at the moment. With one thing and another, that bottle of gin I brought with me from Boston has vanished." She took the top off the teapot and poured hot water in to warm it. "So, the drink I offered you that first day in the hotel will have to wait a while longer."

"Then I'll have something to look forward to."

"Perhaps," she said. She looked at him and smiled. "Well, we can hope."

He watched as she went through the routine of making the tea, spooning the leaves into the pot, then pouring in the boiling water.

"I have some biscuits, if you're interested. I know I'd like one. You'll find them in that cupboard over there. Middle shelf."

He found the biscuits, and she arranged everything on a tray. Stride carried it into the living room and placed it on the coffee table. He saw that she'd moved things around since his last visit, the day she told him about Cake standing in front of the house. He also saw that some of the pictures of her father had been removed.

"I'm making myself as comfortable as I can." She looked up from pouring the tea. "Although, to be honest, I'm having trouble achieving a lot of comfort in this place. The biggest problem, of course, is my feelings about my father. We didn't have much of a relationship before all this happened, and with all the awful things I've learned about him since I came here, well, that's made it almost impossible."

"It is a lot to deal with," Stride said.

"I try and focus on the positive things I know about him. He obviously had some good qualities. He was a good soldier, and he served his country well. He also must have been a good officer, to inspire the kind of loyalty that this man Cake demonstrated the night he was killed." She stirred some sugar into her tea. "Do you know what will happen to him? To Cake, I mean?"

"No, I don't," Stride said. "It's up to the Crown to decide what happens next."

"In my father's case, it was obviously a mercy killing. He was already dying. But that's not the case with Patrick Whelan, is it?"

"No, it isn't. After Cake shot your father, he followed Whelan to his rooming house and killed him. Strictly speaking, that was murder, and it was premeditated. But I believe the Crown understands that this is anything but a straightforward case."

"I don't suppose you have much say in what happens?"

"I don't. But I've talked to the Crown Attorney, and I've told him what I think. Dr. Butcher has too."

"He's the Coroner?"

"Yes. He's also a respected physician, and a veteran of the Great War. His opinion will count for a lot. I really don't think there's much chance that Cecil Cake will ever stand trial."

"I do hope not," she said.

"And how are you doing?"

"With my father's estate, you mean?" Stride nodded. "That's going to be a slow process. There's a possibility that the British or Irish governments, or both of them, could make a claim on the estate. After all, his business here was started up with the money he stole in Ireland, north and south. There's also the matter of the men he killed in the process. There might be a statute of limitations on the robberies, but not on the murders. Barnes Wilson is one of the people working on the file. He's told me that movement on something as complicated as this will be very slow. In the end, they may just drop it altogether, as being more trouble than it's worth. He doesn't really know at this stage."

"How do you feel about it, personally?"

"About inheriting an estate that's based on blood money? I don't want it. And, happily, I don't need it. If they confiscate everything, I won't grieve at all. Just as long as it's settled, and I can get back to the life I had before I came here.

Before all this happened."

"Back in London."

"Yes. I have a business there. I took a holiday—actually a leave of absence—to try and settle some things with my father, but I want to get back there, back to work. And sooner rather than later."

"What do you do?"

"I'm part of a group who've been in the construction business since the last year of the war. We rebuild houses that were damaged in the Blitz. You'd have to go to London to appreciate the amount of destruction there is to deal with. But we are making progress." She read his look of surprise. "I'm not just a pretty face, you see. I actually know how to do things."

"I never doubted that."

"It wouldn't surprise me if you did. Men always doubt that women can do serious and practical things. There was a time when that was more the case than it is now, but the war changed a great many aspects of our society. Women discovered that we could do almost anything we put our hands to. Even die in wars, if it came to that."

"I know." It was all he could think to say. She'd really taken him by surprise.

"Yes, I expect you do." She picked up a spoon and stirred her tea again. "Look, please forgive my little outburst. My friends tell me I shouldn't carry a soapbox around with me."

"Perhaps not. But I don't disagree with anything you said."

"Well, thank you for that. And you'll understand there's been a lot of backsliding over the last two years, since the war's ended. The men have come back home, looking for jobs, and taking them. And that irritates me, sometimes, even if they are entitled. They did bear the brunt of it, after all. But we won't go all the way back to where things were in the twenties and thirties. I think this really is a new world."

"I know," he said again. It didn't seem to be his day for intelligent conversation. He tried to change the subject. "So you'll be here for a while yet?"

"Yes, I will. Just this morning I wrote to my partners and told them not to expect me in London for at least another month."

"If you like, I can show you around the place a bit while you're here. While the weather's still decent. There are interesting things to see, and do. It's not all rain and fog."

"I'd like that. And thank you, I'll look forward to it. Maybe you'll even let me take the wheel of your MG. You'll see I'm a very good driver."

"I believe you." He swallowed the last of his tea and looked at his watch. "I'm afraid I have to go."

"I'm pleased you stopped by." She walked him to the door. "And I am sorry about my little lecture. I won't do it again."

"I didn't mind. Really."

"You will call me? Please? I really am looking forward to driving about with you."

"Yes, I will call. I'll look forward to it, also."

It was late afternoon of the same day when Stride arrived at Tom Butcher's house on Waterford Bridge Road. Butcher himself answered the door.

"Hazel's off for the evening. Her sister is hosting a family gathering at her home in Topsail, and that's not something I'd want to interfere with. She's made a lamb stew for us. I think we'll manage all right."

Stride followed him to the kitchen. A large pot was steaming on the back of the stove. The rich aroma made him realize how hungry he was. He hadn't eaten anything substantial since breakfast, and not much even then. The biscuits he'd eaten with the tea he had with Catherine Darnell hadn't amounted to much.

"I've just spent a few minutes at Harrison Rose's house," Stride said. "With his daughter."

"Mrs. Darnell. And how did that go?"

"I told her what I knew about the case, and about Cake. She expressed the hope that he wouldn't go to trial."

"Good for her," Butcher said. "And I have some news for you on that. I had a talk with the Crown's office just about an hour ago. They've decided they won't be proceeding to a trial for Cake. Just what they will do, or how they'll word their decision, isn't something they know just now. They're working on the language. But there definitely will not be a trial."

"That is good news."

"Very good news." Butcher took two crystal glasses from the cupboard and held up a bottle of single malt. He poured two ounces in each. "I know that Demerara's your preference, Eric, but I'd like you to give this a try. I think you'll like it."

"I'll take your word on that." He took the glass from Butcher and sipped it. "This will do very nicely."

"I thought it would. So, how is Mrs. Darnell?"

"Trying to come to terms with everything that's happened, and everything she's learned about her father. He left her a complicated legacy."

"And you're not just talking about the property," Butcher said. "She'll be staying here for a while to deal with it all?"

"For a month, at least. I've offered to show her around a bit."

"That will probably do you both good." Butcher lifted the lid off the pot and used a wooden spoon to stir the stew. "Any news from your lady, by the way? From Dianne?"

"No, nothing at all."

"Well, I suppose you expected that. Is she even in town?"

"I don't think so. She's taken unpaid leave from her job. An indefinite absence, they told me."

"And her husband?"

"He leaves this week for Washington to take up his new posting at the Pentagon. I got that information from a friend at Pepperrell."

"I see," Butcher said. He lifted the lid of the pot again and stirred it once more. "We'll give that stew another ten minutes." He led the way from the kitchen to the living room. He placed his drink on an end table and took out a cigarette. "And how are you, Eric? You look weary. Are you all right?"

"I've had better moments, Thomas, but I'll manage. I'm having a hard time getting Cecil Cake out of my mind. No one should have to go through what he's been through."

"Neither him, nor the thousands of others," Butcher said. "There are many more casualties of war than are listed in the official statistics of the dead and wounded."

"I'm concerned that he won't get the care he needs and deserves. I have a recurring nightmare that Cake ends up in an institution that has neither the ability nor the interest to look after him properly. I would hate to hear that he's locked up somewhere, rotting away in solitude."

"I understand your concern, Eric. And I promise you that I will do whatever I can to make sure that doesn't happen. There are people who care about him. And common decency isn't as rare a commodity as sometimes seems to be the case."

"Thank you, Thomas. I needed that reassurance." Stride cradled his drink in both hands, staring down into the glass.

"I think it's just as well that Dianne's not in town," Butcher said. "You need some time to yourself. You've things to sort out." Butcher lit his cigarette and put his feet up on a hassock. "Time's the great healer, so they say." He smiled at Stride across the space between them. "You'll understand that's not an original thought."

"I didn't think it was," Stride said. "I'm almost certain I've heard it before."

AFTERWORD

This novel is based, to a significant degree, on actual historical events. The parts involving the Newfoundland Regiment in 1915 and 1916—later the Royal Newfoundland Regiment—are very much based on fact. The regiment's first significant combat involvement in the First World War was the ill-fated Gallipoli campaign, where the Newfoundlanders joined the British, the Australians and others in a bloody and futile standoff against the Turks, who were allied with the Germans. Readers familiar with that campaign will recognize the Gallipoli battle described in the book as a fictionalized version of the Battle of Caribou Hill, an actual event.

The Newfoundland Regiment also participated in the first day of the Battle of the Somme in July 1916, the poorly planned and ultimately disastrous assault on the German positions on the Western Front, which cost the lives of almost 20,000 men in the British Army on that first day alone. The Newfoundland Regiment was almost annihilated, taking more than 90 percent casualties, among the highest of all the regiments involved. Among the dead that day was my mother's brother, Arthur James Rendell. July 1, 1916, is still remembered and commemorated in Newfoundland as a national tragedy.

The "Battle of Ville Ste-Lucille" described in the novel is based closely on the Battle of Monchy-Le-Preux in April 1917. In the actual battle, nine officers and men of the British Army held off a superior force of Germans until reinforcements could be brought up. The two officers were awarded the Military Cross; the seven men received the Military Medal. One of those men was my father's brother, Private Donald Wilfred ("Fred") Curran.

The part of the novel that involves the Irish Republican Army (IRA) is also based on historical fact. A character who appears briefly in the book, General Hugh Tudor, was an actual person. General Tudor lived the last years of his life in Newfoundland, and he was the target of an IRA assassination squad, sent to St.

John's from Ireland. The assassination attempt was unsuccessful.

A brief note on names is appropriate. Throughout this book, as in my two previous books, I refer to the Newfoundland Constabulary, which was its name at the time. In 1979, the designation "Royal" was added. Similarly, the Newfoundland Regiment was renamed the "Royal Newfoundland Regiment" in September 1917, an honour granted by King George V in recognition of the Regiment's valour in the battles of Ypres and Cambrai. That was the only instance of this honour being granted to a regiment of the British Army in the First World War.

As in my previous two books, I have used a large number of published works to obtain accurate historical information. An important source was *The Fighting Newfoundlander*, by Colonel G.W.L. Nicholson, CD; this is the official history of the Royal Newfoundland Regiment, published in 1963 by the Government of Newfoundland (since renamed the Government of Newfoundland and Labrador). A large number of other published works, too numerous to list, were also used. As usual, the Internet was an invaluable source of information.

ACKNOWLEDGEMENTS

F
ew books are written without assistance of various kinds, and *Death of a Lesser Man* is no exception.

I am grateful to Robin McGrath for suggesting the idea of writing a novel referencing General Hugh Tudor and the IRA. I am especially grateful to Verna Relkoff for guiding me through a number of drafts of the book, and helping me turn an awkward first effort into the book that now exists. I also wish to thank my agent, Morty Mint, for his help and encouragement.

As usual, a number of friends and family members read drafts of the book, and contributed their comments and encouragement. In no particular order, they are: Stephen Knowles, Janet Martin, Bridget McNeill, Meredith Stroud Curren, Kristina Curren, Michael and Betty Corlett, John Joy, Alex Brett, Terry Thomas, David Cole, Wilfred Thomas and Suzanne Beaulieu.

I am grateful to my publisher, Gavin Will, without whose involvement this book would not exist.

Finally, I want to express my very sincere thanks to my editor, Charis Cotter, for her extensive work on the final published version of the book.